I AM DEATH

About the author

Born in Brazil of Italian origin, Chris Carter studied psychology and criminal behaviour at the University of Michigan. As a member of the Michigan State District Attorney's Criminal Psychology team, he interviewed and studied many criminals, including serial and multiple homicide offenders with life-imprisonment convictions.

Having departed for Los Angeles in the early 1990s, Chris spent ten years as a guitarist for numerous rock bands before leaving the music business to write full-time. He now lives in London and is a Top Ten *Sunday Times* bestselling author.

Visit www.chriscarterbooks.com or find him on Facebook.

Also by Chris Carter

The Crucifix Killer
The Executioner
The Night Stalker
The Death Sculptor
One by One
An Evil Mind

CHRIS CARTER

I AM DEATH

SIMON &
SCHUSTER

London · New York · Sydney · Toronto · New Delhi

A CBS COMPANY

First published in Great Britain by Simon & Schuster UK Ltd, 2015
This paperback edition published in 2016
A CBS Company

1 3 5 7 9 10 8 6 4 2

Simon & Schuster UK Ltd
1st Floor
222 Gray's Inn Road
London WC1X 8HB

www.simonandschuster.co.uk

Simon & Schuster Australia, Sydney
Simon & Schuster India, New Delhi

A CIP catalogue record for this book is available from the British Library

B format paperback ISBN: 978-1-4711-6938-0
A format paperback ISBN: 978-1-4711-5621-2
eBook ISBN: 978-1-4711-3226-1

Typeset in the UK by Hewer Text UK Ltd, Edinburgh
Printed and bound in Great Britain by CPI Group (UK) Ltd, Croydon, CR0 4YY

MIX
Paper from
responsible sources
FSC® C020471

Simon & Schuster UK Ltd are committed to sourcing paper that is made
from wood grown in sustainable forests and support the Forest Stewardship
Council, the leading international forest certification organisation. Our
books displaying the FSC logo are printed on FSC certified paper.

In all of my novels, I have always tried my hardest to use factual locations in and around the city of Los Angeles. For that reason, I feel the need to apologize. To better suit the plot in *I Am Death*, I have taken the liberty of creating a couple of fictitious establishments and localities.

One

'Oh, thank you so much for coming in at such short notice, Nicole,' Audrey Bennett said, opening the front door to her white-fronted, two-storey house in Upper Laurel Canyon, a very affluent neighborhood located in the Hollywood Hills region of Los Angeles.

Nicole gave Audrey a bright smile.

'It's no problem at all, Ms. Bennett.'

Born and raised in Evansville, Indiana, Nicole Wilson carried a very distinctive Midwestern accent. She wasn't very tall; about five foot three, and her looks weren't exactly what fashion magazines would call striking, but she was charming and had a disarming smile.

'Come in, come in,' Audrey said, ushering Nicole inside with a hand gesture, seemingly in a hurry.

'Sorry I'm a little late,' Nicole said, stepping inside as she consulted her watch. It was just past 8:30 in the evening.

Audrey chuckled. 'You've got to be the only person in the whole of Los Angeles who considers anything under "ten minutes" as being late, Nicole. Everyone else I know calls it "fashionably on time".'

Nicole smiled, but despite the comment, she still looked a little embarrassed. She prided herself on being a very punctual person.

'That's a beautiful dress, Ms. Bennett. Are you going anywhere special tonight?'

Audrey pursed her lips and twisted them to one side. 'Dinner party at a judge's house.' She leaned forward toward Nicole and her next words came out as a whisper. 'They are sooooo boring.'

Nicole giggled.

'Hello, Nicole,' Audrey's husband said, coming down the arched staircase that led to the house's second floor. James Bennett wore an elegant dark-blue suit with a silk striped tie and a matching silk handkerchief just peeking out of his jacket pocket. His butterscotch-blond hair was combed back, and as always, not a strand seemed to be out of place.

'Are you ready, honey?' he asked his wife before quickly checking his Patek Philippe watch. 'We've got to go.'

'Yes, I know, I'll be right there, James,' Audrey replied before turning to face Nicole again. 'Josh's already asleep,' she explained. 'He's been playing and running around all day, which was great, because by eight o'clock he was so exhausted he was dozing off in front of the TV. We took him to bed and he crashed out before his head hit the pillow.'

'Oh, bless him,' Nicole commented.

'From the amount of running the little devil did today,' James Bennett said, as he approached Audrey and Nicole, 'he should sleep right through to the morning. You should have an easy night.' He grabbed Audrey's coat from the leather armchair to his right and helped his wife into it. 'We've really got to go, honey,' he whispered into her ear before kissing her neck.

'I know, I know,' Audrey said as she nodded toward the door just past the river-rock fireplace on the east wall of their large living room. 'Help yourself to anything you like from the kitchen. You know where everything is, right?'

Nicole nodded once.

'If Josh wakes up and asks for any more chocolate cake, do not give it to him. The last thing he needs is another sugar rush in the middle of the night.'

'OK,' Nicole replied, renewing her smile.

'We might be quite late tonight,' Audrey continued. 'But I'll call you later just to check everything is all right.'

'Enjoy your night,' Nicole said, accompanying them to the door.

As Audrey took the few steps down from her front porch, she looked back at Nicole and mouthed the word 'boring'.

After closing the door, Nicole went upstairs and tiptoed up to Josh's room. The three-year-old boy was sleeping like an angel, his arms wrapped around a stuffed toy creature with huge eyes and ears. From the bedroom door, Nicole stared at him for a long while. He looked so adorable with his blond flock of curly hair and rosy cheeks that she felt like cuddling up to him, but she wouldn't dare wake him up now. Instead, she blew him a kiss from the door and returned downstairs.

In the TV room, Nicole sat and watched about an hour of some old comedy film before her stomach started making noises. Only then she remembered that Audrey Bennett had said something about a chocolate cake. She looked at her watch. It was definitely time for a snack, and a slice of chocolate cake sounded just perfect. She exited the room and went back upstairs to check on Josh again. He was in such a deep sleep, he hadn't even moved positions. Returning downstairs, Nicole crossed to the other side of the living room and casually opened the kitchen door, stepping inside.

'Whoa!' she yelled in a fright, jumping back.

'Whoa!' the man sitting at the breakfast table, having a sandwich, yelled a millisecond after Nicole. Instinctively, and also in a fright, he dropped the sandwich and kicked back from the table, standing up immediately and knocking over his glass of milk. His chair tipped over behind him.

'Who the hell are you?' Nicole asked in an anxious voice, taking a defensive step back.

The man gazed at her for a couple of seconds, confused, as if trying to figure out what was happening. 'I'm Mark,' he finally responded, using both hands to point at himself.

They stared at each other for a moment longer, and Mark quickly realized that his name meant absolutely nothing to the woman.

'Mark?' he repeated, turning every sentence into a question, as if Nicole should've known all this. 'Audrey's cousin from Texas? I'm here for a couple of days for a job interview? I'm staying in the apartment above the garage in the back?' He used his thumb to point over his right shoulder.

Nicole's questioning stare intensified.

'Audrey and James told you about me, didn't they?'

'No.' She shook her head.

'Oh!' Mark looked even more confused now. 'Umm, as I've said, I'm Mark, Audrey's cousin. You must be Nicole, the babysitter, right? They said you'd be coming. And I'm sorry, I really didn't mean to scare you, though I guess you've already paid me back in kind.' He placed his right hand over his chest, tapping his fingers over his heart a few times. 'I almost had a heart attack just now.'

Nicole's stare relaxed a fraction.

'I flew in this morning for a big job interview downtown this afternoon,' Mark explained.

He was dressed in what looked to be a brand new suit, very elegant. He also looked quite attractive.

'I just got back from it about ten minutes ago,' he continued. 'And suddenly my stomach reminded me that I hadn't had any food all day.' He tilted his head to one side. 'I can't really eat when I get nervous. So I just came in for a quick sandwich and a glass of milk.' His eyes moved to where he was sitting and he chuckled. 'Which is now all over the table and starting to drip on to the floor.'

He picked up his chair and looked around for something to clean up the mess. He found a roll of paper towels next to a large fruit bowl on the kitchen counter.

'I'm a little surprised that Audrey forgot to tell you I was staying over,' Mark said as he began mopping up the milk from the floor.

'Well, they were in a bit of a hurry,' Nicole conceded, her posture not as tense as moments ago. 'Ms. Bennett asked me if I could get here for eight o'clock, but the earliest I could make it was eight-thirty.'

'Oh, OK. Is Josh still awake? I'd like to say goodnight if I could.'

Nicole shook her head. 'No. He's out like a light.'

'He's a great kid,' Mark said, as he bundled up all the soaked paper towels and dumped them in the trashcan.

Nicole kept her full attention on him. 'You know,' she said, 'you look a little familiar. Have I met you before?'

'No,' Mark replied. 'This is actually my first ever visit to LA. But it's probably from the photographs in the TV room and in James' study. I'm in two of them. Plus, Audrey and I have the same eyes.'

'Oh . . . the photographs. That must be it,' Nicole said, a

hazy memory playing at the edge of her mind, but not quite materializing.

A distant cellphone ringtone broke the awkward silence that had followed.

'Is that your phone?' Mark asked.

Nicole nodded.

'That's probably Audrey calling to say that she forgot to tell you about me.' He shrugged and smiled. 'Too late.'

Nicole smiled back. 'Let me go get that.' She exited the kitchen and returned to the living room, where she retrieved her cellphone from her bag. The call was indeed from Audrey Bennett.

'Hi Ms. Bennett, how's the dinner party?'

'Even more boring than I expected, Nicole. This is going to be a long night. Anyway, I'm just calling to check that everything is all right.'

'Yes, everything is fine,' Nicole replied.

'Has Josh woken up at all?'

'No, no. I just checked on him again a moment ago. He looks like he's out for the count.'

'Oh, that's great.'

'By the way, I just met Mark in the kitchen.'

There was some loud background noise coming from Audrey's side.

'Sorry, Nicole, what did you say?'

'That I just met Mark, your cousin from Texas, who's staying in the garage apartment. I walked in on him having a sandwich in the kitchen, and we scared the hell out of each other.' She giggled.

There was a couple of seconds' delay before Audrey replied.

'Nicole, where's he? Has he gone up to Josh's room?'

'No, he's still in the kitchen.'

'OK, Nicole, listen to me.' Audrey's voice was serious, but shaky at the same time. 'As quietly and as quickly as you can, go get Josh and get out of the house. I'm calling the police right now.'

'What?'

'Nicole, I don't have a cousin named Mark from Texas. We don't have anyone staying in the garage apartment. Get out of the house . . . *now*. Do you underst—'

CLUNK.

'Nicole?'

'NICOLE?'

The line went dead.

TWO

Detective Robert Hunter of the LAPD Robbery Homicide Division pushed open the door to his small office on the fifth floor of the famous Police Administration Building in Downtown Los Angeles and stepped inside. The clock on the wall showed 2:43 p.m.

Hunter looked around the room slowly. It'd been exactly two weeks since he last entered his office, and he had been hoping to come back to it relaxed and with a golden tan, but instead he felt totally exhausted and he was sure that he'd never looked as pale as he did now.

Hunter was supposed to have gone on his first vacation in nearly seven years. His captain had demanded that he and his partner take a two-week break after their last investigation ended sixteen days ago. Hunter had planned to go to Hawaii, a place that he'd always wanted to visit, but on the day he was supposed to fly out, his close friend, Adrian Kennedy, who was also the director of the FBI's National Center for the Analyses of Violent Crime, asked Hunter for his help in interviewing an apprehended suspect in a double homicide investigation. Hunter had found himself unable to say no, so instead of flying to Hawaii he ended up in Quantico, Virginia.

The interview was meant to take no more than just a

couple of days, but Hunter had got sucked into an investigation that changed his life for ever.

He and the FBI had finally closed the case less than twenty-four hours ago. With the investigation concluded, Kennedy had tried one more time to convince the once prodigy kid to join the Bureau.

Hunter grew up as an only child to working-class parents in Compton, an underprivileged neighborhood of South Los Angeles. His mother lost her battle with cancer when he was only seven. His father never remarried and had to take on two jobs to cope with the demands of raising a child on his own.

From a very early age it was obvious to everyone that Hunter was different. He could figure things out faster than most. School bored and frustrated him. He'd finished all of his sixth-grade work in less than two months and, just for something to do, he sped through seventh-, eighth- and even ninth-grade books.

It was then that his principal decided to get in contact with the Los Angeles Board of Education. After a battery of exams and tests, at the age of twelve Hunter was given a scholarship to the Mirmam School for the Gifted.

By the age of fourteen he'd glided through Mirmam's high school English, History, Math, Biology and Chemistry curriculums. Four years of high school were condensed into two and at fifteen he'd graduated with honors. With recommendations from all of his teachers, Hunter was accepted as a 'special circumstances' student at Stanford University.

By the age of nineteen Hunter had already graduated in Psychology – *summa cum laude* – and at twenty-three he received his Ph.D. in Criminal Behavior Analysis and Biopsychology. That was when Kennedy tried to recruit him into the FBI for the first time.

Hunter's Ph.D. thesis paper, titled 'An Advanced Psychological Study in Criminal Conduct', ended up on Kennedy's desk. The paper had impressed Kennedy and the then FBI Director so much that it had become mandatory reading at the NCAVC. Since then and over the years, Kennedy had tried several times to recruit Hunter into his team. In Kennedy's mind, it made no sense that Hunter would rather be a detective with a local police force than join the most advanced serial-killer tracking task force in the USA, arguably in the world. But Hunter had never shown even an ounce of interest in becoming a federal agent, and had declined every offer made to him by Kennedy and his superiors.

Hunter sat at his desk but didn't turn on his computer. He found it funny how everything about his office looked exactly the same, and totally different at the same time. Exactly the same because nothing had been moved or touched. Totally different because something was missing. Actually, not something, someone – his partner of six years, Detective Carlos Garcia.

Their last investigation together, before the enforced two-week break, had put Hunter and Garcia in pursuit of an extremely sadistic serial killer, who chose to broadcast his murders live over the Internet. The investigation had taken them both to the brink of sanity, almost claiming Hunter's life, and placing Garcia and his family in a situation he swore he would never allow to happen again.

Just before their break, Garcia had revealed to Hunter

that upon his return he wasn't sure if he would come back to work at the Robbery Homicide Division and the Homicide Special Section. His priorities had changed. His family had to come first, no matter what.

Hunter didn't have a family. He wasn't married. He had no kids. But he fully understood his partner's concern, and he was sure that whatever decision Garcia came to, it would be the right one for him.

The Homicide Special Section of the LAPD was an elite unit created to deal solely with serial, high-profile murders and homicide cases requiring extensive investigative time and expertise. Due to Hunter's background in criminal behavior psychology, he headed up an even more specialized group within the Special Section. All homicides where overwhelming brutality and/or sadism had been used by the perpetrator were tagged by the department as 'UV' Crimes (Ultra-Violent). Hunter and Garcia were the LAPD's UV Unit, and Garcia was the best partner and friend Hunter had ever had.

Hunter finally leaned forward and reached for the button to power up his computer, but before he'd managed to press it the door to his office was pushed open again and Garcia stepped inside.

'Oh!' Garcia said, looking a little surprised as he checked the wall clock. 'You're earlier than usual, Robert.'

Hunter's eyes flicked to the clock – 2:51 p.m. – then back to his partner. Garcia's longish brown hair was tied back in a slick ponytail, still wet from a morning shower, but his eyes looked tired and full of worry.

'Yeah, a little bit,' Hunter replied.

'You don't look so tanned for someone who's just been to Hawaii.' Garcia paused and frowned at Hunter. 'You did

take your vacation, right?' Hunter was the biggest worka-
holic Garcia had ever met.

'Sort of,' Hunter said, with a half-nod.

'And what does that mean?'

'I took my break,' Hunter explained. 'I just didn't go to
Hawaii in the end.'

'So where did you go?'

'Nowhere special, just visiting a friend back east.'

'OK.'

Garcia could tell that it hadn't been something as simple
as that but he also knew Hunter well enough to know that
if he didn't want to talk about a subject, he wouldn't, no
matter how much anyone pushed him.

Garcia approached his desk but didn't sit down. He
didn't turn on his computer either. Instead, he opened the
desk's top drawer and began emptying it of its contents,
placing everything on the desktop.

Hunter observed his partner without uttering a word.

Garcia finally looked at him. 'I'm sorry, buddy,' he said as
he began emptying the second drawer, breaking the
awkward silence that had taken over the room.

Hunter nodded once.

'I thought long and hard about all this, Robert,' Garcia
opened up. 'Actually, I spent every second of the past two
weeks thinking about it, considering all the possibilities,
measuring everything up, and I know that on a personal
level, I'll probably never stop regretting this. But I also
know that I can never put Anna through anything like that
again, Robert. She means everything to me. I would never
forgive myself if anything happened to her because of the
job I do.'

'I know that,' Hunter replied. 'And I don't blame you,

Carlos, not even a little bit. I would've done the same thing.'

Hunter's heartfelt words brought a very feeble 'thank you' smile to Garcia's lips. Hunter picked up on his partner's embarrassment.

'You don't owe anybody any sort of explanation, Carlos, least of all me.'

'I owe you everything, Robert,' Garcia interrupted him. 'I owe you my life. I owe you Anna's life. It's because of you that both of us are still alive, remember?'

Hunter didn't want to talk about the past, so he moved the subject along as swiftly as he could.

'How's Anna doing, by the way?'

'She's surprisingly OK for someone who went through what she did,' Garcia said, as he finished emptying the desk drawers. 'She's staying at her parents for a couple of days.'

'She's a very strong woman,' Hunter admitted. 'Physically and mentally.'

'She is indeed.'

For a moment the awkward silence came back to the room.

'So where are you going?' Hunter asked.

Garcia paused and glanced at Hunter. This time he looked a little embarrassed.

'San Francisco.'

Hunter was unable to hide his surprise.

'You're leaving LA?'

'We decided it would be best if we did, yes.'

Hunter had not seen that coming. In silence, he nodded his understanding. 'SFPD's Robbery Homicide Division will be lucky to get you.'

Garcia looked even more embarrassed now. 'I'm not staying with the Robbery Homicide Division.'

Hunter's surprise turned into confusion. He knew how long and hard Garcia had fought to make Homicide Detective.

'Special Fraud Division,' Garcia said at last. 'Equivalent to our WCCU.'

Hunter thought he'd heard wrong.

The WCCU was the LAPD's White Collar Crime Unit, which conducted specialized major fraud investigations involving multiple victims and/or suspects. It dealt with offences such as embezzlements, complex grand thefts, and bribe and theft cases involving city employees or public officials. Inside the LAPD, the WCCU was better known as the type of unit detectives got stuck with, not asked to be transferred to.

Garcia lifted both hands in surrender. 'I know, I know. It sucks. But at the moment that's the only position they've got going. Anna also loved that it's a less risky job. After what happened, I can't blame her for that.'

Hunter was about to mention something when the phone on his desk rang. He picked it up, listened for about five seconds, then placed the receiver back on its cradle without saying a word.

'I've got to go and see the captain,' he said, getting up and stepping away from his desk.

Garcia did the same. They stared at each other for a long moment. Garcia was the one who stepped forward, opened his arms and hugged Hunter as if he were a lost brother.

'Thank you, Robert,' Garcia said, looking at Hunter. 'For everything.'

'Don't be a stranger,' Hunter said. Sadness underlined his tone.

'I won't.' As Hunter got to the door, Garcia stopped him. 'Robert.'

Hunter turned and faced him.

'Take care of yourself.'

Hunter nodded and exited the room.

Three

They were staring at him again.

The dark-haired girl and her friends.

They'd stare, giggle, and then stare again. Not that he minded. Eleven-year-old Ricky Temple was used to it by now. His hand-me-down clothes, bushy black hair, ultra-skinny body, pointed nose and umbrella ears never failed to get him noticed. Noticed and laughed at. The fact that he wasn't very tall for his age didn't help much either.

Five different schools in the past three years due to his father's string of unsteady jobs, and the story had been the same everywhere. Girls would make fun of him. Boys would push him around and beat him up. Teachers would praise him for his high grades.

Ricky kept his eyes on the exam paper on his desk. He'd finished it at least twenty minutes ahead of anyone else. Even though his eyes were on his paper, he could feel their gaze burning the back of his neck. He could hear their ridiculing giggles.

'Something funny with the exam, Miss Stewart?' Mr. Driscall, the eight grade mathematics teacher, asked in a sarcastic voice.

Lucy Stewart was a stunning girl, with vivid hazel eyes, fringed, straight jet-black hair that looked just as beautiful in a ponytail as it did when loose, and a captivating smile. Her skin was incredibly smooth for a fourteen-year-old. While most girls her age were already beginning to struggle with acne, Lucy seemed to be immune to it. Every boy in Morningside Junior High would do anything for her, but she belonged to Brad Nichols, or so he said. Ricky always thought that if he looked up the definition of *asshole* in a dictionary, Brad Nichols' picture would be right there.

'Not at all, sir,' Lucy replied, shifting on her chair.

'Have you finished, Miss Stewart?'

'Almost there, sir.'

'So stop giggling and get to it. You only have another five minutes.'

An uneasy bustle swept through the classroom.

Lucy's exam paper was half unanswered. She hated math. In fact, she hated most school subjects. They were of no use to her. Especially when she knew she was destined to be a Hollywood superstar.

Ricky chewed on his pencil and scratched the tip of his nose. He wanted to turn around and defy her stare by looking straight back at her. But Ricky Temple rarely did what he wanted to do. He was too timid . . . too scared of the consequences.

'Time's up everybody! Drop your exam papers on my desk on your way out.'

The school bell rang and Ricky thanked God for it. Another week gone. He had the entire weekend to look forward to. He just wanted to be alone doing what he loved doing – writing stories.

Ricky changed into shorts before stuffing his books inside his faded green rucksack and grabbing his rusty bicycle from the rack by the school entrance. He couldn't wait to get away from that place.

Taking West 104th Street, he cut through South 7th Avenue. Ricky loved the houses in this part of town. They were big and colorful with beautiful front lawns and flower gardens. Several of them had swimming pools in their back-yards, a far cry from the squalid apartment he shared with his aggressive father in Inglewood, South Los Angeles. His mother had left them without ever saying goodbye when Ricky was only six. He never saw her again, but he missed her every day.

Ricky had promised himself that one day he would live in a big house with a large backyard and a swimming pool. He was going to be a writer. A successful writer.

Ricky was so absorbed in his thoughts that he didn't hear the sound of the other bicycles approaching from behind. By the time he noticed them it was too late.

One of the five bicycles leveled up to the left of Ricky's front wheel, squeezing him against the high-curbed side-walk. Out of panic, instead of braking, Ricky increased his speed.

'Where the fuck you think you're going, freak?' the hooded rider shouted from under the blue and white bandanna that was covering the bottom half of his face. 'You don't belong in this neighborhood, you ugly and skinny fuck. Go back to your dirty slum.'

Two of the other riders were also screaming abuse at Ricky, but he was too scared to properly hear them.

Ricky ran out of room as his front wheel started to scrape against the curbstones. His whole body was shaking with fear. He knew he was about to fall. Suddenly, a second hooded rider leveled up to him and kicked out, hitting

Ricky's left leg and sending him and his bike flying over to the sidewalk. He hit the ground hard and at speed, skidding a full yard, enough to scrape the skin on his hands and knees almost clean off. His bicycle tumbled over him, landing heavily on his legs.

'Woo hoo! Ugly boy fell off his bike,' Ricky heard one of the kids say as they headed off, laughing out loud.

Ricky lay still for a moment, his eyes shut tight as he fought back tears. He thought he heard the sound of hurried footsteps.

'Hey, are you OK?' a male's voice asked.

Ricky opened his eyes to blurred images.

'Are you all right?' the voice asked again.

Ricky felt someone lifting his bike off his legs. His hands and knees hurt as if they'd been scalded with boiling water. He looked up and saw a man kneeling next to him. He was dressed in a dark suit with a crisp white shirt and a red tie. His brown hair was wavy and pleasantly tousled above a prominent brow, high cheekbones, and a strong chin that was covered by a neatly trimmed goatee. His pale-blue eyes showed concern.

'Who were those kids?' the man asked, jabbing his chin in the direction that the gang had ridden off in. He had a somewhat angry look on his face.

'What?' Ricky said, still a little disoriented.

'I was just on my way to pick up my son from school when I saw a bunch of kids bump you over.' He indicated his car, which was hastily parked with two wheels up on the sidewalk on the other side of the road. The driver's door was still open.

Ricky followed the man's gaze. He knew that the kids on the bicycles were Brad Nichols and his gang of asshole friends, but he said nothing. It would make no difference anyway.

'Hey, you're bleeding,' the man said with serious concern, as his eyes moved first to the boy's hands, then to his knees. 'You've got to clean that up before it gets infected. Here.' He reached inside his breast pocket and handed Ricky a couple of paper tissues. 'Use this for now, but we need to wash it with disinfectant soap and warm water pretty sharpish.'

Ricky took the tissues and dabbed them against the palms of his hands.

With the fall, his rucksack had opened, scattering his books on to the sidewalk.

'Oh!' the man said, first helping Ricky to his feet, then helping him collect his books. 'You go to Morningside? So does my son.' He paused as he handed one last book back to the boy, looking rather surprised. 'You're an eighth grader?'

Still in silence, Ricky nodded carelessly.

'Really? You look like you're about ten.'

'I'm eleven,' Ricky replied, a hint of annoyance in his voice.

'Sorry,' the man said, acknowledging his mistake and backpedaling as quickly as he could. 'I didn't mean to offend you in any way, but still. You're quite young for eighth grade? My son is ten, and he's just finishing fourth grade.'

Ricky placed the last book back into his rucksack. 'I entered school one year earlier than most kids, and because of my grades they made me skip sixth grade.' This time there was pride in his words.

'Wow! That's amazing. So I'm in the presence of a real child prodigy here.'

Ricky finished clearing the blood from his hands before looking down at his bike and its twisted front wheel. 'Shit!'

'That's pretty damaged,' the man agreed. 'I don't think you're going to be riding anywhere else on that bike today.'

Ricky looked like he didn't know what to do. The man read the boy's uneasiness.

'Listen,' he said, consulting his watch. 'I'm a little late to pick my son up from school so I have to go, but if you like, you can wait here and on our way back John and I can give you a ride back to your house. I'll be five minutes. How does that sound?'

'Thanks, but I'll be OK. I can't go home like this anyway.' Ricky began dabbing the paper tissues against the scratches on his knees.

The man's eyebrows arched in surprise. 'Why not?'

'If I turn up at home bleeding, with a broken bike, that gang of kids will look like heavenly angels compared to what my father will do to me.'

'What, really? But it wasn't your fault. They ganged up on you.'

'That doesn't matter.' Ricky looked away. 'Nothing ever matters.' The hurt in the boy's voice was palpable.

The man observed Ricky for an instant as he picked his bike up from the ground.

'OK, how about if John and I drive you home? I'll then speak with your father myself and tell him what happened. I'll tell him that I saw everything and that none of it was your fault. He will listen to an adult.'

'I told you, it won't make any difference, OK? Nothing ever makes any difference. Thank you for your help, but I'll be fine.' Ricky started limping away, dragging his bike.

'Hey, wait up, kid. If you're not going home, where are you going, limping and dragging that heavy thing behind you? You really need to clean those wounds up properly.'

Ricky carried on walking. He didn't look back.

'OK, I've got a better idea. Hear me out,' the man said, taking a couple of steps toward Ricky. 'My boy, John, is a nice kid. A little quiet, but a nice kid, and he could seriously use a friend – and it looks like, right now, so could you. I can load your bike into the back of my car, we pick up John from Morningside, and I'll drop you guys at his mother's place. It's not that far from here. She's got a swimming pool and all. And she can also attend to your hands and knees.'

The words 'swimming pool' made Ricky finally pause and look back at the man.

'I can then quickly run your bike to a shop. The same shop where I got John's bike. I'm sure they can fix that wheel in no time.'

Ricky looked like he was measuring his options.

The man checked his watch again. 'C'mon!' He pressed his lips together for a moment. 'Look, I'll be honest with you, all John does when he's not in school is read comic books and play games . . . alone. Here . . .' the man reached for his wallet, took out a photograph, and showed it to Ricky. 'You might've seen him around school?'

Ricky squinted as he looked at the photograph of a skinny kid with short, light-brown hair.

'Maybe. I'm not sure.'

The man didn't look surprised. Junior high students would never mingle with elementary ones. Not even outcasts like Ricky Temple.

'Anyway,' the man continued. 'He really, really could use a friend. I know that he's only in fourth grade, but he's a smart kid, he really is, and he's got loads of games that I'm sure you'll be into as well. You guys could play together.'

He gave Ricky a moment. 'C'mon, you've got nothing to lose, and I'll get your bike fixed for you, what do you say?'

Ricky scratched his chin.

One more quick look at his watch. 'OK, so just wait right here for five minutes. I'll go pick up John and come back. You can meet him first, then you decide.'

'He likes comic books?' Ricky asked.

The man chuckled. 'That's putting it mildly.'

Ricky shrugged. 'He sounds like he could be a cool guy.'

'He is. He really is.'

'OK then,' Ricky conceded.

The man smiled and carried Ricky's bike across the road. After placing it in the back of his car, he got into the driver's seat.

'We still have to get those hands and knees properly cleaned up,' the man said as he geared up and got the car in motion. He turned right, then at the end of the block he swung left.

Ricky frowned as the man drove past the entrance to Morningside school.

'You just missed the school.' Ricky turned to look at the driver.

The man was looking at him with an evil smile on his lips.

'Relax, kid.' His voice had changed. Gone were the warmth and the soft tones, substituted by a firm, cold and throaty voice.

'There's nothing anyone can do for you now.'

Four

The crammed, open-plan space that formed the LAPD's Robbery Homicide Division was located just down the hall from Hunter's office. There were no flimsy partitions or silly booths separating the messy labyrinth of desks. Identification was made either by desk nameplates, when they could be seen, or by shouting a detective's name and waiting to see who would raise their hand and shout back 'right here'.

Even at that time in the morning, the RHD sounded and looked like a beehive, alive with movement and buzzing with incomprehensible noise that seemed to come from every corner.

Captain Barbara Blake's office was at the far end of the floor. It wasn't a large room by any means, but it was spacious enough. The south wall was taken by bookshelves overflowing with hardcovers, the north one by a few framed photographs, commendations and achievement awards. The east wall was a floor-to-ceiling panoramic window, looking out over South Main Street. Directly in front of her mahogany twin desk were two bourbon-colored, Chesterfield leather armchairs. A rectangular black and white rug centered the room.

Hunter gave the door three firm knocks. A second later, he heard a voice from inside say, 'Come in.'

Captain Blake was sitting behind her desk, with the phone receiver held firmly to her left ear.

'I couldn't care less how you do it,' she said into the mouthpiece, lifting a hand at Hunter, ushering him inside and indicating that she'd be two seconds. 'Just get it done . . . today.' She slammed down the phone.

At least in here, nothing has changed, Hunter thought.

Barbara Blake had been captain of LAPD's Robbery Homicide Division for the past five years. Upon taking over from the previous captain, it hadn't taken her long to establish a reputation as a no-nonsense, iron-fist leader. She certainly was an intriguing woman – tall, elegant and very attractive, with long black hair and piercing dark eyes that could either calm you or make you shiver with a simple stare. Nothing and no one intimidated her.

'Robert,' she said, getting up. She wore a tailor-made, light-gray suit with a white viscose blouse, black shoes and a thin black belt. Her hair was styled into a bun, and her small pearl earrings matched her necklace. 'Welcome back.' She paused for a short instant. 'I'm sorry that your vacation didn't turn out to be a vacation at all.'

Despite not knowing the true extent of the revelations brought on by the investigation Hunter had been involved in during his short time with the FBI, there was real sentiment in Captain Blake's tone of voice.

Hunter's reply was a simple nod.

The captain walked around to the front of her desk and paused, her forehead creasing slightly.

'Where the hell is Carlos?' she asked, instinctively tilting her body to one side to look past Hunter.

Hunter mirrored her questioning look.

'He's down the corridor, in the office, packing.' He used a thumb to point over his shoulder.

'Packing?' The forehead creasing turned into an even more bewildered look. 'Packing what?'

Hunter looked just as confused – Garcia had to have spoken to the captain about his transfer.

'His stuff.'

The captain's stare turned blank.

'San Francisco? Their Fraud Division?' Hunter said with a subtle headshake. 'Just like our WCCU?'

Blank morphed into total perplexity.

'What the hell are you talking about, Robert?'

Right at that moment, the door to Captain Blake's office was pushed open and Garcia stepped inside.

'Sorry I'm late, Captain. I had to sort out a few things on my desk.'

Looking completely lost, Hunter turned to face him.

'Wow,' Garcia said with a prankster's smile on his face. 'You ate up all that crap like a hungry baby, didn't you? Frisco? Their Fraud Division? Really, Robert? C'mon!'

Captain Blake stiffened a smile. She didn't have to ask. She had already figured out what had happened.

'Son of a—' Hunter said before a huge smile appeared on his lips.

'Maybe you're getting old, buddy,' Garcia joked, tapping Hunter on the shoulder as he moved inside. 'Losing your touch and all. I thought you'd be able to call my bluff straight away.'

Hunter bowed his head, accepting it. 'Maybe I am getting too old for this.' The smile was still on his lips. 'I really never saw this coming. Even after you mentioned the fraud division. That should've been my clue.'

'Or maybe I'm just that good,' Garcia said, renewing his smile. 'That hug at the end was a great touch, wasn't it? A few more seconds and I would probably have managed a few tears too.'

'You didn't have to,' Hunter said. 'I had already bought the whole thing by then.'

'OK,' Captain Blake said, breaking up the joke, her tone quickly moving from playful to serious. She reached for two files that were on her desk. 'Playtime is well and truly over, boys. Welcome back to the UV Unit.'

'So what have we got, Captain?' Garcia asked.

Captain Blake handed a file to each detective. The hesitation in her voice wasn't for effect.

'A fucking nightmare, that's what.'

Five

After the man had taken him captive, Ricky was undressed and beaten to unconsciousness. When he finally came to, he was hosed down with a powerful jet of freezing water and then beaten again, this time with a thick belt that broke his skin and left him bleeding. A few lashes were all it took before he passed out once more.

Ricky's eyelids flickered in rapid succession for a long moment before he finally managed to force them open, but it made no difference. The darkness inside the small, windowless cell was absolute. In spite of that, his drowsy eyes first moved left, then right, as if searching for something before almost closing again. The blur of confusion that had enveloped his brain was so intense, he was unsure if any of this was true, if he was really awake or not.

But then came the pain – powerful, unmistakable and immediate like a nuclear blast, spreading through every atom of his body with unimaginable speed and doing away with the doubt.

This was no nightmare. This was something much, much worse.

That realization brought with it fear on a scale Ricky had never experienced before.

He coughed, and that seemed to enrage the pain further.

Colored sparkles of light exploded just behind his eyelids, and with each explosion he felt as if a nail was being hammered deep into his skull. He was about to succumb to the pain and allow it to drag him back into oblivion again when he heard a noise coming from somewhere to his right.

Ricky froze.

Clunk.

It sounded like the door to his cell was being unlocked.

The boy's terrified eyes darted in that direction and he waited.

Clunk, clunk.

Two more rotations of the lock, a pause, and then the door began to open.

Sheer fear made Ricky reflexively recoil on the cold cement floor, burying his face into his arms and bringing his knees up to his chest, in a defensive, human-ball position. With his movement came more agonizing pain and the bone-chilling sound of metal scraping against metal, as the thick chain firmly shackled to his right ankle rattled against the metal loop fixed into the crude brick wall.

Tears automatically welled up in his eyes, his throat constricted and his breathing became erratic. His heart hammered inside his chest as if trying to beat its way out of his body.

The light bulb encased in the metal wire box at the center of the ceiling blinked a couple of times before engaging. As it did, it brought with it an electric buzz that made it sound as though the room had suddenly been swarmed by angry wasps. Ricky had been lying in darkness for such a long time that, even though he closed his eyes, the light burned at his eyeballs.

The sound of his captor's boots clicking against the floor

as he entered the room fired a new stream of white-hot panic through Ricky's small and fragile body. He began shivering uncontrollably. He didn't have to look. He knew the man was there because he could smell him – a bitter, sour, and sickly sweet fear-inducing mixture of scents that scared the little boy down to his soul. If evil had a smell, Ricky was sure that that was it.

The man's nauseating odor ripped through Ricky's nostrils and scraped at the back of his throat like cat claws.

Ricky wanted to be strong, just like he always was when he was bullied in school by Brad Nichols and his gang, but he was so terrified he had practically lost control of his actions.

'Please ... don't ... don't beat me again.' The words escaped his lips without his consent.

There was no reply. All Ricky could hear was the man's heavy breathing as he stood by the door, and to him the man sounded like an angry, fire-breathing dragon.

'Plea— Please.' His voice came out weak and in spurts.

The footsteps got closer.

Ricky curled into an even tighter ball and squeezed his eyes, bracing himself. He knew what was coming and the anticipation hurt almost as much as the blows.

'What's your name, kid?' The man's voice filled the room with undeniable authority, but it sounded very different from when they had spoken near Ricky's school. It was now throaty, firm, and cold.

Ricky froze. Was this a different person again?

The boy's breathing became even more labored.

'Look at me.' The words sounded like they'd been delivered through angry, clenched teeth.

Ricky was too scared to move.

'Look. At. Me.'

The human ball that Ricky had turned into slowly began to come undone.

'Open your eyes, and look at me.'

Ricky finally lifted his head from his arms. His eyelids flickered again, this time for a little longer while his eyes adapted to the light. At last, he opened his eyes and stared at the stranger standing in front of him.

Who was this man?

'You don't recognize me, do you?'

Ricky breathed out, unable to answer.

'Maybe you would if I spoke like this and told you a little more about my son, John. The shy kid.' Effortlessly, the man's voice transformed into the same voice he had used when he'd helped Ricky up from his bike fall. 'Well, John doesn't really exist.' The man chuckled.

Ricky's eyes widened in surprise. The man standing in front of him also looked completely different. His goatee was gone. So was his wavy brown hair. In its place was a perfectly shaved head. The pale-blue eyes that had once showed concern were now of the deepest shade of brown, bordering on black.

'Don't look so surprised, kid. Changing your appearance isn't really that hard.'

Ricky was still shivering.

'So,' the man said. 'Let me ask again – what's your name?'

Ricky's lips moved, but his voice failed him.

'What was that? I didn't hear you.'

The man took a step forward. Ricky's arms jerked toward his face to protect it. The man paused and waited, observing the boy.

'Richard. My name is Richard Temple.' The boy's voice was barely louder than a whisper.

'Umm.' The man nodded as he scratched his chin, apparently missing his goatee. 'But everyone calls you Ricky, right?' His voice was back to being throaty and cold.

The boy nodded.

'Well, not anymore.' The man sucked in a breath through his nose as if getting ready to spit. 'I'll tell you a secret. You were supposed to die here. I was supposed to do whatever I wanted with you and then kill you.'

Tears began to roll down Ricky's cheeks.

'But I've decided that that's not what I'm going to do. At least, not yet.'

Ricky couldn't tear his eyes from the man's face.

'Let me tell you this – life, as you knew it, is over, do you understand? You'll never leave here. You'll never have a friend again. Not that I think you had any. You'll never go to school again, or play outside again, or see your family again, or do anything again other than obey me. Is that clear?'

Fear kept Ricky from replying.

'Is. That. Clear?'

Ricky saw the man's fingers close into a fist, and fear made him nod.

'You'll do everything I tell you to do. You'll not open your mouth unless I give you permission to speak. You'll not eat unless I give you permission to eat. You'll not drink unless I give you permission to drink. If you try to escape, I will know, and I will punish you. If you disobey any of my rules, I will know, and I will punish you. Do you understand?'

The boy nodded again.

'This is a new beginning for you,' the man continued. 'And since it's a new beginning, you need a new name, because I don't like yours.' He wiped the back of his right hand across his lips, and for an instant the man looked like he was pondering something. 'You know what you look like, all awkward and skinny?' He didn't wait for an answer. 'A squirm. You look like a squirm.' A short pause. 'I really like that.' He smiled. 'So that's your new name – Squirm. Every time I call your name, you will answer "Yes, sir". Do you understand, Squirm?'

The boy didn't know what to do other than look totally and utterly petrified.

'DO YOU UNDERSTAND, SQUIRM?' The man's yell reverberated against the brick walls like a death call.

'Yes, sir.' His voice was drowning in tears.

The man smiled as he walked back to the cell door.

'Welcome to your new life, Squirm. Welcome to hell.'

The door closed behind him with a muffled thud like a coffin lid.

Six

Captain Blake waited while both detectives checked the file in their hands. It opened with an 11x8-inch colored portrait of a woman.

'Her name was Nicole Wilson,' the captain began, leaning back and sitting against the edge of her desk. 'Twenty years old. She was born and raised in Evansville, Indiana, where her parents still live. About a year ago, after being accepted into law school at CSULA on a full academic scholarship, she moved here to Los Angeles. Her records show that she was an outstanding student. For pocket money, and when her college schedule allowed her, she would sometimes babysit a few nights a week. This was supposed to be her first college summer break, but instead of going back to Indiana to see her folks, she decided to stay around because she managed to land a temp job, running errands for a small law firm in downtown LA. One of her professors helped her get the job.'

Hunter and Garcia studied the opening photograph for a moment. Nicole Wilson had a round face, with expressive olive-shaped eyes complemented by a petite nose and full lips. Her cheeks were dusted with a handful of freckles, and her hair was light brown in color, coming down to the top of her shoulders.

'Seven days ago,' Captain Blake continued, as Hunter and Garcia moved past the opening photograph and on to the second page of the file – Nicole Wilson's fact sheet – 'Nicole was babysitting for Audrey and James Bennett, a wealthy couple who live in Upper Laurel Canyon, when she was abducted.'

Hunter's questioning gaze moved from the fact sheet to Captain Blake.

'Yes,' the captain confirmed, reading the unspoken question in her detective's eyes. 'She was abducted while she was babysitting, not on her way to work, or on her way back. The perpetrator took her from inside the house.'

Hunter's attention returned to the file. He flipped to the next page and skimmed through it. 'No struggle?'

'Forensics found no sign of it,' Captain Blake replied, then paused for a second, observing both detectives before nodding once. 'I know what you two are thinking – that the perpetrator was probably known to Nicole, and that she willingly allowed him into the house, hence the lack of evidence of a struggle. The same thought came to me when I first read that file, but no, that doesn't seem to be the case here.'

'How come?' Garcia asked.

Captain Blake shrugged and moved over to the espresso machine on the corner by the bookshelves. 'Because the perpetrator tricked Nicole with a bogus story.' She chose a coffee capsule and inserted it into the machine. This was her second cup since she'd arrived at her office less than half an hour ago.

'A bogus story?' Hunter frowned.

'That's correct. Coffee?'

Both detectives shook their heads.

The captain watched the last drops of coffee trickle into

her cup while she clarified: 'It looks like the perpetrator pretended to be Ms. Bennett's cousin from Texas, who was supposedly staying over at their garage apartment.' She took a moment, allowing Hunter and Garcia to absorb the information before moving on. 'Audrey Bennett doesn't have a cousin from Texas. They had no one staying over at their garage apartment.' She dropped a single sweetener tablet into her cup. 'And get this, the perpetrator was having a sandwich in the kitchen when Nicole walked in on him.'

Curiosity and intrigue flooded Garcia's face.

'He was having a sandwich?'

'According to Ms. Bennett, yes.'

'Wait a second.' Hunter lifted a hand. 'I'm guessing that if Nicole was babysitting for the Bennetts, they were out of the house at the time?'

'That's correct,' Captain Blake confirmed. 'They were attending a judge's dinner. James Bennett is a high-flying lawyer.'

'So if they were out of the house, how does Ms. Bennett know about the perpetrator posing as her cousin?'

'Well, that's where it starts to get creepy,' Captain Blake said, sipping her coffee. 'The perpetrator allowed Nicole to answer a call from Audrey Bennett and tell her about the man she had met in the kitchen, before taking her.' She indicated the file in Hunter's hands. 'A very detailed transcript of the interview Missing Persons did with Audrey Bennett is in there, next page along. It also includes her entire account of the phone conversation she had with Nicole.'

Hunter and Garcia turned to it.

'How did the perpetrator gain access to the house?' Hunter asked.

'As yet unknown,' the captain replied. 'There were no

signs of forced entry but the back door was unlocked. The problem is, Ms. Bennett can't remember if she had left it that way or not. But even if she hadn't, Nicole could've unlocked it for some reason and forgot to relock it, there's no way of confirming that. And there's also the possibility that the perpetrator could've simply picked the lock. Forensics said that there was no damage to it, but we all know that with the right knowledge and tools, door locks aren't that hard to breach.'

Hunter nodded and carried on reading.

'Ms. Bennett called the police immediately after disconnecting with Nicole,' Captain Blake added. 'But by the time they got to the house – twenty-two minutes later – Nicole was gone.'

'Any CCTV cameras around where the Bennetts live?' Garcia asked.

Captain Blake shook her head. 'None. You'd have to go all the way to the bottom of Hollywood Hills to find one.'

'How about the boy she was babysitting?' Hunter asked, reading from the file.

'Joshua, three years old,' the captain confirmed. 'He wasn't touched. They found him asleep upstairs, just the way his parents had left him. The boy heard and saw nothing.'

'Are Nicole's parents rich?' Hunter asked.

'Not by any stretch of the imagination. Father is a schoolteacher. Mother works in a local supermarket.'

'So the perpetrator broke into a wealthy family's house to abduct the babysitter?' Garcia this time. 'Not the boy?'

'As unnatural as it sounds, yes,' Captain Blake answered, having one more sip of her coffee. 'And that's our first tricky question – why? Why complicate things for himself?

He could've made his job a lot easier by taking Nicole either before she got to the Bennett's house, or after she left. A simple approach and grab job. Why increase his risk by breaking into the house and taking her from inside?'

Both detectives understood their captain's concern very well. They all knew a street abduction made collecting left-behind clues and evidence like fingerprints, fibers, hairs and so on infinitely harder, not to mention the fact that everything gets exposed to the elements. Clues could easily be blown away by a gust of wind, washed away by rain, or contaminated in many different ways. But if a perpetrator breaks into a confined space like a house, the risk of third-party contamination decreased exponentially, and he allowed the police an elements-free and much more focused area to work with.

'One of two reasons,' Garcia replied, first looking at Hunter, then back at Captain Blake. 'He was either too stupid to figure out that he would increase his risk of being identified, or he was confident enough to know that he wouldn't leave anything behind.'

Hunter nodded his agreement.

'And if he was so bold as to be having a sandwich in the kitchen and to allow his victim to answer a phone call before making his move,' Garcia carried on, 'I don't think that we're looking at reason number one here, are we, Captain?'

Captain Blake finished her coffee, placing her cup on her desk.

'No,' she finally replied. 'Forensics scrutinized the house for two whole days. Everything they found was matched either to the Bennetts or to Nicole Wilson herself. The unsub left absolutely nothing behind.'

'Did the FBI get involved?' Garcia asked.

The captain shook her head. 'No. The Adult Missing Persons Unit didn't request any help from the Bureau. As I've said, Nicole Wilson was twenty years old, not a minor, which means that the Lindbergh Law doesn't apply to her.'

Hunter got to the end of the dossier. There was nothing else. 'So when was her body found?'

Captain Blake walked back behind her desk, opened the top drawer on the left and retrieved two new files.

'In the early hours of this morning. It was left on an empty field by Los Angeles International Airport. And if the house-break-in-sandwich-eating scenario wasn't creepy enough – have a look at this shit.'

Seven

Squirm waited by the metal sink in the kitchen. He kept his eyes low, tracing the black-and-white squares on the old linoleum floor he had just cleaned to as much of a shine as it would go. His hands were shackled in front of him. A half-foot-long heavy metal bar kept them apart, but each end had been specially fitted with a rotating cuff, allowing Squirm's hands some restricted movement, enough for him to handle a mop and scrubbing brushes. From the center of the metal bar, a long chain connected it to the loop that had been fixed into the east wall. Every room in the house had one, like power points, including the bathroom. Squirm was always shackled to a wall, no matter where he was. There were metal loops built into the walls in the basement too, but he was never allowed down there.

Actually, the basement scared Squirm speechless. Screams came from down there – desperate, full-of-fear-and-over-flowing-with-pain screams. The kind that would haunt one's dreams for ever. He'd heard them for the past few days. A woman's voice, pleading, begging for the man to let her go. She even yelled out her name once. Or at least Squirm thought it was her name – Nicole.

The screams stopped sometime yesterday. He hadn't heard her since.

The man was also in the kitchen, sitting at the small, square breakfast table a few feet in front of Squirm. He was having his usual breakfast which consisted of a bowl of cereal, a cup of coffee, a few slices of cheese, a raw egg, and some toast. His full attention was on the newspaper on the table, by his coffee cup. He didn't even seem to acknowledge the boy's presence.

Squirm's stomach growled like a confused dog and that made every muscle in his body go rigid. He was not supposed to make a sound. The man had told him that.

Terrified, the boy's eyes flicked to the man for just a split second before quickly focusing on his manacled hands. The cuffs, even though they allowed him some movement, were fitted tight around his tiny wrists and his morning cleaning chores had dug them further into his flesh. A thin circle of fresh blood decorated each wrist like a crimson bracelet.

The man didn't look up.

Squirm's stomach growled again, this time for a while longer. He hadn't eaten anything for a whole day. There had been nothing for breakfast, lunch or dinner the day before. He was so hungry he could feel his legs weakening under him.

The man finally finished eating and stood up. He paused by the kitchen door and looked back at the boy.

'Lucky morning for you today, Squirm.' He nodded at the table. 'I'm not that hungry. You can finish that up.'

Squirm looked at what was left but didn't move. He was too scared to. The man had left him a bite of dried toast, about a sip of coffee, and three, maybe four spoonfuls of cornflakes with milk.

'Go on, Squirm, eat,' the man ordered.

Squirm rushed to the table, his shaking hands first

reaching for the piece of dried toast. He grabbed it and immediately shoved it into his mouth, as though if he didn't eat it fast enough it would all be taken away from him again. It tasted like the most delicious piece of toast he'd ever eaten.

The man watched him.

Squirm grabbed the coffee cup and drank whatever was left in it in one single gulp. It tasted so bitter his entire face scrunched up. He had never liked coffee, not without milk and sugar, but right now he would take whatever he got.

Squirm then reached for the bowl of cereal and the plastic spoon.

'Nah-ah,' the man said with a headshake. 'You know the rules, Squirm. No spoon. No cutlery. Use your hands, like the dirty animal you are.'

Squirm dropped the spoon, grabbed the bowl with his right hand and brought it to his lips, but the metal bar between his wrists made it all too awkward, and though he managed to tip some of it into his mouth, a whole spoonful spilled down his chin and on to the table and floor.

'Are you throwing food away, you useless piece of shit?' the man asked angrily, taking a threatening step toward the boy.

'No, sir, no, sir, no, sir. I'm sorry. I'm sorry.'

As carefully as he could, the boy placed the bowl back on the table and looked down at the tiny mess he had created.

'Lick it all up,' the man said. 'Lick it up now.'

Squirm bent down, bringing his mouth to the table. He first sucked all the milk off the table surface, before using his tongue and lips to collect each cornflake that had spilt out of the bowl.

'The floor too,' the man demanded, indicating it with his

index finger. 'You better eat that up right now, or else . . .' He began undoing his belt.

In a flash, Squirm got down on his hands and knees and began sucking the milk from the floor. When he was done, he once again used his tongue and lips to collect the cornflakes.

'I want that floor looking just the way it did before you dirtied it. I want it shining, do you understand?'

'Yes, sir. I'll mop it again, sir.'

'No. I don't want you to mop it again. The privilege of using a mop is gone. I want you to lick it clean.'

Squirm paused for just a moment.

Slam.

The belt hit Squirm across the middle of his back so hard that his already weak arms gave in and his head went crashing against the floor, making his eyes flutter.

'Did I stutter, Squirm? I said lick . . . the . . . floor.'

Anger thickened the air.

It took Squirm a moment to regain his balance and get rid of the dizziness. Without another ounce of hesitation, he began licking the floor where he had spilt his cornflakes.

'That's right, Squirm, nice, long strokes.' The man walked over to the table, grabbed the cereal bowl and emptied the rest of its contents on to the floor. 'Now finish your breakfast,' he said, laughing.

Squirm never stopped. He carried on licking every drop of milk and every tiny piece of cornflake from the floor. When he was done with the cornflakes, the man made him lick the entire kitchen floor. By the time he was done, Squirm's tongue was bleeding.

Eight

Hunter and Garcia flipped open the murder file that Captain Blake had given them. This one also began with a photograph, but this time it wasn't a portrait. It showed Nicole Wilson's body as it had been found in the early hours of the morning. She was dressed in blue jeans, a black T-shirt under a half-unzipped light-gray California State University sweatshirt and black sneakers – no socks. She had no make-up on, and her hair looked wet, with the fringe plastered against her forehead. There was no blood on her, on her clothes, or on the ground surrounding the body. No cuts or wounds were visible either. No apparent cause of death, but Hunter and Garcia immediately understood why Captain Blake was so concerned. The body had been left lying on its back on an empty green patch of grass. The arms were stretched out to her sides in a horizontal line, palms facing up. The legs had also been stretched out and pulled apart as far as they would go, creating a V shape. The overall image was of a human star and that was what sent alarm bells ringing. From experience, they all knew that specific body positioning hinted strongly at one thing – ritual. And ritual killers rarely struck only once.

The next photograph was a close-up of Nicole's face. Her skin had turned a light shade of purple and acquired a waxy, semi-shiny texture. Her lips had gone white from the lack of blood circulation, and even though her eyes were closed Hunter could tell that they had already begun to sink a little deeper into her skull. But what most caught the LAPD detective's attention were the abrasions at the edges of her mouth, together with the small patch of skin that began at the corner of her lips, ran across her cheeks and disappeared behind her neck. It showed a very slight change of color, a little darker than the rest of the skin on her face, and that indicated that she'd been gagged with an overly tight restraint.

Hunter slowly flipped through the next few pictures and paused when he came to the ones showing a close-up of Nicole's hands and feet. The skin around her wrists and ankles showed abrasions and a change of color that were similar to the ones on her face, but the marks were a lot more prominent around her ankles, which was a little strange. She had obviously been gagged, tied up and kept that way for a considerable amount of time, but for some reason the restraints around her ankles seemed to have been a lot tighter than the ones around her wrists or mouth.

The last photograph was a wide-angle shot of the location. Only then could Hunter and Garcia see that Nicole's body had been left in the shade of a tall and bushy tree, with large, bright-green, heart-shaped leaves.

Hunter checked his watch – 7:48 a.m.

'When is the autopsy being performed?' he asked. 'Has anyone expedited it?'

He knew that if the body had been found in the early hours of the morning there was no way it would still be on location. The heat of summer would speed up the decomposition process and vital clues, if any had been left on the body, ran a severe risk of being lost.

'Yes,' Captain Blake replied. 'As you know, heinous crimes, or anything that belongs to the UV Unit, take priority with the coroner. As far as I know, it will be top of the list this morning with Doctor Hove.'

Nine

Los Angeles County's Chief Medical Examiner, Doctor Carolyn Hove, had once again woken up too early, this time two hours before her alarm was due to go off.

It hadn't always been like this. Doctor Hove had never had problems sleeping until her husband of twenty years passed away a year and a half ago, and now the nights seemed longer and lonelier than ever.

She opened her eyes, but didn't move. Lying on her back, she simply stared at the white ceiling, pondering if she should try and get back to sleep or not.

What is the point? she thought. Her brain was now wide-awake. Sleep had most certainly left the building, and any attempt to get it back would be futile. She knew that well enough. She'd tried it plenty of times before.

Decision made, she wasted no more time, getting up and making her way into the kitchen where she prepared herself a strong cup of black coffee. After a quick shower, another cup of coffee and a small but very healthy breakfast, she was ready to leave.

At that time in the morning, and with less traffic than usual, it took her just twenty-two minutes to cover the almost ten miles between her home in West Hollywood and the coroner's office on North Mission Road.

As the doctor swiped her security card at the door of the main building and stepped into the lobby, the young, tall and wiry attendant sitting behind the reception counter looked at her without much surprise.

'Couldn't sleep again, Doctor Hove?'

'Something like that,' she replied with a feeble smile.

'I really don't know how you do it, Doc. I just can't function if I don't get a good night's sleep. Have you tried cherry juice, or chamomile and lavender tea? They work wonders for me.'

'I don't really have a problem falling asleep,' she explained, approaching the counter. 'What's tricky is staying in that state for long enough.'

The attendant nodded once. 'Oh, I see. Yep, I hate it when that happens too.'

'So what did we get overnight?' the doctor asked while she checked something on her cellphone.

'Let me have a look.' The attendant turned his attention to the computer on the counter in front of him and quickly typed something in. 'Not that busy a night, Doc, you'll be glad to know,' he said after a few seconds. 'Only ten new bodies. Five male, four female, and a kid. Five of them seem to be drug related, one from sexual play, and four, including the kid, are homicides.'

Doctor Hove nodded, unsurprised. She had been the Los Angeles County Chief Medical Examiner for three years, and a senior medical examiner for the city of Los Angeles for twenty years prior to that. When it came to violent deaths, very little ever shocked her.

'Oh, wait,' the attendant said, as the doctor began to turn away. 'One of the bodies is flagged as urgent.'

Doctor Hove chuckled. 'Yeah, well, they usually are. Everyone always needs their results ASAP.'

'I know,' the attendant replied, raising his eyebrows. 'But this one says LAPD's UV Unit.'

That made Doctor Hove pause, turn around and return to the counter. 'Who is it?'

The assistant brought up the file on his screen.

'Female, twenty years of age, already identified as Nicole Wilson. No apparent cause of death. She was brought in just a couple of hours ago, Doc.'

The doctor chewed on those facts for a moment. She knew that UV Unit detectives would be calling or dropping by first thing in the morning, and then every hour after that until they had their results. She quickly made her decision.

'OK. Can you please get someone to take her body to theater one?'

The attendant checked the clock on the wall to his left. 'You're going to autopsy her now?'

Usually when Doctor Hove came in early she dealt mainly with paperwork.

'That's the idea.'

'But as I've said, she just came in about two hours ago, Doc,' the attendant retorted, looking slightly surprised. 'She hasn't been prepped or anything.'

Before any autopsy examination, the body needs to be prepared for the post mortem – undressed, then sprayed with fungicide and thoroughly washed with disinfectant soap. That job usually fell to the morgue orderlies, but their shift wouldn't start for at least another hour and a half.

'It's OK,' Doctor Hove replied. 'I'll prep the body myself, it's not a problem.'

'You're the boss,' the attendant said, noting something down on a notepad. 'Would you like me to find you an assistant for the autopsy? I can probably find you one while you're prepping the body.'

'No need. I'll be fine on my own.'

After scrubbing up and disinfecting her hands, Doctor Hove made her way to Autopsy Theater One. The body of Nicole Wilson had already been wheeled in and transferred to one of the two stainless-steel tables that occupied the middle of the spotlessly clean, white linoleum floor.

Nicole Wilson was lying on her back, arms loosely resting by her side. Livor mortis, the discoloration of the body by the settling of blood, showed that the body had most probably been moved after death. She had not been killed in the location where she was found. Rigor mortis had also come and gone, which told the doctor that she'd been dead for over twenty-four hours. Her facial features were now essentially unrecognizable.

Doctor Hove first freed the body from its shoes. There were no cuts to Nicole Wilson's feet or toes, but the doctor immediately noticed the tiny abrasions and color change to her ankles – ligature marks. Next, she removed the CSULA sweatshirt, which had bits of grass and dirt stuck to it. As each item of clothing was taken from the body, it was carefully placed into a clear-plastic evidence bag, which would later be handed over to forensics for further examination. Blood, urine and hair samples would also be collected, and oral and anal swabs taken.

As the doctor removed the victim's sweatshirt, the first thing she noticed were the ligature marks on the woman's wrists. Not surprising, since she had already found restraint marks on her ankles.

Using a pair of safety scissors, Doctor Hove proceeded to slice open Nicole Wilson's T-shirt. As it came undone, she paused, her eyes slowly running up and down the woman's torso.

'Jesus Christ!'

After reaching for her digital camera and documenting everything, Doctor Hove finished undressing the body, sprayed it with fungicide and used a hose with a powerful water jet to methodically wash and disinfect every inch of it. With that over, she turned on her digital voice recorder and started the official examination.

She began by stating the date and time, followed by the case number. After that, she described the general state of the body. Now it was time to move into all the grisly details.

Using a magnifying headset with a directional light, Doctor Hove began by checking the skin around the neck. There were no suspicious bruises. A quick touch-examination also revealed that neither Nicole Wilson's larynx nor her trachea had collapsed. The hyoid bone in her neck also didn't seem to be fractured. There was absolutely nothing to suggest that she had been strangled by hand, or any other method.

Using her thumb and index finger, Doctor Hove pulled open Nicole's eyelids and, with the help of the magnifying headset, carefully studied her eyes. As expected, her corneas were cloudy and opaque, but what the doctor was looking for were minute red specks that could be dotting her eyes or their lids, called petechiae. These tiny hemorrhages in blood vessels can occur anywhere in the body, and for a number of reasons, but when they occur in the eyes and on the eyelids it's usually due to blockage of the respiratory system – suffocation or asphyxiation.

Doctor Hove saw none. It also didn't seem like Nicole Wilson had died from lack of oxygen.

Her next step was to check all of Nicole's cavities for any signs of aggression, sexual or otherwise. She began with her mouth, pulling it open and first checking for any trauma or skin and teeth color alteration. Certain poisons will leave a clear indication of having being used by either burning the fragile skin inside the victim's mouth, or leaving a residue that will discolor the teeth and tongue, or both. Doctor Hove found no primary indications of poisoning, but she'd have to wait for the results from the toxicology tests to be completely sure.

She was about to move on when something caught her attention.

'Wait a second,' she whispered to herself, turning the light on her magnifying headset back on and squinting at the inside of Nicole Wilson's mouth. 'What do we have here?'

She examined the victim's throat for a moment.

'I'll be damned.'

Carefully, the doctor moved the head left, then right, then down a fraction. She had no doubt about it, there was definitely something lodged in the victim's throat.

From the instrument table to her right she grabbed a digital camera and proceeded to photograph the object undisturbed, snapping three shots from different angles. Once that was done, she retrieved a pair of surgical fishing forceps and inserted them into Nicole's mouth. It took her just a couple of seconds to pinch the edge of the object she could see. It looked like a thick piece of paper. Cautiously, she began extracting it from the throat.

'What the hell?'

What at first looked like a paper fragment just kept on coming – three, four, five inches long before it finally came loose. The piece of paper had been tightly rolled up into a tube, then inserted into Nicole Wilson's throat.

Doctor Hove deposited the rolled-up piece of paper on to an aluminum tray on the table, grabbed her camera once again, and snapped a couple more shots.

She put the camera down and very slowly started to unroll the paper tube.

Despite everything she'd seen in all her years as a pathologist and medical examiner, and she'd seen things that defied belief, as she held the unrolled tube of paper in her hands, Doctor Hove had to pause for breath.

'Oh fuck!'

Ten

The day outside was bright and warm, with a cloudless blue sky that could've belonged in the Caribbean. Even at that time in the morning, and with the breeze that blew from the west, temperatures were already getting up to 68°F.

Garcia drove while Hunter re-studied Nicole Wilson's fact sheet and the photographs in both files the captain had given them. As they merged on to Harbor Freeway, heading towards the airport, Hunter's cellphone rang inside his pocket.

'Detective Hunter, Homicide Special,' he answered on the second ring.

'Robert, it's Doctor Carolyn Hove at the LA County Coroner.'

'Oh, hi, Doc.' Hunter wasn't expecting her call so soon.

'I'm not sure if "welcome" is the right word, but . . . welcome back.'

'Thanks.'

Doctor Hove sounded tired, which Hunter knew wasn't that unusual due to her workload and the problems she faced when it came to sleeping. Not that she had ever discussed it with him or anyone else for that matter, but Hunter knew about her husband, and he had recognized the telltale signs of insomnia over a year ago, just after her loss. He was well qualified to do so.

Hunter was an insomniac himself. He had struggled with it most of his life. It'd started mildly, just after his mother lost her battle with cancer. As the years went by it intensified, but Hunter quickly learned that his insomnia was nothing more than his brain's defense mechanism so he didn't have to deal with the ghastly nightmares that tormented him almost every night. Instead of fighting it, he simply learned to live with it. He could survive on three, sometimes two hours of sleep a night for weeks.

'I just finished the autopsy on case 75249-6. Young female identified as Nicole Wilson. According to the case file, you're the lead, is that correct?'

'Yes, that's right.'

'OK.' Hunter heard the sound of pages turning. 'I think that you'll want to have a look at what I found, Robert.'

'Sure, Doc. But we're just on our way to the location where the body was found. We'll drop by the morgue in, let's say –' he consulted his watch – 'two hours, give or take.'

There was a heavy pause. When Doctor Hove spoke again, there was something else in her tone of voice – trepidation – that was very unusual.

'Trust me, Robert, I really think that you should have a look at this first.'

Eleven

The main facility of the Los Angeles County Department of Coroner on North Mission Road was an impressive building, both in size and architecture. Showing hints of Renaissance and neoclassicism, the large hospital-turned-morgue was fronted by terracotta bricks with light-gray details. Old-fashioned lampposts flanked the extravagant entrance stairway, and from the exterior alone one would be forgiven for thinking that the inspiration for such lavish design had come from the old town of Prague, or the historic universities of Oxford.

Garcia parked in the area reserved for law enforcement officials and both detectives took the stairs up to the main building in a hurry. They pushed open the large glass doors that led into an awfully busy, but pleasantly air-conditioned, lobby and stepped inside.

Neither Hunter nor Garcia were too surprised as to the number of people mingling around the reception foyer. As the busiest coroner in the whole of the USA, the Los Angeles County Department of Coroner could receive anywhere up to one hundred bodies a day. The LACDC was also the only department of coroner in the country with an official gift shop, where one could purchase sweatshirts, baseball caps, mugs, skeleton bones and a multitude of other items, all carrying the legitimate logo of the Los Angeles morgue.

Hunter and Garcia zigzagged their way through a group of Japanese tourists and approached the main reception counter. The middle-aged African-American woman behind it looked up from her computer screen, removed her reading glasses and gave them a smile that was both warm and sorrowful at the same time.

'Hello, gentlemen, how can I help you?' She spoke in the same tone and volume as a librarian.

Morgue receptionists' greetings were pretty much the same all over the USA. They never greeted anyone with the words 'good morning', 'good afternoon', or 'good evening'. Usually, a person visiting a morgue would struggle to find anything good about the day they were having.

'LAPD Detectives Hunter and Garcia to see Doctor Carolyn Hove,' Hunter said, producing his credentials. Garcia did the same.

'She's expecting us,' Hunter added.

The receptionist allowed her eyes to hover over both detectives' badges for a moment before reaching for the phone on the counter in front of her, but before she was able to dial the heavy metal door on the east wall was pushed open by Doctor Hove herself.

'Robert, Carlos,' she said. 'You guys made it in good time.'

Doctor Hove wore a white lab coat with a photo card clipped to her left pocket. She was holding a blue file in her right hand.

'Hey, Doc,' Hunter and Garcia said at the same time, greeting her warmly.

Doctor Hove was a tall and slim woman with deep penetrating green eyes. Her long chestnut hair was bundled up into a bun and tucked under a factory-style hairnet. A surgical mask hung from her neck.

'Once again,' she said. 'I'm not sure if this really applies, but . . . welcome back, both of you.' She paused and her eyes narrowed a fraction as she looked at Hunter. 'Though, I must add that you don't look like you just came back from a break, Robert. Are you sure you've been away?'

'Oh, I'm sure.'

Garcia stifled a smile.

'So,' Hunter asked, his eyes focusing on the file in her hand. 'What have you found, Doc?'

She didn't follow his gaze. Instead, she tilted her head in the direction of the door she'd just come out of.

'I think you both better come with me.'

Twelve

Hunter and Garcia followed Doctor Hove past the reception counter, through a set of double swinging doors and into a wide corridor with strip lights on the ceiling and shiny floors.

As they entered the corridor, they were all greeted by a cold, antiseptic odor that lingered in the air and scratched the inside of their nostrils as if it were alive.

Hunter hated that smell. No matter how many times he'd been through these corridors, he just couldn't get used to it. He subtly scratched his nose and did his best to breathe only through his mouth.

They passed a couple of closed doors with frosted-glass windows on the left side of the corridor, before turning right at the end of it and into a second, narrower hallway. There they came across three lab technicians, also in white medical scrubs, standing around a coffee machine. None of them looked their way.

They pushed through a set of double swinging doors and, as they did, they all had to squeeze against the wall and wait for a trolley wheeled by an orderly to go past. The body on the trolley was covered by a white calico sheet. Balanced on its torso was a box of test tubes containing blood and urine.

Garcia made a face and looked the other way.

At the end of that corridor, they finally reached a small anteroom. Another set of double doors with two small frosted-glass windows stood directly in front of them. Above the doors, in big black letters, a plate read – Autopsy Theater One.

'Here we are,' Doctor Hove said, as she punched a six-digit code into the keypad to the right of the door. It buzzed loudly, and then the door unlocked with a hiss like a pressure seal.

Most people who have never been inside an autopsy room would expect the air to be heavy with the smell of a compound like formaldehyde – something many associate with biomedical labs and the preservation of a body or part of it, human or otherwise. Instead, Hunter detected a faint scent of antiseptic and industrial soap. The temperature inside the autopsy rooms was also a few degrees below what would be considered comfortable. Within minutes, an unprepared visitor would be shivering in here from the temperature alone.

The room was relatively spacious. A large double sink hugged the west wall, with a central channel that led to a drain. Next to it was a metal counter with a multitude of tools, including a Stryker saw. Parked against the north wall, in neat rows, were three empty trolleys. The center of the room was taken by two stainless-steel examination tables. The body on the furthest of the two was completely covered by a white sheet. Just above the table, circular and powerful halogen lights were suspended from the ceiling.

Doctor Hove gloved up and approached the table. Hunter and Garcia followed, each grabbing a pair of latex gloves themselves.

The doctor positioned herself on the other side of the

table from the two detectives and pulled back the sheet, revealing Nicole Wilson's naked body. Her skin had begun to turn a pale, ghostly shade of white. Her eyes had sunk deeper into their sockets, and her thin lips had now lost all color. Her hair looked wet and messy, with some of it sticking to the sides of her face. Clearly visible was the large Y incision that started at the top of each shoulder, ran down between her breasts and the front of her stomach, and concluded at the lower point of her sternum. A second large incision had also been made around her head, running across the top of her forehead to open her cranium, which indicated that her brain had been examined. Hunter found that a little peculiar, but he knew the doctor would explain it in due time. Both incisions had been stitched up with thick, black surgical thread. All that gave Nicole's body a plastic, Frankenstein-mannequin look, a far cry from the person she had once been.

As the white sheet was pulled back, Hunter and Garcia paused, looked at each other for a split second, then back at the body. What caught them by surprise wasn't the ugliness of the two incisions, or the roughness of the black thorn-like stitches. They had seen those more times than they cared to mention. What had made them pause was the incredible number of open wounds that covered most of the victim's torso and thighs. They all looked to be fresh lacerations, probably no more than three to four days old, varying in sizes and orientation – some were horizontal, some diagonal, some vertical.

'What the hell?' Garcia breathed out.

'I know,' Doctor Hove agreed. 'I was as surprised as you are when I undressed the body as I prepped it for the post mortem earlier today.'

Both detectives approached the table, bending down slightly to have a better look at the cuts.

'What we have here is a combination of two types of wounds,' the doctor announced. 'As you can plainly see, they all vary in size – the smallest being just over an inch long, and the largest measuring five and three quarter inches. No two lacerations are the exact same size.'

She placed her fingers over the sides of one of the cuts and pressed it down, spreading it open.

'None of the cuts is deep enough to have reached a major organ, artery or vein.'

She repeated the process with a couple more cuts.

'They're essentially all flesh wounds.'

'Torture,' Garcia stated rather than asked.

'No doubt,' Doctor Hove replied.

'You said that they were a combination of two types of wounds,' Hunter queried. 'What do you mean, Doc?'

Doctor Hove shrugged and tilted her head to her left. 'To be more precise, not two types of wounds, but wounds inflicted by two different instruments.'

Garcia repositioned himself by the foot of the examination table.

'Some, like this one for example,' she indicated a diagonal wound just above the body's right nipple, which looked to be about three inches long, 'were made by a laser-sharp instrument. Maybe a kitchen knife, or perhaps a surgical scalpel. Very clean. No serrated edges. Further analyses showed that some of the cuts created by such an instrument were made from right to left, some from left to right. The ones that aren't horizontal in orientation also vary. Some were made starting at the highest point and moving down. Some, the exact opposite.' Doctor Hove moved her index finger from the lowest point of the wound to the highest. 'That makes it impossible for us to tell if the assailant was right or left-handed. To me, it looks like the killer was having fun. He enjoyed torturing her.'

Hunter and Garcia kept their full attention on the body.

'He took his time,' Hunter added, his eyes tracing the cuts. 'To him it was almost like putting brush strokes on to a canvas.'

'There's no doubt that he took his time,' the doctor confirmed. 'As I've said, some of the cuts were made by a very sharp instrument, but not all of them.' She directed their attention to the lower half of the body. 'Like most of the wounds inflicted on her legs and back.'

Hunter took a step closer to examine the wounds to her thighs. Neither detective was surprised to hear that the victim also had lacerations to her back.

'These cuts weren't created by a sharp instrument,' Doctor Hove continued.

'So what was used?' Garcia asked.

'A whip.' The answer came from Hunter. He had seen similar injuries before.

'That's correct,' the Doctor agreed. 'But not the kind used for sexual play, or what have you. What was used here was a proper leather bullwhip. The kind used to tame animals. I counted and recounted them. She received sixty lashes. But they were expertly controlled. Hard enough to break the skin and cause extreme pain, but light enough so it wouldn't cut too deep into her flesh and cause excessive bleeding. That would've no doubt driven the victim into unconsciousness too often. He didn't want that to happen. The same level of control was applied to the laser-sharp cuts which, by the way, also amount to sixty – hard enough to break the skin and rupture flesh to cause pain, but light enough to not cause excessive bleeding.' Doctor Hove lifted her finger to emphasize her next point. 'The interesting thing here is, healing progress differs slightly from one batch of wounds to another.'

'Batch of wounds? What do you mean, Doc?' Garcia asked.

'Front of the torso, back of the torso, front of the legs, back of the legs, and buttocks.' The doctor paused, her words hanging in the air for a moment, like smoke. 'And that means that they were inflicted upon her at different times, most probably daily. In my opinion, she was flogged and tortured for five days, give or take a day.'

'Was she sexually assaulted?' Hunter asked.

'Repeatedly. But unfortunately for us the assailant was careful enough to protect himself. I could recover no trace of semen, foreign blood, or any other bodily fluids.'

As a sign of respect, the room went silent for a moment.

Hunter walked over to where Garcia was and bent over to have a closer look at the victim's neck.

'I found no signs that she was either strangled or suffocated,' the doctor added, anticipating Hunter's question. 'X-rays also revealed no broken bones. Toxicology will be another day or two, and if the killer used any sort of drugs on her prior to her death we should get a result for traces of it soon enough, but we won't get a positive result for poisoning. That's not how she died.'

'So what was the cause of death, Doc?' Garcia asked.

'I'll get there in a minute, Carlos,' Doctor Hove said, paused, and called their attention to the marks on the body's wrists, ankles and cheeks. 'First let me show you a peculiarity about these. These marks indicate that she was very tightly restrained, and for a considerable amount of time. Most certainly while she was being tortured and violated. The restraint used on her wrists was some sort of thin rope. Probably nylon. Probably very easy to obtain from a multitude of stores. But I found no residues to examine, so that's just an educated guess.'

'On her wrists?' Garcia asked with a frown.

Doctor Hove nodded. 'And that's what I mean by peculiarity. Her captor used different restraints on her ankles – stronger, harder, thicker. From the pattern left on her ankles, I'd say he used a metal chain.'

'And why would he do that?' Garcia again. 'I mean, why two different types of restraints?'

Doctor Hove allowed her gaze to move around the room aimlessly, almost as if she was trying to pass the question on.

'More torture,' she finally replied. 'The kind that won't show externally.'

'Whoa.' Garcia lifted a hand. 'Are you saying that her internal organs were also damaged? I mean, due to torture?'

'One was,' Doctor Hove replied. 'And that'll finally bring us to the cause of death, which baffled me throughout the entire post mortem examination until I examined her brain.'

Doctor Hove's words seemed to chill the air inside the autopsy room even further.

'Her brain showed signs of being damaged?' Garcia asked. His eyes moved to Nicole's head. 'With no visible external trauma? Was her cranium injured?'

'No. Her cranium was intact.'

Garcia raised his eyebrow questioningly.

Doctor Hove retrieved two sheets of paper from the instrument table behind her and handed one to each detective. 'What caused her death was oedema of the brain.'

Garcia frowned at the sheet. 'Wait a second, Doc, isn't oedema some sort of swelling?'

'Well, swelling is a consequence of it,' the doctor clarified. 'More precisely, oedema is an excessive build-up of fluid in the body's tissues, which will often cause swelling and can result in further damage. It's most common in the feet and ankles, but it can occur anywhere in the body – the lungs, the eyes, the knees, the hands, and in rarer cases, the brain.'

'So you're saying that her brain swelled up because of fluid excess?' Garcia again.

'That's correct.'

'What sort of fluid?'

'Her own blood.'

Thirteen

Garcia looked at Hunter, then at the body, then back at Doctor Hove.

'She died due to an excessive build-up of her own blood inside her brain?' he asked. 'And that was induced by the killer? How?'

'By keeping her upside down for long enough,' Hunter answered in a subdued voice. 'That would explain the difference in restraints from her wrists to her ankles. They needed to be stronger to be able to hold her body weight.'

'Correct again, Robert,' Doctor Hove agreed, moving closer to the head of the examination table, and resting her hands by Nicole's ears. 'If you understand the process, oedema of the brain isn't very difficult to achieve. You see, it all rests on the difference between arteries and veins. Arteries are thick-walled vessels that carry blood away from the heart and into the organs of the body.' Like a medical professor addressing her students, she pointed at Nicole's chest, and then moved her hand away, spreading her fingers at the same time as she explained. 'Even upside down, the heart will continue to distribute blood through the arteries just as strongly as it would right side up. That blood travels with a lot of pressure, due to it being forced into the arteries by the pumping of the heart. So, right side up, upside down ... it makes no difference. Blood will always travel with the same force away from the heart. Veins, on the other hand, are thin-walled vessels that carry blood from the organs of the body back into the heart for repumping. They have essentially no pressure in them, and they rely on gravity, inertia and the force of skeletal muscle contractions to help push blood back to the heart.'

Doctor Hove coughed to clear her throat before continuing.

'With no skeletal muscle contractions happening inside the skull, if you reverse gravity by placing someone upside down for long enough, blood will still travel normally from the heart, through the arteries, and into the brain, but it will cease to travel through the veins back to the heart. So what you have is a build-up – blood coming into the brain, but not getting out.'

The doctor paused, the look on her face just a little more somber than a moment ago.

'With a build-up of blood in the brain, after a while blood will start to leak from the capillaries, accumulating inside the cranium, increasing pressure, and causing the brain to swell. And with that comes a hell of a lot of pain – head, ears, eyes, nose ... every heart pump would probably feel like thunder was exploding inside her head. All the killer had to do was suspend her by her feet, nothing else. Gravity does the rest. He didn't even have to be in the room anymore. The pressure would've just kept on building up inside her head until it brought her gradual loss of consciousness, and then finally death as the brain would signal either respiration to fail, or the heart to stop pumping blood.'

Uneasily, Hunter shifted his weight from one foot to another.

'How long?' Garcia asked. 'How long before she died?

How long could one stand all that pain before the gradual loss of consciousness and death?'

Doctor Hove gave the detective a subtle, unsure head-shake. 'It would depend on several factors, Carlos, like strength and health of the victim. She appears to have been very healthy – good muscle tone, non-smoker, strong lungs, healthy liver and kidneys. But even if I'm wrong, the killer could've prolonged the whole process for as long as he wanted simply by returning her to a right-side-up position, decreasing the pressure in her brain, and then starting it all over again an hour or so later.'

'Do you have an approximate time of death?' Hunter asked.

'Supposing that her body was always kept at room temperature after death,' the doctor explained, 'and I found no indication to the contrary, I'd say that she's been dead for about thirty hours, give or take a couple.'

Hunter and Garcia knew that Nicole Wilson had been abducted seven days prior to her body being found, which meant that her killer could indeed have tortured her for five and a half consecutive days.

Before she spoke again, Doctor Hove took in a deep breath and held it for several seconds.

'But that's not all,' she finally said.

Hunter and Garcia both looked at her, surprised.

'Everything I've told you about this victim . . . about how she was tortured, about how she was murdered . . . I'd say none of it is scary in comparison to this.'

'In comparison to what, Doc?' Garcia asked.

The doctor turned and retrieved something else from the instrument table behind her – a clear plastic evidence bag containing a white piece of paper.

'To this.'

'And what is that?' Hunter this time.

Doctor Hove looked down at the evidence bag for a couple of seconds before locking eyes with Hunter.

'This is a note from the killer. He left it lodged inside her throat.'

'Wait. What?' Garcia asked, lifting a hand as if he hadn't heard it properly.

Hunter didn't move.

'This piece of paper was first rolled up into a tube,' the doctor explained, 'then carefully inserted into the victim's throat.' She handed the plastic evidence bag to Hunter. 'The note speaks for itself.'

The piece of paper inside it was about eight inches long by five wide. Plain white. No lines. Across the center of it, written in blood, were three words.

I AM DEATH.

Fourteen

After leaving the LACDC, it took Hunter and Garcia forty-eight minutes to reach the location where Nicole Wilson's body had been found – a large, unoccupied green field just a stone's throw away from Los Angeles International Airport. The field itself was half a mile long by a quarter of a mile wide. Most of it was densely populated by bushy trees like wax myrtles, white ash and California pepper trees, with the exception of two small areas occupied by untreated grass and a few small shrubs and bushes – one on its west side and a much smaller one on its southeast side, where the body had been left. Oddly enough, as if it had decided to run away from the forest-like field, a lonely tree stood in that southeast clearance. Nicole Wilson's body had been placed just a few feet from it.

Neither detective said much throughout the entire trip. They were both lost in their own thoughts, silently running over everything Doctor Hove had thrown at them and trying their best to make sense of a senseless act.

But even in silence, they both shared one certainty – a killer who was bold enough to write a message in blood and carefully place it in his victim's throat, knowing full well that it would be found during the post mortem examination, a killer confident enough to call himself DEATH

– didn't do it for fun. He didn't do it just to tease the police, or to inflate his own ego. He did it for one reason. To let everyone know that this wouldn't end here.

At the southwest end of the airport, Garcia turned right on to Pershing Drive, and geared down his car.

The area had been cordoned off and a perimeter had already been established by the police. Due to its semi-secluded location there were very few curious onlookers hanging around. The ones that had ventured their luck were being kept too far back to be able to catch a glimpse of anything interesting, and looked bored and ready to give up at any second.

A single reporter was trying his best to obtain any kind of information from the officers by the yellow tape that read: Police Line – Do Not Cross.

Despite decreasing numbers in recent years, murder in LA was still a very common occurrence – on average, one person was murdered every thirty-nine hours in the City of Angels. Though newspapers and TV news stations still covered a number of them, murder just didn't constitute big news anymore, unless the crime was shrouded by some sort of attention-grabbing factor, like a celebrity being involved, extreme violence or it being attributed to a serial killer.

As Garcia approached the perimeter at the other end from where the reporter was, a uniformed officer signaled for him to turn left and move on, but instead Garcia simply slowed down further. Irritated, the officer shook his head and murmured something to himself before taking a couple of steps toward Garcia's car.

'Sir, as you can see the road is closed,' the officer said in a bored voice, first indicating the police line, then gesturing to his left. 'You need to go around the—'

Garcia lifted his left hand, interrupting the officer and displaying his credentials.

The officer stopped midsentence and nodded apologetically. 'Sorry, sir.'

As he handed Garcia the crime-scene logbook so he and Hunter could sign it, a Boeing 777 finished its approach on the west route and touched down on runway 7R, its engine noise so loud and powerful Garcia's car windows rattled.

'You can park on the road right over there, sir, by that black and white unit,' the officer said, collecting the logbook.

Garcia did exactly that.

Two other uniformed officers stood under the shade of a tall and leafy tree next to some more yellow tape that denoted a smaller, internal perimeter. A third officer was sitting inside his Ford Interceptor, apparently text messaging someone. Most activities, including crime scene forensics, had already ceased.

All the officers looked up as Hunter and Garcia stepped out of the car. They didn't need to flash their badges; the officers knew that the only people allowed past the police line would be CSIs or detectives. With zero concern, they returned their attention to whatever it was that they were doing.

From where Hunter stood, just by Pershing Drive, he paused and studied his surroundings. Garcia joined him and did the same for several seconds.

The location had been very well picked out. The field was well away from prying eyes, sandwiched between the airport and a water treatment plant. There were no residential homes within a one-mile radius of it. The road they were on, which was parallel to the field and provided its only access route, served only as a shortcut between Culver

Boulevard and Dockweiler Beach. Traffic would be minimal during the day, and even less so at night.

Only two yellow evidence-number placards had been placed on the field. The first, displaying the number 1, had been positioned in a direct line with the large tree by which the two officers were standing, about eight feet east of it. It marked the spot where Nicole Wilson's body had been found. The second placard – 2 – was located not too far from where Hunter and Garcia stood, about fifteen feet in from the road. From the report they'd read, Hunter and Garcia knew that it indicated where forensics had found depressions on the grass – probably caused by a heavy vehicle, like an SUV, probably the one used by the killer. But the depressions were on grass, not dirt or mud, which meant that forensics had been unable to obtain any tire tracks. The best they could do, if they were correct in their assumption, was to identify where the killer had parked.

As both detectives started walking toward evidence placard number 1, an Airbus 320 took to the skies from runway 7R. Garcia cringed at the deafening sound, bringing his hands up to cover his ears.

The two officers who were standing by the tree, shading themselves from the sun, turned to face the detectives.

Hunter and Garcia would have preferred to view the body *in situ*, but since they had only been handed the case several hours after the body had been discovered, they had to content themselves with the photographs taken by the CSI team, and the odd, star-like shape created by white tape that forensics had used to outline the body's exact position on the ground.

Despite the tape, Hunter retrieved a photo from the folder Garcia had with him, went down on his haunches and placed it on the grass, right at the center of the white outline.

Garcia squatted down next to him.

Nicole's body had been left with her extended right arm pointing west, in a straight line with the lone leafy tree. Her right leg pointed southwest. Consequently, her left arm and leg pointed east and southeast respectively. Her head pointed north.

Hunter's eyes flicked from the picture to the tree and the surrounding vegetation several times.

Garcia ran his palm against the grass around him. Despite it being untreated, it wasn't very high – about two to three inches long, maybe four in some places. It felt dry, which was understandable because Los Angeles had seen nothing but cloudless skies and a beating sun for the past two weeks. Not a drop of rain.

'There's no give on the ground whatsoever,' Garcia said, his fingers still moving back and forth on the grass. 'That's why forensics got no footprints anywhere.'

Across the road at LAX, another airplane approached and touched down.

Garcia stood up, his eyes searching the vicinity once again. Something didn't sit right with him.

'Why would the killer dump her body right on this spot?' he asked.

He was facing west, looking at the leafy tree. There were dense clusters of trees north, south and further west, past the lonely tree. Pershing Drive and the airport were east, directly behind him.

'I was just asking myself that same question,' Hunter said.

'The killer clearly wasn't attempting to hide the body,' Garcia added. 'Just look around. There are thicker clusters of trees just about everywhere on this field. He could've hidden the body behind any of them. Why place it here, in the most exposed spot there is? Plus, this guy was arrogant enough to write us a note just to tell us his chosen name – DEATH. And I say "us" because he knew the note would be found during the autopsy examination. Not to mention the whole role-playing abduction game that he played with the victim. This guy's got an ego, Robert, and it's a big one. He's confident, seemingly intelligent and knowledgeable. He knows it, and he wants us to know it as well. If such a person wanted to hide a body, he wouldn't dump in a city field. He would've simply made it disappear. No traces. No witnesses. Nothing. He dumped the body here because he wanted it found.'

Hunter agreed with a nod. 'But something still isn't right,' he said.

Garcia looked around again.

'One thing we know,' Hunter continued, 'is that perpetrators who place their victims' bodies into specific positions or shapes, with the intention of them being found that way, are very particular about everything, every detail. Most of them to the point of OCD.' Hunter indicated the photograph of the body *in situ*. 'The position of the hands, feet, head, the hair, the clothes and the makeup, if any, the surroundings . . . it all has to perfectly match the picture in the perpetrator's head.'

Above them another aircraft approached for landing. Hunter waited for the sound to die down before moving on.

'This guy put a lot of time and effort into what he did – the abduction, the torturing, the kill method, the positioning as he disposed of the body, the note in her throat . . . everything was done with tremendous attention to detail.

There's no way he would want us to miss any of it. He wants us to know how good he thinks he is.'

'I agree,' Garcia said. 'And that's why this is bothering me. He would've wanted the body found, and fast, before the elements started to eat at it, before something or someone disturbed its placement. For that, this whole site is wrong. It's too secluded, too far back from the road ... wait a second.' Garcia lifted a hand as he looked at Hunter.

'Who found the body?' Hunter asked. 'Who called it in?'

'I was about to ask you the same question,' Garcia said, already searching through the file he had with him, looking for the 911-occurrence sheet. 'Who would've come across a body way out here?' A few more page flips. 'OK, here it is.' Garcia pulled a sheet out of the folder. As he read it, his forehead creased with doubt. 'Anonymous call, made by a male cyclist at 12:39 a.m.'

The green field they were in sure as hell wasn't a city park. It looked more like a small forest than anything else, squashed between an airport and a water treatment plant. People didn't walk their dogs there. They didn't go for runs, or cycle about in a place like that, especially not at night.

'A cyclist riding past here at around half past midnight spotted the body?' Garcia repeated, pointing to Pershing Drive. 'From that road? That's what, about thirty to forty yards away? In pitch-black darkness?' He chuckled at the idea. 'I don't think so.'

Fifteen

Taking extra care not to damage her recently manicured pale-pink fingernails, Grace Hamilton opened the FedEx package. Inside, she found a standard, brown paper legal-size envelope addressed to the Mayor of Los Angeles, Richard Bailey. Across the front, in large red letters, were the words URGENT – PRIVATE & CONFIDENTIAL.

She reached for the FedEx wrapper and checked the sender's name on the back. Tyler Jordan.

Grace frowned at it. It wasn't a name she recognized. The address was local, somewhere in Victoria Park, Central LA. Despite having a fantastic memory for names and addresses, she couldn't remember seeing it before either. The space for the sender's contact number had been left blank – typical.

She pulled her chair closer to her computer desk and called up the application that allowed her to go into Mayor Bailey's contacts book. After typing in her password, she entered the family name 'Jordan' and clicked 'Search'. She got three matches, none of them were Tyler. None of them from Los Angeles. She tried 'Tyler Jordan' as a double-barreled name, first with a hyphen, then without.

Nothing.

Grace didn't find that strange at all. It wasn't unusual for members of the public to mark their mail 'urgent', or 'for your eyes only', or 'private and confidential', in the hope that it would reach the mayor's desk unopened. But that rarely happened.

Mayor Bailey received hundreds of letters from members of the public every month, but it was Grace's job to make sure that he didn't waste his valuable time reading the sort of rubbish that got sent in on a daily basis.

Whoever Tyler Jordan was, it didn't look like he, or she for that matter as Tyler could be male or female, was known to Mayor Bailey. That fact alone already placed the envelope in the 'not so urgent' stack, but elections were just around the corner and Grace couldn't afford to ignore something potentially important.

She called up an Internet map application and entered the address on the back of the envelope. What she got was a boarded-up grocery store on an empty concrete lot.

Strange, she thought, but that only served to heighten her curiosity.

Grace knew that, before reaching her desk, every single postal item had already been thoroughly scanned by security for harmful chemicals and explosives, so it wasn't like she was taking a health risk. But x-ray machines and other security devices couldn't read any internal text, or make out any included images.

In the two and a half years she'd been working for Mayor Bailey, she'd seen obscene drawings, threatening letters, hate mail, pornographic pictures of people offering themselves to him (female and male), conspiracy theory plots . . . the list was almost endless.

Anything deemed remotely threatening was passed on to

the Secret Service. Anything viewed as indecent or obnoxious went straight into the shredder by her desk.

Grace stared at the envelope in her hands for a short while, then at the 'not so urgent' mail pile on her desk. She pursed her lips.

'Oh, what the hell,' she said seconds later as she slid open the envelope. One more crazy letter or silly picture wouldn't really make a difference to her. If there was one thing that Grace Hamilton was not it was prudish.

What she got was a second envelope. This one was crispy white, similar to the ones sent with wedding invitations. On the front of it someone had typed the words – DO NOT IGNORE THIS.

Now Grace was really intrigued.

She checked the back of the new envelope. No sender's name or address. Not that she really expected to find any.

She bit the right side of her bottom lip, considering.

A couple of seconds later, her decision was made. She reached for the sword-shaped letter opener on her desk, tore open the top of the envelope and tilted it so its contents could slide out.

The first item to drop on to Grace's desk was a white piece of paper that had been folded in half. Something had clearly been written inside. She could make out the outlines of the letters.

The second item was a Polaroid photograph.

It slid on to her desk face down.

Grace paused, amused by the irony of it all. One more decision to make – what to look at first, the picture or the folded piece of paper?

In her head, she eeny meeny miny moed between the two items.

The picture won.
She reached for it and turned it over.
Her heart skipped a beat.
'Oh, sweet Jesus!'

Sixteen

Garcia's gaze stayed on the 911-occurrence sheet for just a moment longer before finding Hunter's face.

'OK,' he said. 'We need to listen to this call.'

Hunter nodded, looking at Garcia's Honda Civic. They could access it through the onboard police computer. They quickly made their way back to the car.

After navigating through a couple of screens, Garcia finally found the emergency-line log record.

'Here it is,' he said as he double-clicked the icon for the sound file.

DISPATCHER (female voice): 'Nine-one-one, what's your emergency?'

MALE VOICE: 'Umm, I think I just came across a dead body. She looks dead.'

The voice sounded a little rushed, but not exactly nervous.

DISPATCHER: 'You said you *came across* a female body?'

Keyboard clanks.

MALE VOICE: 'That's right. I was just riding my bicycle, then suddenly, there she was on the grass.'

DISPATCHER: 'And she isn't moving at all?'

MALE VOICE: 'I'm telling you, she looks dead.'

DISPATCHER: 'Is she a friend of yours? Do you know her name?'

MALE VOICE: 'No, I've never seen her before.'

DISPATCHER: 'OK, sir, can you tell me your location?'

MALE VOICE: 'Yeah, I was cycling north on Pershing Drive, just by the airport – LAX, past the Hyperion water treatment plant.'

There was a pause as the dispatcher waited for the caller to carry on, but he said nothing else.

DISPATCHER: 'OK, sir, that's great, but can you be a little bit more specific? Pershing Drive is quite a long road.'

MALE VOICE: 'Once you pass the treatment plant, heading north, there's a large field full of trees on the left. She's just on the grass by a tree that's a little detached from all the other trees. I'd say maybe about . . . maybe three hundred yards past the plant.'

DISPATCHER: 'Have you tried talking to her, or waking her up? Maybe she was just tired, or had a little too much to drink and fell asleep by the tree. Can you see any liquor bottles by her side? Any trace of vomit on her clothes or on the ground by where she's lying?'

MALE VOICE: 'No, I haven't touched her, and you're not listening to me.'

The voice got a fraction more anxious. He pronounced the next three words very slowly.

MALE VOICE: 'She looks dead.'

DISPATCHER: 'Yes, sir, I *am* listening to you. I just need to establish the correct service to dispatch. Can you see any blood around her, or on her person?'

MALE VOICE: 'No, I can see no blood.'

DISPATCHER: 'OK, and are you sure she isn't breathing? Can you check for a pulse?'

MALE VOICE: 'No, I'm not touching no dead body. Look, you need to send the police up here. Fast.'

DISPATCHER: 'They're already on their way, sir, and they'll be with you very shortly. Can I please have your—'

The caller disconnected.

Hunter and Garcia gave each other a measured stare.

'I want to listen to this again,' Garcia finally said, double-clicking the sound file one more time. Another airplane took off and Garcia increased the volume a touch.

Hunter checked his watch, sat back and closed his eyes, but his attention wasn't on the dialogue anymore.

When the file had finished playing, Garcia breathed out. 'This is all wrong,' he said.

Hunter checked his watch again.

'At night,' Garcia continued, 'not even *Superman* could have spotted the body from this distance. There's no way a cyclist saw her all the way over there from here.'

'Especially when that call wasn't even made from here,' Hunter said.

Garcia's forehead creased. 'What do you mean?'

'There's something missing from the recording, Carlos.'

Garcia's stare became more purposeful and he instinctively looked at the onboard computer screen and the sound file icon again.

A Boeing 767 began its run up the runway and Garcia realized what he had missed.

'There are no background airplane noises,' he said.

They were next to LAX, the third busiest airport in the USA with an aircraft either taking off or landing every forty to sixty seconds, day and night. The roar of jet engines was practically constant. Even with the windows shut, they could still hear it. Hunter had timed it – the call had lasted one minute and forty-two seconds. Even during the night, when air traffic was reduced, they should've heard at least two planes either landing or taking off.

'There are no airplane noises,' Hunter confirmed.

'Sonofabitch,' Garcia said, switching off his car stereo.

'Like you've said, this guy is very confident.' Hunter tilted his head to one side. 'And he wants to play.'

'The killer made the call. We need to get a copy of this recording to audio forensics.'

Hunter agreed.

Garcia regarded him for a couple of seconds. 'But we're not going to get anything from it, are we?'

'I don't think so,' Hunter replied. 'If we do, it will only be because the killer wants us to.'

Seventeen

After leaving the green wooded area by LAX, Hunter and Garcia drove to Nicole Wilson's abduction site – Audrey Bennett's house in the Hollywood Hills. Hunter had no intention of bothering Ms. Bennett for another interview. He knew that there was nothing else she would be able to tell him that she hadn't already told Missing Persons, and Hunter had thoroughly read the interview transcript twice over. What he really wanted was to have a look at the outside of her property and its grounds. He wanted to understand how easy it had been for the killer to gain access to it, break into the house and take Nicole from inside without being noticed. And as Hunter had expected, it'd been particularly easy.

One didn't actually drive up to the Hollywood Hills as much as crawl up. The roads were steep and twisty with so many abrupt changes and so few signs that even residents who'd been living there for years found it easy to get lost. The beauty of it, some said, was that it was exactly that sort of confusion that made Upper Laurel Canyon and Hollywood Hills so desirable to the people who lived there. Who'd need a gated community when few could find their way around anyway?

Audrey Bennett's house was located just off an elbow

bend on Allenwood Road and, like all the other houses on that side of Upper Laurel Canyon, there was no gate, wall, or even a decorative fence protecting any part of her property. No surveillance cameras either. Any visitor, known or unknown, could very easily walk on to the grounds of the house and, if so desired, all the way around to its backyard without being restricted by even the flimsiest of doors.

After asking Ms. Bennett's permission, Hunter and Garcia took their time studying the house, grounds and backyard before taking to the road. As they started walking, they saw two little girls dressed in pink ballet outfits come running out the door of one of the neighboring houses. A short and plump woman followed. The three of them jumped into a blue SUV that was parked on their driveway. As they drove off, both girls waved at Hunter and Garcia from the back seat.

Slowly, both detectives walked from Allenwood Road all the way down to Laurel Pass Avenue. On their way back up to the Bennetts' house, they also walked the length of Carmar Drive, which branched out to the left of the main road. Twice they passed a group of kids on skateboards, none older than thirteen years old, who were making the most out of the steep hills and tight bends.

'Who needs to go to a gym?' Garcia said, wiping his brow with the palm of his hand. With the sun high in the sky, the temperature at that time of the day had hit 82°F. 'Just go up and down these roads once a day and you'll be as fit as an athlete. Just look at this.' He pointed at his face. 'I'm sweating like a pig.'

Hunter paused and watched the kids skate for a few moments. As they reached the bottom of the long hilly road, collected their skateboards and began the long walk back up to the top, a new thought entered his mind. He quickly returned to Garcia's car, picked up the files that Missing Persons had sent over to the RHD and started flipping back through them.

'Something wrong?' Garcia asked.

'I'm looking for the report on the door-to-door Missing Persons conducted around the area at the beginning of their investigation.'

Reflexively, Garcia's eyes scanned the house across the street from them, then the one next to it, before going back to Hunter.

'Why?'

'They drew a blank, didn't they?' Hunter asked. 'No one remembered seeing anything out of the ordinary on the night Nicole was abducted. No vehicles that didn't belong. No conspicuous characters lingering around. Nothing.'

'Yeah, that's correct,' Garcia confirmed it. 'But this is a very quiet road. We've been here for almost an hour and we've seen one car drive by, the one with the ballet girls. Do you find it surprising that the killer managed to get in and out of here without anyone seeing him?'

Hunter carried on flipping through the pages. 'No, not really. But I just need to check on something.'

Hunter finally found the file he was after and quickly reread it before handing it over to Garcia.

'Check this out,' he said, tapping his index finger twice at the top of the page.

Garcia read it, made a face, looked up and down the road one last time, then read it again.

'Oh, man,' he finally said. 'We're going to have to get some uniforms back up here again.'

Eighteen

The Missing Persons investigators had knocked on every door on Allenwood Road and questioned everyone in the houses, including staff if there were any. No one had seen anything. But, up on those hills, that was hardly surprising.

Hollywood Hills might have given out the impression of being a laid-back neighborhood, but the truth was it was more like a secret society with unspoken rules. The reason why so many actors and musicians loved those hills so much was because no matter what happened up here, people tended to keep their mouth shut and to mind their own business. Up on those hills, nothing ever seemed excessive. No one, no matter how odd they looked, no matter how flamboyantly or minimally dressed they were, ever seemed suspicious or out of place. Over the years, Hollywood Hills' residents had been practically conditioned to look the other way.

The mistake that Missing Persons had made was that they had only questioned people about the night of the abduction.

So far, from the little they had, Hunter and Garcia had already deduced that this killer was very meticulous, and though he could've abducted Nicole Wilson from a multitude

of locations, he had chosen to do it from inside the Bennetts'
house. Why?

Other than the killer wanting to show off how bold and
arrogant he was, the obvious answer was because Allenwood
Road was a very quiet street, which severely reduced the
risk of the killer being spotted as he dragged his victim out
of the house and into a vehicle. But the twist was – neither
detective had known how quiet the road really was until
they had driven up there.

And the killer wouldn't have known either without
checking for himself.

'The killer must've made at least one recon trip up here
prior to the abduction night,' Garcia said.

Three houses to their left, a man who looked to be in his
early sixties stepped out of the front door carrying a golf
bag, placed it in the trunk of the Mercedes E-Class that was
parked in front of the house, jumped into the driver's seat
and slowly drove away.

'That's what I would've done,' Hunter accepted it. 'If all
I wanted to do was to figure out if this road was quiet
enough or not. But that wouldn't have been enough for this
guy. He's too careful. He would've wanted specifics.' He
pointed to the car as it drove away. 'And for that, he
would've had to survey this road for days.'

Garcia looked a little unsure. 'Specifics?'

'Routine,' Hunter replied. 'Every street has one. Especially
one as exclusive as this. We all do it, Carlos. We all stick to
routines because we're creatures of habit. We go to the gym
at specific times, on specific days, or out for a game of golf,
or poker nights, or ballet classes, or long walks, or whatever. This killer has planned this abduction too well to risk
being spotted coming out of this house carrying his victim

by someone going out or coming back from a yoga class. He would've wanted to know how this street works. He would've wanted to know its routine.'

Hunter turned and faced the Bennetts' house.

'But would you like to know something that wasn't a routine?' he asked.

Garcia thought about it for a second. 'The evenings Nicole Wilson babysat for the Bennetts.'

'Exactly. It happened sporadically. They would only call her when something came up. And according to what Ms. Bennett told Missing Persons,' Hunter nodded at the files sitting on the passenger seat, 'she'd called Nicole around noon on the day she was abducted asking if she could babysit that night. It was sort of a last-minute thing. And without knowing beforehand which day he would strike . . .'

'The killer would've had to have surveyed this street for an entire week,' Garcia agreed. 'Know its movements, its habits, day by day.'

Hunter nodded. 'It wouldn't have been foolproof, but it sure would've given him a much better idea of what he should try to avoid. We need to run a door-to-door again. Maybe, if we're lucky, somebody might've noticed something on the days leading up to the abduction.'

Nineteen

For the first time in two weeks dense rain clouds began gathering over Central Los Angeles, announcing that a new summer downpour was imminent, which wasn't all that surprising given how hot it had been in the past few days. By the time Hunter and Garcia got back to the Police Administration Building, bullet-sized raindrops were coming down in torrents.

While Garcia went back to their office to go over some paperwork, Hunter drove on to Ramirez Street in Downtown Los Angeles where the LAPD Missing Persons Unit's Special Division was located. He had received a call from Detective Troy Sanders, saying that he'd be more than happy to meet up with Hunter, and that he'd be in his office that afternoon.

Detective Sanders was the head of the MPUSD, but also the detective who'd been in charge of Nicole Wilson's abduction investigation.

Hunter found Sanders by the vending machine at the far end of the Missing Persons detectives floor, which, in all fairness, was a carbon copy of the Robbery Homicide Division's – a simple, open-plan space housing a chaotic labyrinth of desks. The noise level resembled a fish market on a Sunday morning.

Sanders was in his early forties and, at exactly six foot, was as tall as Hunter, with a shaved head, a prominent brow, a strong chin and wide shoulders. His eyes, clear and pale blue, contrasted nicely with his tanned skin, and the intense gaze in them suggested both experience and knowledge.

After grabbing a can of soda, a couple of candy bars and a packet of mints from the vending machine, Sanders ushered Hunter into his office, which by comparison was smaller, but a lot tidier, than Hunter and Garcia's.

'Mint?' Sanders offered as he opened the small can of Ice Breakers.

'No, thank you. I'm OK.'

Sanders popped two into his mouth. 'Maybe it's only me, but it's like this job leaves a bad taste in my mouth on a daily basis. I eat tons of this stuff.'

Hunter could easily sympathize with Sanders.

'OK. I've got the file here, ready for you,' Sanders said as he walked over to his modest desk and retrieved a green folder that sat on top of a tall and very neatly arranged pile.

Hunter wasn't too surprised by the number of cases sitting on Sanders' desk. The LAPD Missing Persons Unit investigated somewhere between two and three hundred adult missing person reports per month, and at least double that number when it came to children under the age of sixteen. Contrary to public belief, and despite the fact that approximately seventy percent of all reported adult missing persons were found, or voluntarily returned within seventy-two hours, a new federal law prohibited the observance of a 'waiting period' before accepting a missing persons case. That meant that an investigation had to be launched, and a file had to be created, for every single accepted report.

'Unfortunately, I'm not sure how much help this will actually be,' Sanders said, passing the folder to Hunter. A look of disappointment came over him. 'What we managed to find out isn't much.'

The Missing Persons report opened with the same portrait photograph of Nicole Wilson that Hunter and Garcia had seen in the file Captain Blake had handed them that morning, followed by her fact sheet. Hunter skipped the basic information and quickly scanned the report, which indeed was very brief. It stated that Nicole Wilson was about to start her second year of law school at CSULA, that she sometimes babysat a few nights a week for extra cash, and that just a few weeks ago, at the end of her first year in college, she had managed to land a summer job, running errands and archiving reports for a law firm in downtown LA. Apparently she was also a very quiet and reserved person, preferring to spend her free nights studying in her room or at the library instead of partying in the City of Angels. From what Sanders' team had gathered, most of her life revolved around college campus and a very small number of college friends, so initially that had been exactly where they had concentrated the bulk of their investigation. But summer break had made talking to students and teachers around campus a little harder than usual. Most of the interviews had been conducted over the phone.

Sanders and his team had followed certain abduction investigation guidelines to the letter. In the case of someone like Nicole Wilson, they were simple – a young and attractive woman goes missing without a ransom request or any known family feud, and sitting at the top of the 'people of interest' list would be: the boyfriend (if any), followed by ex-boyfriends, and anyone who had shown a romantic interest in Nicole (male or female). But according to the few people Sanders had managed to talk to, Nicole Wilson hadn't been dating anyone. In fact, it seemed like she hadn't dated anyone since she'd started college just over a year ago.

Sanders and his team had also spoken to everyone who worked at the small law firm Nicole had been running errands for since the beginning of summer – two attorneys and one secretary. They all had watertight alibis for the night in question, and pretty much a perfect score when it came to their past. As far as Sanders could tell, none of them had any motive either.

'All the interview transcripts are in here,' Sanders said, handing Hunter a second folder, this one yellow in color.

Hunter took the file before asking, 'Have you checked her dorm room?'

'Thoroughly. No diary or anything similar,' Sanders replied, anticipating that that had been the reason why Hunter had asked his question. He then handed Hunter a list of all the items he and his team had found in Nicole's dorm room.

'We did find her laptop,' Sanders added, pointing to the fifth item on the list. 'Computer forensics took about a day to breach its security, since then we've been sieving through all its files, including her emails. So far, we've found nothing relevant. I'll get someone to drop her laptop to you in the next hour, if that's OK, together with a list of all the files we've already been through.'

Hunter saw sadness and disappointment creep into Sanders' eyes and he understood exactly why. If Nicole Wilson had been murdered only hours after being abducted, there would've been very little anyone could've done, but she hadn't. The killer had tortured her, seemingly for almost six days, before finally ending her life. That meant that Missing Persons had had five days, or around one hundred and twenty hours, to get to Nicole, but they didn't get anywhere near her or her captor. No matter how experienced or seasoned a Missing Persons detective was, in these sorts of circumstances the feeling of failure wrapped up in guilt can run them over like a speed train.

'Sure, that'd be great. Thank you,' Hunter agreed.

Sanders popped another mint into his mouth before extending the round tin container in Hunter's direction.

Once again, Hunter declined.

'You've read the transcript of the telephone conversation between Miss Wilson and Ms. Bennett, right?' Sanders asked. 'Just before her abductor took her.'

Hunter nodded.

'I'll tell you this much, I have ten years with the LAPD MPU, half of them with the Special Division. I've seen some crazy shit, and I've investigated some really arrogant bastards, but I've never come across anyone with this level of confidence, or an abduction this clean. Forensics spent two days fine-combing the entire house and its grounds, and they got nothing that didn't belong. Not a single hair. Not a speck of dust. This guy left absolutely nothing behind, other than a forensic black hole. That's not an easy thing to achieve.'

Hunter looked at the detective for a couple of seconds. Sanders didn't have to voice it for Hunter to know that he feared exactly what he and Garcia already knew – Nicole Wilson was only the beginning.

Twenty

Their fifteen minutes were up. This had been one hell of a boring meeting, but with elections just around the corner Mayor Richard Bailey had to endure several of those on a daily basis, and he did it with a perfect smile on his lips and a look of total interest on his face. If there was one thing Richard Bailey had learned since joining the world of politics over a decade ago, it was that every vote counted, and the two women sitting before him represented a group of over one thousand voters from South Los Angeles.

'I completely understand your views,' Mayor Bailey said, addressing the stick-thin blonde woman who had just finished a five-minute-long monologue that he had paid no attention to. Their chairs had been strategically positioned with their backs toward the round clock on the wall behind them inside the mayor's office. That way, while facing them, Mayor Bailey could always keep track of the time without appearing rude by consulting his wristwatch every couple of minutes.

'And if I get to serve another term,' he continued, dishing out another very well-rehearsed look that made sure his visitors understood what those words really meant, 'I will certainly put those views forward to the relevant committees. You have my word.'

He stood up and adjusted the sleeves of his jacket.

The women followed suit.

'It's been an absolute pleasure, ladies, and I want to thank you for taking the time to come and see me,' he said, offering his hand. His handshake was as well crafted as his entire performance – strong enough to show strength and authority, but not too overpowering. He escorted both women to the door, before giving them one last 'goodbye' smile.

His personal assistant, Grace Hamilton, was standing in the outer office, holding a legal-size envelope.

As always, Grace was impeccably dressed. Today she wore an extremely well-fitting navy-blue suit with a silky white blouse, but the look on her face was far from her usual tranquil and smiling one.

'Richard,' she said, taking a step forward once the two women were gone.

Mayor Bailey had insisted that she call him by his first name. The request hadn't been a flirtatious move, though he did enjoy flirting and was very good at it, but because he didn't like formalities in his office . . . and it made him feel younger.

He locked eyes with his assistant and paused for a heartbeat. Her eyes were full of fear.

'Grace, is everything OK?' There was nothing fake about his expression or tone of voice. The concern in them was all real.

Grace Hamilton never discussed anything with the mayor in his anteroom.

'Could I have a word in private, please?' Her voice sounded edgy and urgent.

'Of course,' he replied with a single nod before stepping to one side and ushering her into his office.

Grace closed the door behind her and followed Bailey to his large oak desk.

'What's the matter?' Bailey asked, turning to face her.

'This arrived this morning,' she finally said, lifting up the envelope she had with her. 'It was addressed to you, and marked as "urgent – private and confidential".'

Bailey looked at Grace. 'Yes? So? We get enough of those every week. Did you check the contents?'

'I did,' she said, nodding. 'It's a photograph.' She paused as if she needed to catch her breath. 'And a note.'

Bailey's eyes moved to the envelope.

Grace handed it to him.

Without sitting down, Bailey opened it and reached inside. The first item he brought out was the 4x6 Polaroid photograph.

Grace looked away in disgust.

Bailey glanced at the image and froze. A pit immediately opened in his stomach and threatened to swallow him whole.

'What the fuck?'

The photograph was of a woman's face, but it was far from a glamorous one. Her dark-brown hair seemed dirty and drenched in sweat and was sticking to her clammy forehead and the sides of her face. Tears had caused her eye makeup to smudge and run down her cheeks, drawing thin dark lines that should've run down to her chin, but they hadn't. Instead, they had been collected by the thick fabric gag that had been tied so tight around her mouth it had stretched her face awkwardly and cut into the edges of her lips. Just past the gag, blood had finished the thin-line design that her tears had started. But what seemed to squeeze Bailey's heart inside his chest was the look in the woman's eyes – pleading, full of fear and totally void of hope. It was the look of someone who deep inside knew nobody would come for her in time.

Bailey looked at Grace, his expression a mixture of repugnance and confusion.

She finally looked back at him.

'Is this for real?' he asked. 'I mean, with all this digital-photo-enhancing crap today, who can be sure, right?'

'I don't think so,' Grace replied, her voice unsteady. 'That's a Polaroid picture, Richard. Like in the old days. I don't think they can Photoshop those.'

The mayor looked back at the picture. 'No, you're right,' he agreed. 'Do you know who this woman is?'

Grace shook her head. 'I've never seen her before. You?'

'No, me neither.'

A couple of jittery seconds went by.

'I was unsure whether I should bring this to you, or hand it straight to the police or the Secret Service.'

Bailey placed the photo on his desk but continued to stare at it. His palms were damp with sweat, his mind full of questions. True, over the years he had received a ton of crazy mail, but never something like this. His mind worked fast.

'How was this delivered, Grace?'

'It came in a FedEx envelope. The address is bogus. It's a boarded-up grocery store.'

Bailey's left eyebrow rose inquisitively.

'Do you still have it? The envelope, I mean?'

'Yes, of course. I'll go get it.' Grace began backing away from Bailey.

'Grace, wait,' Bailey called again. 'Do we have latex gloves anywhere in the office?'

'Umm . . .' Her eyes narrowed as she looked back at

him. 'Not in the office, I don't think so.' She hesitated a second. 'But maintenance will have them. Their personnel all wear them.'

'Call them and get them to bring us a couple of pairs ASAP.'

'Right away, sir.'

'Also,' Bailey stopped her again, 'do we have some sort of sealable plastic bags? Something we keep documents in?'

Grace thought for a moment. 'I've got a box of sandwich bags in my drawer. They've got zip seals.'

'They'll do. Bring them over.'

Grace nodded and quickly walked out of the office. A few minutes later she returned with the FedEx wrapper, a box of latex gloves and a box of plastic see-through sandwich bags. She handed everything to Bailey, who immediately slipped a pair of gloves on before checking the sender's information at the back of the FedEx envelope.

'Tyler Jordan?' he whispered to himself, frowning.

'I checked it against your address book,' Grace explained. 'But there was no match, that's why I proceeded to open the package.'

Bailey was sure that the sender's name and address would be bogus, but he would still have it verified.

'Have you shown this to anyone else?'

'No, of course not.'

'So other than you, no one else has touched this picture?'

'That's correct,' Grace replied with an anxious nod.

Bailey doubted that whoever had sent him the package had been stupid enough to leave fingerprints anywhere but, again, he needed to make sure. He retrieved a couple of sandwich bags from the box and placed the photo and the FedEx wrapper inside them.

'There's still a note inside, Richard,' Grace reminded Bailey, nodding at the envelope on his desk.

He had been so taken aback by the photograph and the desperate look on the woman's face that he had forgotten all about the note Grace had mentioned earlier. He took the envelope, tipped it over and allowed the piece of paper to slide out on to his hand.

Grace held her breath.

Bailey unfolded the note and his eyes stayed on the script for several seconds, the words barely making any sense to him until he got to the last couple of sentences. That was when his whole demeanor changed.

If Grace hadn't known better, she would've sworn that what had consumed the Mayor of Los Angeles had been fear.

For the briefest of moments, Bailey seemed paralyzed. Then, like a missile, his hand shot in the direction of the phone on his desk.

Twenty-One

Four days earlier

The man sitting in seat 9A was, by cabin crew standards, the perfect passenger. As he boarded the plane, he smiled politely at all the attendants and then waited patiently for the passengers crowding the aisle in front of him to place their hand luggage inside the appropriate compartments. There was no trace of annoyance from him, no exasperated folding of the arms, no irritated 'excuse me's, and no uncomfortable shifting from foot to foot. Once he'd taken his seat, he hadn't asked for a single thing, not even a glass of water.

Despite all the stewardesses onboard flight number 387 from Sacramento to Los Angeles being young and very attractive, there had also been no flirtatious looks from passenger 9A, nor any awkward attempts at cheesy pick-up lines.

The man had caught the attention of Sharon Barnard, the youngest of the three stewardesses on board, and she was curious about what he did for a living. His clothes gave little away; a dark-gray suit and a crisp white shirt with a perfectly knotted black-and-white tie. He could've been just another businessman, like half the passengers on that early morning flight, but he was missing all the typical gadgets – the briefcase, the laptop computer or tablet, and the smartphone.

While some passengers read, some slept, some worked, some played games on their tablets or listened to music, passenger 9A did nothing. He kept his seat in the upright position, his hands together in his lap and his eyes forward, staring straight ahead. At first Sharon wondered if he was meditating, but when she walked past his seat and asked him if he'd like anything to drink, he answered her immediately and courteously, saying that he was all right. She asked him if he was going to Los Angeles on business, and he replied that he was returning from business. He lived in Los Angeles.

That had brought a smile to Sharon's lips.

'Tom,' Sharon said to the head steward, who was also her best friend and housemate. 'What do you think of that guy in seat 9A?'

Tom smiled at her teasingly. 'Are you asking me if he's gay, darling?'

Tom Hobbs was twenty-three years old, very attractive, single and gay. One of his biggest talents was his sixth sense for spotting other gay males without even speaking to them. He stepped out from behind the partition and casually looked down the aisle.

'Yep, he's one hundred percent hot,' he replied. 'I clocked him as soon as he stepped on to the aircraft.' Tom smiled again, then pouted his lips at Sharon. 'And I can see that so did you.'

Sharon didn't look embarrassed. 'As you've said,' she replied, 'he's hot.'

'No doubt there, and you might just be in luck, honey,' Tom continued. 'Because he's definitely straight.'

Sharon smiled. 'You really think so? He hasn't looked at any of us girls.'

'Oh, I'm positive, darling.' Tom glanced at 9A again. 'Yep, that man likes pussy.'

'No wedding band either,' Sharon said.

Tom grinned at her. 'Look at you, you vixen, scouting the customers and all, way ahead of the competition. I *like* your style.'

'You better, I've learned it from you.'

Tom lifted his hand for a high-five.

Sharon slapped it.

'Though,' she said, 'I can't help thinking that he looks familiar somehow.'

'Really?'

'Yeah. Maybe it's the eyes, or that strong chin, but I keep on thinking that I have seen him before. Do you remember seeing him on a previous flight at all?'

Tom looked at passenger 9A once again. 'Umm, no darling. A hunk like that, I would definitely remember if I had.'

Sharon also didn't think that she had seen him on a previous flight, but she was almost certain that she had seen him before somewhere.

'OK,' she said, moving things along. 'So what do you think he does for a living?'

When flying together, Tom and Sharon sometimes played a guessing game over a few chosen passengers. It helped pass the time.

'Umm.' Tom wiggled his head from side to side for a second. 'He definitely works out. You can tell by his arms. His biceps are about to rip through his sleeves. But he also comes across as the calm type. Nothing seems to bother him, and he has one hell of an intense stare. Have you checked those big brown eyes?'

Sharon nodded. 'Oh yes.'

Tom smiled again. 'Silly me for asking. Well, I'd say he's either a psychologist, or some sort of therapist . . . maybe sports.' He then mimed a shiver. 'Ooh no, even better, I'd say he's a sexual therapist.'

'Psychologist.' Sharon liked that thought.

'Cabin crew, please take your seats for landing,' the announcement came through the speakers.

Less than ten minutes later the Boeing 757 touched down on runway two at Los Angeles International Airport.

Once again, passenger 9A waited patiently for all the other passengers in front of him to collect their hand luggage and clear the aisle. As he walked past the crew at the front of the plane, he gave them all a single courteous nod and mouthed the words 'thank you'. His eyes sought no one in particular and Sharon felt a little disappointed. She had a special smile, coupled with a sexy wink prepared just for him. All she could do was watch as he walked away. She really would've liked to get to know him a little better.

What she had no way of knowing was that passenger 9A already knew everything he needed to know about Sharon Barnard.

Twenty-Two

Hunter's cellphone rang less then ten seconds after he had stepped back into his office at the Police Administration Building.

'Robert, where are you?' Captain Blake said as soon as he answered.

'Just got back to the PAB, Captain, why?'

'Is Carlos with you?'

'Yes.'

'I need to see you both in my office – right now.'

When Hunter and Garcia got to the captain's office, she was sitting behind her desk, attentively looking at something that was lying flat on her desktop. From where they were standing, neither detective could tell what it was.

'OK,' she said, finally lifting her stare to meet theirs. 'First question – are we really dealing with some sort of ritualistic killer here?'

'It's too soon to tell, Captain,' Garcia replied. 'As things stand, there's not enough evidence to say for certain either way.'

'How about the positioning of the body?' she countered. 'Set out to look like a five-point human star? Isn't a five-point star a pentagram? And aren't pentagrams widely known to be associated with devil worshiping and all?'

'Not exactly, Captain,' Hunter replied.

Captain Blake looked at him and waited. He said nothing else.

'What do you mean, Robert?' she asked finally.

'Pentagrams are ancient figures that have been used throughout history to symbolize a number of things,' Hunter explained, 'such as strength, unity, power, secrecy. Several different religions have adopted it in different contexts, including Christianity. In fact, the pentagram has long been believed to be a potent protection *against* evil.'

Both Garcia and Captain Blake looked a little surprised.

'The symbol that has been associated with evil and devil worshiping,' Hunter continued, 'is an inverted or reversed pentagram, with two points projecting upwards, and that's because an inverted pentagram symbolizes overturning the proper order of things.'

Hunter paused, giving Captain Blake a few seconds to weigh everything up.

'In our case,' he added, 'there's no way to tell, Captain. Yes, the victim was positioned in a way that resembles a five-point human star, but we don't know if that star is right side up or upside down, because we have no way of telling what the killer's point of view was. If we consider the standard geographic coordinates – north being up and south being down – then the victim was not left in an upside down position.'

Captain Blake frowned at Hunter.

'Her head was pointing north,' he explained.

'I'm actually scared to ask how you know all this about pentagrams, Robert,' Captain Blake said, sitting back on her chair.

Hunter shrugged. 'I read a lot.'

'But of course you do.' Her eyebrows arched sarcastically. 'OK,' the captain lifted her right hand, accepting Hunter's argument, 'for now, let's forget the pentagram shape and focus on the body itself. Doesn't specific victim positioning suggest some sort of ritual?'

'Usually, yes,' Garcia agreed. 'But as I've said before, Captain, right now we don't have enough evidence to be sure either way. What if this killer positioned the body that way just to try to make us believe that he really *is* a ritual-istic killer, just to send us down the wrong path? He seems to be smart enough to be able to come up with something like that.'

Captain Blake chewed on that thought for a couple of seconds.

'How about a cult?' she asked, getting up from behind her desk and moving around to the front of it. 'Could we be dealing with some sort of cult here, instead of a single individual?'

'No,' Garcia replied. 'We're not dealing with a group or any sort of cult here, Captain. This is a single individual.'

'You sound very sure.'

Garcia proceeded to tell Captain Blake everything that the autopsy examination had revealed. She listened to his account without interrupting, her expression changing according to the level of surprise or disgust she was feeling at what was being said.

'So this note the killer left lodged inside the victim's throat,' she said when Garcia was done, 'it was written in blood?'

'That's right.'

'Whose blood, the victim's?'

'We don't know yet,' Garcia answered. 'That's what we're

expecting it to be. We should hopefully get an answer from the forensics lab sometime this afternoon.'

'I'm a little confused,' the captain said, lifting a hand again. 'How does that answer my question as to why you sounded so sure that we're not dealing with a cult here, Carlos?'

'The note.'

The penny finally dropped.

'I Am Death,' Captain Blake said in a half-whisper. 'Not *We* Are Death.'

Hunter nodded. 'This guy's got an ego, and a big one. This is his work, his "masterpiece", no one else's, and he really wants us to know that.'

One didn't need to be a detective to pick up the look of deep concern on Captain Blake's face. A concern that clearly went beyond Garcia's account of the autopsy findings.

'Captain,' Hunter asked. 'What's going on?'

Captain Blake reached for something on her desk.

'A fucking hell of a lot.'

Twenty-Three

Captain Blake picked up a small, see-through plastic bag, which was what she had been looking at when Hunter and Garcia entered her office a few minutes earlier. Inside the bag sat a 4x6 Polaroid photograph. She handed it to Hunter and Garcia.

'Here, have a look.'

Garcia took the bag and turned it over so they could see the image. The photograph was of Nicole Wilson.

'What the hell?' Garcia's gaze paused on Hunter for a split second before moving back to his captain. 'How did you get this?'

'I didn't.' Captain Blake leaned against her desk. 'The mayor did.'

There was a hesitant moment as both detectives exchanged another concerned look.

'The mayor?'

'Yes. He received it earlier this morning, via FedEx.' She reached for plastic bag number two and handed it to Garcia again. 'As you can see, it was marked as "urgent – private and confidential".'

Hunter and Garcia checked the FedEx wrapper.

'Tyler Jordan?'

'Bogus name, as expected,' the captain replied. 'Bogus

address as well. Apparently it's a boarded-up shop – everything else still needs to be checked.'

'Did the mayor know Nicole Wilson?' Hunter asked.

Captain Blake shook her head. 'According to him, he's
never seen her before. But we all know that public safety
has always been at the forefront of Mayor Bailey's
campaign, so once he saw that picture he immediately got
on the phone to Chief Bracco. Bracco left this office about
five minutes before you got here. That's how I have these.
He wanted them to go to forensics ASAP, but I wanted you
to see them first.'

'Does the chief know that Nicole Wilson's body was
found in the early hours of this morning?' Hunter asked.

'He does now.' Captain Blake paused and drew in a deep
breath. 'But that's not all.'

Hunter and Garcia's attention moved from the photo
and the FedEx wrapper back to her. Once again, she reached
for something that was on her desk – a third see-through
plastic bag.

'The photo came with a note,' she said, handing the bag
to Hunter.

The white piece of paper that sat inside the plastic bag
had a crease down its center where it had been folded in
half. Like the note found in Nicole Wilson's throat, the
words had been handwritten, but this time not in blood.
The killer had used a red ballpoint pen.

People in this city put their trust in law enforcement
agencies like the LAPD, and sometimes even the FBI, to
keep them safe, to help those who can't help themselves,
to right them when they're wronged, to protect them,
and to seek justice no matter what.

Those agencies are supposed to be the best of the best. The experts when it comes to reading people and discerning good from evil. But the truth is that they only see what they want to see. And the problem with that is that when they play at being blind men, people suffer . . . people get tortured . . . and people die.

So now I have a question. If any of these so-called experts stood face to face with someone like me, if they looked straight into my eyes, would they see the truth inside me? Would they see what I have become, or would they falter?

The woman in the picture certainly saw it. She felt it on her flesh.

And before the sun rises tomorrow, someone else will see it and feel it too. And trust me, what she's been through is nothing compared to what is still to come, unless these so-called experts are able to stop me.

Well, are they?

FOR I AM DEATH.

'Jesus,' Garcia said after reading the note a couple of times over.

'And from what you've told me so far,' the captain said, 'I guess we can confidently say that he's not bluffing.'

Silence filled the room for several seconds. Garcia was the first to break it.

'What I don't get is, why the mayor? This note refers to law enforcement agencies like the FBI, and ourselves, nothing really to do with the mayor's office. If Mayor Bailey didn't know Nicole Wilson, why send the picture and the note to his office? Why not send it directly here to the PAB or to Chief Bracco's office?'

'I've been asking myself that same question,' Captain Blake said. 'And with today's technology, why post it instead of emailing it?'

'Two reasons,' Hunter replied, his full attention still on the note. 'If the killer had emailed it, there'd be no guarantees that the mayor would've gotten it. Something like this could've easily been automatically flagged as spam or junk mail by some sort of firewall program, and have been completely discarded without anyone actually opening it. No way this killer would've run that risk.'

Captain Blake accepted it with a head nod. 'And the second reason?'

'The shock effect. The credibility. Seeing a handwritten, original note, and a Polaroid photograph, two tangible items, something that the mayor could actually handle, packs a much bigger punch then something the mayor could only see through his computer screen. It makes the threat a lot more real. That's also the reason why the killer used a Polaroid, instead of a regular photo.'

Garcia nodded. 'An attached photo could've been Photoshopped to the last pixel. A Polaroid is practically impossible to touch. As Robert said, it gives the killer credibility.'

'OK,' the captain agreed. 'But why send it to the mayor?'

'Urgency,' Hunter replied. 'If this package had come straight here to the PAB and to your office, would you have informed Chief Bracco, or the mayor?'

'No, of course not.'

Hunter nodded once. 'And if it had gone straight to Chief Bracco's office, do you think he would've informed the mayor?'

Captain Blake caught up with Hunter's logic.

'No,' she agreed. 'There'd be no need to worry the mayor. But send it directly to the mayor a couple of weeks before an election, and you start a hierarchical panic chain reaction – the mayor, who's obsessed with citizen safety, takes it straight to the chief of police, who brings it straight to me.'

'As I've said,' Hunter added. 'This guy's got a big ego, and he wants to play, but he wants to make sure he's playing against the right opponents. As he wrote on his note – *the best of the best* – because in his mind, he deserves nothing less. Getting the mayor involved would guarantee he got what he wanted.'

'Well, so, he's in luck,' the captain said, walking back behind her desk. 'Because you two are supposed to be the best I have.'

Twenty-Four

Night had already recolored the sky by the time Sharon Barnard opened the door to the house she shared with Tom Hobbs in Venice, in the Westside region of Los Angeles. Today she had worked a return flight from LAX to Kansas City, where for three and a half hours each way, she had endured a battery of cheesy pick-up lines and humorless anecdotes, all of them from overweight businessmen who smelled of cheap cologne and did a piss-poor job of hiding their wedding bands.

She smiled in relief as she finally closed the door behind her, put her cabin crew suitcase on the floor and began rubbing the back of her neck with both hands. Her neck and shoulder muscles felt a little stiff, but it was nothing that a long shower followed by a nice bottle of wine and some relaxing music couldn't fix. And tonight she had the house to herself. Tom had flown to San Francisco that morning, where he'd spend the night, probably partying somewhere in the Castro, the largest gay neighborhood in the USA, before flying back tomorrow afternoon.

Both Sharon and Tom had been away for a day and a half. The house had been locked, all the windows shut and the curtains drawn. With the early August heat, the place felt like a sauna. Sharon opened one of the living room windows before crossing over to the kitchen and grabbing a cold bottle of beer from the fridge to cool her down.

In spite of it not being a career choice she had ever really considered until just a year earlier, Sharon loved her job as a stewardess.

Ever since she was a young girl, Sharon had always dreamed of becoming a nurse, and that was due in part to her obsession with the television series *ER*. She had the entire collection on DVD. She had watched every episode at least ten times, but still she just couldn't get enough of it. But *ER* was not the only reason. Sharon had always had a kind heart, and helping people in need satisfied her in a way that very little else ever did. The interesting thing was that she had never even considered being a doctor, and that was indeed *ER* and Nurse Carol's fault – Carol Hathaway had always been her favorite character and she wanted to be just like her. But Sharon was a very down-to-earth person. She fully understood that a nurse's reality would certainly be very different from the half-glamorous life she saw on the little screen.

With that in mind, Sharon decided to follow the advice of her school counselor and the school nurse, and straight after high school she enrolled herself into the Licensed Practical Nurse program where she showed tremendous talent and aptitude, graduating top of her class twelve months later. Though LPN gave her the initial skills she needed, dealing with real patients would prove to be a whole different ballgame.

Her plan was to try to gain practical experience as a working nurse for at least one year before going back to school and enrolling into the Associate Degree in Nursing

program, which would then allow her to become a registered nurse.

Upon graduating from the LPN program, and with the
help of two of her tutors, Sharon was immediately offered
a nursing position at the Cedars-Sinai Medical Center,
ranked among the top three medical centers and hospitals
in California. She jumped at the chance, and was assigned
to the neurological ward, commonly known as the coma
ward. And that was when everything went sour.

Only six days after she first started working on the ward,
Sharon saw the arrival of a nine-year-old black girl named
Joan Howard. Joan had been playing alone on the sidewalk
right in front of her house when she was practically run
over by an eighteen-year-old kid who, just for the fun of it,
had decided to see how fast he could go on a bicycle. The
bicycle collided with Joan with such force that she was
projected forward and through the air several yards. She
landed on the road, hitting her tiny head against the asphalt
and fracturing her cranium in two places, causing her brain
to hemorrhage. The kid on the bicycle was never caught.

'A miracle,' the head nurse at the coma ward had told
Sharon on her first day on the job. 'That's pretty much the
only thing that can make most of our patients wake up and
get out of here, and trust me, you will probably see some
miracles happen right in front of your eyes in this place. But
they are very few and far between. What I'm trying to tell
you is – don't get attached, don't be too human, don't
succumb to your emotions, because it will only hurt you and
compromise your professionalism. Be objective. Most of the
patients in this ward are half dead. That's why they're here.'

And a miracle had been exactly what Joan's family and
everyone else had hoped for. Nothing else could help. The

doctors had done all they could do. But as the days started to melt into weeks, and the weeks into months, hope began to fade, except for Sharon, who wasn't able to follow the head nurse's advice and had fallen in love with the little girl. Maybe it had been because Joan reminded Sharon of her best childhood friend, who had been murdered when she was ten years old during a gang drive-by shooting, just east of MacArthur Park, where she used to live.

At first, Joan's father, who was a single parent, would come in every day after he'd finished work and spend several hours by his daughter's bed, holding her hand, reading her stories, singing her songs, and combing her hair, but soon hope abandoned him too. First he started spending less and less time with his daughter every day, then the visits became less frequent.

Sharon caught up with him one night as he was leaving, and with teary eyes begged him not to desert his daughter. Even without ever having seen one, she tried to explain to him that the sort of miracles that happened in that ward depended as much on the families not giving up on their loved ones as it did on divine intervention. Joan's father looked like he had aged ten years in just a few months. He said nothing to Sharon. He simply stared at her with heavy, pain-stricken eyes for a whole minute before turning and walking away in silence.

He didn't come back the next day.

And that was the night Joan passed.

Sharon had been unable to hide her distress after the little girl's death, and that made her question her willingness to become a nurse. She decided to take some time off and rethink. During her break, her old school friend, Tom Hobbs, suggested that she looked into becoming an air stewardess. Sharon decided to give it a try. She told herself that she had nothing to lose.

That had been just over a year ago, and she hadn't looked back since.

In her bedroom, Sharon opened another window, turned on the portable stereo system on her bedside table and switched to the radio. 'Maps' by Maroon 5 came on and she immediately began swinging her hips to the beat as she sang the words. It was one of her favorite songs. While doing so, she undressed and finished her bottle of beer. She thought about having a second one, but she didn't handle mixing drinks very well. It usually gave her a horrible headache and a zombie-like hangover, and she was really looking forward to her bottle of wine.

Sharon grabbed a freshly washed towel from the cupboard in the corridor and walked into the bathroom. She got the shower running but didn't get under it. Instead, she took a step back, faced the mirror above the washing basin and regarded herself for an instant – first her left profile, then the right one. After a few seconds of deliberation, she decided that she was relatively happy with her figure, though, in her mind, there was always room for improvement.

She finally stepped under the shower, leaned forward, placed her forehead against the white tiles and allowed the strong jet of lukewarm water to sluice over her head, shoulders and back. It felt like a dream. As soon as the water came in contact with her skin, her tense muscles began to relax.

Shower over, she wrapped herself in her towel and returned to the kitchen.

Sharon and Tom had quite a nice selection of wine, and tonight she felt like having something fruity and refreshing.

'Perfect,' she whispered to herself as she selected a bottle of New Zealand Gewurztraminer from the fridge, uncorked it and poured herself a glass. She had just returned the bottle to the fridge when her cellphone rang. She had left it on the kitchen counter. She closed the fridge door before reaching for her phone and checking the display screen. She didn't recognize the number.

'Hello?'

'Hi, Sharon.'

The male voice didn't sound familiar to her.

'Umm . . . Hi. Sorry, but who's this?'

'Would you like to take a guess?'

Sharon frowned at the phone. She just wanted to relax and enjoy her wine. She was in no mood to play games with anyone.

'No, I wouldn't, actually. And if you don't tell me who you are, this call is over.'

'OK, how about if I tell you that I'm the one waiting at the end. Will that do?'

'Waiting at the end? At the end of what?'

First the voice at the other end chuckled at the question. When it spoke again, the words came out slowly, and in a tone that could only be described as morbid.

'Life, Sharon. I am the one waiting at the end of life, for I am death.'

Sharon didn't scare easy, but there was something about this voice that sent a chill trickling down her spine.

'You know what? That's one horrible joke, whoever you are.'

'Who said it was a joke?'

'Fuck you, you sick freak. Don't call me again.' In a burst of anger, Sharon almost slammed her cellphone against the sideboard but she stopped herself just in time.

A few seconds later, it rang again – same number. Sharon just let it ring out.

A few more seconds after the ringing had stopped, a text message came through.

C'mon, answer your phone, Sharon. Don't you want to play?

Sharon knew that she should just ignore it, but after such a long day her anger got the better of her. She quickly typed a reply.

Go fuck yourself, freakshow. Whoever you are, I'm blocking your number.

Ping.

Just moments after Sharon had replied, a new text message arrived.

You know what? Forget about the phone. Let me ask you something. Did you remember to lock your front door?

Clunk, clunk, clunk.

All of a sudden, the handle on her front door twisted three times in quick succession.

'Jesus!' Sharon jumped back, almost dropping her cellphone. Her frightened stare shot toward the door. 'What the fuck?'

Thankfully, she had locked the door.

Ping. A new message.

She looked down at her phone again. Only then did she realize that she was trembling.

C'mon, open the door, Sharon. I'm right outside. Let's have some fun.

The handle on the front door moved again, this time a lot slower, and only once.

'Oh my God! Oh my God!'

As Sharon began panicking, her eyes immediately filled with tears.

Ping.

OK, who needs the door anyway? Maybe I can get in some other way.

The pause that followed was suddenly punctuated by desperate fear.

Oh fuck, Sharon thought as the memory came back to her. *The window.*

Despite how frightened she actually was, Sharon's survival instincts took over and she exploded toward the living room window. She never knew her legs could move that fast. As she slammed it shut and drew the curtains, her towel came undone and fell to the floor. She was way too scared to care.

Between heavy breaths, her terrified gaze flitted between the door and the window for a long moment. Finally, her brain, which had gone momentarily numb, re-engaged.

What the fuck are you waiting for, Sharon? she told herself. *Call 911 now.*

She quickly tapped the numbers into her cellphone and pressed the 'call' button.

Nothing. No dial tone.

'What the hell?' She looked at the display screen. She had not one signal bar. 'How can this be?' she yelled at her phone through clenched teeth. Just a moment ago she'd received a new message.

What Sharon had no way of knowing was that every time the caller got off the phone, he switched on his own cellphone signal scrambler.

Instinctively, she stretched her arm out and moved it around, searching for a signal.

Nothing. Not even half a bar.

'Shit. Shit.'

Her brain turned another rusty wheel.

'Landline.'

She rushed toward the phone on the counter in the kitchen, but just as she was about to snatch it from its cradle, it rang.

Stunned, Sharon brought it to her ear.

'Hello?'

'Let's play a game, Sharon.'

Sharon froze.

'And it starts like this. Lights out.'

In that instant, her entire house fell into darkness. Sharon let out another terrified scream. Her eyes circled the room but she saw nothing.

'Oh my God, what the hell is happening?' she said into the phone in a shaky voice. 'Who are you? Why are you doing this to me?'

Sharon still had her cellphone in her hand. She swiped her thumb across the screen and turned on the flashlight application.

'Do you know what your mistake was, Sharon?' The voice came through the landline receiver once again.

Sharon could do nothing but breathe hard.

'You went for the wrong window.'

Terror ripped through her heart as she remembered – her bedroom window.

Panicking and completely out of ideas, Sharon frantically moved her cellphone around. The weak light that came from the tiny flashbulb at the back of it cast shadows everywhere, but as those shadows passed over the door that linked the living room to the corridor, she saw a human silhouette move across it.

The next time she heard the man's voice, it did not come from the receiver by her ear. It came from behind her.

'I'm already inside.'

Twenty-Five

As he finally placed his pen down on his desk, Hunter noticed that his hands were shaking. Beads of cold sweat had also formed on his forehead.

He stood up, and as he did his knees clicked noisily. He'd been sitting down for way too long. He stretched his long frame and the stiff muscles in his back and legs responded with what felt like a thousand painful pinches. Hunter forced the stretch even more, this time bringing his neck into it. It clicked just as noisily as his knees.

Damn, he thought, grinding his teeth. *Carlos is right. Maybe I am getting too old for this crap.*

Hunter had just spent the last three hours transcribing and re-transcribing every word from the note the killer had sent Mayor Bailey that morning. He'd made twenty-five copies of it, trying to match the killer's handwriting as best as he could.

And he'd done a great job.

The exercise was simple. Hunter wasn't trying to memorize the note word for word, though, after recopying it so many times, that was exactly what had happened. But no, what he was really trying to do was to get some sort of insight, however small, into the killer's mind, into the killer's way of thinking. He was trying to think like the killer did, to feel what the killer felt when he wrote those words. He was looking for hidden meanings and word tricks. Trying to read between the lines.

After three laborious hours, Hunter had come up with very little. To him, it felt as if the killer knew that the note would be scrutinized to its very last detail. Every word, every letter, analyzed and reanalyzed – physically and psychologically – and the killer had locked every door; he had left no openings, no pathways into his psyche.

Hunter knew that carrying on any longer would bring him no better results.

He poured himself another large cup of black coffee, returned to his chair and half swiveled it around to face the old-fashioned picture board by the east wall. Despite how young their investigation was – less than twenty-four hours old – the board was already plastered with information and photographs.

Forensics had come back with the results of the test that had been run on the blood used to write the note that had been left lodged inside the victim's throat – I AM DEATH. As Hunter and Garcia were expecting, the killer had used Nicole Wilson's blood to write it, but according to the forensics report, it didn't seem as though he had used a brush to do it. Instead, he had used his own fingers, dipping them in his victim's blood before carefully inscribing each letter. Not surprisingly, forensics had found no fingerprints, partial or otherwise. The killer, no doubt, had been wearing gloves.

The second note, the one that Hunter had spent the last three hours transcribing, had been sent over to the forensics lab, together with the Polaroid photograph of the victim in captivity, immediately after he and Garcia had left Captain Blake's office earlier that afternoon.

Hunter was no graphologist, but he didn't need a forensics report to tell him that the notes had been written by the same person. Despite the killer using his fingers to inscribe the first note, and a red pen to write the second, his handwriting was impressively steady.

The killer had written both notes in cursive handwriting, and his calligraphy was firm but gracious. Despite the paper having no guiding lines, all the letters stood in perfect symmetry to one another, and they flowed in beautifully measured strokes and shapes. This told Hunter that the person they were looking for was meticulous, organized, paid particular attention to detail, and prided himself in everything he did, including how he murdered his victims.

Twenty-Six

The man finished tying his victim to the chair, got up and calmly walked over to the kitchen. After filling a large glass with water from the fridge, he strolled back to the center of the room and stood directly in front of her.

Sharon Barnard was still unconscious, her ankles zip-tied to the chair's legs, her arms firmly secured behind her back. Her head was low, her chin resting against her chest, her mouth semi-open, her lips a little out of line, falling to one side. The man studied her for an instant – the details of her facial structure, the symmetry of her neckline, the intoxicating beauty of her naked body. Sharon was undoubtedly a very attractive woman . . . but not for long.

The man stood with his legs shoulder-width apart, steadied his body and threw the water on to her face.

As the ice-cold liquid came into contact with her skin, Sharon jolted awake and immediately sucked in a lumpy breath. Her head jerked back in a fright. Her eyelids flickered like butterfly wings for a long moment, while from her lips came indecipherable, frightened sounds.

The man waited patiently, his hands now tucked behind his back.

Sharon finally managed to open her eyes. Her confused

and drowsy gaze moved right, then left, ultimately settling on the figure in front of her.

One . . . two . . . three seconds went by before Sharon looked properly at the man. There was something in his light-blue eyes, something in the way he looked at her that felt terribly familiar. She had met him somewhere before, Sharon was certain of it, but where?

She forced her memory.

Nothing.

It didn't matter how tightly she closed her eyes, or how much she begged her brain to remember it, her memory just wasn't able to make the connection.

Sharon opened her mouth in an effort to speak, or scream – she wasn't sure herself – but her breathing was still too erratic, catching in her throat. Her diaphragm was unable to overcome her fear.

Not a sound came out.

Her lower jaw trembled, then her entire body, as if all of a sudden an arctic front had just climbed in through her window and clothed her.

The man waited patiently, his hands still tucked behind his back. No movement whatsoever, just a cold stare locked on to her eyes like a predator stalking its prey.

Sharon kept her petrified gaze on his for God knows how long. It was like she had been hypnotized by those deep, penetrating eyes. She trembled again, this time something that came from deep inside her, shaking her core, and that finally made her break eye contact. Her eyes moved right, then left again, but she was too frightened to understand what was happening to her, or where she was.

At last she tried moving, first her legs, then her arms, but as she did so unbearable pain shot up from her feet and legs, and through her arms and shoulders. A pain so intense it made her gag. Her eyes rolled back into her head and she almost passed out again.

Amused, the man waited patiently, his hands still tucked behind his back.

As Sharon regained consciousness, she realized that the reason why she was unable to move was because she'd been tightly tied down to the chair she was sitting in. Cold water was still dripping from the tips of her wet hair on to her chest, stomach and thighs. She drew in a deep breath and steadied herself. Finally, a distant memory began to materialize inside her head. The phone call, the male voice at the other end, the sick joke about him being 'death', the door, the window, the fear. As she remembered, her expression changed.

Sharon looked back at the man, pleading. That was when she realized something that her eyes had certainly noticed before but her brain had failed to register – over his clothes and shoes the man was wearing a see-through, hooded, plastic coverall. Only his face was exposed, nothing else. Then Sharon noticed his clothes through the coverall – not your regular everyday attire. He wore some sort of black, shiny jumpsuit, made out of something that hugged his body like a second skin. What came to her mind was – latex.

The man held her stare for another second, then his lips stretched out slowly. Sharon couldn't tell if that was a smile or not. If it was, it was like none she'd ever seen before. It carried no humor, no sarcasm, no sympathy, no apathy, no feelings of any kind. A completely emotionless facial expression that only served to scare her more.

Sharon drew in another lumpy breath, and despite her fear, she felt her voice come back to her.

She moved her lips, and every word came out through tears.

'Plea . . . please. What do you want with me? Wh . . . why are you here? Please . . . just let me go. I'll do anything you want.'

The smile, or whatever it was, disappeared from the man's lips. He was done waiting. It was time to do what he was there to do. He moved his hands from behind his back, revealing what he was holding.

Sharon's gaze first focused on his right hand, then on his left.

Panic turned into terror.

In an effort to clear her tears, she squeezed her eyes as tightly shut as she could. When she opened them again, the man had moved two steps closer.

'Oh, God, no. Please don't do this.'

'Do you know who I am?' he asked. His voice carried no emotion.

All Sharon could do was shake her head.

'Oh, Sharon, Sharon. You disappoint me. I told you on the phone. Don't you remember?'

Tears came back to her eyes.

'I. Am. Death.' He smiled again. 'And I have come for you.'

Twenty-Seven

When Garcia got to the office at 7:31 a.m., Hunter was seated on his chair with his back toward the door. His hands were behind his head with his fingers interlaced together. His legs were extended in front of him, the heels of his boots resting on the edge of his desk. He was staring at the picture board as if it was the first time he was seeing any of what had been pinned to it. There was an empty coffee mug by his computer keyboard, together with two candy bar wrappers. Garcia glanced at the coffee machine in the corner – empty. From the door, he also noticed the transcribed notes on Hunter's desk. A couple of them had fallen on to the floor.

'Did you spend the night in here?' Garcia asked, stepping inside and closing the door behind him. It wouldn't have surprised him if Hunter had.

'No, not really,' Hunter replied, without diverting his attention from the board. 'I went home and had a shower.'

'But no sleep.' Garcia didn't phrase it as a question.

Hunter shrugged. 'In the words of the great American poet, Jon Bon Jovi, I guess "I'll sleep when I'm dead".'

Garcia chuckled. 'Carry on this way and it won't be long, my friend.' He moved around to his desk, placed his rucksack on the floor and fired up his computer. 'So what time did you get here this morning?'

Hunter's gaze moved to the clock on the wall just above the board.

'About a quarter past five.'

Garcia didn't have to ask. He knew the reason why Hunter had gotten to the office so early – the threat the killer had added to the note he'd sent Mayor Bailey: *And before the sun rises tomorrow, someone else will see it and feel it too. And trust me, what you've seen is nothing compared to what is still to come, unless these so-called experts are able to stop me.*

'Have we got anything?' Garcia asked, the play completely gone from his tone. 'Any new nine-one-one calls?'

Hunter finally moved his heels from his desk, sat up straight and swiveled his chair to face his partner.

'No, nothing yet.'

Both detectives knew that didn't mean anything.

'I checked with FedEx about the package that was delivered to Mayor Bailey yesterday,' Garcia said, loading something up on to his computer screen.

'And?'

'The package was dropped off two days ago, just before lunchtime, at a FedEx Express drop box just outside Union Station.' Garcia tilted his head to one side and followed it with a sigh. 'Get this, neither of the two CCTV cameras on that corner of the station picked up anything. In fact, they were both concentrating on something else.'

Hunter queried with an eyebrow lift.

'Yep. He created a diversion,' Garcia confirmed. 'Small, homemade smoke bomb hidden inside a trashcan. Nothing major, just a single Ping-Pong ball wrapped in aluminum foil with a short fuse. Good to create enough smoke to get the attention of the cameras, but not enough to create panic. So, for at least a minute, everything else got overlooked.'

'He would've needed just a second or two to drop the package into the box,' Hunter said.

Garcia nodded emphatically with his next words. 'This guy is careful. No unnecessary risks. Better to be safe than sorry.' He then jerked his chin at the mug and the wrappers on Hunter's desk. 'Was that breakfast?'

Hunter's left eyebrow lifted again. 'More like a late night come early morning snack.'

'Well, I really need a fresh cup,' Garcia said, now indicating the coffee machine. 'Would you like some?'

'Have you managed to get any more of that stuff from Minas?'

Hunter had always liked coffee, but unlike most people he knew he didn't drink it for the caffeine. He needed no help staying awake or with his energy and alertness levels. He simply and truly enjoyed the taste of it, the stronger the better. But Hunter was no connoisseur, unlike Garcia who had been brought up by a father who admittedly was a coffee fanatic.

Garcia was born in Sao Paulo, Brazil. The son of a Brazilian federal agent and an American history teacher, he and his mother had moved to Los Angeles when he was only ten years old, after his parents' marriage collapsed. Even though he'd lived in America most of his life, Garcia could still speak Portuguese like a true Brazilian. His father was a very attractive man with smooth dark hair, brown eyes and olive skin. His mother was a natural blonde with light-blue eyes and European-looking fair skin. Garcia had inherited his father's olive-tone skin and brown hair. His eyes weren't as light blue as his mother's but they had definitely come from her side of the family. He had a slim frame, thanks to years of track and field, but his build was deceptive and he was stronger than anyone would've guessed.

When Garcia had found out that Hunter enjoyed coffee just as much as he did, he had been more than happy to share a few secrets with his partner. One of those secrets was a special blend of Brazilian coffee produced only in the southeastern estate of Minas Gerais, by a small independent farm with a unique recipe. It was grounded finer than most blends and roasted at a lower initial temperature, preventing it from over-roasting and giving it a stronger but smoother taste. It had quickly become Hunter's favorite blend, but the only shop that sold it in the whole of Los Angeles had closed down.

Garcia smiled and from his rucksack retrieved two one-kilo bags of the special blend, placing them on Hunter's desk.

'Someone I know just got back from Brazil last night.'

Hunter's face told a happy story.

'Yes,' he said, looking like a kid who'd just received the Christmas present he was hoping for. 'I'd love a fresh cup of coffee.'

As he walked over to the coffee machine, Garcia picked up one of the transcribed notes from the floor. The handwriting was an almost perfect match to the original. He craned his neck and looked over his partner's shoulder at the pile of copies on his desk.

'You transcribed the note?'

Hunter shrugged. 'A few times, yeah. I was trying to look at it from different angles.'

'You mean, think like the killer.'

This wasn't the first time that Hunter and Garcia had had to deal with a killer who liked to taunt the police with written notes or images.

'I didn't go as far as transcribing it,' Garcia said, placing the note back on Hunter's desk before filling the machine with ground coffee and adding water. 'But I also barely slept. Every time I closed my eyes,' he nodded at the notes, 'that's what I saw.'

'And?' Hunter's interest grew.

Garcia shook his head. 'I'm not sure what to think, Robert. To me, most of it comes across as if this killer is your "straight out of a textbook sociopath". You know – delusions of grandeur and all. He probably believes he's above everyone else in every aspect, especially intellectually, being way too smart to ever make a mistake or get caught. That's the reason for the note, isn't it? Defiance. Come catch me if you think you can.'

Hunter agreed with a silent nod.

'What he did to the first victim,' Garcia continued, the expression on his face morphing into one of disgust, 'the abduction, the torture, the violation, everything – shows that he has achieved such a high level of emotional detachment from other human beings that he's now clearly unable to feel anything other than anger, or rage, or perhaps repugnance. There's no remorse, guilt, compassion, pity, love, nothing – no sort of affectionate sentiment of any kind. I'm not even sure if he ever did feel those things.'

The coffee finished brewing. Garcia filled two cups and took one over to Hunter.

'Thanks,' Hunter said. The strong aroma of the special brew made him smile.

'And then there's the really scary part,' Garcia said.

'Which is?' Hunter asked.

'This.' Garcia pointed at the killer's sign-off on his note – I AM DEATH. 'Giving yourself your own pseudonym?' He chuckled. 'That's the pinnacle of arrogance, isn't it? Son of Sam, The Happy Face Killer, The BTK Killer, The Zodiac Killer, Jack the Ripper, whoever . . . they all did it because they all believed that they were special.'

'Back to delusions of grandeur,' Hunter said.

'And then some,' Garcia agreed. 'But what we do know about serial killers who like to name themselves is that they've been planning their murders for a long time, and they intend to carry on murdering for even longer. That's the scary bit. That's why they like to torment the authorities with notes, or images or what have you. Because a letter to the authorities constitutes a very bold challenge – the note is like a formal invitation to turn the investigation into a cat-and-mouse chase – a game where they create the rules, and they can change them whenever they see fit. And since they decided to turn it into a game, they might as well make it fun. And we have just been dragged into that game.'

Hunter couldn't disagree with anything Garcia had said.

What Garcia also knew was that killers who liked taunting authorities with messages tended to hide clues deep within those messages, sometimes in cryptic format. And Garcia knew no one better at reading between the lines than Hunter.

'OK,' Garcia said, once again indicating the transcribed notes on Hunter's desk. 'Now it's your turn. Have you come up with anything?'

Hunter gave his partner a shabby shake of the head. 'The note clearly isn't written in riddle format, and if there is any double meaning to anything I haven't been able to find it. In fact, the more I read it, the more I copied it, the more of the opposite feeling I got.'

'Opposite feeling?' Garcia looked a little confused. 'What do you mean?'

'Whoever wrote this note put a lot of effort into it, Carlos, carefully choosing every word. And here's the twisted bit. He didn't do it to confuse us, on the contrary. He did it to leave the least amount of doubt possible.'

Twenty-Eight

Garcia paused what he was doing, turned toward his partner and allowed his gaze to settle on the note on Hunter's desk.

'OK,' Hunter said. 'Let's try to break this down into parts.'

He slid a copy of the note to the edge of his desk. His coffee had finally cooled down enough for him to have his first sip. It tasted like paradise.

'Have a look just at the first and second paragraphs and tell me what you think they mean. Don't try to read between the lines or find any double meanings to anything. Just read them and tell me what you think.'

Garcia didn't bring his chair around. Instead, he just leaned over Hunter's desk, placing both hands on the desktop.

People in this city put their trust in law enforcement agencies like the LAPD, and sometimes even the FBI, to keep them safe, to help those who can't help themselves, to right them when they're wronged, to protect them, and to seek justice no matter what.

Those agencies are supposed to be the best of the best. The experts when it comes to reading people and discerning good from evil. But the truth is that they only see what they want to see. And the problem with that is that when they play at being blind men, people suffer . . . people get tortured . . . and people die.

Garcia read the paragraph three times before scratching his chin and looking back at Hunter.

'He's preaching, being condescending even, reminding us of who we are, what our job is, what the public expect of us, and what happens when we fail or make a mistake.' There was a short pause. 'There's also a blatant accusation, saying that we see only what we choose to see. And this line –' he pointed to it on the note – '"*And the problem with that is that when they play at being blind men, people suffer . . . people get tortured . . . and people die.*" Though very aggressive,' Garcia continued, 'it doesn't sound like a threat. It sounds like a statement.'

'You're exactly right,' Hunter agreed. 'There's no other way of interpreting those two paragraphs, Carlos. They're clear and concise. No ambiguity, no sarcasm, no play on words, no double meanings, and nothing hidden between the lines.'

Garcia's attention didn't deviate from the note.

'Now, have a look at the third paragraph and tell me what you think. Again, forget double meanings and all. Just read it like a letter.'

So now I have a question. If any of these so-called experts stood face to face with someone like me, if they looked straight into my eyes, would they see the truth inside me? Would they see what I have become, or would they falter?

Garcia thought about it for a moment. 'It's . . . a challenge,' he said. 'He's defying us to go find him. To pick him out of a crowd. To identify him. That's the invitation to the game. As you've said before, he wants to play.'

'Right again,' Hunter said. 'But there's something else. Something not actually hidden. You just need to read it carefully.'

Garcia frowned and reread the paragraph a couple more times. 'OK,' he said, standing up straight and shrugging. 'I'm missing it, then. What else? What am I not seeing?'

'He's not only challenging us to pick him out of a crowd, Carlos. He's questioning if we'd be able to see what he has *become*. That's a very powerful statement.' Hunter had another sip of his coffee. 'Think of what that word actually means.'

'He's telling us that he wasn't always like this,' Garcia said, looking at Hunter, his voice a touch more excited then a moment ago. 'He wasn't always a monster, a killer. He's not your textbook sociopath because he wasn't born that way. He, for the lack of a better word, became that way.'

Hunter nodded slowly.

'Something changed him.'

Twenty-Nine

The man woke up as the first rays of the morning sun seeped through the dirty curtains covering the window on the east wall of his small bedroom. Out on the streets, garbage trucks were already noisily moving around and, far off in the distance, a couple of sirens wailed like coyotes barking at the moon.

He'd finished with Sharon Barnard in the early hours of the morning, but he'd felt too tired to drive all the way back to his place, a two-storey house somewhere north-east of Los Angeles. He'd found the property many years ago, hidden away in the middle of nowhere, surrounded by nothing but empty terrain. He had paid cash for it and used false documentation, which meant that the house could never be traced back to him. Because the building had been so run down, he'd got it for an absolute bargain. After years of repairs and heavy modifications, which he did himself, he ended up with just the perfect place. No matter how much noise anyone made from inside his house, no one would ever hear it. No one would ever come for them.

The one-bedroom apartment he was in at the moment was just a crash pad somewhere in East Los Angeles. He had paid a year's rent in advance, all in cash. He really only used it from time to time, when circumstances demanded. Just like this morning.

As soon as the man opened his eyes, he swung his feet off the single bed, sat up straight and rubbed his face vigorously with both hands. He didn't have a watch, and there was no clock anywhere in the room, but it didn't matter. He knew exactly what time it was.

He reached for the medicine bottle that was on the bedside table, poured two capsules into his hand and flung them into his mouth. He didn't need any water to wash them down. He simply filled his mouth with saliva, threw his head back with a jerk, and down they went. He walked naked to the window, his feet padding across the worn-out and scratched wooden floorboards. Outside, city life was slowly trickling on to the streets.

The man crossed over to the bathroom and paused before the small mirror on the wall just above the washbasin. He could barely recognize the stranger staring back at him now. So much had changed over the years. He would never be the same again. He knew that full well but it didn't matter. Not to him. Not anymore.

In his reflection he saw the proud glint of accomplishment deep inside his eyes, and that caused him to smile, something he didn't do too often.

He brushed his teeth and then stood under a warm shower, washing meticulously from his head down, before using a brand new razor blade to shave off every strand of hair from his body, including his head, a ritual he repeated every morning. When he was done, he dried himself and returned to his bedroom.

From the wardrobe he retrieved the only two items that hung there – a dark suit and long-sleeved white shirt. The tie rack on the back of the wardrobe door held a single black and white striped tie. There was a solitary drawer at the bottom of the wardrobe. It contained one pair of white boxers, a pair of black socks and a large plastic laundry bag. He slipped on the boxers and got dressed, then took the bed sheet, the pillowcase and the cover sheet and stuffed them into the laundry bag, together with the clothes he'd been wearing the night before.

He walked into the living room, grabbed a red pen and a loose sheet of paper from the bottom drawer of an old two-drawer cabinet, and took a seat at the wooden table that faced the window.

The man barely had to think about what he wanted to write. He'd gone through it in his head a thousand times, until he had it worded perfectly, just the way it needed to be.

Once he was done, he carefully folded the note in half and slipped it into a brown paper envelope. This time, the note wasn't addressed to the mayor, or any other politician. He didn't need to use the same trick again because this time he knew exactly who to address it to – Detective Robert Hunter, LAPD Robbery Homicide Division.

'OK, Detective,' he said in an angry voice. 'Let's see how good you really are.'

Thirty

Despite leaving San Francisco International Airport fifteen minutes late, US Airways flight 667 landed at Los Angeles International Airport exactly on time, at 08:55 a.m.

Tom Hobbs had been the lead flight attendant on the fully booked, one hour and twenty-five minute flight, and he had struggled through every second of it. By the time the flight touched down, Tom's brain was turning to mush.

He staggered through the airport, pulling his inflight case behind him. He felt tired, hungover and nauseated, but the worst was now behind him. Or so he thought.

Tom slipped on his sunglasses and stepped out of the building into another scorching hot summer's day. Outside he paused for an instant, trying to decide what to do. He had driven to the airport yesterday morning. His car was parked at the Central Terminal Area parking lot, building 2A, but he was in no state to drive. He felt shivery, his headache was now so intense it could wake the dead, and he hadn't eaten anything yet; courtesy of the cocktail of drugs he had consumed overnight. Finally, deciding to listen to reason, Tom chose to leave his car where it was and take a cab home.

The almost ten-mile trip from Los Angeles LAX to the house he shared with Sharon in Venice took the cab driver just under half an hour. Twice Tom almost asked the driver to pull up by the side of the road. The stop and start motion, due to traffic lights and road congestion, brought him to the verge of being sick, but somehow he managed to hold it all in.

'You OK back there?' the cab driver asked, checking Tom through the rearview mirror. He was sloshing on the backseat with his head propped against the window, his eyes closed.

Tom's reply was barely audible.

'Buddy, you all right? Do you need me to stop? You don't look so good.' The driver asked again, this time reducing his speed.

Tom forced his eyes open. 'No, it's OK. I'll be all right.' His voice sounded hoarse and fatigued. 'I just need to get home and get some sleep.'

'Rough night?' The driver followed the question with a dubious smile.

Tom saw it, and didn't like it.

'No, just bad food. I'll be OK once I get home and get some sleep.'

The driver didn't make any more small talk, but stepped on it and kept checking on Tom via the rearview mirror every couple of minutes. The faster he got to Tom's address, the better. The last thing he wanted was to have to clean up puke from his back seat.

Tom stepped out of the cab and squinted at how bright the day seemed, even through his dark glasses. The glaring light made him feel sick again. He took an enormous deep breath, hoping that that would be enough to keep his nausea at bay.

'I've gotta stop partying like this,' he said to himself as he started toward the house. But that certainly wasn't the first, and probably wouldn't be the last time he'd recited those exact same words. The flesh was weak, he had admitted to that many times.

As he paused before his front door, his stomach roared so loudly he thought that maybe his large intestine was now devouring the small one. But despite how hungry he felt, Tom would think about food later. All he wanted right now was to collapse in bed and sleep until tomorrow morning.

He reached for his key and slid it into the door lock. His stomach roared again, this time louder and for longer, making him curl over a little with pain. OK, maybe he would have to eat a candy bar or something before heading for bed, just to try to calm the storm brewing inside his belly.

Tom tried rotating the key, but it didn't move.

'Hum!'

He tried a couple more times.

Nothing.

'What the hell?' He twisted the doorknob. The door was unlocked. Tom found that very strange. They never forgot to lock the door, not even when they were *in* the house. Venice wasn't the most secure neighborhood in LA.

'Sharon,' he called, pushing open the door.

The first thing that hit him was the smell, an odd combination of putrid and bittersweet that seemed to rip its way though his nostrils before lodging itself at the back of his throat, choking him and making him gag. He felt a drop of bile come up through his esophagus and spill into his mouth. For some reason, instead of spitting it out, he swallowed it back down.

Tom squeezed his eyes tight behind his shades. The smell

had also made his eyes water. He took off his sunglasses and rubbed his eyes.

'What the fuck? Sharon?' he called again. Had she left a whole chicken outside the fridge in this heat?

He coughed a couple of times before finally looking up and into his living room. His eyes were still half blurred, so it took them a few seconds to refocus.

For a moment Tom hesitated, his tired and confused brain struggling to make sense of the grotesque images his visual nerves were sending in. Reality had just morphed into the sickest nightmare he'd ever had.

'*What?*'

His whispered voice caught in his throat as a rush of adrenalin took over his body. It fired bullets of uncontrollable fear down his spine and into his heart. Bitter bile shot back up from his stomach but this time it wasn't only a drop, and this time it would've been impossible for Tom to swallow it all back down.

Sick exploded out of his mouth before he collapsed on to the floor and into the pool of blood his living room had become.

Thirty-One

'Something changed him?' Captain Blake asked with a frown. She was sitting behind her desk, nursing a fresh cup of coffee. 'How so, Robert?' Her hair was loose, tucked behind her ears, and she wore a black pencil skirt with a tight-fitting plum cotton blouse. She had asked Hunter and Garcia to come to her office as soon as she arrived at the PAB.

'I'm not really sure how, Captain,' Hunter replied. 'But what I'm very certain of is that he chose the words he used on his note very carefully, doing his best to avoid doubt. He ends his third paragraph by writing: "*Would they see what I have become, or would they falter?*" He could very easily have written "see what I am?" Or "who I am?" Or "the monster in me?" Or something along those lines.'

'But he didn't,' she said, leaning back in her chair.

'No, he didn't. I'm sure that he picked the word "become" for a specific reason.'

'And you think that is because he wants us to understand he wasn't always a psychopath. That something in the course of his life changed him. And whatever it was that happened to him, it made him decide to start killing people.'

Hunter nodded.

'Like what, for example?'

Hunter shrugged. 'He doesn't allude to anything in his note, so right now that's impossible to tell. Every individual reacts differently to different situations, Captain, you know that. Everybody's got a different breaking point. For some people, it takes a lot for that switch to flick inside their heads, if it ever does. For others, not so much. Even a physical disease can potentially turn someone into a murderer.'

'Wait a second,' the captain said. 'Physical disease?'

Garcia also looked at Hunter sceptically.

'Yes,' Hunter confirmed. 'History is littered with different cases. In America, Charles Whitman is probably the most famous example.'

Captain Blake paused for a moment, searching her memory. The name finally came back to her. 'Charles Whitman? Wasn't he the Texas Bell Tower sniper?'

'That's right,' Garcia said, now remembering it as well.

Charles Whitman was a former US Marine who became one of the most famous mass murderers in US history. On 1 August 1966, he started his killing spree by murdering his wife and then his mother. Once they were dead, he drove up to the University of Texas in Austin, where he was studying for a degree in engineering, and, armed with numerous firearms and several hundred rounds of ammunition, got up on to the highest point on campus, the main building's clock tower. From there, he indiscriminately shot random passersby for almost two hours until he was finally shot dead by Austin police officer Houston McCoy. In those two horrible hours, Charles Whitman managed to kill fourteen people and injure thirty-two.

Understandably so, the press quickly branded Whitman a monster – but that was until the police discovered the note Whitman had left behind. A suicide note, or what essentially became a suicide note because Whitman was certain that he would die that day.

The note shocked everyone. In it, Whitman confessed that he himself found his behavior completely inexplicable. He began his note by stating that he adored his wife and mother, and that he had no idea why he was doing what he was doing. He went on to explain that in the past few months he had simply been consumed by excruciating headaches, like nothing he had ever experienced before, and those headaches brought with them overwhelming feelings of rage and destructive impulses which he found harder and harder to resist.

Because he was certain that he would be killed that day, Whitman ended his note by begging the authorities for his brain to be autopsied for signs of physical disease. The authorities complied, and it was discovered that Charles Whitman had a brain tumor that seemed to be just a few months old. The tumor was located in the hypothalamus, and it was pressing on to his amygdala. The coroner confirmed that Whitman's terrible headaches were certainly caused by the tumor. In the USA, Whitman's case opened a whole new door to the way psychologists and psychiatrists approached the mental state of a supposedly sociopathic murderer.

'So you're saying that our killer could have a brain tumor now?' Captain Blake asked in a semi-sarcastic tone.

'He could,' Hunter admitted. 'But that's not what I'm saying, Captain. I'm just trying to reinforce the fact that, with the little we have, it's impossible to do anything else other than speculate at this time, and that will lead us nowhere. We all know this.'

'And you don't think that you're reading too much into

every word this nut case has written?' the captain shot back. 'You don't think that he could've sent us that note just to fuck with us? As Carlos has suggested – to throw us down the wrong path? We all know that it has happened plenty of times before. After all, the note promised that we'd have another victim before sunrise today.' The captain turned toward the large panoramic window and pointed at the sky. 'Well, the sun has certainly risen, and we've got nothing yet. He could be bluffing for all we know, Robert. That note could be nothing but a gimmick.'

'That's not what the note says, Captain,' Hunter came back.

Captain Blake glared at him. 'Is it not?'

'No. The note says that before the sun rises tomorrow, which is today, someone else will *see* it and *feel* it too. He's talking about the monster that he has become. He's telling us that before the sun came up today, someone else would have suffered and died by his hands. The note says nothing about the victim being delivered to us. If he decides to do the same thing he did with Nicole Wilson and call it in via the switchboard, that call could come in this afternoon, tomorrow, next week, or any time after that. We're dancing to his tune here, Captain, and he can change the beat any time he likes.'

Mulling those words, Captain Blake reached for her cup of coffee and had a sip.

'And no,' Hunter added, 'I don't believe that he sent the mayor that note with the intention of fucking with us. The Polaroid and the victim's mutilated body are proof that he's more than serious.'

Captain Blake was about to say something else when the phone on her desk rang.

'Give me a sec,' she said as she took the call.

No words were needed. The look in her eyes as she stared back at her detectives told them all they needed to know.

The killer wasn't bluffing.

Thirty-Two

The house was in a pleasant-looking *cul de sac* down a small private road in Venice, just a couple of blocks away from Venice Beach. It was painted white, with blue-framed windows, a hipped roof, and a small front yard that seemed to be in urgent need of some attention. A knee-high, white wooden fence surrounded the property, which was set back from the road, isolating it even more from its neighbors. But the fence was there simply for decoration, not security. It wouldn't stop anyone from getting to the house, or moving around toward its backyard. Access to every door and window was kid's play.

There was a single garage to the right of the house, but the only cars on the driveway were a police vehicle and a forensics van. Despite the house being tucked away at the end of a private and very quiet road, the crowd of curious onlookers that had gathered outside the police perimeter was already substantial and seemed to be growing fast.

Garcia pulled up by one of the three black and white units that were parked on the street, just outside the house. The press was also there, crowding up the area even more.

A couple of reporters recognized the UV Unit detectives as they stepped out of Garcia's car and immediately started shouting questions from across the road.

They fell on deaf ears. Without even turning to acknowledge them, Hunter and Garcia simply flashed their credentials at the two policemen guarding the perimeter's edge and stooped under the yellow crime-scene tape.

A third police officer who was standing to the left of the house's front porch saw the two new arrivals and began making his way toward them.

'You guys from the UV Unit?' he asked as he got closer.

The officer was in his early forties, with natural suntanned skin, a cleft chin and a thick, black horseshoe mustache, which he clearly dedicated a lot of upkeep time to. His eyes were as dark as night, but the look in them was hesitant, scared even.

'Yes, that's us,' Garcia replied, indicating the badge clipped to his belt. Hunter did the same.

'I'm Sergeant Perez, with West Bureau,' he said, extending his hand.

Both detectives shook it and introduced themselves.

'West Bureau took the nine-one-one call earlier today,' the sergeant informed them. 'I was first response. First through the door.'

They began moving toward the house.

'OK, so what do we have in there?' Garcia asked.

Sergeant Perez stopped walking and allowed his worried expression to shift from Garcia to Hunter.

'I'm not actually sure I know how or what to call it.' His tone of voice was cautious. His gaze settled on the house before him and he gave both detectives a subtle, disbelieving headshake. 'I've been an officer for over twenty years, all of them with the LAPD. God knows I've attended crime scenes words wouldn't be able to describe, and nothing can erase them from my memory. But in there –' he nodded his head again in the direction of the house – 'nothing I've ever seen comes close. Inhumane is the only word I can think of. Way beyond sadistic.'

That explains the heavy press presence, Hunter thought. Word of the sort of violence used by the perpetrator had obviously been leaked to the media, which wasn't surprising. Not only did they scan police radio frequencies 24/7, but they also paid informers inside the force for that sort of intelligence, and they paid well.

They reached the front porch, where a couple of forensic agents were hard at work. The first was checking the wooden floorboards for footprints or any sort of residues that could've been left behind. The second one was dusting the door handle and frame. A couple of bloody handprints were clearly noticeable against the door's light-blue color.

'Anonymous nine-one-one call?' Hunter asked.

To their surprise, Sergeant Perez shook his head.

'Nope. The victim's housemate found the body,' he said, tilting his head toward the black and white unit parked in the driveway. The unit's passenger door was open. Sitting on the passenger seat with his feet on the ground, his elbows resting on his knees and his face buried in the palms of his hands was a tall, thin man who looked to be in his late twenties or early thirties. His short, dark-brown hair was completely disheveled, and he was wearing what was undoubtedly an air steward's uniform. Part of his white shirt and the front of his dark-blue jacket seemed to be covered in blood.

'His name is Thomas Hobbs,' Sergeant Perez continued, reading from the notepad he'd retrieved from his police belt. 'Twenty-three years of age. Born and raised here in Los Angeles, Pomona Valley. He shares this house with one other person, Sharon Barnard, who, according to Mr. Hobbs, and he had to base this conclusion purely on the jewelry she wore, appears to be the victim. They both work for US Airways.'

'Wait a second,' Garcia interrupted. 'Appears to be the victim?'

Garcia was six-foot two. Perez was five-foot six. The sergeant had to look up to meet the detective's stare.

'I guess you'll understand when you walk in there.'

Garcia shot a worried glance at Hunter.

'Mr. Hobbs had been away for a day and a half,' Sergeant Perez explained. 'This morning he was head steward on a flight from San Francisco back to LA. He wasn't feeling too well, so after he landed he decided to leave his car at LAX and take a cab home. He found the victim as soon as he opened his front door.'

The sergeant shifted his weight from foot to foot.

'Unsurprisingly, the sight was way too much for him and he collapsed. That was before he made the nine-one-one call.' Perez flipped a page on the notepad. 'As he passed out, he fell forward and into his living room. That explains the blood on his clothes. He's still in shock so getting any coherent information out of him at the moment is a monstrous task, but you're welcome to try it if you like. It took me half an hour to get these few details.' He wiggled the notepad he was holding.

'Any information on the "possible" victim?' Hunter asked.

'Very little,' Perez replied, consulting his notepad again. 'Name is Sharon Barnard. Twenty-two years old. Also born and raised here in LA. We did a quick check with US Airways. She finished her last shift – a return flight to Kansas

City – yesterday afternoon. She landed at LAX at seventeen twenty-five. We have no indication that she went anywhere else once she left the airport, so we're assuming that she came straight home. With rush-hour traffic and without stopping anywhere for groceries or anything, she would probably have got home some time between eighteen thirty hours and nineteen hundred hours.'

Hunter and Garcia nodded their understanding.

'Any signs of a break-in?' Hunter's question was directed more at the forensic agent checking the front door.

The agent stopped dusting the doorframe, looked back at the detective and shook his head.

'Nothing here. The frame isn't broken or cracked. The lock hasn't been picked or tampered with. We've got a couple of fingerprints from the door handle. Judging by size alone, one of them is definitely female. The bloody hand-prints –' he indicated the one just above the doorknob, and the one on the outside frame – 'belong to the guy who found the body.' He nodded toward the police unit on the drive-way. 'He used the door and the frame to steady himself as he got up from the floor after fainting.'

'Have you found a breaching point?' Hunter asked. 'Any idea of how the perpetrator got in?'

'No, nothing yet. Apparently the front door was unlocked when the housemate got home,' the agent revealed. 'All the windows are unbroken, and they were all closed and shut from the inside. The back door was also locked.'

'Here,' Sergeant Perez said, handing Hunter and Garcia two brand new Tyvek coveralls inside sealed plastic bags.

Both detectives took the bags, ripped them open and started suiting up. When they were done, they pulled the hoods over their heads and each slipped on a pair of latex gloves.

'I would sincerely suggest that you go for the nose masks too,' Sergeant Perez commented.

Nose masks in place, they stepped up to the front door. The forensic agent who had been dusting the door handle and frame took a step to his right and pulled the door open.

'Mind the blood,' Sergeant Perez said as he turned and walked away.

At last Hunter and Garcia stepped into the living room and immediately paused. Their eyes tried to take everything in, but their brains struggled to comprehend the scene in front of them.

Garcia breathed out, and his words came out as a whisper. 'What the fuck?'

Thirty-Three

The front door of the house opened straight into a small and sparsely decorated living room, with an open-plan kitchen at the back. A square table was positioned about four feet in front of the stove, which centered the cooking counter. The refrigerator was on the far left, just by the door that led into a short hallway and then deeper into the rest of the house. No windows were open, and all the curtains had been drawn shut, but the room was bright with light courtesy of the two high-powered crime-scene lamps that had been mounted on to tripods and placed at opposite corners of the room.

The living room area was covered with a beige, loop pile carpet. A tall, black-wood module occupied most of the west wall. On it were a few decorative items. No TV. A dark-blue fabric sofa with a matching armchair and a black coffee table had been positioned a few feet from the module, toward the center of the room.

Hunter and Garcia breathed out almost at the same time, but neither said a word, their gaze still taking in the entire space, which had been completely bathed in blood – the furniture, the decorative items, the walls, the ceiling, the curtains . . . everything was covered in splatters of crimson red.

The carpet under their feet had soaked a large amount of blood, but it was now covered by a thick, protective, see-through plastic sheet, which indicated that forensics had already photographed and vacuumed the floor for fibers, hairs, traces and residues. The protective sheet was to avoid any forensic agent, detective, or whoever else entered the crime scene from spreading their bloody footprints, since it was practically impossible to move around the living room without treading on a pool of blood.

Even with the nose masks on, the nauseating smell of human flesh in the early stages of decomposition still filled the room, forcing both detectives to breath mostly through their mouths.

The words I AM DEATH had been written in huge bloody letters across the carpet, just a few feet in front of what was undoubtedly the centerpiece of the sickening canvas that the living room had become. That centerpiece was Sharon Barnard.

She was naked and tied to a metal-framed chair, which was facing the front door. Her ankles had been securely fastened to the chair's legs by plastic zip ties. Her arms had been pulled behind the chair's backrest and zip-tied at the wrists. Her whole body was covered in blood. Blood that had come from her face and cascaded down her torso and legs before soaking the carpet beneath her feet. A face that simply wasn't there anymore.

'Her face was sanded off.'

The words came from the forensics agent who was by the high-powered lamp at the east end of the room. He was about six-foot one, with an athletic body, high cheekbones and a strong jaw. Unlike Hunter and Garcia, he wore no nose mask. The smell of putrid flesh didn't seem to bother him.

Garcia turned to face him, but Hunter kept his attention on the victim in front of him.

'I'm Doctor Brian Snyder,' the man said, moving toward the detectives. 'I'm the lead forensic agent assigned to this scene.'

'Detective Carlos Garcia, LAPD UV Unit. You're new,' Garcia added, without any malice. Mike Brindle was the lead forensic agent who attended most UV crime scenes. Hunter and Garcia had worked with him for years.

'To LA maybe,' he replied. 'But I've been a forensic agent for over ten years. I just got transferred from Sacramento.'

With an apologetic face, Garcia said, 'Welcome to Los Angeles. This is Detective Robert Hunter.'

Hunter finally faced the forensic doctor, his expression asking a silent question.

Doctor Snyder read it and nodded to confirm his previous statement. 'Yes, you heard it right, Detective. The perpetrator used a powerful random circular sander on her face,' he said, as he indicated the machine inside a large plastic evidence bag that was resting on the kitchen counter. 'The type used to sand off hard wood and metal,' he added. 'That explains the blood splatter pattern around this room, and why it reaches as far as the ceiling, the walls, and the curtains.'

The machine on the kitchen counter was gray in color, with a strong, rubber-coated grip handle. The on/off button sat on the upper part of the handle, just level with the operator's thumb. Very easy to control. Like most items in that living room, the handheld sander was also drenched in blood.

'If the killer used a handheld sander on her face,' Garcia cut in, 'that means he would've been covered in blood himself.'

'Oh, there's no doubt about that,' the doctor confirmed. 'And that would explain the several footprints you can see around the living room and in the kitchen.' He indicated a few of the footmarks that littered most of the beige loop pile carpet and the kitchen's tiled floor. 'Given the footprint pattern,' the doctor moved on. 'I'd say that the killer was wearing some sort of protective clothing. At least around his feet. His shoe size seems to be eleven.'

Garcia looked at his partner and pulled a face. He and Hunter knew that around sixty-eight percent of the male population in the USA wore size eleven shoes.

Hunter cautiously stepped forward and approached the body. Garcia and Doctor Snyder followed. With each step, the blood-soaked carpet squished under their weight and against the thick plastic sheet, creating a squealing sound reminiscent of rubber flip-flops walking on a wet floor.

Because the victim's head was slumped forward and downwards, hiding most of what would've been her face, Hunter had to squat down in front of her to have a better look. What he saw was truly grotesque. Her face had been almost entirely scraped off, from her forehead all the way down to her chin. All that was left was a gooey mess of flesh, muscle, cartilage and blood. Most of her facial bones were fully exposed. Her left eyeball had come into contact with the sander. Her cornea, pupil, iris, and ciliary body had been obliterated, releasing the jelly-like substance that makes up most of the ocular globe, deflating the eyeball, and leaving the eye socket lined with nothing more than a gelatinous matter and the exposed optic nerve. Her right eye, on the other hand, had been completely spared. It lay intact, speckled with blood, and wide open, with a dead, soul-chilling stare. It seemed that all the suffering she had been put through and all the agonizing terror she had felt had been immortalized on the surface of her right eye like a snapshot.

Her nose was also completely gone. It had been sanded down all the way to the nasal bone. Her lips weren't there anymore, and in their absence the victim's superior and inferior dental arcs had been fully exposed. Some of her frontal teeth had also come into contact with the sander's surface.

Garcia squatted down next to Hunter. All he managed was a couple of wide-eyed seconds before his guts forced him to look away.

'Jesus Christ.'

He got back on to his feet.

Doctor Snyder gave Hunter a moment before he spoke again.

'Rigor mortis has started to set in, but it's not in its full stage yet.'

Both Hunter and Garcia knew what that meant – the victim had been dead for less than twelve hours.

Hunter checked his watch.

'So she died some time in the early hours of this morning, not last night.'

'I'd say so, yes,' the doctor agreed. 'But you'll have to wait for the autopsy report for a more precise timeframe.'

Hunter finally pulled his gaze away from the victim's disfigured face and slowly began checking the rest of her body – torso, stomach, legs and feet. Standing up, he also studied her nape, shoulders and upper back. Unlike Nicole Wilson, this victim didn't seem to have any cuts or abrasions to any other part of her body. The killer hadn't sliced her skin with a sharp or blunt instrument, nor had he flogged her with a bullwhip like he had done to the first victim.

'It doesn't seem like any vital organs have been affected.' Garcia addressed Doctor Snyder. 'Any guesses as to the cause of death? Did she bleed out from her facial wounds?'

The doctor's gaze moved around the room, pausing for an instant on the largest pool of blood directly underneath the victim's chair, before meeting Garcia's questioning look.

'Without a proper post mortem I can't be one hundred percent sure, Detective, but it's likely to have been a combination of the amount of blood she lost and the tremendous pain she was put through. Her heart would've been working three times as fast as normal to try to replace the lost blood. As you can see, all the nerves around her face were completely exposed, which means that her brain would have been receiving pain signals by the truckload every second. That would've stressed out her heart and her brain even more. In situations like these, it's not uncommon for the heart to just give up, or for the brain to signal respiration to cease, and the lungs to simply stop taking in oxygen.'

'And how long would that have taken?' Garcia spoke again.

'That's impossible to tell,' Doctor Snyder replied. 'It depends on two main factors – the victim's physical and mental strength. First impression is that physically she was strong enough, as you can see for yourself. Young. Good muscle tone. Not overweight. How strong her heart was is also a key factor, but mental strength is pretty much what dictates your fate in circumstances like these. How badly did she want to live after having her face ripped from her? Your brain can keep on willing your body to fight, or simply tell it to give up. For her, death could've come within five minutes or after several hours.'

Hunter approached the kitchen counter and the evidence

bag containing the circular sander. It wasn't a brand new model, but it also wasn't a dated one, which made identifying the store in which it had been bought a lot harder. Hunter checked the underside of the handle. The serial number had been filed off.

'The killer left it on the floor,' Doctor Snyder offered. 'By the victim's chair. No attempt to hide it whatsoever.'

Next to the sanding machine were two smaller evidence bags. They each contained a single 125mm sanding disk. Both had been used and were blood-soaked.

'The disks were found in the trashcan,' the doctor said, joining Hunter by the kitchen counter and indicating the plastic trashcan on the opposite corner from where the refrigerator was. Several bloody footprints revealed the killer's path as he crossed the kitchen floor in the direction of the trashcan, and then came back out to where he had tied up his victim.

Garcia returned to the living room. He was intrigued by the footprint pattern.

Hunter took a minute to study the used disks. His next few words confused everyone.

'She lasted way over five minutes.'

Thirty-Four

'I'm sorry?' Doctor Snyder queried.

'You said that death could've come within five minutes, or after several hours,' Hunter clarified. 'I can't tell you for sure how long she lasted, but it was way over five minutes.'

Hunter's confidence puzzled the doctor.

'Could I ask what makes you so sure?'

Hunter moved to the other side of the kitchen counter, being careful to avoid the footprints on the tiled floor.

'Because the killer paused not only once, but *twice*, and calmly walked over to that trashcan to discard the used sand disks.' Hunter gave the doctor a chance to absorb the weight of his words.

'If the victim was already dead,' Doctor Snyder said, realizing what he'd missed, 'what was the point in changing the disks and carrying on with the torture?'

Hunter stayed silent.

'But that still could've happened under, or just over, five minutes?' Snyder insisted. 'Five minutes would feel like an eternity of pain when you have a high-power sander pressed against your face, don't you think?'

Hunter, who had been checking the trashcan, returned to the kitchen counter and grabbed hold of one of the evidence bags containing a discarded sanding disk. 'Are you familiar with sanding machines at all?' he asked. 'Do you do a lot of DIY?'

'Not particularly, no. Why?'

'These disks are fiber based, not aluminum oxide, or ceramic,' Hunter explained. 'That makes them a little lighter than most. The grit size is CAMI one thousand, which means it's a microgrit. In this case – ultra fine. The higher the grit size, the less abrasive the sanding action. In the US, CAMI one thousand is the finest sand disk grit you can get. These are only good for the final sanding and polishing of thick finishes, not for stripping wood, metal, plastic, or anything else, really.'

Again, Hunter allowed his words to sink in for a couple of seconds.

'If the killer had used a lower grit disk,' Hunter continued, 'the damage to her skin, muscle and bones would've happened to a much higher extent, and a lot faster.'

Doctor Snyder breathed out slowly while looking back at the victim. 'So, by picking the right type of disk, he would've kept her alive for longer and, by doing so, prolonged her suffering.'

Hunter nodded. 'Theoretically, yes.'

'Like I said,' Garcia commented after a silent pause. 'Welcome to Los Angeles, Doctor, where the "freaks" come out to play.'

'So are you a DIY kind of guy then?' the doctor asked Hunter.

'No, not really.'

'So how come you know so much about handheld sanders?'

'He reads a lot,' Garcia offered, anticipating his partner's usual answer.

Hunter shrugged. 'I do, but that's not the reason.'

Garcia paused and looked at him, intrigued.

'About a year ago,' Hunter explained, 'I helped a friend of mine redecorate her living room. I had to use a machine very similar to that one.'

Garcia went back to studying the footprint pattern on the carpet. A couple of minutes later, something caught his eye. He squatted down to get a better look at it.

'Robert,' he called out moments later. 'Come have a look at this.'

Hunter and the doctor joined him.

Garcia drew their attention to a spot on the carpet about five feet slightly to the left of the victim's chair, just by a cluster of footprints.

Hunter and Doctor Snyder squatted down next to Garcia, and he indicated a specific blood splatter among the hundreds on that side. Not the smallest, but not the largest one of them either.

Hunter and the doctor looked at it, frowned, then bent down further, bringing their faces just inches from the carpet.

'Wait a second,' Doctor Snyder said, getting up, walking over to his forensics bag in the corner and retrieving a large magnifying lens. 'This might help.' He handed it to Hunter.

With the help of the lens, Hunter considered the bloodstain for a long moment. From a few feet up, looking down, it looked just like all the other splatters, but once he and Doctor Snyder got closer, they noticed its odd shape.

A splatter is a drop of liquid that travels through the air and splashes against a surface or object, creating an irregular shape as it does. And that was the problem. The shape of this specific splatter wasn't irregular. It looked almost like a perfect half moon.

Hunter's gaze alternated between the splatter and the victim a couple of times, and he was obviously weighing up something in his mind. Then, just as Garcia had done a couple of minutes earlier, he placed his pinky finger at the center of the splatter and pressed down on the carpet. A few seconds later, his attention moved to the hundreds of other splatters that surrounded the half-moon one.

'What are you looking for?' the doctor asked.

'A second splatter, similar in shape to that one.'

Garcia had already been looking for the same thing. He found it first.

'Right here,' he said, now calling their attention to a spot in the carpet that was about a foot and a half from where the first splatter was. It wasn't quite the same. This one was a lot rounder than the first one. Nearly a full circle, in fact, but it was hollow. There was no center to it. All that could be seen was its round edge. The second splatter also seemed to fall in an almost direct line with the first one.

Hunter checked it, once again pressing his finger against the carpet at the center of it. Across from it, also in a direct line, there were no splatters but a puddle of blood. Hunter calculated something in his head, then used his finger again, this time as though he was searching for something somewhere inside that puddle.

'So what do you think those are?' Doctor Snyder asked.

Hunter and Garcia had both seen similar splatters and carpet depressions before.

'Foot marks,' Hunter replied, standing up again and indicating one of the forensic lights. 'From a tripod. Similar to that one, but a little smaller. It was set right here. Its weight left slight indentations on the carpet where each foot would've been. The third leg sat on that puddle of blood, that's what I was prodding for.'

The doctor's eyes narrowed.

'The killer filmed it.'

Thirty-Five

Squirm woke up in fright as the heavy door to his dark cell was hastily thrown open by his captor. It slammed against the inside concrete wall with purpose, shaking the entire room and sending a thunderous blast reverberating through the air.

Like a startled rat, the boy's skinny legs kicked out wildly as he desperately scrambled his way to the corner where his dirty mattress met the damp wall. When he got there, he immediately curled himself into a ball, bringing his thin arms up to protect his already scarred head.

He hadn't done anything wrong. Or at least he thought he hadn't. He had cleaned the kitchen, the living room and his captor's bedroom, just like he had to every day. He had scrubbed the floor, the shower tray, the plughole and the toilet bowl in the bathroom to as clean as it would get, and to prove it, he had licked around the toilet rim and drunk from its water. He never made any noise. He spoke only when spoken to, stayed as far away from the basement as he could, and he only ate when given permission.

Every day, after breakfast and cleaning duties, Squirm was locked back into his cell and left there until the evening, when his captor would come in and either beat him up, sodomize him, or both. After that, Squirm was usually allowed to feed on leftovers. Usually, not always.

But it wasn't nighttime yet. It couldn't be. Squirm was sure of it. He had no watch, and no way of telling the time, but something told him that, at a stretch, it was early afternoon. Then again, his captor needed no excuse to storm into Squirm's cell whenever he felt like it and allow his anger and sexual deviance to rain over the small boy like a meteor shower.

With a mixture of anger and limb-trembling fear, Squirm's whole body tensed as he ground his teeth and waited for the first blow. Hand, belt, or whip. He never knew. But this time that first blow never came.

'C'mon, get on your feet, Squirm,' 'The Monster' said from the door.

In his head, Squirm called him 'The Monster' because, whoever he was, that man was no human being.

Squirm thought he'd heard wrong. Not the man's words, but his tone of voice. It seemed to carry no rage whatsoever. Thinking back, it reminded him of the first time they'd met, just near his school. A day Squirm knew he would curse for the rest of his life.

'C'mon, Squirm, get up on your feet and come with me. I wanna show you something.'

Yes, Squirm had heard right. The man's tone was calm and inviting, almost playful.

Squirm slowly moved his arms out of the way and looked back at his captor. His eyes took a moment to adjust to the light that seeped through from the corridor outside. 'The Monster' was standing just inside the cell, staring straight at him. No anger in his expression either.

'C'mon, c'mon,' he said again, clapping his hands twice.

'We don't have all day. Let's go.' He tagged his last words with a subtle head-jerk. He then turned, stepped back out through the door and waited.

Squirm couldn't quite grasp what was going on, but he sure as hell didn't want to make 'The Monster' wait. In a flash, the boy jumped to his feet, took in a deep breath of damp, mold-smelling air, and followed his captor outside.

The man took Squirm up the squeaky wooden stairs to the second floor and into a padlocked room that he'd never been allowed in before. The room was relatively small, about sixty square feet, with a dark-gray linoleum floor and a single window at the center of the west wall, which had been boarded up with steel plates. No one could see out or in. The walls and the ceiling were all painted black and completely bare. A corner lamp cast the room in a glow of cold orange light. The space was also bare of furniture, save for a two-seater black leather sofa that sat to the right of the entry door, and faced a projection screen mounted on to the opposite wall. The sickly sweet and musky aroma that came from the room was like nothing Squirm had ever smelled before. It made his stomach crumple inside of him, and without even registering, the boy held his breath and squeezed his lips together as tightly as he could.

As he glanced inside the sinister-looking room, Squirm noticed that the sofa had been covered by some sort of thick, impermeable plastic sheet.

'I like to call this my cinema room,' 'The Monster' said, stepping inside and proudly widening his arms, as if about to hug an invisible friend.

Squirm paused at the door, his frightened gaze darting about the room.

'It's perfect, isn't it?' 'The Monster' smiled. 'So, would you like to watch a film with me, Squirm?' He sounded animated, like a caring father talking to his son.

Squirm finally breathed in again, and immediately he felt like throwing up. His gaze traveled to 'The Monster' but he didn't know how to reply. The man saw the boy's doubt and helped him out.

'But of course you would, isn't that right, Squirm?' 'The Monster' nodded twice to emphasize the decision he had made on the boy's behalf.

Wide-eyed, Squirm hesitated. For some reason, that room scared him more than his dungeon cell.

'Isn't that right, Squirm?' 'The Monster' repeated, his voice now firm and menacing.

Squirm felt his whole body quiver as he finally acknowledged the question with a single nod.

'Great, so come over here and have a seat.' 'The Monster' gave the sofa a couple of taps with his right hand.

With guarded steps, Squirm closed the door behind him before moving into the room and sitting where the man had indicated. As he took his seat, the plastic cover squeaked under his weight.

'The Monster' picked up the remote control that was balanced on one of the sofa's arms and sat down next to the boy.

Unsure, and now covered in goosebumps, Squirm kept his gaze fixed straight ahead, too scared to look at his captor.

'Oh, I think you'll like this one, Squirm. It's a new release.' 'The Monster' clicked the 'play' button and sat back.

Squirm, his body as rigid as a plank of wood, sat at the edge of his seat, his arms extended, his hands clasped together and tucked between his bare thighs.

As the first images filled the screen, Squirm frowned. There was no title, no opening credits, no mood-setting soundtrack. Instead, the film cut straight to a close-up of a woman's face, who looked to be in her early twenties. Her blue eyes were full of tears, bloodshot, and puffed up from crying. Her long blonde hair was loose, falling over her shoulders.

'Plea . . . please,' she said, looking straight at the camera. 'I'll do anything you want. Please don't hurt me.' Her voice wavered with every word.

The shot panned out gradually to reveal the woman's full body, and the sight made Squirm swallow dry. She had been stripped naked and tied to a chair that had been placed at the center of what looked like somebody's living room.

'Isn't she pretty, Squirm?' 'The Monster' asked with a smile.

The boy, transfixed by the playing images, was unable to say anything back.

'Her name is Sharon,' 'The Monster' continued. 'I like that name, don't you?'

No reply.

'Say her name, Squirm,' 'The Monster' demanded.

The boy's attention finally moved from the screen to the man at his side. 'What?'

'What's her name? Say her name back to me. I just told you what it was. Weren't you paying attention?'

'Yes, sir, I was.' Squirm's words sounded almost as frightened as the woman's.

'So say her name. And you'd better not get it wrong.'

'Sh . . . Sharon. Her name is Sharon.'

'The Monster' held the boy's gaze for a long while, his face a blank mask.

'Isn't that right, sir?' Squirm asked in a pleading voice.

At last, the man's lips parted into a smile and he sounded happy again. 'Yes, that's exactly right. But don't look at me, Squirm. Look at the screen. It gets much better.'

Squirm did as he was told.

'Whizzzzzzz.' From the speaker, a loud, mechanical sound filled the room, startling Squirm and making him jump in his seat. On the screen, Sharon screamed in petrified terror and turned her face away as she began sobbing uncontrollably.

'Please . . . no, no, no.'

Using whatever strength she had left, she ferociously wiggled her body on the chair, trying desperately to break free, but to no use.

Suddenly, from Sharon's left someone else entered the shot. It took Squirm a few seconds to realize that the person now on-screen was the man sitting by his side – 'The Monster'. He was dressed in some strange outfit, covered from head to toe in what looked to be a handmade, see-through plastic jumpsuit. In his hands he carried a small machine, which was the source of the loud whizzing noise.

'Do you know what that is, Squirm?' 'The Monster' asked, indicating the machine.

Squirm shook his head.

'It's an electric sander. Fantastic little machine. Very powerful.'

Squirm looked back at 'The Monster' with shocked eyes, as he felt a new shudder run up and down his spine.

'The Monster' smiled at him. 'That's right, Squirm, you've got it. I'm going to sand off her face. Just look.' He pointed at the screen.

The boy didn't move. Couldn't move.

'Look,' 'The Monster' ordered, grabbing the boy's chin, and forcing his face in the direction of the screen again.

Panic had completely consumed Sharon, who was now frantically screaming and jerking her body in the chair, but her efforts didn't seem to bother 'The Monster'. On the contrary, they seemed to excite him more. He stepped closer and brought the sander to within just a couple of inches of her face. Feeling the wind and the heat produced by the 420-watt rotating disk, her panic went through the roof and she wet herself.

The boy just couldn't look anymore. Instinctively, he closed his eyes and turned his head away.

SLAP.

'The Monster' hit him across the face so hard it sent Squirm flying off the sofa and on to the floor. The boy's vision was immediately flooded by sparkles of light.

'The Monster' pressed the 'pause' button.

The boy brought a hand to his tender cheek. Tears began rolling down his face. Blood began dripping from the corner of his mouth.

'Open your eyes, and sit back here, Squirm. If you even think about closing them again, or looking away, then you'll really understand how painful an electric sander can be because I will sand all the skin off your back. Do you understand?'

Squirm sucked in a ragged breath. 'Yes, sir. I'm sorry, sir.' On weak legs, the boy got back to his feet and returned to the sofa.

'Good boy.'

His captor pressed 'play' again. On the screen, Sharon had stopped moving. Her fear was so intense it had paralyzed her. It seemed like all she could do was hope for a miracle, but that miracle didn't come.

As the machine touched her face, blood and skin began spitting from the sander in all directions, creating a rain of red mist. The scream she let out was so guttural and full of pain, it blocked out the bone-chilling grinding noise from the machine.

Squirm could feel he was about to be sick, but he knew that if he looked away or closed his eyes, 'The Monster' would hurt him like he'd never been hurt before. Out of options, the boy did the only thing he could think of so he wouldn't close his eyes – he brought his hands to his face and, using both of his thumbs and index fingers, he forced his eyelids open and continued to stare at the screen.

Thirty-Six

'Detective Garcia, Homicide Special,' Garcia said into the mouthpiece of his cellphone, answering the call after the second ring. He and Hunter had just got back to the Police Administration Building after spending most of their morning and afternoon at the crime scene in Venice.

'Detective, this is Officer Woods.'

Officer Garry Woods was in charge of the new door-to-door that was being conducted in Hollywood Hills. With the events of that morning, Garcia had forgotten about it.

'Sir, you asked me to inform you directly if anything came up.'

'Yes, that's right.'

'Well, I think that we might've come across some new information for you here.'

'OK. We're on our way.'

Through late afternoon stop-and-start traffic, the drive from South Central back to Upper Laurel Canyon in Hollywood Hills took Hunter and Garcia close to an hour and ten minutes. Once they finally got there, they found Officer Woods and his partner waiting for them inside their black and white unit, which was parked directly in front of house number 8420, ten doors away from the Bennetts.

'Detectives,' Woods said, stepping out of his car and greeting Hunter and Garcia. He was about forty-five years old, with straight, rust-colored hair, full lips, longish, bushy eyebrows, and deep-brown, almost black eyes. He looked like a pensive wolf in a police uniform. His partner, who looked like he was counting the minutes until the end of his shift, stayed inside the unit.

Hunter and Garcia returned the greeting.

'OK,' Woods began. 'Just as we were instructed to, we knocked on every door from the top of this road, all the way down to Laurel Pass Avenue, including the houses on Carmar Drive.' He pointed to the street they could see branching out of Allenwood Road on the right. 'That's sixty-nine properties in total. We spoke to everyone who was available this time, including minors.' He allowed his gaze to bounce from Hunter to Garcia, then back to Hunter. 'I must admit; in this neighborhood, it all sounded like a wild goose chase at first. As expected, just as the previous door-to-door showed, nobody could remember seeing anything or anyone out of the ordinary, mainly because there's no such thing as *ordinary* up on these hills, if you know what I mean. But about halfway through the search, we came across something that sounded at least interesting.' He paused and gave both detectives a shrug. 'It could also be nothing at all, but that's not my decision to make. I'm just reporting it as instructed.'

'OK,' Garcia said. 'So what have we got?'

'Right here,' Woods said, and he turned and faced house number 8420, a two-storey, redbrick home with a hipped roof, a neatly cropped front lawn and paths edged with orderly flowerbeds. Two cars were parked on the driveway – a white GMC Yukon and a metallic-blue Tesla S.

'The information came from a kid,' Woods said, nodding his head in the direction of the house. 'His name is Marlon Sloan. Thirteen years old. Seems quite intelligent, but he's as shy as shy can be.' He reached for his notepad. 'Would you like me to just relate to you what the kid told me, or talk to him yourself?'

Hunter sensed some hesitation in Officer Woods' tone. 'Why? Are you unsure of what he told you?'

As Woods tilted his head slightly to one side, his eyebrows lifted like two hairy caterpillars trying to kiss.

'Like I said,' he began. 'The kid is terribly shy. As he was telling me his story, he barely maintained eye contact. He also seemed a little nervous, almost scared. That could be just the way the kid is, or something else. I'm not sure. But I know you detectives like to read people while you talk to them, that's why I asked.'

Garcia nodded at Officer Woods before facing Hunter. 'Well, since we're here, we might as well talk to the kid.'

A few seconds after Officer Woods rang the doorbell, the door was opened by a five-foot-six woman in her early forties, who was more charming than attractive. She wore a black dress with spaghetti straps, black stockings and low-heel work shoes. Her naturally wavy auburn hair fell down to the top of her shoulders, framing a small, round face.

'Hello again, Ms. Sloan,' Woods said.

The woman's gaze stayed on the officer for just a fraction before moving questioningly to the other two people standing at the door.

As Hunter and Garcia finished introducing themselves, a pale and skinny kid with short blond hair and thin

wireframe glasses appeared at the door a few feet behind
Ms. Sloan. He was about an inch taller than his mother. He
wore blue jeans and a black T-shirt with a sugar skull on it.
Underneath the skull, in white letters, was a band name –
Aesthetic Perfection.

Hunter tilted his head to one side to catch the kid's
attention.

'Hi there,' he said, with a subtle hand-wave. 'I'm Detective
Robert Hunter of the LAPD, and this is my partner, Detective
Carlos Garcia. You must be Marlon, right?'

The kid nodded in silence. Eye contact was established
for no more than a second before he looked away.

Woods looked at Hunter and Garcia with a gaze that
said: 'I told you the kid was shy.'

'Hi, Marlon,' Woods said, looking over Ms. Sloan's
shoulder. 'These are the detectives I said might have a few
more questions for you. Do you mind telling them again
what you told me earlier?'

'I'm sorry,' the boy's mother cut in, sounding a little
annoyed, 'but this seems like a waste of time, ours and
yours. He won't tell them anything that he hasn't already
told you.' She checked her watch. 'And we've got a therapist's appointment in less than an hour.' She turned and
faced her son. 'We need to get going.'

Hunter was observing the boy, and as his mother
mentioned the word 'therapist' Marlon looked away to his
left, pressed his lips against each other and tucked his hands
deep into his jean pockets. A negative reaction that indicated he wasn't so keen on his therapist sessions.

'We'll take as little of your time as we possibly can, Ms.
Sloan,' Hunter said calmly, trying to reassure her and the
boy. 'But this really is important.'

Before Ms. Sloan could voice a reply, Hunter addressed the boy directly.

'Marlon, we would really appreciate your help. If you could give us just a few minutes of your time, please.'

Marlon finally stepped forward, joining his mother at the door.

'Do you mind if I see your credentials?' he asked. This time, eye contact was held for a while longer than before.

The question caught everyone by surprise, even the boy's mother, who looked at him as if he was being rude.

'Of course,' Hunter said, reaching for his LAPD identity and handing it to Marlon. Garcia did the same.

The boy studied them carefully and for a long moment, as if he were an expert in telling a forgery from the real thing.

'Homicide,' he said, returning the IDs to both detectives.

'Excuse me?' Ms. Sloan said, surprised, first looking at her son, then at Hunter and Garcia. She had failed to notice that detail when she first looked at the detectives' identification. 'Homicide?'

'That's correct, ma'am,' Hunter said, handing her his credentials one more time. 'Unfortunately, what started as an abduction from the house just down the road to yours has now sadly escalated to a homicide. The woman's body was found yesterday morning. That's why we're revisiting every house.'

'Oh my God!' Ms. Sloan said, returning the credentials to Hunter, her annoyed demeanor completely dissipating. 'I'm so sorry to hear that. I had no idea.' She placed her arm around her son's shoulder in a protective, tight hug.

'At this time, any information, no matter how trivial it

might seem to others, could be very important to us,' Hunter reinforced.

'Of course, of course,' Ms. Sloan replied apologetically, before taking a step to her left. 'Please, why don't you come in?'

Thirty-Seven

Hunter, Garcia and Officer Woods followed Ms. Sloan and Marlon through a small anteroom, past a turned staircase and into the living room. Antique furniture decorated the large and very pleasant space. The walls, covered by widely striped wallpaper of deep-green and olive hues, were adorned with several oil paintings, all of them originals. A large, green and white shaggy rug centered the room, together with an impressive set of Victorian carved mahogany sofas and armchairs. Hanging from the center of the ceiling, a very elegant crystal chandelier bathed the room in calming light.

Ms. Sloan guided the group to the seating area. She and her son took one of the sofas. Hunter and Garcia took the other. Officer Woods took one of the framed armchairs. As they sat down, Ms. Sloan placed her arm around her son's shoulder once again.

Hunter had kept his attention on Marlon. Officer Woods was right, the kid was terribly shy. He felt uncomfortable and awkward around people, especially strangers, and coping came in the form of minimum interaction, a shielded, timid posture, and little or no eye contact. As a result of how he felt, Marlon had built a defensive wall around him, probably subconsciously. In today's world, not that rare a behavior. His mother's hug seemed to embarrass him.

Hunter didn't want to take much of their time, but he also wanted to try to make Marlon feel as at ease as he possibly could.

'That's a great band, by the way,' he said as he and Garcia took their seats, indicating the boy's shirt.

Marlon's eyes slowly moved from the floor back to Hunter. Doubt and surprise were written all over the boy's face. This time, he didn't break eye contact.

'You know Aesthetic Perfection?' His tone, unlike his expression, carried a lot more doubt than surprise.

Hunter nodded. 'I've seen them live a couple of times.'

Marlon adjusted his glasses on his nose and regarded the detective for an instant.

Hunter could tell that he was being studied.

'Really?' Marlon finally said. The doubt in his tone had turned into scepticism. 'Do you have a favorite song?'

The kid is clever, Hunter thought. *And very guarded.* He had taken Hunter's friendly comment and turned it into a test.

'I wouldn't say I have a favorite song,' Hunter replied. 'I like most of their stuff, especially the last two albums, but if I had to pick, maybe "Antibody", or "Pale", or "Lights Out". How about you, do you have a favorite song at all?'

The kid hesitated again, visibly taken aback by a response that he wasn't expecting. In consequence, his tense posture and expression finally relaxed. Unintentionally, his lips spread into a ghost of a smile.

'"Antibody" *is* a great song,' he admitted. 'I like "Inhuman" a lot too. But I agree, most of their stuff is awesome.' He studied Hunter a moment longer. 'Do you know a band called God Module?'

Hunter looked deep in thought for a couple of seconds. 'No, I don't think I do.'

'If you like Aesthetic Perfection, you'll like them. You should check them out.'

'God Module.' Hunter nodded. 'Thanks. I will do.'

Ms. Sloan followed their quick conversation with a half surprised, half intrigued look on her face. Very rarely had she seen her son deliberately engage a stranger in conversation.

'I'm sorry.' Hunter addressed Ms. Sloan. 'I know that you're pressed for time.'

'Umm . . . yes, we are a little.' She looked at her son.

'Marlon,' Hunter began. 'Could you just run us through what you told Officer Woods earlier?'

The boy nodded. 'Sure. I was asked if I remembered seeing either a vehicle or maybe someone hanging out in the street in the past weeks. Like a non-resident, or a car that I hadn't seen before.'

'That's right,' Hunter confirmed.

'I'd like to point out that Marlon doesn't really like to leave the house, you see,' Ms. Sloan intervened. 'He doesn't feel so comfortable outside.'

'Mom,' Marlon stopped her, sounding annoyed and embarrassed at the same time. 'So what if I like to stay in the house? I still have eyes, don't I? And my room has a large window, which I like to look out of.' He subtly wiggled his shoulder, freeing himself from his mother's embrace.

'So you saw something from your window?' Hunter asked in a calm and steady voice, bringing Marlon's attention back to him and to the reason why they were all there.

'Yes, I did,' the kid replied, now scooting a couple of inches away from his mother. 'I have a pretty good view of most of the street from my bedroom window.'

While outside, Hunter had already noticed the very strategic position of the Sloans' house in relation to the street and the Bennetts' home.

'OK, so what was it that you saw?'

'Well, let me give you a little bit of background first,' Marlon began. 'About four weeks ago there was some sort of problem with one of the telephone poles out on the street. The one just outside number eight-four-five-six, to be precise.' He pointed north. 'All the phones around here were dead.'

'Yes, I remember that,' Ms. Sloan interrupted again.

Before continuing, Marlon looked at her as if to say: *Just let me speak, Mom.*

'OK,' he carried on, 'late that afternoon, a couple of AT&T engineers came by and fixed everything. I saw them working on the cables up at the top of the post.'

Hunter nodded but said nothing, allowing the kid to continue at his own pace.

'What to me seemed strange,' Marlon continued, 'was that two days later another engineer was back here, working on the same telephone pole.'

Garcia frowned. 'Why did you find that strange?

Marlon readjusted his glasses one more time. 'Well, first, because there was no problem with the phone lines anymore. The problem had been fixed two days earlier. Second, because this engineer was by himself, using a telescopic ladder to get to the cables at the top of the post. It's a pretty high post. The AT&T engineers that were here before him had a basket-crane truck.'

Garcia peeked at Hunter, who kept his eyes on the kid.

'And then,' Marlon continued, 'about a week or so ago, that same lone engineer was back working up on the same telephone pole. Again, with a telescopic ladder, not a basket-crane truck, but this time I saw him leaving.' Marlon paused, maybe for effect, maybe to take a breath. 'He wasn't driving an AT&T van, or any company van. He was driving a Yukon that was parked on the other side of the road. It was just like Mom's, but his was black. He placed the ladder on the roof rack and took off.'

'About a week or so ago?' Hunter asked.

'Yes,' Marlon confirmed. 'I think it was about two or three days before the police came knocking the first time.'

This time Hunter and Garcia exchanged a semi-concerned look.

A loud crackling noise came from the radio attached to Officer Woods' belt. He quickly reached for it, while getting up.

'Please excuse me, ma'am.' He turned toward the detectives. 'I've been waiting for some information to come in. This will be it. I'll wait for you outside.' He addressed Ms. Sloan again, who was about to get to her feet. 'It's OK, ma'am, I can see myself out.' He turned and left the room.

Hunter resumed his questioning. 'Did you manage to get a good look at this engineer?'

'I only saw him from the back, while he was up on the post,' the boy answered with a disappointed look. 'He was tall, like the two of you. And he wasn't fat, like the two AT&T engineers.'

'Was he skinny, muscular?' Garcia this time.

'I couldn't tell. He was wearing a jacket.'

'An AT&T work jacket?'

'I can't remember, but I don't think so.'

'How about hair color?'

Once again, the kid shook his head, disheartened. 'Sorry, I couldn't really see it. He was wearing a baseball cap. I wasn't really paying much attention to him or anything. It didn't really look like he was doing anything wrong. I only thought of it because the officer who just left came asking. The only non-residents I've seen around the street in the past weeks were the AT&T engineers, this third engineer I told you about, and the police. That's it.'

Everyone understood where the kid was coming from.

'How about his vehicle?' Hunter asked. 'You said it was a black GMC Yukon?'

'Yeah, it was.'

Hunter saw Ms. Sloan consulting her watch one more time.

'And you said it had roof racks,' he asked.

'Yeah, it did.'

'Did you notice anything else about the car at all? Like . . . were there any big bumps or scratches on the bodywork? Bumper or window stickers? Anything you can remember, really.'

Marlon looked down at his hands. 'No, sorry. Only that it was a black Yukon.'

Hunter and Garcia exchanged one more look. There was nothing else they needed from Marlon or his mother, who was now looking rather impatient again.

Both detectives got up, thanked Marlon and Ms. Sloan, and made their way to the door. As Ms. Sloan saw them out, Hunter turned to face her.

'The therapist session you're taking Marlon to now, is that for his social anxiety and panic disorder?'

Ms. Sloan frowned at Hunter, mainly because she was surprised by his accurate diagnosis. Her next few words were a lot more guarded than before.

'Yes . . . it is.'

Hunter glanced at Marlon, who was standing just behind

his mother. He had heard the question and now looked a little embarrassed.

'How long now?' Hunter asked. 'How long has he been going to therapy?'

A deeper frown from Ms. Sloan this time.

'I'm sorry, but I fail to see how that is any of your concern, Detective?'

'It hasn't helped a great deal, has it?'

Ms. Sloan looked offended.

'You should stop with the therapist,' Hunter said.

Behind his mother, Marlon came close to a smile.

'Excuse me?' Ms. Sloan said.

'You should stop with the therapist,' Hunter repeated.

'And why on earth would I want to do that?'

Hunter's gaze found Marlon before returning to the boy's mother. 'The sad truth is that therapy and shrink visits are mainly hogwash. It's in their financial interest to keep their patients coming back. Marlon's condition is a lot more common than you might think, Ms. Sloan. And though you might think you're helping by being overly protective of your son, you're not.'

Ms. Sloan glared at Hunter. Anger crept into her eyes.

He ignored her look and addressed Marlon. 'Every week, just try to walk a block outside your comfort zone, Marlon, however far that might be. If you can't manage a block, try half a block. Find a park bench and have a seat. When your breathing calms down, ask a passing stranger for the time. Next week, ask two. The week after that, three. Next month, walk another block outside your new-found comfort zone, and repeat what you did before. Before you know it, you'll be making new friends and the whole anxiety thing will be behind you.'

Ms. Sloan's glare morphed into an intrigued stare.

'You don't need a therapist's mumbo-jumbo to crack this thing, Marlon. You can do it yourself. One small victory at a time.'

Thirty-Eight

Cautiously, Squirm raised his left hand and brought it to his face, but the tips of his fingers touched nothing. They paused less than half an inch from the swollen flesh that now surrounded his left eye.

Back in the projection room earlier that day, his trick had worked. By using both of his thumbs and index fingers, he had managed to force his eyes open and keep them that way while those horrific images played on the large screen before him. 'The Monster' didn't seem to mind it. In fact, he had laughed out loud, telling Squirm it was an ingenious move.

'I like that, Squirm,' he said as he used his dirty fingernail to pick something from between his teeth. 'You were faced with a problem, and you came up with a smart alternative. That's clever. I like clever.'

Without noticing, Squirm's breathing had become labored. He'd never seen so much blood. He'd never heard screams like the ones coming from that woman – guttural and overwhelmed with pain, drowning in terror, and completely void of hope.

Sharon, that was her name. The man had made him repeat it a number of times while the film played on. Squirm would never forget that name for as long as he lived.

On the screen, Sharon had finally passed out. Somehow she had managed to endure the pain for a lot longer than anyone would've imagined. Several minutes, in fact. Squirm actually thought that she'd finally let go of the desire to live and accepted the inevitable. That the film and her suffering would finally be over. But he couldn't have been more wrong.

The images played on, and Squirm watched as 'The Monster' turned off the sander, placed it on the floor and walked over to where the camera was. Once he got to it, he zoomed in on the grotesque mess that her face was turning into. Lumps of skin and flesh hung loosely from her forehead and brow. Blood surged from her wounds in sheets. It ran down on to what was still left of her face, moving past her chin and down to her naked torso, but Squirm could see that Sharon was still breathing.

The ordeal was far from over.

'Keep your eyes open, Squirm,' 'The Monster' had said, excitement coating his words. 'It's just about to get really good.'

Squirm felt like something had gained life inside his stomach and had begun crawling its way up the inside of his chest. Shock had forced the boy's mouth to fall half open. His hands were shaking and he had to keep readjusting his fingers so as not to let go of his eyelids. Cold sweat had begun trickling down his face and back.

The screen flicked to black for a moment, then it started again.

'I had to stop filming.' For some reason, the man sitting beside him had decided to explain. 'It took me the best part of twenty minutes to wake her up again. But I'll tell you something, Squirm, she was one tough bitch.' He let out a croaked, over-enthusiastic laugh that made the boy's skin crawl.

The new segment started from where the previous one had left off. More blood and tiny chunks of skin began flying up, propelled by the sander's rotating disk, before cascading back down over everything like rain.

'Next time, maybe you can watch it live, Squirm, what do you say? Wouldn't you like to be in that room with us?'

Whatever had begun crawling its way through Squirm's insides gained momentum. All of a sudden, it rushed up through his throat with incredible speed.

Squirm hadn't thought it possible, but Sharon's screams had gotten even louder, assaulting the boy's ears with the effect of piercing needles. He was still doing his best to hold his eyes open, but there was no stopping the crawling creature from his stomach which had burst into the kid's mouth in avalanche style.

Squirm's body jerked forward violently and he projectile-vomited the little that he had in his gut all over the dark-gray linoleum floor. Some of it reached the screen.

'You ungrateful sonofabitch,' 'The Monster' had barked, jumping up from his seat. He was careful not to step on the mess Squirm had made on the floor.

The boy looked up at the man with total panic in his eyes. 'I'm sorry, sir. I'll clean it. I'm sorry.' He fell to his knees and used his hands to try to collect what he had regurgitated on to the floor.

POW.

The man's opened hand connected with the side of the kid's face, just by his left eye, with such force it sent the boy tumbling across the floor. He only stopped when his head smashed against the wall. Squirm's eyes rolled back into his head a fraction of a second before he collapsed on to the ground like an empty sack of potatoes.

Without caring, 'The Monster' grabbed the unconscious boy by the hair, dragged him downstairs and threw him back in his cell.

Thirty-Nine

'What was that about?' Garcia asked Hunter as both detectives joined Officer Woods by his black and white unit outside.

'Nothing, really. Just trying to give the kid a tip.'

'OK,' Woods said as he finished writing something in his notepad. 'I've just come off the radio with Operations. Before you guys got here, I had asked them to run a quick check on what Marlon had said. That was the info I was waiting for.'

Hunter and Garcia were quietly impressed by Officer Woods' approach. Most officers would have left all the checking to the detectives.

'Anything?' Garcia asked.

'You tell me,' Woods began, reading from his notes. 'There really was a fault with the phone lines reported last month. AT&T sent two engineers to fix it on the twelfth, and yes, they did have a basket-crane truck with them. The fault was fixed that same day. Since then, AT&T has had no other reports, and they have no knowledge of any other faults with the phone lines in this area. They also said that they did not send any other engineers up here for a subsequent check since the fault was fixed. Not on the fourteenth of last month, or at any other time for that matter, and that includes last week.'

'And it couldn't have been a different phone company?' Garcia asked.

'No,' Woods replied. 'No other supplier services this area.' He closed his notepad. 'It seems like you have got yourselves a mysterious telephone engineer.'

'Marlon said that they were working on the telephone pole in front of property number eight-four-five-six,' Hunter said, looking north.

'That's correct,' Woods confirmed. 'And that's the one, right over there on the corner.' He pointed at the T-shaped telephone pole directly in front of a white-fronted, single-storey house that sat right where Allenwood Road bent sharply left, about thirty yards north of where they were standing.

Hunter and Garcia walked over to have a better look. Officer Woods followed.

It was a regular-looking telephone pole, brown in color, and made of southern yellow pine. It stood somewhere between thirty-five and forty feet tall. A total of seven telephone cables ran through it – five at the very top, through the horizontal arm of the T, and the remaining two just a few feet beneath the first five, through the long, vertical arm.

Hunter and Garcia spent less than ten seconds looking up at the post before both of them came to the same conclusion.

To reach the first of the cables, an engineer would have to climb about thirty to thirty-five feet. No wonder the AT&T engineers used a basket-crane truck to get up there. On the other hand, a single engineer, even with a long telescopic ladder, would be facing a very tough and somewhat danger-ous task.

Hunter walked around the pole, checking it from both sides.

'Do those cables service this whole street?' Garcia asked, still looking up at the pole.

'I'm not sure,' Woods replied. 'But I would say so.' He observed the two detectives for a moment.

'Do you think it was him?' Garcia asked his partner.

Hunter paused and looked north, where the road bent left and disappeared behind property 8456.

Garcia waited.

Hunter then looked south, in the direction of the Sloan and Bennett houses. If Marlon was at his bedroom window, Hunter wasn't able to see him. The angle of the window in relation to the pole's position, coupled with the way the light reflected off the glass, made it virtually impossible for anyone standing at the pole to see inside.

'Yes,' Hunter finally replied. 'I think it was him.'

Garcia's gaze moved to the telephone cables. 'Do you think he bugged the phone lines?'

Hunter looked up at the pole one more time. 'There's no reason why he would've needed to do that,' he replied. 'If that's what he wanted, then it would've been a lot easier, and less risky, to do it via the telephone exchange box.'

'So if you think that this mysterious telephone engineer was your man,' Woods said. 'What was he doing up on the telephone pole?'

Hunter looked north again. Past the pole, the road bent sharply left and disappeared behind the house they were standing in front of, impeding his view. From where he was, he could see no other houses, which meant that no other houses could see him either. He then turned and looked south. From that point, he had a clear and unrestricted view of every house on Allenwood Road, including the Bennetts'.

Hunter finally answered Woods' question with another question.

'How difficult do you think it would be for someone to place some sort of camera up there?'

Forty

Night arrives slowly in the summertime, gently gaining ground like a silent soldier. First, lazy shadows find the alleyways, then they start creeping across sidewalks, up walls and through windows, until finally darkness takes hold. By the time Hunter and Garcia got to the coroner's office, after receiving a phone call from Doctor Hove just half an hour earlier, darkness had stealthily found its way into almost every corner of Los Angeles, with the exception of a sliver of purple sky that still colored the horizon over Santa Monica, but that too was fading fast.

At the crime scene in Venice, besides the several bloody footprints retrieved from the carpet in the living room, forensics had also managed to collect a number of fibers, hairs and traces of dust. Everything had been bagged and taken back to the lab for further examination. Due to how careful they all knew this killer was, hopes weren't high, but they weren't dead yet either.

Sharon Barnard's cabin crew suitcase had been left in the living room by the front door. Inside it they'd found a used change of clothes, a toiletries bag, a makeup bag, and a tablet computer, which was password protected. Her cellphone was found on the kitchen counter, its screen locked by a six-digit combination. Both electronic items had been passed to the LAPD Computer Forensics Unit.

Forensics had also discovered a large number of finger-prints all around the house, but just like the ones found on the front door and handle, an initial, naked-eye analysis by the forensics team expert told them that they probably came from only two sources, one of them almost certainly female. The natural conclusion was that the prints had probably come from Sharon Barnard herself and her house-mate, Tom Hobbs. Due to the large number of fingerprints found, confirmation was only expected to come some time in the next twenty-four to forty-eight hours.

Tom Hobbs was still in shock, and waves of anxiety, which were triggered by involuntary memory flashes, came and went throughout the day, throwing him into fits of tears and panic attacks. The LAPD had managed to get in contact with his parents, who came and took him with them back to Pomona Valley, but not before a medic was forced to sedate him. Hunter would try to interview him again tomorrow.

After identifying themselves to the receptionist sitting behind the counter at the LA County Coroner, Hunter and Garcia were told that Doctor Hove was waiting for them inside Autopsy Theater One, the same theater they were in the day before.

In silence, Hunter and Garcia navigated their way through the shiny corridors and double swinging doors until they reached the small anteroom leading to Autopsy Theater One. Hunter hit the buzzer by the electronic keypad to the right of the door. Five seconds later, the doors hissed open.

Despite knowing to expect it, the low temperature inside the autopsy room still made Garcia shiver as he stepped inside. It did every time.

'Robert. Carlos.' Doctor Hove greeted both detectives with a nod of her head. She wore a regular light-blue lab gown, with her nose mask hanging loosely around her neck. Her hair was pulled back and tied up in a bundle at the top of her head. She smiled, but there was no way of disguising the drained and exhausted look of someone who'd been working for hours on end under artificial light.

Sharon Barnard's body was laid out, uncovered, on the stainless-steel examination table at the center of the room. The mess of muscle and flesh that her face had become had now taken on a brownish, dry-meat color. Her right eye, the one that had been spared by the handheld sander, had gone completely milky, and the rest of her skin now looked ghostly white.

Doctor Hove approached the instrument counter on the other side of the examination table. Hunter and Garcia were right behind her. She picked up two copies of the autopsy report and handed one to each detective.

'Unfortunately,' the doctor began, her voice sounding as tired as she looked, 'this post mortem examination hasn't revealed a great deal.' She switched on the high-powered halogen lights above the autopsy table.

Hunter and Garcia blinked a couple of times while their eyes got used to the enhanced brightness.

'As you can plainly see –' she directed their attention to Sharon Barnard's torso, arms and legs – 'unlike the first victim, this one shows no signs of having been physically tortured prior to the total disfiguration of her face. No whipping marks or cuts of any kind. None to her back either.' She turned and indicated the chart on the wall behind her, which itemized the weight of the deceased's brain, heart, liver, kidneys and spleen. 'All of her internal organs, including her brain, were in as good a condition as could be expected for a healthy twenty-two-year-old female.'

Hunter and Garcia flipped to the second page on the report. Just as the lead forensics agent at the crime scene, Doctor Brian Snyder, had guessed, the cause of death had been heart failure induced by acute loss of blood.

'Again, unlike the first victim,' Doctor Hove continued, 'this one showed no indication of having been sexually assaulted.'

That discovery surprised Garcia a lot more than it did Hunter. In truth, Hunter was half expecting it. When he had examined Sharon Barnard's body *in situ* that morning, he had seen no bruises or abrasions of any sort to her inner thighs, nor around her groin region.

'Also,' the doctor added, 'this time there was no message. Nothing was left in her throat or anywhere else in her body.'

Garcia nodded as he explained, 'The message was left on the carpet inside the victim's house. Written in her own blood.'

Doctor Hove's face was colored by intrigue. 'What was the message?'

'Same three words as before, Doc. I Am Death. That's it. Nothing more. Written all in capital letters.'

The doctor's gaze returned to Sharon Barnard, and to what should've been her face. 'I will admit that, bar being shot in the face by a close-quarters shotgun, the trauma to her facial muscles and nerves was as severe as I've ever seen.'

'The difference is,' Hunter said in a somber voice, moving around to the other side of the table, 'when you're shot in the face by a close-quarters shotgun, chances are you'll die instantly. No pain.' He shook his head. 'The killer didn't want that to happen here.'

Everyone went quiet for a moment.

Garcia, whose gaze had returned to Sharon Barnard's body on the examination table, let out a heartfelt breath.

'I don't get this. I don't get any of this. How can a killer completely switch his MO this way? I've never heard of a case like this.'

'That's exactly the same thought that has been with me since I started the post mortem,' Doctor Hove said. 'If I hadn't been told, I would've never guessed, or found out through the examination, that this victim belonged to the same killer who had tortured and murdered the victim from yesterday morning's autopsy.'

'Exactly,' Garcia agreed, bowing his head in the doctor's direction before looking at Hunter. 'We've dealt with killers who like to experiment before, Robert. Killers whose MOs slightly change from one murder to the other, but this is nothing like that. Here, the break away from the previous MO is too severe. Like the Doc said, this could've been a completely different killer. If not for the fact that he likes to authenticate his work by signing it, we would've never known both murders were related. We wouldn't even be in this autopsy room.'

Out of frustration, Garcia stated what Hunter and Doctor Hove already knew.

'His first victim was abducted and tortured for arguably five-and-a-half days before she was murdered. Her body was covered in whipping marks and lacerations – one hundred and twenty in total. We all know that, when used, abduction and prolonged torture accounts for a large portion of the killer's MO. That just simply didn't happen here.' He nodded at the body on the table. 'The second victim was never abducted. She was subdued and murdered inside her own home in a matter of hours, not days. Also, the first victim's cause of death could easily be considered a non-violent method. He kept her upside down long enough to induce oedema of the brain. Painful? Yes. Violent? Not quite. Now just look at this.' Once again, Garcia pointed to Sharon Barnard's body. 'He scraped her whole face off with an electric sander and left her to die. Painful? Hell, yes. Violent? Like nothing I've ever seen before.'

Garcia took a step back from the autopsy table and folded his arms in front of his chest. The coldness of the room was starting to get to him.

'And my last point,' he continued, 'which baffles me more than all the others, is the fact that victim one was raped repeatedly.' He shrugged as he spoke. 'People who are dominated by sexual compulsion to commit ever-increasingly savage and brutal crimes will *never* find enough satisfaction in their acts to the point that it will make them spontaneously stop. We all know this. They simply can't stop themselves. Nevertheless, we just found out that victim two wasn't even touched.' Garcia paused for breath. 'Looking at both crimes, the only similarities we have, other than the "I AM DEATH" bullshit, is that both victims were female and in their early twenties. That's it. Nothing else matches. Not even the level of violence.'

Hunter tucked his hands deep inside his pockets. 'I

know all this, Carlos, and you're right on every point. Sociopaths who are guided by powerful MOs such as sexual gratification, extreme sadism, and victim abduction followed by torture and death rarely detour from those MOs. And even when they do, it's usually an escalation, or a slight variation, not a total detachment like we have here. I've been wracking my brain trying to come up with a plausible theory to explain any of this since I first laid eyes on her this morning.'

Garcia looked at Hunter questioningly.

'The only thing I could come up with was that this killer is lacking that uncontrollable urge.'

Garcia greeted Hunter's statement first with silence, then by looking back at Sharon Barnard's disfigured face.

'The uncontrollable urge,' Hunter repeated. 'That compulsive desire inside of them that so many can't even explain themselves and are completely helpless against. Like you said a minute ago – they simply can't stop themselves. I don't think that that's what drove this guy to abduct, rape, torture and kill Nicole Wilson, or to invade Sharon Barnard's home and mutilate her the way he did. That's not why he's doing what he's doing.'

A thoughtful silence descended on the room one more time.

'So why is he?' Doctor Hove asked eventually.

Hunter shook his head. 'I'm not sure what's driving him yet. But this guy is not out of control, Doc. He's not losing an internal battle against his urges. On the contrary, he's *completely* in control of everything he does. He abducts, he rapes, he tortures, he kills, not to satisfy some overpowering desire inside of him.'

Hunter faced the body.

'He does it because he wants to. He's showing us that he can be any sort of killer he wants, morph from one type to another in no time at all. Because he's not driven by compulsion. He's a killer by choice.'

Forty-One

Garcia was the one who knocked on Captain Blake's door. She had called both detectives into her office for an unscheduled meeting, which wasn't at all unusual. The surprising fact was finding Chief of Police James Bracco in her office, also waiting for them.

Captain Blake was standing by the bookshelf on the south wall, while Chief Bracco had taken one of the two Chesterfield armchairs that faced her desk. He was nursing a full cup of coffee, from which no steam was visible. His posture and facial expressions were tense to say the least.

As Hunter and Garcia stepped into the well air-conditioned office, Chief Bracco immediately stood up and turned to face them. Instead of his usual raven-black police uniform with four silver stars on each side of his shirt collar, he wore a well-tailored suit, silvery-gray in color, with the jacket open to reveal a blue tie and a white dress shirt underneath. His horseshoe mustache matched his peppery hair.

'Detectives,' he said, taking one step forward and offering his hand.

No introductions were necessary. Despite taking over from the previous Chief of Police just over eight months ago, both detectives had met Chief Bracco at least a couple of times before.

They all shook hands, and then Hunter's gaze quickly moved to his captain. Hunter could tell that some of Chief Bracco's anxiety had rubbed off on her.

'OK, you both know that I'm not a man to beat around the bush,' the Chief of Police began, placing his untouched cup of coffee on the small coffee table between the two armchairs. His voice was firm but slightly hoarse, as if he was either fatigued or had just come out of a bad cold. 'So I'm not going to waste your time or mine with bullshit conversation.'

Captain Blake returned to her desk, but instead of taking a seat she stood behind her chair, resting her forearms on the backrest.

'Despite doing our best to keep the specifics of this investigation as airtight as possible,' Chief Bracco continued, 'there's no avoiding it anymore, the case will make the news by tomorrow.' He lifted his right index finger to stop anyone from asking any questions before he was finished. 'Our press office is expected to issue a statement by tomorrow morning. As far as we know, the press isn't aware of any of the grisly details, like the level of violence used or the fact that this psycho likes to call himself "Death".' The chief's eyebrows arched ironically. 'As original as that might sound. They also have no idea that this morning's murder is directly linked to the body that was found in the early hours of yesterday by LAX, so there will be no mention of the term "serial killer". Not by the press, not at the conference tomorrow, and not by any of us. I'm sure I don't have to remind anyone in this room how sensationalist the LA press can be. Hell, they practically invented the term. If any of this leaks, it will start a city-wide panic that I'm sure will spiral out of control faster than a skunk's fart. And I hate that goddamn smell.'

Chief Bracco readjusted his tie before moving on.

'As we all know, for some reason this douchebag decided to bring Mayor Bailey into the loop with the picture and the note that was sent to him yesterday. With elections just around the corner, it's no surprise that the mayor is now freaking the fuck out.' He paused for a moment while his gaze moved from one detective to another. 'Frankly, I must admit that so am I. At least a little bit. This investigation is only two days old – *two days old* – and we already have just as many bodies. This killer seems to be on a roll.' He breathed out, shaking his head. 'Though I haven't visited the site, I saw the crime-scene photographs. Who the fuck murders someone by scraping off her face with an electric sander?'

No one said anything because they all thought it was a rhetorical question.

They were wrong.

Chief Bracco pinned Hunter down with a gaze that could've curdled milk.

'I understand that you have a Ph.D. in criminal behavioral psychology, Detective Hunter.'

Hunter's reply was a subtle nod.

'And that there's no one more experienced than the two of you when it comes to cases of this nature.' His eyes moved to Garcia, then back to Hunter.

'So please, humor me this once. What type of creep are we after here, other than one with a massive hard-on for killing people?' He nodded at Captain Blake. 'Barbara has already told me that, despite the star positioning of the first body, neither of you believe we're dealing with a ritualistic killer here. So who are we after?'

Hunter studied the Chief of Police for a beat.

'It's too soon to tell, sir,' he replied. 'We are still trying to analyze the little data we have so far. As you've just mentioned, we've been on this case for less than forty-eight hours.'

'I understand that, Detective, and as I've also said, in that short amount of time this psycho has already given us two bodies. I'd say that that's plenty to analyze, wouldn't you?' Chief Bracco shook his head. 'I'm not asking for an official psychological profile here, Detective. I would just like to know your personal opinion of this guy.'

Hunter stayed quiet, and once again the Chief of Police watched him, this time with an intense, searching gaze, but Hunter's expression revealed nothing. Chief Bracco checked his watch.

'I'm meeting the mayor and the Governor of California in just under an hour. Would any of you like to take a guess as to what the main topic of conversation will be?'

This time it *was* a rhetorical question.

'So, for my own peace of mind, Detectives, so that I at least half believe the crap that I'll be selling them in sixty minutes' time, and subsequently to the LA press at the conference tomorrow, please give me something.'

'All I have are hunches and suppositions, sir,' Hunter finally said. 'Nothing concrete.'

'I appreciate that, Detective,' Chief Bracco said, lifting a hand to stop Hunter before he gave him any more excuses. 'And a hunch is all I'm asking for. All of us here know that that's all criminal profiling is – a hunch, a best guess based on the evidence found so far, nothing more. It's not an exact science and it never will be. So please, Detective, hit me with your best hunch. What kind of sick bastard are we after here? Is he delusional? Is he schizophrenic? Does he hear voices in his head? What?'

'No. He's not delusional, or schizophrenic, and I don't believe that he hears voices in his head, sir.'

Hunter felt too tired to launch into a whole psychological explanation to back up his opinion. Instead, he moved on to the facts.

'What we do know is that he's methodical, patient and very disciplined. His risks are well calculated. He never rushes because he knows he doesn't have to. He never leaves anything behind because his planning is practically flawless. He isn't the type to panic easily if things don't go exactly to plan because he knows that he can improvise at the drop of a dime. He's comfortable getting into character. He's comfortable lying, and he does it very well and without hesitation.'

'And you're basing all those assumptions on what, exactly?' Chief Bracco asked, sounding intrigued as opposed to condescending.

'Everything this killer has done so far has worked out perfectly for him, sir,' Garcia took over. 'No mistakes. No glitches. Not a speck of dust left behind that he didn't want to leave behind. His timing with his victims has been impeccable. The risk of anyone running into him while he was with any of them was practically non-existent because it was calculated to the very last detail. None of it, sir, including the fact that he's so elusive and so thorough, is down to luck.'

The Chief of Police mulled his words for an instant. 'Wait a second, are you saying that you think the killer knew beforehand that both victims would be alone on the night he acted?'

Garcia nodded. 'We're very sure he did.'

'How? How did he know?'

'That we don't know yet, sir,' Hunter replied. 'But that kind of information isn't very hard to come by if you know where to look. A lot of people will freely offer it on social media network sites.'

'Goddamnit.' Chief Bracco knew Hunter was right. No matter how often he reminded her of the risks, his own daughter was constantly posting similar information about her daily schedule on her Facebook page.

'So if you think that he knew his victims would be alone on the nights he acted,' Chief Bracco said, 'then you must also believe that he picked them beforehand.'

Hunter nodded. 'They weren't picked at random, sir. There's a reason why he chose them.' It was Hunter's turn to lift a hand to stop Chief Bracco before he could ask his next question. 'And no, sir, at the moment we don't know what that reason is, but we are doing all we can to find out.'

'Any links between the victims?'

'We don't know yet, sir.' Garcia was the one who replied this time. 'We basically just got back from the crime scene and the coroner's office, but we already have a team working on it. If there's a link between them, I'm sure we'll find it.'

'How about the note and the photograph that were sent to Mayor Bailey?'

'Clean,' Garcia answered with a headshake. 'No prints whatsoever. We're still waiting on ink, paper and handwriting analyses.'

'How about the package's point of origin?'

Garcia quickly told him about the smoke bomb diversion at the FedEx drop box.

Chief Bracco ran his thumb and index finger over his mustache a couple of times.

'So if I got this right,' he said, facing both detectives, 'in short you're saying that the freak we're after is careful, very patient, well organized, resourceful, and probably highly intelligent.'

Hunter agreed. 'You wanted to know who this killer is, sir?' His gaze paused on Captain Blake before returning to Chief Bracco.

'This killer is your perfect predator.'

Forty-Two

It was coming up to 4:45 a.m. when Hunter finally got back to his one-bedroom apartment on the third floor of a dilapidated building in Huntington Park, Southeast LA.

After leaving his office at around 9:00 p.m. the night before, Hunter had decided to drive around the city. He did that often enough. For some reason that not even he could explain, driving around at night through the streets of Los Angeles somehow calmed him. Helped him think.

As he left his office, he could tell that sleep, if it came at all, would've been restless and dotted by nightmares. In the morning, he would feel worse than if he'd stayed up all night, so he'd decided to stay up all night.

Hunter aimlessly drove around the streets of Central, East and South LA, then The Harbor and South Bay, before crossing the city all the way over to Santa Monica. The clock on his dashboard read 2:22 a.m. when he finally decided to park his car and go for a walk on the beach.

Hunter loved the beach, but unlike most, he preferred it at night.

He liked watching the sea at that time. The undisturbed sound of waves breaking against the sand, together with the quietness of the early hour, reminded him of his parents and of when he was a little kid.

His father used to work seventy-hour weeks, jumping between two awfully paid jobs. To help out, his mother would take any work that came her way – cleaning, ironing, washing, whatever she could find. Hunter couldn't remember a weekend when his father wasn't working, and even then they struggled to make ends meet. But despite their struggle, Hunter's parents never complained. They played the cards they were dealt and, no matter how bad a hand they got, they always did it with a smile on their faces.

Every Sunday, after Hunter's father got home from work, they used to go down to the beach. Most times they got there once everyone else had already left and the sun had already set. But Hunter didn't mind. In fact, he preferred it. It was like the whole beach belonged to him and his parents. After Hunter's mother passed away, his father never stopped taking him to the beach on Sundays. Sometimes, Hunter would catch his father wiping away tears as he watched the waves break.

As Hunter finally locked his car and made his way up to his apartment, he never noticed the black GMC Yukon hiding in the shadows around the corner from where he'd parked.

Sitting patiently in the driver's seat, the man observed Hunter with a black look on his face.

Forty-Three

Without switching on any lights, and more out of habit than hunger, Hunter walked into the kitchen, pulled open the fridge door and glanced inside. As always, there wasn't much choice – a couple of pieces of fruit, a carton of milk, a can of some cheap energy drink that he was sure one day would punch a hole in his stomach and a half-full pack of chili-flavored beef jerky. He loved those things, and even though it made them tougher and chewier, he preferred to have them cold.

He stared at the items inside his fridge for a long minute, but reached for none. Despite having had almost no food since that morning, unsurprisingly, Hunter's appetite was non-existent.

The images of Nicole Wilson's beaten body, together with the ones of Sharon Barnard's totally disfigured face, seemed to have etched themselves on to the inside of his eyelids. Every time he closed his eyes, there they were – one, raped and tortured to death, the other, just an incomprehensible mess of ripped skin, torn flesh and blood. Both made to suffer the unimaginable, at the hands of a true monster.

Hunter closed the fridge door, bringing the kitchen and the apartment back to darkness, but didn't move. Instead, he used his right hand to massage the stiff muscles at the back of his neck and shoulders. The tips of his fingers came into contact with the jagged, ugly scar on his nape and he paused, feeling the leathery, lumpy skin. A simple reminder of how close to death his job had taken him, and of how resolute and lethal the mind of an evil murderer can be. As memories began to poke at his brain, he let go of his neck and shook his head, banishing them back to the darkest corners of his mind. A place he did his best never to visit.

In the bathroom, despite the warm night, Hunter leaned back against the tiled wall and welcomed the powerful, hot shower jet that almost burned his skin. The discomfort caused by the heat was balanced out by how much it helped his tensed muscles to relax. By the time he shut off the water, his tanned skin had gone a light shade of red and the tips of his fingers looked like old prunes.

Back in the living room, wrapped in a white towel, Hunter switched on a floor lamp and dimmed its intensity to 'medium'. That done, he approached his drinks cabinet, which was small but held an impressive collection of single malt Scotch whisky, which was probably his biggest passion. Though he had overdone it a few times, Hunter sure knew how to appreciate the flavor and quality of a good single malt, instead of simply getting drunk on it.

His eyes scanned from bottle to bottle. One thing that he knew for certain was that he needed something strong, but at the same time comforting and soothing. He didn't have to search long. His decision was made as soon as his eyes grazed over the eighteen-year-old bottle of Auchentoshan.

'This should do nicely,' Hunter said, reaching for it.

He poured himself a double dose, added about a fifth of water and dumped himself on the black leatherette sofa, which faced a TV set that hadn't been turned on in over six months. In fact, since the Super Bowl game back in February.

He sipped his drink, letting the robust and spicy taste of the Scotch, which had hints of woody almonds, brown sugar and vanilla, engulf his taste buds for a moment.

Mollifying, no doubt about that.

Despite how hard he tried not to think of the case, the images of what he'd seen in the past two days had nowhere else to go. All they did was tumble over themselves inside his mind. One grotesque scene morphing into another, like a well-edited horror film on a never-ending loop.

Hunter finished his Scotch and decided to have a second one. His palate had gotten used to the single malt's powerful flavor, so this time he had it neat, no water. Instead of going back to the sofa, Hunter walked over to the window on the north wall and looked outside. Everything looked still. Even the moon, coyly peeking out in its initial state of waxing crescent, seemed scared of the evil that now lurked around the City of Angels.

Hunter's gaze moved to the lights in the distance. From his window he couldn't see much, but he could still see the tip of the unmistakable conglomerate of high-rise buildings that formed the central business district of the city, otherwise known as Downtown LA.

Hunter finished his second Scotch and put his glass down on the window ledge.

'Where are you hiding, you sonofabitch?' he whispered to himself, his gaze slowly scanning the horizon.

Hunter's body felt tired, but he could tell that his brain was still wide awake. Going to bed would make no difference. All he would do was toss and turn under the sheets, fighting a battle he knew he would never win, so instead, he decided to have one more drink. As he turned away from the window and faced the inside of his living room, he paused, frowning.

'What the hell?'

On the floor, about a foot from his front door, he could see a brown paper envelope. He didn't really have to search his memory. He knew that it hadn't been there before. Someone had slid it under his door.

Hunter's eyes sought the clock on the wall – 05:47 a.m.

He could think of no reason why any of his neighbors would need to place a letter under his door, much less at this time at night.

Immediately, every muscle in Hunter's body went into alert mode. He quickly moved over to the chair where he had left his gun holster, unclipped the lock, pulled out his semi-automatic HK Mark 23 and thumbed the safety off.

His front door was locked. Of that he was absolutely certain. The door chain was also securely locked in place.

The corridor outside his front door was about fifty feet long, servicing eight apartments, with the stairs and the elevator at the east end of it. The hallway lights were acti-vated by means of a very sensitive motion sensor, so if anyone stepped out of their front door, or surfaced from the stairs or elevator, the lights would immediately come on. And they would stay on for sixty seconds.

Hunter could see no light seeping through from under his front door. If someone was outside, he or she had remained totally still for some time.

With careful, noiseless steps, Hunter crossed his living room. As he reached the envelope and looked down, what he saw made every muscle on his body tense up.

The envelope had been slid under his door face up. There was no stamp and no recipient's address, just a single line written across the front of it in red ink – Detective Robert Hunter, LAPD Robbery Homicide Division.

Hunter didn't need to look any closer to know that those words were in the killer's handwriting.

Forty-Four

Adrenalin shot into Hunter's veins like an angry buffalo stampede. For the moment, he disregarded what the envelope on the floor might contain and quickly positioned himself to the right of the front door, pressing his back flat against the wall. Waiting. Listening.

Thirty seconds.

Nothing.

Sixty.

Not a sound.

Ninety.

Dead quiet.

One hundred and twenty.

The lights outside were still off.

With his left hand, Hunter undid the security chain before turning the key in the lock, keeping it all as quiet as he could. When that was done, he waited another ten seconds before turning the handle and pulling the door open. Immediately, the motion sensor outside picked up the door movement and activated the lights.

Hunter's apartment was the last one down the corridor, at the opposite end from where the elevator and stairs were. Being the last door on the left meant that there was nothing to the right of his front door except a solid wall. No one could

hide there. With that in mind, and still with his back flat against
the wall on the inside of his door, Hunter stretched his neck
and looked down the corridor, in the direction of the stairs.

There was no one there.

Holding his weapon with a firm two-hand grip, Hunter
finally stepped out of his apartment and into the corridor,
his aim moving left then right, searching for a target.

He found none. The hallway was empty.

From his position, he could see that the elevator was on
the ground floor. As far as he could see, the stairs also
looked clear. Whoever had slid that envelope under his door
was now long gone.

Hunter breathed out and thumbed the safety back on,
but the tenseness in his muscles remained. Once he
breathed in again, he felt an awkward surge of emotions
rush through his body, as if he had breathed in more than
just oxygen. He felt exactly as he had done so many times,
as he stepped into a brutal crime scene for the first time.
He felt like he was standing where evil had once been.

Back inside his apartment, with the door safely locked
behind him, Hunter grabbed a pair of latex gloves from the
bathroom and finally turned his attention to the envelope
on the floor. At the back of it, there was no sender's address.

Hunter got back into his living room and lifted the envelope against the floor lamp. The only thing he could make
out was a folded-in-half sheet of paper. The color was
uniform throughout it, which indicated that there was nothing else in there other than the sheet of paper.

Hunter walked over to the kitchen and grabbed a knife
from the drawer before carefully tearing the envelope open
at the top. A couple of seconds later, he began reading the
killer's new note.

Forty-Five

Tom Hobbs parents' house was located down a quiet road, just a block away from Pomona's Holy Cross Catholic Cemetery. The sedatives the medics had given Tom the day before had had their desired effect. He had slept for twelve consecutive hours and, despite the fact that the trauma of what he'd seen would stay forever in his mind, he had finally overcome the initial shock stage.

Tom's mother, a very elegantly dressed woman in her fifties, showed Garcia into the white two-storey house, which was surrounded by a well-kept cluster of small evergreens.

While Mrs. Hobbs went upstairs to fetch her son, Garcia began browsing the bookshelves in the lavishly decorated study. They were packed full of classics, from Tolstoy and Victor Hugo to Jane Austen and Charles Dickens.

At the far end of one of the bookcases, Garcia found several picture frames neatly arranged on a shelf. All of them of Tom and his family.

Garcia pulled his attention away from the photographs and turned around as he heard steps coming to the study door. Tom Hobbs was standing next to his mother. He wore faded blue jeans, an old pair of black All Stars and a long-sleeved white shirt that looked to be at least two sizes too big.

'Hello,' Garcia said, stepping forward and offering his hand. 'I'm Detective Carlos Garcia of the LAPD. We met yesterday at your place, but you might not remember.'

Tom looked a mess. His hair was disheveled and flattened at the back. His striking eyes, now framed by dark circles, were puffed up and red from crying, and the skin on his face seemed blotchy and dehydrated.

'I'm . . . not sure if I remember or not,' Tom said, shaking Garcia's hand, his tone beaten. 'My mind is still a little hazy about yesterday.' He let go of Garcia's hand and broke eye contact. 'I really hoped that I would wake up this morning and find out that it had all been just a horrible nightmare.' His voice caught on his throat. 'But it's all true, isn't it?' He looked back at Garcia.

'Unfortunately.'

Tom's mother kissed him on the cheek.

'I was wondering if I could ask you a few questions?' Garcia said, breaking the silence. 'Not about yesterday, but about Sharon Barnard. As I understand it, you knew her better than anyone else.'

Tom nodded. 'She was my best friend.'

'Do you mind?' Garcia asked, indicating the sofa set. 'I'll be as brief as I can.'

Tom turned to face his mother. 'Mom, could you give us a moment, please?'

Mrs. Hobbs looked back at Garcia with a look that said: *Please, don't upset my son.*

Garcia had seen that look many times. He gave her the subtlest of nods.

Mrs. Hobbs left the study, closing the door behind her.

'Please have a seat, Detective,' Tom said, taking one of the armchairs himself. Garcia took the other.

'I apologize for my mother,' Tom added. He sat at the edge of his seat with his arms crossed in front of his chest. He kept on squeezing them tight against his body every now and then, as if he was feeling cold.

'There's no need to apologize. I was also an only child. My parents were just as overprotective.'

For a moment, Tom frowned.

Garcia read his doubt and explained. 'The photographs on the family shelf.' He indicated the picture frames. 'Other than your parents, you're the only person in them.'

Tom nodded as he looked at the picture frames.

Garcia began with basic questions, mainly to allow Tom to relax, even if just a little bit. Tom Hobbs had known Sharon Barnard for over six years. They had gone to Claremont High School together and they'd been best friends since ninth grade. According to Tom, Sharon never had any enemies, neither in school nor at work, or at least not in the proper sense of the word.

Within five minutes, Tom was sounding more relaxed. His arms had uncrossed and he had moved back a little from the edge of his seat.

Garcia had no doubt that neither of the two murders had been a crime of passion, but experience told him that it was very probable that at some point prior to the murders this killer had come into direct contact with his victims. He needed to start there.

'Do you know if Ms. Barnard was seeing anyone?'

Tom chuckled uneasily. 'Sharon just isn't the relationship type, if you know what I mean, Detec—' He stopped himself and his eyes saddened again. It would take him some time to be able to automatically refer to his best friend in the past tense. 'I'm sorry.'

'It's OK.'

'Sharon *wasn't* the relationship type,' Tom tried again. 'Even through high school, she only dated a couple of guys, and neither lasted any longer than just a few months. But with the job we do? Always away, never really around.' He shook his head at the thought. 'It's quite hard to find a partner who is willing to put up with that sort of schedule. Not that she was actually looking for one.'

Garcia understood those restrictions perfectly. His job, although very different, carried a very similar downfall.

'Any casual affairs?' he asked.

For the first time, a hint of a smile grazed Tom's lips. 'You want to know if she had "sex buddies"?'

Garcia nodded. 'Unfortunately, I do have to ask a few questions of a more personal nature.'

Tom lifted a hand. 'There's no need to apologize, Detective. I totally understand that it's your job. And yes, of course she did. Sharon is—' Another heartfelt pause. '*Was* a very attractive woman. She got a lot of male attention, sometimes even female. Yeah, she used to get approached all the time, especially by married men. But she never went anywhere near them. "Man with a wedding band is a problem times ten." She used to say that all the time.'

Garcia gave Tom a sympathetic smile.

'Do you know if any of Ms. Barnard's affairs were based here in Los Angeles?' Garcia asked.

'No. None. That was one of her "little rules".' Tom used his finger to draw quotation marks in the air. 'She had a few of those. She wouldn't "play" close to home.'

'And why was that?'

Tom shrugged. 'To avoid unwanted complications – now and in the future.'

Garcia nodded his understanding. 'Had Ms. Barnard ever mentioned any one of her casual affairs becoming too forceful with her? Too insistent, wanting to move things to the next level when she didn't?'

Tom didn't take long to answer. 'No. Never. Of course some of the guys she saw wanted to be more to her than just a casual fling. As I've said, Sharon was a very attractive woman, and most guys would love to properly date someone like her, but as far as I know, every time anyone mentioned maybe moving things to the next level, she ran a mile.'

Garcia kept an eye on Tom's body language and facial expressions. Since he had begun to relax, he had stayed that way, which was a very good sign. His answers also flowed spontaneously, with no hesitation, and weren't preceded or followed by any sort of nervous telltale signs, which indicated that he wasn't trying to hide anything.

If this killer really had directly approached Sharon Barnard prior to the murder night, it didn't sound as though he had done it as a lover. Garcia decided to move away from this line of questioning.

'And had she mentioned anything about anyone else she'd met recently?' he asked. 'Not a lover, or anyone trying to pick her up, but maybe someone who had approached her at the supermarket, or a coffee shop, or on the streets . . . anywhere, really. Someone new whom she had chatted to for a little while but had made no sexual advances on her.'

This time Tom took a little longer to reply.

'No, I can't recall her saying anything.'

'Are you sure?'

Tom took another moment.

'Yes, I'm pretty sure.'

This killer was also very comfortable in assuming different identities. He'd proved that when playing out the 'cousin' scenario with Nicole Wilson. From that, Garcia had to assume that he was also very good at disguising himself. If he really had come face to face with Sharon Barnard prior to the murder night, chances were he didn't do it as himself.

'How about mentioning anything about someone that she might've seen before, but was unsure? Maybe a face that she thought looked familiar, but she couldn't quite place? Did she ever comment on anything like that?'

Tom scratched his left elbow and his eyes squinted one more time as he thought about it.

'In our line of work, that happens quite often, Detective. It's not uncommon for some of us to get scheduled anywhere up to fifteen flights a week. As you can imagine, that's a lot of faces to greet, smile at, serve, smile at some more and then say goodbye to as they disembark. Some of them we might remember well for one reason or another, but most just get logged into our subconscious and we tend to forget about them. If I had a penny for every time I heard one of my colleagues say "That person looks familiar", I'd be a billionaire.'

Garcia understood that very well, but he still had to try.

'Yes, I imagine it happens a lot,' he said. 'Probably more often than in any other profession, but still, do you recall Ms. Barnard recently mentioning anything about someone whom she thought looked familiar?'

'Hmm . . .' Tom frowned. 'Actually, come to think of it, I do.'

Forty-Six

Garcia's eyebrows arched slightly at Tom's response because, in all honesty, he was about to give up on the interview.

'A passenger caught her eye not so long ago. Attractive man, tall, well built, well dressed, very polite, very quiet too.'

'You saw him?'

'Yeah, we were working the same flight. Sharon really had the hots for him.' Tom proceeded to tell Garcia about Sharon asking him what he thought of the passenger, and their little guessing game.

Garcia kept his voice steady and void of any excitement because he knew that this could mean absolutely nothing at all. As Tom had said, as a flight attendant, Sharon Barnard would've seen a staggering number of faces over the past year and throughout her whole life. Garcia was well aware of the fact that a person's subconscious doesn't only spit recent memories and images back at them. It can go back months, years, decades even. But there was also a chance that the passenger could be the man they were looking for. Garcia needed more details.

'You didn't happen to catch his name, do you?'

'No, sorry, Detective.'

'It's OK.' Garcia moved forward in his seat. 'So this

passenger showed no signs of recognizing Ms. Barnard, even though she thought he looked familiar?'

Tom shook his head. 'Not as far as I know. If he had, she would've jumped at the chance, I'm telling you.'

Garcia wasn't sure if that was a good or bad sign.

'Did this passenger look familiar to you at all?' Garcia asked. 'Do you think that maybe you have seen him on a previous flight or something?'

'No, not to me. Truth be told, he was quite a hunk. If I had seen him before, I'm very sure that I would remember.' Tom looked at Garcia curiously. 'Do you think that this passenger could've had anything to do with what happened to Sharon?'

'Probably not,' Garcia admitted. 'But we're checking absolutely everything.'

Those last words seemed to comfort Tom.

'Can you remember which flight it was?' Garcia asked.

Tom chewed on his bottom lip. 'Not exactly, no, but I know that it wasn't that long ago.'

'Past week? Two?'

'Umm . . .' Some more squinting. 'I don't think it was any longer than in the past week.'

'And you're sure you can't remember which flight it was? That would really help.'

Tom rubbed his eyes as he thought back. 'I'm sorry,' he said after a long while. 'I can't remember. My mind is in such a mess.'

'That's not a problem,' Garcia reassured him. He decided to try a different approach to narrow it down as much as he could. 'How many flights did you and Ms. Barnard work together in the past week, do you know?'

'I'm not quite sure, but let me go get my cellphone and I'll find out.'

As Tom got to the door, he paused and looked back at Garcia.

'Would you like a drink, Detective? Coffee, juice, water?'

'No, I'm fine for now, thank you very much.'

Tom left the study. When he came back, he was holding a smartphone in his right hand.

'We did five flights together last week,' he announced even before he had returned to his seat.

Damn! Garcia thought. That was still a hell of a lot of passengers.

'Is there anything else you can remember about the flight that could maybe narrow it down a little further?'

Tom looked pensive. 'It was a morning flight, I remember that.' He checked his cellphone again. 'OK, Sharon and I worked only three morning flights last week. We did an out/in from LA to Frisco on Monday. We flew out from LAX at six a.m., landed at around seven-hirty at San Francisco International Airport, quick turna-round, left Frisco at eight-thirty a.m. and landed back at LAX at around ten. The other flight began as an overnight. We flew out to Sacramento on that same Monday night, but the flight back was on Tuesday morning.'

Tom lifted a hand and made a face at Garcia, as if he had just remembered something else.

Garcia waited.

'OK,' Tom said. 'I just remembered that the passenger we are talking about was on a flight back to LA, not on an outward flight.'

'Are you sure?'

'Yes, I'm pretty sure. I remember that, after we landed, Sharon and I had a quick sandwich and a cup of coffee at

Brioche Dorée in terminal four. I remember it because she kept on looking around and over her shoulder to see if she could spot him again.'

Down to two flights.

'Anything else you remember that might help us identify who that passenger was?' Garcia asked. 'Or maybe narrow it down a little bit more?'

Garcia saw Tom's eyes widen a fraction and his eyebrows lift. He had remembered something else.

'He was sitting toward the front of the plane,' Tom said, triumphantly. 'I remember it because I could see him well from the plane's front galley. That's where Sharon and I were playing our passengers' game. But as far as I can remember, he wasn't right at the front, so I would discard rows one through six, maybe. I'd say he was somewhere between rows seven and fourteen.'

Garcia wrote that down in his notebook. That was a good start. With the mayor and the Governor of California so involved in this case, he would have no problem getting the passenger manifest from the airline.

'And is this the only passenger that you remember Ms. Barnard mentioning anything about looking familiar to her recently?'

Tom nodded. 'Like I've said, Detective, that sort of thing happens a lot, but yes, he's the only one that comes to mind right now.'

'Is it OK if I ask a police sketch artist to come see you some time this afternoon?'

'I'm not sure I remember him that well, Detective?'

'Anything helps,' Garcia countered. 'And these sketch artists are pretty good at what they do.'

Tom looked down at his feet for a second. 'Yes, of course.

Anything I can do to help catch the sick bastard that did that to Sharon.'

'Just one more thing,' Garcia said.

'Sure.'

'I take it that, also because of the job you do, yours and Sharon's circle of friends is quite tight?'

'Yes, I guess you could say that.'

Garcia reached into his pocket and retrieved a photograph he had brought with him. It was the portrait shot of Nicole Wilson.

'Do you happen to know if Sharon knew this woman? If they were friends, perhaps?'

Tom took the photograph and examined it for several seconds, before returning it to Garcia and shaking his head at the same time. 'No, I don't think so. I've never seen her before. Is she a stewardess as well?'

'No, she's just someone we interviewed yesterday who said she knew Ms. Barnard,' Garcia lied.

'Oh.' Tom nodded. 'Maybe she did. I just don't remember ever seeing her.'

Garcia got to his feet. 'Thank you so much for your time, Mr. Hobbs. You've been a great help.'

They shook hands and Garcia handed Tom one of his cards. 'If you remember anything else, no matter how small it might seem to you, please don't hesitate to contact me. It could be very important to us. My cellphone number is on the back.'

Tom took the card and looked at it for a quick second before placing it in his back pocket.

'Of course I will.'

Tom walked Garcia to the front door.

'Detective,' he called as Garcia stepped on to the footpath that took him across the property's front lawn.

Garcia turned around to face him.

'You will catch the psycho who did that to Sharon, won't you? Please tell me you will.' His eyes glassed over one more time as he waited for Garcia's reply.

Garcia nodded once. 'Yes, we will catch him.'

As he began walking toward his car, Garcia hoped that his words had come out with a lot more conviction than he'd felt.

Forty-Seven

Alison Atkins had arrived in LA twelve years ago, at the tender age of sixteen. Back then she didn't call herself Alison. Her real name was Kelly, Kelly Decker, but she swore that she would never use that name again. She could never use that name again. For her own safety.

Like so many before her, Alison's suitcase was fairly empty of clothes, but overflowing with dreams and hopes. But unlike most who came to the City of Angels, her dreams and hopes weren't for stardom, or a career in Hollywood or in the music business. All she really wanted was a better life. A normal life. And any life would be better than the one she had left behind in Summerdale, Alabama – population less than a thousand people.

Alison was an only child, born into a strict Jehovah's Witness family. Her father was a storeowner. Due to complications, and the fact that Jehovah's Witnesses aren't allowed to receive blood, her mother had passed away while giving birth to her. Her father blamed the baby and not the stubbornness of his own faith for his wife's death. That blame was made overly clear to Alison throughout her childhood and young teenage years.

With an iron fist, her father demanded that Alison follow the rules of his chosen religion to the letter. She was not allowed to associate herself with a worldly person – one who is not a Jehovah's Witness. She also wasn't allowed to salute the flag of her country, recite the pledge of allegiance, stand for or sing the national anthem or vote. Alison had also never celebrated a single one of her birthdays. Her father's chosen religion forbade her to do so. But the date had never really gone unnoticed, as her father would always spank Alison's naked back with birch branches until her skin was raw. He then would lock her inside a dark room with no food or water for twenty-four hours, so she could reflect on what her coming into this world really meant – a dark day full of suffering and pain.

Despite being an extremely religious man, Alison's father was a vicious brute who used physical force to impose his ways. Alison couldn't remember a single day, while living under his roof, where he hadn't either yelled at her and made her feel like she had been a mistake, or slapped her across the face at least once. And those were the good days. Some of the beatings and castigations she received were so severe she would pass out. But he was also very skilled in his brutality – no deep skin rupture, and no broken bones ever.

Alison's father remarried when she was only three years old and her stepmother was just as cruel as he was. She knew of all the beatings; in fact, she administered many of them herself and was present throughout most of the others, always cheering her husband on.

When Alison turned fourteen, her father told her that she was now a fertile woman and therefore was 'ripe' to bear children of her own. And 'ripe' had been the exact word he'd used.

One night, Alison overheard her father telling her step-mother that he had already chosen the man whom Alison would marry – the eighteen-year-old son of a fellow Jehovah's Witness family from Tennessee they had met a year earlier. Those words had filled Alison with more dread than any of the beatings she had ever received. She promised herself that she would rather die than marry into her family's faith.

Alison was no thief, but as desperate panic took over she saw no other way out. A few days after overhearing their conversation, as her father and stepmother slept, she grabbed half of the earnings that her father's store had taken over the past few days and broke out of the house. Overnight, Alison jogged for seventeen miles, non-stop, until she got to the city of Fairhope, where she bought a one-way bus ticket to the City of Angels.

She sat on that bus for forty-eight hours and 2030 miles, planning the start of her new life. That was when she came up with the name Alison Atkins. Both names, first and family, came from outdoor billboards she saw during the two-day trip. The first was advertising the new album from some singer called Alison Krauss. She had never heard of her, but she loved that name and how beautiful the singer looked. A decision was made in just a few seconds. Kelly had all of a sudden become Alison. She also promised herself that she would find out what Alison Krauss's music sounded like.

Alison saw the second billboard during a scheduled stop. This one was advertising some sort of diet plan. Alison had already planned on a complete change in the way she looked, behaved and sounded – hair color, hairstyle, body shape, accent, posture, the way she walked, everything she could change about her old self, she would. Her first thought upon seeing the billboard was that maybe she should give that Atkins Diet a try. Her second thought was: *I like the sound of the name Atkins.* A moment later, she began repeating the name out loud – Alison Atkins, Alison Atkins, Alison Atkins. She liked it . . . very much.

Yes, her new name brought a smile to her face. To her, it sounded like a new beginning. Maybe starting over wouldn't be so difficult after all.

She was wrong.

Life in Los Angeles proved to be a lot harder than Alison had anticipated. Once she finally got there, she found a cheap room on the south side of the city. The landlord asked for no identification, which suited Alison just fine, but finding a job with no proof of ID didn't turn out to be quite as easy, especially for someone who looked so young. With just about everything in LA a lot more expensive than back in Summerdale, the little money she had with her ran out a lot faster than she had expected.

The landlord, a short and bald man with dirty nails and weather-beaten skin, who always smelled of stale sweat and fried chicken, told Alison that he would cut her a deal. If she was nice to him, he would be nice to her, and she could stay without having to worry about paying rent. Alison, in her naivety, thought that the landlord was really trying to help her, and when he asked her to come to his apartment, she truly believed that she would probably clean his room and kitchen for him, or perhaps cook his meals.

The landlord was as streetwise as they came. He knew that a place like his, in a city like Los Angeles, attracted a particular crowd. It had always done, and he'd seen plenty of young girls and women just like Alison, frightened to death of the life they'd left behind in some 'shit-kickers-ville' town somewhere, to know that they'd probably rather die than go to the cops. Going to the cops meant giving them their real names, showing them some ID and telling them where they were really from. That wasn't something they were prepared to do. At least not yet, anyway.

Until then, Alison had believed that her mother's death, as she gave birth to her, and her father's angry beatings throughout her life were the worse that could ever happen to her. That night Alison discovered a new type of fear and pain. A new type of body and soul violation that she'd never thought possible. She thought that she'd discovered hell.

Once the landlord was done with her, a terrified and bleeding Alison returned to her room, gathered her few belongings and ran away for the second time in just a few weeks – once again, in the middle of the night. That night, for the first time, Alison began to believe what her father had yelled at her so many times – that she had been a *mistake*, that she should never have been born, that she had been put on this earth as a punishment, and that she should suffer, *always*. But Alison didn't want to suffer anymore. All she wanted was to end it all.

It was around six in the morning when, by chance, she ran into Renell, a thirty-two-year-old African-American woman who had gone through everything Alison had gone through, and much more.

Renell worked for a charity group whose main purpose was to help women who had been victims of domestic abuse and violence, be it by partners or parents.

Renell's charity sheltered Alison that night and for several nights after that. They also gave her food and medical assistance and, when she was well enough, helped her find some decent work.

As luck would have it, or not, Alison's story was very

similar to Renell's, whose real name had once been Alisha. They became best friends, and it was Renell who, through her street contacts, arranged for Alison to get some sort of documentation with her new chosen name.

Now, twelve years later, they were still best of friends.

Forty-Eight

It was just coming up to lunchtime by the time Garcia got back to the Police Administration Building. A few white clouds had gathered over downtown Los Angeles, providing it with a much-needed break from the incessant summer heat, even if only in the form of a few scattered shadows.

'We might have a little crack here,' he said in an animated voice as soon as he entered the office.

Hunter, who was sitting at his desk running over a few paper files, paused what he was doing and turned to look at his partner.

Garcia immediately proceeded to tell him about the passenger who had caught Sharon Barnard's attention on the morning flight.

'Operations is already on it,' he said. 'They're contacting US Airways and the FAA for the passenger manifest of both flights.' He lifted a hand. 'OK, I'm sure that if this is our guy, he no doubt used a bogus name and probably wore some kind of disguise, but if we establish that it could be him, with the manifest we could then get in touch with the passenger who was sitting next to him. Maybe he or she noticed something Tom Hobbs didn't. Also –' this seemed to be what excited Garcia the most because his eyebrows lifted like a drawbridge – 'LAX is packed full of CCTV cameras, including the transit corridors. If this is our killer,' Garcia nodded, 'we'll get some sort of footage.'

Garcia was so focused on the possibility of some sort of breakthrough, however small it might be, that until that moment he'd failed to notice the see-through, plastic evidence bag on Hunter's desk. He paused and craned his neck sideways.

The evidence bag contained the brown paper envelope that had been slid under Hunter's door in the early hours of the morning.

Garcia repositioned himself to have a better look at it. As he did, his breathing froze for a second. He didn't need to compare it to know that handwriting.

'What the fuck is that, Robert?'

'It's exactly what you think it is.' Hunter slid the evidence bag towards his partner.

'It was delivered here?' Garcia asked without reaching for it.

'No. Somebody slid it under my door some time in the middle of the night.'

Garcia looked at Hunter as if what he'd just said made no sense.

'Under your door? As in – under the door to your apartment?'

Hunter confirmed it with a nod.

'Somebody slid it under your door? Somebody who?'

Hunter shook his head. 'By the time I noticed the enve-lope, the person was long gone.'

'The killer?

'I can't think of anyone else, can you?'

'Holy shit, Robert. Are you telling me that the killer

dropped by your apartment to deliver that? He was standing just outside your front door?'

Another nod from Hunter. This time, the movement looked a little more defeated than the previous one.

'It looks that way. Yes.'

Garcia ran both hands through his hair, pausing as they reached the back of his head. 'What the hell, Robert? Why? Why would he do that?'

'I have a suspicion as to why, but I'd like you to read the note first and tell me what you think.'

Despite their investigation not being in the news yet, it wouldn't have been hard for the killer to get hold of Hunter's address. All he needed to do was place a call to the PAB and ask for the name of the detective in charge of the investigation. Once he had Hunter's name, obtaining his address wouldn't have taken any longer than five minutes.

'Has forensics seen this?'

'Not yet,' Hunter replied. 'I wanted you to read it first.'

'Sure,' Garcia said, picking up the evidence bag and walking over to his desk. As he sat down, he pulled open the top right-hand drawer, reached inside it and retrieved a pair of latex gloves. After gloving up, he turned his full attention to the envelope.

Forty-Nine

It was a typical American diner with a flickering sign outside that read 'Donny's' in large red letters. The diner was located on a strip mall, just a few blocks away from the heart of the financial district in Downtown LA. Despite it being daytime, the inside was lit by the glow of neon and the sequence of lights from a large jukebox. All the booths and tables were taken, which wasn't really surprising because the food was good and inexpensive, and the coffee much better than that served at many of the chain coffee shops found all around the city. Yes, Donny's was constantly busy, and lunchtimes were the rush hour of the rush hour.

As a table for two vacated, Alison Atkins, the oldest of the four waitresses working the floor that afternoon, sprayed its surface with some disinfectant soap, wiped it clean with the cloth that she kept hanging from her work apron and signaled Rita at the door to let her know that she could seat two new customers. Rita immediately sent the couple that had been waiting for the past ten minutes in Alison's direction.

As the couple walked past table seven, the second table to the right from the front door, they paid little attention to the man who was sitting alone at it. The man, in return, seemed lost in thought, oblivious to the loud chatter and constant movement that was going on all around him. To the outside world, it looked like the only thing the man was interested in was the double espresso sitting on the table in front of him, which he'd been stirring for the past thirty seconds.

The customer sitting at table seven had come to Donny's diner about an hour earlier. As he'd got to the door, he'd smiled politely at Rita, the young waitress who greeted him, and asked for a table for one. No tables were available at that time but he said that he didn't mind waiting, and wait he did, for almost twenty minutes. Once he was finally seated, he once again waited patiently for the waitress to come back to him and take his order, which took her close to another ten minutes. He did all that waiting with no irritation whatsoever, as if he had all the time in the world and not a worry in his life.

He finally stopped stirring, tapped his teaspoon against the edge of the espresso cup, placed it down on the saucer and brought the cup to his lips. He had to admit that the coffee at Donny's certainly deserved its reputation.

'Is everything OK, sir?' Alison asked, coming up to his table and giving the customer her usual magnetic smile.

Alison had stayed true to the promise she had made herself all those years ago while sitting inside that Greyhound bus, heading to Los Angeles. She had completely changed the way she looked, her accent, her posture, the way she walked . . . everything. There was nothing left of the young Kelly Decker from Summerdale, Alabama. Alison had also grown up to be a very attractive woman. Her longish, copper-blonde hair sparkled with life under any light, even when tied back in a work-style ponytail like that afternoon. Her skin was soft and well cared for, and her piercing eyes

shone with such distinction that it was almost impossible
for anyone not to notice them. Alison had also been blessed
with the sort of metabolism that would make her a billionaire if there were any way she could bottle it. No matter
what she ate, she just didn't seem to put on any weight –
ever. Her long legs were strong and toned like an athlete's,
not from exercising at the gym or at the beach, she never
really had time for either, but from the amount of walking
her job required daily.

Donny, the diner owner, and all the other waitresses had
lost count of the times a customer had slipped Alison a card
with his/her name and number, and told her that she should
be on the big screen instead of slaving away for peanuts pay
and shitty tips in some greasy diner in South Central.

Alison would always take the card, politely smile back
and thank the customer, and then throw it away when she
got to the kitchen.

'You know, Alison,' Rita, and all of the other waitresses,
had told her many times, 'some of those people and offers
could actually be real. This is LA, remember? Hollywood is
just around the corner, girlfriend. It ain't crazy to think that
maybe some of these people mean what they say. This city
is riddled with stories of stars who were discovered while
waiting tables or working behind bars. Maybe you should
think about giving some of them a chance? Wouldn't you
like to get the fuck out of this dead-end job and your shitty
neighborhood? Go live in Malibu or something?'

Alison would always reply the same way.

'I like this job, and I love the area I live in.'

That was actually true. Alison was very content with her
life. But despite that fact, no matter how much time had
gone by, no matter how different she looked, fear would

forever live inside her. The last thing Alison Atkins wanted was to gain notoriety, in any shape or form. She didn't need to be rich or famous to be happy.

The customer at table seven looked up at Alison and smiled back. In all honesty, his smile was just as disarming as hers.

'Yes,' he replied. 'Everything is just fine, thank you very much.'

The man had also completely changed his appearance from when he'd last eaten at Donny's, but his transformation hadn't taken years, merely an hour. In the past years, the man had become a makeup and prosthetic expert. He could make himself look as attractive or as ugly as the situation demanded. He could change his whole persona, including his accent, at the drop of a hat. He could pass for several different people in the same day and no one would ever know. Yes, the customer at table seven truly was a modern-day chameleon.

Today the man had chosen to have longish black hair that came down to his jawbone, dark-brown eyes that were framed by round spectacles, which he didn't need, and a stylish goatee. His cheekbones looked a touch higher than they naturally were, and his teeth whiter and straighter, giving him a nearly perfect smile. He wore dark trousers with black shoes, a matching blazer jacket and an expensive-looking blue shirt.

The other three waitresses working the lunch shift had all tried flirting with the customer at table seven, but he seemed deep in thought throughout – eyes forward, blank stare, no frown. Their attempts went unnoticed.

Alison also found him quite attractive. There was something about him that she found rather familiar, but she couldn't tell exactly what. Neither Alison, nor any of the other waitresses, could remember seeing him in Donny's before.

Despite his eyes not wandering, he'd been observing Alison the whole time he'd been there.

'Oh, I'm so sorry,' the man said, renewing his smile. 'This has been tremendously selfish of me.'

'What has?' Alison looked unsure.

'This place is so busy, there's a line of people outside waiting for a table, and here I am taking all the time in the world just to finish a cup of coffee. I apologize. If you bring me my check, I'll be out of your way in no time.'

His voice was firm, but tender at the same time.

'Oh, don't worry about that,' Alison said with a shake of the head. 'You can take as long as you like.' She checked her watch. 'It's dying down now, anyway.'

'Really?' He turned his neck to look around. The place was still heaving. 'Could've fooled me.'

Alison smiled again.

It was the man's turn to consult his timepiece. 'No, actually, I really do have to go.'

'No problem, I'll get the check for you.'

While Alison returned to the cash register, the man calmly finished his double espresso.

'Here you go,' Alison said, placing the check on the table in front of him.

The man noted the amount, reached for his wallet, and placed a few bills on top of the receipt. Right then, Alison noticed two things. One – the man had put down an extra twenty dollars. Two – his hands looked leathery and shiny, as if he had some sort of thin, protective plastic layer over them. She wondered if it was some sort of treatment for a skin condition.

'Keep the change,' he said, getting up.

'Are you sure?' She sounded doubtful.

'Of course I am.' The man winked so charmingly at Alison, she practically blushed.

In an impulsive move, something Alison almost never did, she threw a question his way, just as he was turning to leave.

'I haven't seen you in here before, have I?'

The man looked back at her. 'No, this is actually my first time eating here.'

'Well.' She returned the wink. 'I really hope you'll come back.'

Their eyes locked for a few seconds and the man nodded, courteously.

Alison never heard what the man whispered as he turned and walked toward the diner door.

'You'll see me a lot sooner than you expect, Alison.'

Fifty

As if handling some sort of dangerous and unstable substance, Garcia extracted the contents from the evidence bag carefully, before retrieving the single sheet of paper from inside the envelope.

The note had been folded in half to perfectly fit a regular business envelope.

Hunter waited while Garcia unfolded it and placed it flat on the desk in front of him. Just like the note sent to Mayor Bailey, this one had also been handwritten in red ink. Once again, the killer had used a ballpoint pen.

So you are the one who is supposed to be the best of the best. The so-called expert who's been tasked with the burden of stopping me, huh? You are the one who is supposed to bring justice to the victims. The one who will look into my eyes and find out what I have become.

Well . . .

How's that going for you so far, Detective Hunter?

Are we having fun yet, or am I moving too fast for you?

Are you still keeping count, or are the bodies piling up too quickly?

One thing I can tell you is that I am looking forward

to the challenge. The question is, will you see only what you want to see, or will you prove me wrong, Detective Hunter? Because you haven't seen anything yet. I am just getting started.

If you are wondering why I am doing what I'm doing, the answer is simple. I am creating history. Or, if you prefer, rewriting it.

Do you want to know who I am, Detective Hunter?

Do you really want to know?

Well, the clues are in the name.

FOR I AM DEATH.

Garcia read the note several times over before finally lifting his eyes to look at Hunter again, who was leaning against the edge of his desk.

'OK. So what do you think?'

Garcia got to his feet, pushed his chair out of the way and approached the picture board.

'Remember when we discussed the note that was sent to Mayor Bailey?' he asked, indicating it on the board. A copy of the first two notes had been pinned side by side. 'We both agreed that the third paragraph constituted a challenge of sorts, right?' Garcia didn't wait for Hunter's reply. 'Well, the way I see it, the whole of this third note, other than it being coated in arrogance, is nothing but *one* big challenge.'

Hunter scratched his chin. 'OK, I'm listening.'

'The problem is,' Garcia continued, 'the killer has now made it personal. Here, have a look.' He walked over to his desk. Hunter followed. Garcia then indicated all five instances where the killer had referred to Hunter by name. 'In fact, he has made it *very* personal, Robert. He went all the way to your *home* to deliver it.'

Hunter nodded his agreement, but allowed Garcia to continue without interrupting him.

'Just look at this.' Garcia returned to the picture board, unpinned the copy of the killer's second note and brought it to his desk. 'At the beginning of this new note he makes several references to his previous one.' Garcia indicated each line on both notes as he mentioned them. '"Best of the best", "So-called expert", "Bring justice to the victims", "See only what you want to see" and "Look into my eyes and find out what I have become". The difference here is, on the previous note all of that sounded like an open invitation to the LAPD, or the FBI, or a special task force, or whoever. But not this time. This time all of those challenges are aimed at a specific subject.' Garcia's eyebrows lifted as he nodded at his partner. 'You, my friend. Whether you like it or not, he's bringing this fight to you.'

So far, Garcia's assessment of the note had been right on the money with Hunter's. Hunter wasn't chasing this killer alone, and he was sure that the killer knew that full well. Nevertheless, this time the killer had made every single challenge personal to Hunter, not to a task force, or the LAPD, or the FBI, or even the UV Unit. The killer had, once again, been very careful when phrasing his written work to leave as little doubt as possible.

'But I don't think that this is "personal" personal.' Garcia used his fingers to draw quotation marks in the air.

Hunter questioned by narrowing his eyes a touch.

'What I mean is, I don't think that this guy's got a personal grudge against you,' Garcia clarified. 'I don't think that this is someone you put away in the past, or someone related to anyone you put away in the past. I'm even willing to bet that your paths have never crossed before, Robert.'

'Because if that were the case,' Hunter agreed, 'he would've made it personal on the first or second note. Why wait until now? And the second note wouldn't have been sent to the mayor. It would've been sent directly to me.'

'Exactly,' Garcia accepted. 'The way I see it, he would've brought this fight to the doorstep of whoever became lead investigator in this case. We were just the unlucky ones.'

Hunter made a face. 'Aren't we always?'

'But now that he has a counterpart, he not only reiterates the challenges of the second note, he goes beyond it. He bullies.' Once again, Garcia indicated on the note:

How's that going for you so far, Detective Hunter?

Are we having fun yet, or am I moving too fast for you?

Are you still keeping count, or are the bodies piling up too quickly?

. . . will you see only what you want to see, or will you prove me wrong, Detective Hunter?

'And then he threatens,' Garcia added.

Because you haven't seen anything yet. I am just getting started.

'After the threats,' Garcia continued, 'he feels the need to explain the reason why he's doing what he's doing. Though it all sounds like bullshit to me.'

'Delusions of grandeur,' Hunter commented. 'You know how most sociopaths are blinded by them. And because some truly believe that they are better, superior to everyone else, they also believe that whatever it is they're doing can't be understood by us mere human beings unless it's explained. And even then, they still don't expect us to fully understand the reasons behind their actions, or the complexity of their geniuses.' Hunter shrugged. 'How could we, when our intellect could never measure up?'

Garcia chuckled, shaking his head at the absurdity of it all. 'So this crackpot truly believes that he's creating history?'

'Or, as he put it, rewriting it?'

'Yeah, but rewriting whose history?'

Hunter turned and faced the picture board. 'I don't know. His own, maybe.'

'And what the hell is this crap at the end?' Garcia said, bringing Hunter's attention back to the new note. 'Is this his attempt at being funny? Let me give you a clue as to who I am, and that clue is in the name – "DEATH". Yeah, hilarious.'

Hunter wasn't really sure what the killer meant by that, but he had a hunch that, whatever it was, it wasn't meant as a joke.

Fifty-One

The stairwell that led down to the underpass reminded Alison of one of those old, black and white B-movies. The ones that weren't supposed to be scary, but were. Her footsteps echoed loudly against the concrete risers and all of a sudden she was painfully aware that she was alone, in a badly lit and isolated underpass.

Alison Atkins had missed her bus stop. She had done three double shifts at Donny's in just as many days, and when she'd boarded the bus almost an hour ago she'd felt the same sort of exhaustion one feels after a long and debilitating illness. She'd sat alone at the back of the bus, as she usually did. Ten minutes into the forty-minute trip to where she lived, Alison had decided to rest her head against the window, just for a moment, so she could close her tired eyes. But it was OK, because she reopened them only five minutes later – or so she thought.

As she sat up and looked out the window, she was overcome by an uncomfortable feeling. The feeling that she was in a place she didn't belong. She quickly rubbed the blur of tiredness from her eyes, turned her head around and looked out the window across the aisle from where she was sitting.

No, she didn't recognize any of it.

She craned her neck and looked at the digital display toward the front of the bus.

She had definitely missed her stop.

'Shit!' she said between clenched teeth, quickly getting to her feet and pressing the 'stop' button.

A minute later, the bus pulled up to the next stop on its route.

Three passengers jumped out with her – two women, counting Alison, and a middle-aged man. The man, who appeared to be in a hurry, quickly headed west. The other woman, who looked to be about the same age as Alison, went north.

Alison paused and looked around. This was an ugly part of town. A part of town that she would never visit during the day, never mind at night.

She checked her watch – five minutes past one in the morning. Her bus route wasn't part of the 'Owl Service' that ran 24/7 in LA – but she knew that her route ran all the way up to two a.m. Alison crossed the road and began walking to the bus stop on the other side. She reached into her bag, but as she rummaged around for her purse, she felt a pit begin to materialize in her stomach.

No purse.

She stopped walking, pulled her bag open with both hands and began fumbling inside it again, this time a little more desperately.

Nothing.

'Oh no, no, no, no, no,' Alison cried out, almost sticking her whole head inside her bag to look for it. Lipstick, foundation powder, makeup brush, loose change, cellphone, a pen and house keys.

Her purse was gone.

'Oh, fuck!'

She knew she'd had it with her when she boarded the bus because she kept her TAP card in it.

While she slept at the back of the bus, she'd of course never noticed the hooded eighteen-year-old kid who had first sat across the aisle from her, before stealthily moving over to her side once he'd noticed how deeply asleep she was. When he left the bus, his pocket was a little heavier, and Alison's bag a little lighter.

'Fuck, fuck, fuck.'

In today's double shift she had made a total of two hundred and twelve dollars in tips.

The pit in her stomach had now turned into a well.

She desperately needed that money to pay her bills.

Alison looked around one more time. The bus stops on both sides of the road were empty, and the streets looked almost deserted. She didn't know the area but she didn't like it one bit. She felt vulnerable.

Feeling cheated and lost, Alison quickly pondered what to do. She could go to the police, but she was certain that there wasn't much they would do. Lorena, one of the other waitresses at Donny's, had also been pickpocketed inside a bus on a different route a couple of months back. She'd gone to the police. They'd taken down all her details, and the pep talk they'd then given her about how she should be more careful and more attentive when in a crowded space had made her feel like it all had been her fault.

Alison decided that the best thing she could do was to get home as quickly as possible.

Hanging on tightly to her bag, she began walking south as fast as she could.

She'd been walking for almost forty-five minutes when

she reached the underpass. She'd been through it plenty of times before, just never this late at night. But the good news was that the underpass was just a five-minute walk from her place.

Alison began walking faster, but as she did so she heard something else other than her own footsteps echo behind her. She looked around wildly for a moment. She could see no one behind or in front of her, but due to the shadows created by the poor lighting, she just couldn't be sure.

Definitely a B-movie horror scene, she thought.

Alison exhaled slowly, as if blowing out hot air would carry with it the ripples of fear that had iced over her heart a moment earlier. The echoes faded around her and she listened to the raspy sound of her own breath.

Seconds later she began walking again, and again she could swear that she heard something else behind her other than the echoes of her own footsteps, but this time she was also overwhelmed by a sense of narrowing. It was as if the walls around her had closed in ever so slightly.

Alison shook her head, hoping that by force of vigorous motion she could cleanse the sensation from within her.

It didn't work. Instead, the sensation grew stronger, moving to plain and simple fear.

She swung her body around to look behind her one more time.

That was when she saw him.

The middle-aged man who had stepped off the bus with her. He had been following her since she'd left the diner. When she'd missed her stop, he'd sat tight. He jumped off when she did, and followed her from a distance.

In the underpass now, he was no more than four steps behind her.

Where the hell had he come from? How was he able to move so fast?

Three steps.

His hand came out of his jacket pocket.

Two.

He was holding something.

One.

Oh my God, is that a syrin—

Too late. The needle had already been plunged into her neck.

Fifty-Two

When Hunter got to their office, Garcia was standing by his desk with his arms crossed in front of his chest and his feet shoulder-width apart, as if waiting for something. His attention, though, was on the several printouts neatly arranged on his desktop.

'What's all that?' Hunter asked, pressing the 'space' bar on his keyboard to wake up his computer.

'Forensic lab reports,' Garcia replied, his gaze not moving from the paper. 'They all came in less than ten minutes ago. I just printed them out.' He grabbed one of the files and passed it over to Hunter. 'The toxicology on our first victim, Nicole Wilson, came back negative,' he announced. 'The killer kept her completely sober for six to seven days while raping and torturing her. We're still waiting on the results from Sharon Barnard.'

He turned to face his partner.

Hunter nodded while he scanned the report.

Garcia leaned back against the edge of his desk. 'If this was any other killer, I would've said that toxicology on the second victim would mimic the first, but with this guy . . .' Garcia shrugged. 'Expect the unexpected. He doesn't even have an MO. It wouldn't really surprise me if we found out that, unlike Nicole Wilson, Sharon Barnard had been drugged to her eyeballs.'

Hunter couldn't argue with Garcia's logic.

Garcia reached for a couple more sheets of paper from his desk, passing them to Hunter.

'OK, moving on,' he said. 'Forensics checked the telephone pole on Allenwood Road. They found no fingerprints, but what they did find were two tiny screw holes that didn't seem to belong. They were high off the ground, just past the first set of telephone cables. They checked them against all the other poles on that road.' Garcia shook his head. 'No other pole had them. AT&T confirmed that the holes shouldn't be there.'

'Camera holder?'

'That's also my opinion,' Garcia agreed. 'According to IT forensics, it could've been easily done. The camera could've either stored the recorded images to some sort of hard drive, or streamed them live over the Internet.'

Hunter seemed unsure. 'Storing it to a hard drive would have meant using a camera bulkier than the killer would've wanted, or having a separate hard drive connected to it. Forensics found only one set of screw holes?'

'That's right.'

'So no separate hard drive. A bulkier camera would've also been easier to spot from the road. I don't think he would've gone for that option.'

'Neither do I. Live streaming would've been the best option by far. IT forensics said that a camera with a wireless Wi-Fi connectivity could've piggybacked the Wi-Fi connection from any of the neighboring houses and no one would've known. Some of those cameras are as small and as light as a credit card.'

'So our killer could've staked out the street from the comfort of his living room, miles away,' Hunter said. 'No suspicious characters or vehicles on the road. Risk of being spotted – zero.'

Garcia nodded again. 'As if we didn't know, this guy is clever.' He pushed one document aside and picked up a new one. 'Forensics also managed to identify the type of pen the killer used to write the note that was sent to Mayor Bailey.'

'So what have we got?'

'The killer used a red, BIC Cristal, *large* ballpoint pen.' Garcia lifted his right index finger as he said the word 'large' to stress the emphasis. 'BIC Cristals are probably the most popular ballpoint pens in the whole of America,' he explained. 'They are inexpensive and can easily be purchased from just about anywhere – corner shops, supermarkets, minimarkets, stationery stores, post offices, you name it. But the interesting thing here is; the most popular BIC Cristals are the medium ballpoints, not the large ones. Those are a little rarer.'

Hunter peered at the copies of the killer's notes pinned on to the picture board before his attention returned to Garcia.

'But still,' Garcia added. 'Even though the large ballpoints aren't as popular, they're still popular enough.'

Hunter could've guessed that would be the case.

Garcia moved on to a new batch of documents. 'We still have nothing relevant from Nicole Wilson's laptop,' he said. 'Nothing from her emails either, but IT forensics have now managed to break through the security on Sharon Barnard's tablet computer and cellphone. I already have someone going over the computer files. So far, nothing of any significance.' Garcia's eyebrows lifted promisingly, as if he had left the best for last. 'But we did get something very interesting from her cellphone.'

Fifty-Three

Hunter, who was still going over the numbers on the last report Garcia had handed him, lifted his eyes to look at his partner.

Garcia searched through the printouts on his desk, then passed two new sheets over to Hunter before explaining: 'These are the transcripts of the very last text message conversation Sharon Barnard had.' He paused and his demeanor changed to something more somber. 'That conversation was between Sharon and the killer.'

Hunter sat up. He hadn't been expecting that. The first text message at the top of the file was time-stamped – 19:23.

C'mon, answer your phone, Sharon. Don't you want to play?

Hunter read those first ten words, paused and looked back at Garcia.

'We've already checked the sender's number,' Garcia said. 'Surprise, surprise – prepaid cellphone, untraceable. No calls or messages were made or sent prior to or after what was sent to Sharon Barnard. All the calls and text messages made and sent from that phone were to Ms.

Barnard's number. After that, the signal died. He destroyed the phone.'

Hunter's attention returned to the file.

Sharon Barnard's reply:

Go fuck yourself, freakshow. Whoever you are, I'm blocking your number.

Then the killer.

You know what? Forget about the phone. Let me ask you something. Did you remember to lock your front door?

No reply from Sharon Barnard.

Killer:

C'mon, open the door, Sharon. I'm right outside. Let's have some fun.

Hunter flipped over to the second sheet.

Again, no reply from Sharon Barnard.

Killer:

OK, who needs the door anyway? Maybe I can get in some other way.

The file came to an end.

Hunter reread the entire transcript a couple of times over. 'Is this it?'

'That's it,' Garcia confirmed. 'We've got nothing else. But the killer called her twice just before sending the first text message. Neither of the calls lasted very long.'

Hunter gave him a questioning look.

'Yeah, we're already in contact with her cellphone provider to see if we can get either a recording or a transcript of those conversations. We might have something by tomorrow.'

Garcia began pacing in front of the picture board. 'Have you ever encountered anyone like this guy, Robert? I mean, he's like a fucking chameleon when it comes to the way he operates.' He indicated the sheets on Hunter's desk. 'Those text messages show another complete change of MO from his previous murder.'

Hunter knew exactly what his partner was talking about.

'He went for pure fear this time,' he agreed, locking eyes with Garcia.

'Exactly. With Nicole Wilson, instead of terrorizing her, he befriended her with that whole horseshit story about being Ms. Bennett's cousin from Texas. He wasn't looking to scare her. He was after her trust. But with Sharon Barnard –' Garcia shook his head – 'He wanted her fear, not her trust.'

'And he certainly got it,' Hunter told him. 'The lack of response to these messages.' He indicated them on the transcript. 'The reason she didn't answer them back isn't because she was ignoring him, it's because she was petrified. She knew he was about to break into her house.'

'So why didn't she try calling nine-one-one?'

'Maybe she did but the call never got through. Maybe she didn't have time. Or maybe, in her panic, she didn't think of it. Thinking straight under that sort of fear is a huge task, Carlos.'

Three knocks sounded on Hunter and Garcia's office door.

'Come in,' Garcia called.

'Detectives,' the man who pushed the door open said, lifting the blue folder he held in his right hand, 'I think you'll want to see this.'

Fifty-Four

That morning, just like every morning since Squirm had been taken into captivity, 'The Monster' unlocked the door to the kid's cell at exactly 5:45 a.m. Squirm had been feeling ill all night. His dinner the night before had been his own vomit, eaten from the floor in the projection room upstairs – and 'The Monster' had made him eat every last scrap. Squirm had puked again, but not until he'd made it back to his cell, away from the man's eyes. This time, shrouded by the fear of what could happen if he dirtied the floor one more time, he did it into his latrine bucket.

'Rise and shine, Squirm,' 'The Monster' said from the doorway, his voice bright and jovial. 'It's a quarter to six. Time for your chores.'

Squirm had barely slept. His left eye remained badly swollen and the pains in his stomach felt like knife stabs. They were a combination of hunger pains and the result of heaving for so long on a completely empty stomach. His head also hurt with a deadly purpose, as if somehow thorns had found their way into his skull, lodging themselves just behind his eyeballs and were now digging at them like crazed woodpeckers. There also came a point during the night when he wasn't sure if he'd gone delirious, or 'The

Monster' had brought a new victim home, because he was certain that he could hear a woman's screams.

'I know you've heard me, Squirm. So get your lazy ass out of bed. Don't make me come over there.'

Squirm was curled up into a ball, lying down sideways on his dirty mattress, facing the wall. As he heard the man's voice, he felt the will to carry on living desert him.

And Squirm didn't fight it.

What was the point in living if he had to go through another day at the hands of this monster?

Squirm knew exactly what was coming because every day always played out the same. He would be beaten up, sodomized, starved, then beaten up some more – most days, until he passed out and was thrown back into his cell, ready for the whole process to repeat itself the next day.

'Get up, Squirm.'

Maybe if Squirm didn't move ... maybe if he didn't respond ... maybe if he disobeyed the man's orders, this would all end? Maybe the man would get angry enough to dish out a beating so severe the boy's fragile body and internal organs would finally give up, and life would at last abandon him.

Was it wrong for an eleven-year-old to want to die?

Squirm didn't think so, because in his mind what *was* wrong was for an eleven-year-old to live in this way.

Squirm had also given up praying, because he simply didn't know to whom he was praying anymore. If there was a God, he had no idea what he had done to piss him off so badly.

Once again, tears came to the boy's eyes. He was tired of them. He was tired of all the pain, and the hunger, and the darkness, and the fear. But most of all, Squirm was tired of living.

As he heard the man take his first heavy step into the cell, the young boy began shivering. Instinctively, his body curled up into an even tighter ball, readying itself for the inevitable.

But Squirm didn't care anymore. In fact, he would rather be dead.

All I have to do, Squirm thought, *is piss him off enough that he won't stop beating me when I pass out. Yes, that's it. I just need to make him angry and that won't take much doing.*

'The Monster' took another step toward the boy.

Squirm drew in a deep breath, as if he was breathing in courage, rolled his body over on the mattress to face his captor and looked him straight in the eye.

It was time to die.

'Fuck you, you sick piece of shit.'

Fifty-Five

Garcia didn't recognize the man standing at the door to their office. Decked out in a well-fitting black suit, a crisp white shirt, and a red silk tie, he was way too well dressed to be a CSI. He also didn't look anything like any of the IT forensics people Garcia had ever met.

'Please come in,' Hunter said, getting to his feet. 'Carlos, this is Detective Troy Sanders,' he said, putting an end to Garcia's questioning look. 'He's the head of the Missing Persons Unit's Special Division based in Ramirez Street. He was also the detective in change of Nicole Wilson's investigation.'

'Please, call me Troy,' Sanders said, shaking Garcia's hand before turning to face Hunter. 'I just came over to hand you this,' he said, nodding at the file he had with him. 'It's the results of the search you asked me to run.'

As Sanders handed Hunter the file, his gaze moved past the RHD detective and settled on the picture board directly behind him. A second later, his eyes widened.

'Jesus Christ,' Sanders whispered under his breath.

Hunter and Garcia followed his stare.

'You already have a second victim?' Sanders asked, his eyes moving about the board.

Neither Hunter nor Garcia said anything.

'When?'

'Her body was found the day before yesterday,' Garcia replied.

Sanders' expression was a mixture of surprise and incredulity. 'A day after the first victim was found?'

Garcia gave him a single, subtle nod.

Sanders frowned as his eyes focused on one particular photograph.

'Sharon Barnard . . . Sharon Barnard . . .'

Reading it from the board, he murmured the name to himself a couple of times, searching his memory for a moment before shaking his head.

'Neither her name nor her face sound or look familiar.' He looked back at Hunter and Garcia. 'Was she ever reported?'

'She was never missing,' Hunter explained. 'There was no abduction this time. Her killer simply broke into her house and murdered her in her living room.'

Sanders' frown intensified, now speckled with confusion. 'No abduction? The perpetrator broke away from his original MO?'

'Don't even get us started on this "MO" business,' Garcia said, lifting his hands in surrender. Strategically, he moved around to the other side of the room, dragging Sanders' attention away from the board.

Hunter quickly joined him.

Garcia moved the subject along. 'So those are the results of a search? What search?' The question was directed more at Hunter than at Sanders.

'Just a long shot, really,' Hunter explained. 'I had forgotten all about it. I asked Detective Sanders to run a search against the national Missing Persons database for cases where an abduction was perpetrated under similar circumstances to that of Nicole Wilson.'

Garcia thought about it for a second.

'I must admit that I hadn't thought about it like that until then,' Sanders added. 'But it made sense. The abduction scene at the Bennetts' house was too clean. Forensics spent two full days in there and they found absolutely nothing – no prints, no fibers, no hairs, no speck of dust that didn't belong, not a thing. In ten years with Missing Persons, I'd never come across such a sterile scene. That level of perfection isn't very easy to achieve, especially alone and on your *first ever* abduction?'

'Right from the beginning,' Hunter took over, addressing Garcia, 'we both had our suspicions that this killer would kill again, remember? That he would become a repeat offender.'

'But what if he already was a repeat offender?' Garcia said, already in sync with Hunter.

Sanders nodded his agreement. 'Exactly. At least when it came to abductions.' He once again indicated the file he'd handed Hunter. 'Well, that long shot might've paid off. Have a look in there.'

Fifty-Six

Fuck you, you sick piece of shit.

Fuck you, you sick piece of shit.

Squirm kept repeating those words in his head and he had every intention of spitting them out in his captor's face, but as 'The Monster's' steps drew nearer and Squirm rolled his body over on the mattress, survival, the most primal of all human instincts, grabbed hold of him in a way it had never done before. Instead of saying what he had rehearsed, the words that came out of the boy's lips were:

'I'm sorry, sir. I'm getting up now.'

Still, Squirm had taken too long to reply. Anger had already colored the man's face. He grabbed the boy by his hair and lifted him off the ground.

In vain, Squirm's hands shot up to his head, grabbing at the man's closed fist. Pain once again took hold of the boy's entire body with the speed of a lightning bolt. He tried screaming, but he was so weak that all his vocal cords could produce was a feeble and muffled 'Urghh'.

'You're going to have to start doing better than this, Squirm. I'm beginning to lose my patience with you.'

'The Monster' let go of Squirm's hair, but with his legs too frail to hold him up, the boy first collapsed on to his knees, then to all fours.

It took all of Squirm's willpower to block new tears from coming to his eyes.

I'm not going to cry anymore, the boy told himself through gritted teeth. *I'm not. Never again.*

'C'mon, Squirm, let's go.'

Still trembling, Squirm got to his feet and followed the man out of his cell and into the kitchen. As always, 'The Monster' had already prepared his own breakfast. This morning it consisted of scrambled eggs, three buttered slices of toast, three bacon rashers, a bowl of cereal with milk and a large glass of orange juice.

Squirm's first chore of the day was to watch the man eat his entire breakfast. No matter how hungry he was, if Squirm's tongue left his mouth and licked his lips, even if only for a split second, his face would be slapped so hard blood would usually drip from his lips at the corner of his mouth. When 'The Monster' was done, if there was any left he would throw it on to the floor. Squirm was then allowed to use his shackled hands to eat it, no cutlery allowed, before washing up after 'The Monster', including all the pans that were already in the sink. After that, the boy had to scrub the entire floor with a brush barely larger than a toothbrush. If 'The Monster' didn't think the floor was clean enough, he would make Squirm lick it in its entirety.

Squirm took his place, standing with his back to the north wall, facing the breakfast table and his captor, who sat at the head of it. What usually happened then was that 'The Monster' would begin eating. He would use his plastic knife and fork to either slice or pick up some food, slowly bring it to his mouth, all the while not taking his eyes off the hungry boy. With every mouthful, the man would tease

Squirm by making appreciative noises, as if he were eating the most delicious food on earth.

Squirm wasn't allowed to close his eyes or look away. If he did, he would be punished.

Fuck you, you sick piece of shit.

The words were still playing in Squirm's mind. They were halfway between his tongue and his lips, but still, the boy's survival instinct was fighting a better battle than his desire to die.

The boy kept his mouth shut.

As 'The Monster' took his place, his gaze moved to the newspaper by his breakfast plate, then to the plate, but he didn't reach for his knife and fork. His gaze moved once again, this time to the boy standing against the wall, facing him.

Squirm was still shaking. He was unsure how much longer his legs would hold him up. But he had stayed true to his word so far and hadn't cried another tear.

The man followed the boy's gaze. Surprisingly, it didn't lead to the food on the table but to the newspaper.

Squirm's captor paused, studying the scenario. He then smiled and did something that seemed absurd. He pushed his plate away from him without having touched a single piece of food.

'You know what, Squirm?' he said. 'I'm not hungry this morning. You can have it. You can have it all.'

Squirm didn't move. He was sure he had heard wrong.

'Here,' 'The Monster' continued, pushing the glass of orange juice and the bowl of cereal away from him as well. 'Have the juice and the cornflakes too. I'm not thirsty either.'

A dream. That's it, Squirm thought. There was no other explanation for the madness that was going on in front of him. *I'm right in the middle of some crazy-ass dream, no matter how real this all seems. Soon it will be 5:45 a.m. 'The Monster' will unlock the cell door and my real day will start.*

'C'mon, eat up, Squirm, before I change my mind.'

The boy still didn't move.

'The Monster' sat back, brought a hand to his face and began to gently run the tips of his fingers against his lips.

'I saw you eyeing up the newspaper,' he said. There was no anger in his voice. 'You want to read it?'

This dream is just getting more and more bizarre. What next? He's going to offer to drive me home? But then, a new thought entered the boy's mind. Pain. Back in his cell, when the man grabbed him by his hair, he'd felt pain – unbearable pain. *You're not supposed to feel pain in a dream, despite how real it might seem.* He had read that once. *So is this craziness real?*

'This is all real, Squirm,' 'The Monster' said, as if he had the power to read the boy's thoughts. He indicated with his hands as he spoke. 'The food is real, this house is real, these walls are real, those shackles are real, your cell is real and I am real. This is really happening to you. Your life isn't yours anymore. It belongs to me and I can do whatever I like with it.'

Squirm's good eye glanced around the room, as if he were unable to find something to focus on. Finally, it returned to the newspaper.

'I know why you want to read it,' 'The Monster' said. 'You're curious to find out about the investigation, aren't you?' He paused for effect and to study the boy one more time. 'You can read it if you like. It makes no difference to me.'

As 'The Monster' mentioned the investigation, Squirm

could sense his breathing picking up speed. He was sure that the police were looking for him. They had to be. He'd been missing for days now, he just didn't know exactly how many. Despite his tumultuous relationship with his father, they were still family and deep inside they still cared for each other. When Squirm hadn't come back home that day, his father would've contacted the school, then the authorities, there was no doubt about that. Yes, he was sure that the police were looking for him, but while at first that thought at least gave him some hope, it now gave him none. If they hadn't found him after so many days, he knew that police efforts would be reduced; after that, the search would lose momentum; and soon, if it hadn't already happened, he would be relegated to just another cold case. Another missing kid who was never found. Another missing persons casualty.

Squirm looked back at 'The Monster'.

That's why you want me to read the paper, isn't it? the boy thought. *Because there's something in there saying that the police have called off the search, isn't there? I'm already just a casualty. Just another statistic. No one is coming to help me. Not anymore. You want me to know that, don't you?*

Squirm felt his heart fold inside his chest.

'C'mon.' The man pointed to one of the other three chairs around the table. 'Sit. Eat. Today you don't have to eat it from the floor.'

Still Squirm didn't move. Was this a trick? Was that monster enticing him to move only so he could beat him up some more?

That made no sense, because that monster didn't need an excuse to beat him up. He did it whenever he pleased.

So what the hell is this?

'The food isn't poisoned either,' the man announced, once again guessing the boy's thoughts. And he'd guessed it right. 'Here. Look.' He reached for his plastic fork, scooped up some scrambled eggs from the plate and ate it, this time without making a single appreciative sound.

Squirm watched in silence.

Suddenly the man's expression went somber, before his eyes widened in terror. He dropped the fork and, with both hands, reached for his throat. His panicked gaze moved to the boy, who was now watching everything with a totally confused look on his face.

'Hellllp.' The man's voice came out strangled. Desperate. His face reddened.

Out of pure instinct, Squirm took one step forward, then stopped.

What the hell is happening?

'Arghhh . . .'

Fuck you, you sick piece of shit.

'Arghhh . . . ha, ha, ha, ha, ha.' The man let go of his throat and began laughing like a kid who had just been told the best joke in the world.

'Did you really think that the food was poisoned, Squirm? What the fuck? Why? Ha, ha, ha, ha, ha. If I wanted to kill you, why would I poison the food? That's no fun.' The play left the man's voice, replaced by a dead serious tone. 'The fun comes from getting your hands dirty, Squirm. From feeling the warmth of blood against your skin. From punishing them. You in sync with their breathing as they're dying, and you taking every breath with them. Until the very last one. Until they breathe no more.' 'The Monster' laughed again. 'You should've seen your face. Shocked and happy at the same time.' He shook his head. 'Sorry, Squirm. The only way you'll get rid of me is if I get rid of you. Besides that, your worthless little life belongs to me.'

Squirm felt like he had fallen down the rabbit hole. That he had somehow transcended worlds.

'No, you're not hallucinating,' the man replied.

Without noticing it, Squirm had asked the question out loud.

'I know that you're wondering what the hell is happening here. Why am I giving you my food without having touched it? Why haven't I thrown it on the floor for you to eat it? Why am I being so . . .' 'The Monster' searched the air for the word. 'Nice.' The man turned his palms toward him, folded his fingers in and checked his nails. 'And trust me, this is the nicest I'll ever be.' He looked at the boy again. 'You want to know why, don't you?'

No reply. No movement.

'Don't you, Squirm?'

'Yes, sir.'

'OK then.' He tapped the tabletop twice with his right hand. 'Sit down. Eat your food. And I'll tell you.'

Fifty-Seven

The file that Detective Sanders handed Hunter opened with a black and white portrait photograph of a man who looked to be in his mid to late thirties. He was an interesting-looking man. His head was clean-shaven, his face round and unremarkable, with a small nose and thin lips, but his light-blue eyes carried an intensity in them that was almost hypnotic. They seemed to be full of intelligence and pain at the same time.

The first thought that came into Hunter's mind as he studied the photograph was that whoever this man was, with the exception of his eyes he had the sort of simple, featureless face that would take to disguising like a cat to free food. The sort of face that would easily blend into a crowd and then disappear.

'Detectives,' Sanders finally said. 'Meet Mathew Hade.'

'OK, and who is he?' Garcia asked.

'Well, following Detective Hunter's guidelines, I initialized a search against the national Missing Persons database for a list of cases where an abduction was perpetrated under similar circumstances to Nicole Wilson's; for example, from inside a house, or where the abduction scene was relatively clean, and so on. I restricted the search to LA only, going back a maximum of twenty years.' Sanders shook his head. 'That gave me no results really worth looking into. I sent Robert an email telling him that the search hit a blank and he asked me to try it again, this time expanding the search to the whole of California. That gave me four different cases.'

Garcia finally moved his gaze from Hade's picture back to Detective Sanders.

'The scenes in those cases were nowhere near as clean as Ms. Wilson's one,' Sanders explained. 'But they were interesting enough. The problem was, two out of the four perpetrators were dead, and the other two are serving life sentences with no possibility of parole. I emailed the results to Robert and he asked me to run one last search.'

'In reality I was ready to give up,' Hunter took over. 'This was just a long shot, anyway. I was just throwing things up in the air, hoping for a sniff of a result.'

'But the new search made sense,' Sanders said, paused, then corrected himself. 'Actually, it wasn't a new search, it was the same search, but Robert figured out what we were doing wrong – we were searching only through closed MP investigations.'

If an investigation was tagged as 'concluded' by Missing Persons, it meant that the perpetrator/s had either been apprehended or shot dead. Of the ones apprehended, only a very small number, the least dangerous ones, the ones least likely to reoffend, would've made parole. The rest would still be inside. The very few who'd manage to break out of prison were again either shot dead or re-apprehended within days. If the search was only factoring investigations that had been concluded by Missing Persons, it was no wonder they were getting poor results.

'So I take it that Mr. Mathew Hade over here is the result

of that search,' Garcia said, nodding at the photograph. 'Or, at least, one of the results.'

'He is indeed,' Sanders confirmed it. 'The case follows,' he said, indicating the file.

As Hunter turned the page, Sanders began relating it.

'In February two thousand and nine, while house-sitting for a friend, a twenty-one-year-old college student named Tracy Dillard went missing in Fresno. The friend had gone back to Arizona on her college break to visit her parents for a couple of weeks. Ms. Dillard was asked to housesit mainly so her friend's cats would be properly fed in her absence. Until this day, Ms. Dillard has never been found.

'Despite no signs of forced entry, the investigators concluded that she had actually been abducted from inside the house. There were no signs of a struggle either. Forensics found no fingerprints, but they did find a few fabric fibers that seemed to belong to some sort of coat. Unfortunately, the fibers were matched to a very common brand of work-man's jacket. At the time, you could pick one up at Wal-Mart for under fifty bucks. They also found a couple of male boot prints in the house's backyard.'

Hunter and Garcia, who'd been following Sanders' accounts on paper, flipped over the page.

'The investigation led Fresno PD's Missing Persons Unit to interview a number of "persons of interest",' Sanders continued. 'Mathew Hade was one of them.'

'How come?' Garcia asked.

'He was a sort of a jack-of-all-trades. A handyman. Extremely clever and adaptable. His IQ was up in the 130s. He was good at just about anything – plumbing, electronics, mechanics, carpentry, roofing, bricklaying, gardening, decorating . . . you name it. If it needed fixing, he could probably do it. He could also build you stuff, if that was the requirement, and apparently he did it all very well.' There was a short pause. 'He was also a trained locksmith.'

Sanders' last few words got Hunter and Garcia's attention.

'On the week of Ms. Dillard's disappearance, Mathew Hade had been doing some roofing work on the same road where she was housesitting, two houses away, actually. That same week, he was also seen out on the street, talking to Ms. Dillard on one or two occasions. He completed all the roofing work a day before she went missing. The boot prints found in the garden matched Hade's shoe size, but the sole pattern didn't match any of the shoes the police found in his house.'

'What shoe size was he?'

'Eleven,' Sanders replied and made a face. 'Yeah, I know, the most common male shoe size in the US.'

'How about the jacket fibers?' Garcia asked.

'Mr. Hade told the police that he did have one of those exact jackets, but it was old and torn, so he had thrown it away a few days prior to his interview.'

'Convenient,' Garcia commented.

'Was he ever arrested?' Hunter asked.

'No. Despite suspicions, police didn't have enough to justify an arrest.' Sanders regarded both detectives for a quick second. 'I know what you're thinking – so this Mathew Hade was a person of interest in a missing persons investigation in Fresno, so what, right?'

Neither detective replied. Their silence spoke for itself.

'Well, I don't blame you, because I thought the same. But there's more,' Sanders added. 'Just turn the page. And here is where it starts to get interesting.'

Fifty-Eight

Despite still being completely confused by what was happening, Squirm drew in a courageous breath and took a couple of wary steps in the direction of the breakfast table. The boy's eyes were fixed on the man sitting at its head. Part of him was still expecting this whole thing to be a trick. He kept anticipating 'The Monster' jumping up from his seat and punching him hard enough to shatter bone, then laughing at how easy it had been to trick him.

But that never happened.

'C'mon, Squirm,' 'The Monster' said, once again tapping the tabletop twice with his right hand. 'Have a seat. Eat your breakfast.' He reached for the newspaper and pushed it across the table as well. 'Have a look at the paper if you like. It makes no difference to me.'

As Squirm got closer, the man pulled out the chair next to him.

'It's not a trick, Squirm,' the man said, reading the fear in the boy's eyes. 'I give you my word. I understand why you're so hesitant. I would've reacted the same way, but this is for real. The food is yours if you want it.'

Squirm's gaze finally moved from the man's face to the breakfast plate and he immediately started salivating. His stomach growled like a sick dog.

'I can actually hear how hungry you are,' the man said, placing his plastic cutlery by the plate. 'Here, today you also don't have to eat using your hands. You can use these.'

At last, Squirm took a seat at the table. Still very concerned, the boy kept his gaze on the man and his hands in his lap.

'It's not going to magically jump from the plate into your mouth, Squirm. And I sure as hell am not going to put it there for you.'

Squirm's hunger finally won the battle and the boy reached for the knife and fork. As he did, the heavy metal chain that shackled his wrists together rattled against the tabletop, almost tipping over the plastic cereal bowl and pushing the breakfast plate off the table.

'Here,' the man said, reaching inside his trouser pocket for a key. 'Let me help you with that.'

He took the boy by the arm and unlocked one of the metal rings around his wrists.

Squirm looked down at his hands. The skin around his free wrist, where the thick metal ring had hugged it for so long, was red, raw and inflamed. Instinctively, he touched it with the fingertips of his opposite hand and as they grazed the ugly wound a burning, stinging pain shot up his arms, but boy, did it feel good?

OK. This must be a dream. This just can't be happening.

The man looked down at the breakfast plate, and followed the look with a jerk of his head. 'Eat.'

Squirm gripped the fork with his free right hand. His good eye scanned the contents of the plate, trying to decide what to go for first. He could barely remember the last time he'd had a civilized hot meal. His hand shot toward the plate and he scooped up as much scrambled eggs as the tiny fork could possibly hold. A millisecond later, the fork was in his mouth. The process was repeated once again, almost too fast for the eye to see. His scrawny cheeks puffed up like inflated balloons from the amount of food the boy had shoved inside his mouth. He could hardly chew it all.

'Wow, hey,' the man said, lifting a hand. 'Easy, Squirm. You're going to make yourself sick. The food isn't going to go anywhere. I told you, you can have it all. I'm not going to take it away from you.'

Squirm still chewed as fast as he could. Once he finally swallowed the first mouthful, he wiped his mouth with the back of his hand. One more time, and still fearfully, he peeked at the man, who seemed totally unconcerned.

The boy reached for a piece of toast.

In silence, the man watched him eat. Squirm still ate fast, but not as fast as his first few mouthfuls. He drank his orange juice in gulps and finished the bowl of cereal in record time, but without spilling a single drop. He was about to eat the last of the food, a piece of bacon rasher, when the man spoke again.

'You really don't remember what day today is, do you?'

Squirm paused before the piece of bacon hit his lips.

'Not at all?' his captor asked.

Squirm frowned, but failed to reply.

'OK, I'll tell you.' There was a forced, full-of-suspense pause. 'Today is your birthday, Squirm.'

Shocked, the boy looked back at his captor. The piece of bacon fell from his fork back on to the plate.

Squirm's life had taken such a drastic turn in the past few days that he had completely forgotten about his own birthday. The last time he had thought about it had been on the day he was abducted, as he was leaving school. Back then, there had been only nine days to go.

The boy's eyes ran the length of his skinny arms all the way to his hands. Dry blood coated his knuckles and every single one of his nails. All of them broken. He had no idea what his face looked like, as there were no mirrors or shiny surfaces anywhere in the house, but Squirm wasn't sure he wanted to know. What he did know was that he had also lost a silly amount of weight. He looked like someone who had been struggling with either anorexia or bulimia.

Oh my God! I've been here for only nine days?

In the boy's mind, it really did feel like a year or more.

'I guess that explains why I'm being nice to you today,' the man said, sitting back in his seat. 'So, happy birthday, Squirm. That breakfast was your present.'

The boy felt tears coming to his eyes, but he remembered his promise from earlier on and somehow found the strength to choke them.

'You're not going to read the paper?'

Squirm peered at it, but his hands didn't move.

'You must be curious about what is going on out there, aren't you? You've been missing for quite a few days now. The police must be going crazy trying to find you, don't you think?'

No reply. No movement.

'C'mon, have a look. I'll help you.' The man reached for the newspaper and flipped it open to the crime section, before placing it back on the table in front of the boy. He watched Squirm's good eye move to it and quickly scan all the headlines.

Nothing.

'Oh!' 'The Monster' said sarcastically. 'Nothing in today's paper. That's strange, isn't it? Would you like to check the earlier newspapers too?'

They locked eyes, or in Squirm's case – eye.

'I've kept them all.' 'The Monster' jerked his head to his left. 'They're in the cupboard. Let me get them for you.' He got up, walked over to the cupboards high on the south wall and opened the second one from the left. From inside, he retrieved a pile of folded newspapers.

'Here they are,' he said, dumping them on the table. 'Every single *LA Times* since the day after I picked you up from outside your school.'

Squirm found it astonishing that 'The Monster' made it sound as though what had happened that day was nothing more than a regular school pick-up.

'Go on,' the man pushed. 'Have a look.'

The boy reached for the first one at the top of the pile, yesterday's *LA Times*, and unfolded it. He found that the papers had already been opened on to the crime section. This time he took a little longer going over the articles and headlines. In the 'Missing Persons' section, he came across a few photographs, most of them of kids around his age or younger. His wasn't one of them. He put the paper down and quickly reached for the next one – the *LA Times* from two days ago. Again, his picture wasn't listed in the 'Missing Persons' section.

A cold, discomforting feeling began to grow inside the boy's stomach.

Newspaper number three.

No pictures of him.

Number four.

A repeat of the previous three.

The discomfort turned to nausea, branching out to some sort of spike that stabbed at his heart.

Five.

Not a thing.

'The Monster' simply observed Squirm, his eyes sparkling with satisfaction.

Six.

No.

Last newspaper. The one dated the day after he'd been abducted.

The boy's picture wasn't there.

If there was still such a thing that Squirm called 'world', it collapsed right in front of him that morning.

OK, this is a dream. It has to be. There's no other explanation for how fucked-up crazy this morning has become.

'Nothing?' 'The Monster' asked, his lips parting into a malicious grin.

Squirm's attention didn't break from the newspapers, which were now scattered all over the breakfast table. His good eye was still searching from paper to paper.

I must've missed it. It's there somewhere. It has to be.

'Looking at them some more isn't going to make your picture miraculously appear on the paper, Squirm. Let me try to save you the trouble. It's not there. It never has been.'

Squirm began shaking.

'Haven't you wondered how come I knew that today was your birthday, Squirm?' The man shrugged. 'I never asked you. You never offered it.'

The boy turned to look at 'The Monster'. All the madness had happened so fast that morning that Squirm had never stopped to think about it.

How did he know it was my birthday?

'That question can be answered by answering another couple of questions.' Once again the 'The Monster' paused, lifting his eyebrows to emphasize his words. 'How come there are no pictures of you in the papers? How come there's no story about the boy who went missing after leaving school a week and a half ago?'

Squirm felt as though something had begun choking his heart inside his chest. He said nothing. He didn't know *what* to say.

'And the answer is – because you were never reported missing, Squirm.'

Fifty-Nine

'Just turn the page,' Sanders said. 'Because here is where it starts to get interesting.'

Hunter did, and Sanders carried on with his account.

'Five months after Ms. Dillard's disappearance, in July two thousand and nine, Sandra Oliver, a twenty-four-year-old bank clerk from Fresno, also went missing. She lived by herself in the west part of town. Once again, the Missing Persons investigation concluded that whoever had taken her had done so from inside her own house and, once again, there was no sign of a break-in or a struggle. The abduction scene was almost a carbon copy of Ms. Dillard's – relatively clean, no fingerprints, no mess, just a few fibers and a couple of shoeprints by the back door. The shoe size and sole pattern matched those found in Ms. Dillard's abduction scene so suspicions of it being the same perpetrator were high.

'Now, guess who'd been working in the neighbor's house the same week of Ms. Oliver's disappearance?' Sanders didn't wait for a reply. 'That's right, our friend Mathew Hade. He'd been doing several minor repairs to the property, as well as remodeling their front garden. All the work was completed just a couple of days before Sandra Oliver went missing. Once again, the police ended up knocking on Mr. Hade's door, and once again they didn't have enough to take him in. The detective in charge of the investigation managed to get a warrant to search Hade's house but they found nothing incriminating. A week and a half after she went missing, Ms. Oliver's body was found on a patch of green grass in the northern part of town.'

Hunter and Garcia's interest grew.

'Now tell me if this sounds familiar,' Sanders continued. 'She was found fully clothed, positioned in a human crucifix shape, with her legs fully extended but close together and her arms wide open, palms up. Ligature marks were found on both of her wrists and ankles.'

Hunter and Garcia both lifted their head to look at the Missing Persons detective.

'Her picture follows,' Sanders said expectantly, nodding at the file.

One more page flip and both detectives were held fast.

Sandra Oliver was a petite woman with very similar features to Nicole Wilson. Just like Ms. Wilson, she had a round face, which was also framed by shoulder-length dark-brown hair.

Hunter checked the next photograph along. It was a crime-scene snapshot, showing the position in which Sandra Oliver's body had been found. If her legs had been spread apart, she would've been left in the exact same position Nicole Wilson was found in, on a similar patch of green grass.

To better compare them, Hunter looked at Nicole Wilson's crime scene photograph pinned to the picture board. This had indeed got interesting.

Sanders' gaze followed his before he added, 'The post mortem concluded that Ms. Oliver was tortured for several days prior to her demise,'

'What sort of torture?' Garcia asked.

'She was severely beaten up. The skin under her clothes was black and blue, covered in bruises and hematomas, but no lacerations. For some reason, her torturer punished her body but left her face completely intact, as you can see from the photographs. According to the coroner, the blunt traumas to her body were inflicted by hand alone – punches to be more precise – by someone with relatively big fists.' Sanders paused for breath. 'Also, whoever punished her was kind of an expert. Superficial injuries only. No broken bones or internal organ damage.'

'Was she sexually assaulted?' Garcia again.

'Repeatedly, but the assailant was smart enough to use a rubber. No semen was found. Unfortunately, the autopsy examination uncovered nothing else that could be construed as a clue to her killer's identity. The investigation hit a wall.'

'Cause of death?'

'She suffocated. The coroner couldn't be any more specific as to how it happened but it wasn't by strangulation.'

Sanders gave Hunter and Garcia a moment to read over the autopsy report.

'But it doesn't end there,' he proceeded. 'A year after Ms. Oliver's body was found, Mathew Hade relocated to Sacramento. Six months after the relocation, a twenty-year-old woman named Grace Lansing went missing in River Park, on the east side of the city. She was taken from inside her parents' house while they were away on a weekend break. Just like Tracy Dillard, the college student who went missing in Fresno, Grace has also never been found.'

'Did Mathew Hade make the POI list in Sacramento again?' Garcia asked.

'He did,' Hunter was the one who answered, reading from the file.

'Working in the proximities?' Garcia half questioned, half guessed.

Sanders nodded. 'He had found a job with a roofing company. The company was making repairs to one of the houses in the same street as Grace Lansing's parents'. Once again, Mathew Hade had no alibi for the night Ms. Lansing went missing but, once again, the police couldn't get anything concrete on him to justify an arrest.'

Hunter continued reading the file.

'I know that all of this might mean absolutely nothing,' Sanders said, lifting up both palms. 'It could all be just a coincidence, but I wanted to bring the file to you and let you decide. Especially because of the last photograph.'

Hunter and Garcia turned to it. It was a mugshot of Mathew Hade. With the exception of maybe a wrinkle or two, he looked exactly the same as he did in the file's first photograph.'

'A mugshot?' Garcia said.

Sanders nodded. 'That mugshot was taken seven months ago. Mathew Hade was taken in because he got involved in an altercation at a bar . . .' Sanders paused.

'OK,' Garcia said.

'In East Los Angeles,' Sanders added. 'Mathew Hade isn't in Sacramento anymore. He's here.'

Sixty

'The Monster' is lying.

That had been Squirm's first thought after hearing the man's words.

He must be lying. Of course my father reported me missing.

The man could see the boy's demeanor changing. He returned to his seat, placed his elbows on the table and interlaced his fingers together, his hands directly in front of his chin.

'You don't believe me, do you, Squirm?' he said, looking at the kid. 'I don't blame you. Why would you? But let me tell you a quick story which might change your mind.'

Squirm kept his gaze on 'The Monster'.

'A few months ago, I was having a quiet drink in this run-down joint not that far from your school. It was late, sometime between one and two in the morning, I think. The place wasn't busy at all. I'd say maybe five or six people, max. I was just there, sitting at the bar, minding my own business, when one of the regulars walks in. The reason I know he was a regular was because the bartender greeted him by name – Pete. Well, this guy, Pete, already looked to be pretty hammered, but since he was a regular, the bartender didn't seem to mind it.

'Pete ordered a bourbon, neat, and took the stool next to where I was sitting. Strange, as the bar was pretty fucking empty, but hey, it's a free country and a man has the right to sit wherever he likes, as long as he isn't bothering anyone.'

Keeping his fingers interlaced, the man used his thumbs to rub his chin.

'Once the bartender brought Pete his drink, he looked at me, probably because I was the only other person sitting at the bar, lifted his glass and in a stroppy way mumbled the word "Cheers". Now I'm a polite guy, so in return I raised my glass and we both had a sip of our drinks. Pete then put his glass down, turned on his stool and slowly looked at me from head to toe. In a seedy bar like that, full of drunken people, that was all that was needed to either start a fight or a conversation. Well, I wasn't in the mood for a fight so that night it was a conversation.

'We shot the breeze for a while, then ended up moving the conversation from the bar to one of the tables, all the while Pete is drinking neat bourbon and I'm drinking cheap whiskey. Once we took the table, Pete began telling me how he hated his life, how his wife had left him years ago for no good reason, and how she had left him stuck with this boy.'

The man was tracking Squirm's reactions, but the boy looked as if he had gone into some sort of trance, with his good eye wide open staring back at his captor. The man continued without missing a beat.

'Pete went on and on, telling me how much of a pain in the ass the boy was, that he had been a mistake that should never have happened and so on. In short, Pete blamed this boy for everything bad that had happened to him in his life. I'm telling you, Squirm, this guy *hated* his son with a divine passion. He told me that there'd been many nights that he'd gotten back home and almost strangled the boy in his sleep. I asked him "Why hadn't he?" and he told me that if he thought he could get away with it, he would.'

The man paused, reached for the bacon rasher that Squirm had failed to eat and placed the whole thing in his mouth. He continued only when he was done chewing.

'That was when I told Pete that there were plenty of ways one could get away with murder. One just needed to know what to do.'

Those words seemed to fill the room with a cold, discomforting air.

'This Pete guy looks back at me,' the man continued, 'and his next few words came out sounding like a challenge.' 'The Monster' spoke with a deep sounding voice. '"Oh, really? OK, big shot, if it's so easy, why don't you do it for me?"'

'The Monster' let those words hang in the air for a moment, giving the boy a chance to take in every syllable.

'I said nothing in return, but this Pete guy didn't want to let go, he kept on pushing. "I'm serious, man. You do the kid and I'll pay you."' 'The Monster' smiled at the boy. 'Obviously Pete had no idea who he was talking to, so I looked him deep in the eye and asked him how much he was willing to pay me. Now, I must admit that I thought that all that crap about getting rid of his boy was just the alcohol talking, that deep down he didn't really mean it, but fuck, was I wrong? He meant every single word.'

Squirm kept his gaze on the man sitting at the head of the table, but his thoughts were elsewhere. In his mind he could picture the bar scene perfectly, and as he did so he felt something come alive inside his stomach. All the food he'd just eaten threatened to come back up, but this time he didn't care.

'So once we'd established that neither of us were joking,' 'The Monster' continued with his story, 'we began to discuss a figure. Would you like to know what that figure was, Squirm? Would you like to know how much your father paid me to take you away and kill you?'

Sixty-One

Detective Sanders was right, Mathew Hade could be nothing more than one enormous coincidence. After all, neither Fresno PD nor Sacramento PD had managed to gather enough evidence on him to substantiate any sort of arrest, despite all the suspicions. But then again, neither Hunter nor Garcia subscribed to the 'coincidence' fan club, especially when those coincidences began to accumulate in the way that they had. The fan club that both detectives did subscribe to, however, was the 'check absolutely everything' one.

As soon as Sanders had left their office, Garcia asked Operations to compile a detailed profile on Mathew Hade, tracing him all the way back to his childhood. The file would take at least twenty-four hours to compile, so at the moment all they had was the little information contained in the dossier Sanders had handed them. Not much, but definitely a start.

The address listed on Mathew Hade's arrest sheet was somewhere in East Los Angeles, not that far from the bar in which he had gotten arrested for getting into a fight. The drive took Hunter and Garcia a little over thirty minutes.

For the duration of the ride, Hunter kept Hade's file open on his lap. He had read and reread the dossier twice over, and every now and then Hunter would flip back to Hade's mugshot and portrait, as if he needed to verify something against both photographs.

'You know,' Garcia said, as he exited Santa Ana Freeway, heading north. He couldn't help but notice how often Hunter had checked Hade's photographs. 'There's something about him that bothers me too.' He jabbed at the mugshot. 'Something about the look in his eyes.'

'Like what?'

'I'm not sure, but just look at them. Look at that stare.'

Hunter did, for the zillionth time.

'It's a dead, cold stare. Full of anger and –' Garcia had to pause and think of the best word to use – 'Determination.'

Hunter nodded his agreement, but said nothing in return. Garcia didn't need to explain what he meant. He and Hunter had come across that sort of stare more times than they would've liked to. It was the kind of stare they both knew never to overlook.

Garcia glanced at Hunter from the corner of his eyes. 'But that wasn't what you were looking at, was it?'

'What do you mean?'

'C'mon, Robert, you've been staring at those pictures as if you're looking for Wally. Well, let me tell you, he's not there. So what is it?'

Hunter regarded the photographs one more time. 'Nothing, really. Just something the killer mentioned in his second note.'

This time Garcia didn't glance at Hunter. He turned to look at him.

'Shit!' he said before quoting: '"If they looked straight into my eyes, would they see the truth inside them? Would they see what I have become, or would they falter?"'

Garcia had also memorized the killer's note.

'I had forgotten about that,' he admitted. 'But now that you've mentioned it, and looking at those photos, one thing is for damn sure – those eyes can certainly tell a story on their own.'

'Well, these are just photographs,' Hunter said, finally closing the file. 'We'll get a better idea once we meet him face to face . . .'

'. . . and look into his eyes,' Garcia finished.

Sixty-Two

Consciousness returned to Alison like waves breaking over a beach, but the pain was always there whether she was conscious or not. It was an odd kind of pain, a dull ache that started on the left side of her neck and spread with the resolve of soldier ants to the rest of her body, but the worst pain came from her wrists – a burning soreness that felt like her hands were being sawn off with a blunt hacksaw.

Her head was slumped forward with her chin almost touching her chest. During periods of consciousness Alison's eyes would flicker and every now and then she could see red toenails resting against the floor. It took her some time to realize that they were her own toenails. She had been stripped naked.

Alison had no idea where she was but it was somewhere dark and hot, with thick rubber foam sheets glued to the walls and metal pipes above her head.

Instinctively she tried moving, but that only served to sharpen the pain in her arms. Something dug deeper into her wrists, as if thin metal rods were being forced between her joints and then twisted to one side. The pain quickly moved up her arm before settling on her shoulders. Right then, she truly believed that her arms were being slowly pulled from their sockets.

Trying to better understand what was happening to her, Alison lifted her chin, a movement that sent waves of nausea rippling through her stomach. Her eyes rolled back into her head and her lids flickered again. She had to summon all of her strength not to fall back into the abyss of unconsciousness.

With great effort, Alison managed to focus on her arms, which were stretched high above her head. Only then did she finally understand why they hurt so much. Her wrists were shackled by a metal chain speckled with blood. The chain had been looped over a thick metal pipe that ran across the ceiling. All of her weight was being supported by her thin arms and the chain was biting deeply into her bloody wrists.

Time dragged interminably. She tried to remember what had happened. Why was she in this hellhole? But the incessant throbbing in her head made thinking an impossible task. Her throat had swollen up so much that she had to practically force every breath into her lungs, and that had caused her mouth to go bone dry.

Braving the pain, Alison looked up once again and studied her restraints as best as she could. The chain around her wrists was fastened by a small, brass padlock. A bigger padlock kept the loop around the ceiling pipe in place.

What the hell is going on? Where was she?

Nothing made sense.

Her eyes had gotten a little more used to the poor lighting, enabling her to look around her surroundings. The floor of the room she was in was made of concrete. It was covered in stains of different sizes but Alison couldn't tell what had created them – oil, water, blood?

Over to her left she saw a short flight of stairs leading up to a closed door. There were no windows in the room, which led her to believe that she was in some sort of sordid basement. To her right, a little more hidden in the shadows, she could see part of a workshop table. Several tools and instruments were lying on its surface. She couldn't make them all out but the ones she saw froze her heart – a circular handheld sander, a pair of bolt cutters, pruning shears, a bullwhip and a selection of medical scalpels and forceps.

She tried to use her feet to push herself up and lessen the stress on her arms but they could barely touch the ground. All she could do was teeter on her toes. The effort produced the exact opposite effect to the one she was looking for, straining her arms even further. The pain made her scream, but the rubber foam that lined the walls muffled the noise as if she were underwater.

But somebody heard her, because seconds later the door at the top of the stairs opened and a male figure was framed in the light behind it. He stood there, in silence, for a moment. His strong arms hung loosely by his sides.

'Wh . . . who are you?' she breathed out, but her voice sounded so weak she was unsure he had heard her. She tried again. 'Why are you doing this to me?'

No reply. No movement.

That only served to fill Alison with even more terror.

'Please . . . please.'

The figure finally reached for a light switch on the outside of the door and a fluorescent bulb, encased in a metal box on the ceiling, blinked into life, flooding the basement with light.

Alison immediately looked away, squeezing her eyes tight to protect them from the sudden brightness. Seconds later, she tried to focus on the figure by the door. His shoes clicked against the stairs as he made his way down to the basement floor. Alison's gaze followed him.

'Please. What do you want from me? Who are you? Why am I here?'

The man walked over to the workshop table in the shadows and paused, facing her. They locked eyes for a long moment.

'You don't recognize me, do you?' he finally said. His voice was deep, cold and guttural – and overflowing with confidence. His posture was firm and strong, like a warrior's ready for battle.

Alison concentrated. No, she didn't recognize him, but she also couldn't shake the feeling that something about him was very familiar to her, especially his eyes.

She didn't have to answer him. He knew she didn't recognize him. His disguises were always flawless.

He turned toward the workshop table and reached for something Alison couldn't see.

'Let me ask you something, Alison.'

The man began unbuttoning his shirt.

Alison felt her body begin to convulse with fear.

'Oh no, no, no.'

He allowed the pause to linger on, stretching the suspense.

'How much do you know about pain?'

He turned to face her.

Her eyes locked on to the object he was holding in his hand and her voice completely failed her.

'Because I know . . . everything.'

Sixty-Three

'OK, this is it,' Garcia said as he parked his car right in front of an old three-storey construction located halfway down a relatively busy road. The building looked tired and in serious need of some attention. Most of the windows looked like they'd never been cleaned, at least not on the outside, and what should've been a front lawn looked more like the remains of an old battlefield.

It didn't get any better on the inside.

The wooden door at the entry lobby creaked loudly as Hunter pushed it open, revealing a small and poorly lit room that smelled of a thousand ashtrays. Water infiltration stains marked the ceiling like freckles on a face. Some of that water had lazily traveled down one of the walls, pushing itself behind the wallpaper and creating blisters that looked ready to pop at any minute. Cigarette burn marks formed an interesting pattern on the old and dirty rug that centered the room.

'Nice. Classy,' Garcia said as he and Hunter stepped inside.

It seemed like the creepy sound generated by the hinges on the old front door was used as a shop bell, because as soon as the noise came to a stop, an overweight Hispanic-looking man promptly appeared behind the counter on the south wall. He smelled of spiced refried beans and Taco sauce, and his greasy hair was stuck to his sweaty forehead as if he'd just finished the toughest exercise session ever known to man.

'What can I do for you gentle—' He paused midsentence, before his shoulders slumped down as if all of a sudden he'd become fed up with life. 'Aww, *chinga tu madre*! Cops.'

Hunter had had a suspicion that this wouldn't be a regular apartment building. From the outside it looked like one of those places that rented their apartments by the hour, day, week, month, or whatever arrangement better suited the customer – no questions asked, just as long as they could make the payments.

'Are we that obvious?' Garcia asked Hunter, looking at him from head to toe.

'No, I don't think so.'

'What? Are you joking, *ese*?' the man said from behind the counter. His Mexican accent wasn't nearly as heavy as he was. 'Your badges are practically tattooed on your foreheads. Yes, you are that obvious. Why do you guys like to bust my balls so much, huh? I'm just trying to earn an honest living here.'

'Yeah, that *is* a wonder,' Garcia said, emphasizing the way he was looking around the entry lobby and bringing his right hand to his face to cover his nose. 'Everything around here looks to be right on the money, and that includes the attitude.'

The man began to murmur something inaudible but Hunter cut him short.

'We're not here to bust your balls,' he said, approaching the counter and displaying his credentials.

'Or to criticize your fine establishment,' Garcia said, coming up behind Hunter. 'And yes, we are cops.'

'I take it that you are the building's superintendent, Mr.?' Hunter said, returning his ID to his pocket.

'Moreno,' the man replied with a sullen face. 'Arturo Moreno and, yes, I am the building's superintendent.'

The sweat stains on his shirt, directly under his armpits, looked like they were growing larger.

'OK,' Hunter said, being careful to place Mathew Hade's portrait photograph, not his mugshot, on the counter. 'We have information that this man lives here. Apartment two-eleven?'

Moreno eyeballed the picture for a little while.

'Um-hum.' He nodded, looking bored. 'But I'd say that "lives" is a very strong word to describe his relationship with apartment two-eleven.'

Hunter's eyebrows lifted inquisitively. 'All right, so how would you describe it?'

'He comes and goes,' Moreno replied. 'Like most people here. Sometimes he'll stay for a week. Sometimes more, sometimes less. And sometimes he'll disappear for the same amount of time. Even longer. He's got no schedule. No one here does.'

'Is he in now?' Garcia asked, his eyes moving to the staircase to the left of the counter. The severely worn-out red and black carpet that lined the stairs was ripped at the edge of every step, some of it so badly Garcia was certain it would constitute a health hazard.

Moreno shook his head. 'No, he isn't. I haven't seen him for . . .' He paused and looked up at the cobwebs on the ceiling, as if the answer was up there with all the dust. 'Five, six days, maybe? Maybe less, I'm not sure. Last time I saw him he was only here for a couple of days. If I remember right, he had a friend with him then.'

'A friend?'

'Well,' Moreno shrugged carelessly. 'They came in together, chatting like they were friends, so I guess that that's what they were.'

'Was this friend male or female?' Hunter queried.

'*Hombre*,' Moreno answered. 'Male.'

'Have you ever seen this friend before?'

Moreno thought about it for just a couple of seconds. 'No. I can't say I have.' He began scratching the back of his neck as if his life depended on it.

Garcia frowned at him before taking a step back. He wouldn't be surprised if the place had a flea or bedbug problem.

'But in this place, *ese*,' Moreno continued. 'A lot of new people come and go with the guests.' He stopped with the scratching and checked his nails, before rubbing them against the front of his shirt. 'You know how it goes, right? What the guests do in their apartments is their own business, *comprendes*? I just take care of the place.'

And you're doing a fine job, Garcia thought, but kept his mouth shut.

'Have you ever seen him bring any women back here?' Hunter asked.

Moreno coughed a laugh. 'Are you for real, *ese*? Yeah, I've seen him bring women here and, before you ask, as far as I am concerned they were all of legal age.'

'Have you seen either of these two women around here?' Hunter asked, now showing the building super a photo of Nicole Wilson and one of Sharon Barnard.

While studying the photographs, Moreno kept his mouth closed and ran his tongue against his upper front teeth. His top lip bulged with the movement.

'Umm . . . nope, they don't look familiar to me.'

'Are you sure?' Garcia insisted.

Moreno kept his gaze on the pictures for a while longer. 'Yep. Positive, *ese*.'

'Who else works here? Like, who takes your place on your day off, or on your once-a-week shower day.'

Garcia's joke was completely missed by Moreno.

'My cousin, *ese*, but he's not around till the end of the week. You can come back then and speak to him, if you like?'

'Maybe we will,' Garcia said.

'You do have the keys to apartment two-eleven, right?' Hunter asked.

Moreno looked at him, then at Garcia, then back at Hunter. 'Yes, of course I do, but don't you need some sort of warrant to go up in there? This place might be a dump, but it's not a free-for-all, *ese*.'

'Oh, sure,' Garcia replied. 'We can go get a warrant if you like, and maybe we'll come back here with more than just a warrant for apartment two-eleven, *ese*. We'll have a warrant for this whole building, including your office back there.' He pointed at the closed door just behind Moreno. 'And while we're at it, we'll bring a few health inspectors and immigration officers with us too. Sound good?'

'Aw, *pinche culero*.' Moreno rubbed his greasy forehead while looking down at the floor.

'*Usted sabe que hablamos español también, ¿no?*' Garcia said, reminding Moreno that he and Hunter both understood Spanish.

Moreno didn't look back at him. Instead, he simply opened one of the drawers behind the counter and picked up a set of keys.

'OK, *ese*, but the only way you're going up there is if I go with you.'

'I wouldn't have it any other way, *ese*,' Garcia said, taking a step back and pointing toward the staircase. 'After you, *compadre*.'

Sixty-Four

By the time they cleared the four flights of stairs that took them up to the second floor, the building superintendent looked like he was about to go into cardiac arrest. His forehead was dripping with sweat and his breathing was so labored he sounded like an asthmatic Darth Vader.

'Are you OK?' Hunter asked as Moreno finally reached the second-floor landing. It had taken him almost two minutes to get through fifty steps.

'*Hijo de perra.*' Those words came out as a gasp. 'Yeah . . . I'm fine, *ese* . . .' he finally replied, in between deep breaths, while holding on to the wall. 'I just need a moment.'

'Yeah, you look fine,' Garcia observed. 'You sound fine too.'

Once again, Moreno simply ignored the sarcastic comment.

Down the short corridor in front of them, a door opened just enough for someone to peek outside, quickly shutting again a second later.

'OK,' Moreno said, standing up straight and wiping his forehead with the palm of his hand. 'Let's just get on with this. The two of you walking these corridors is bad for business, *comprendes*? You guys even smell like cops.'

Garcia frowned at Hunter before quickly bringing his left forearm to his nose, smelling it, then doing the same to his right one.

'You mean, we're making the place smell nice?' he said.

Moreno looked back at him, a reply almost materializing on his lips, but then he thought better of it.

Apartment two-eleven was the first door on the left as they entered the hallway. Moreno was about to slide his master key into the lock when Hunter grabbed his arm, gesturing for him not to. He pulled the building super to one side, moving him away from a direct line with the front door.

'We knock first,' Hunter whispered.

'Why, *ese*? I told you, he's not here.'

'That may well be, but we still knock first.'

Hunter pulled Moreno away so that the two of them were standing against the wall to the left of the door. Garcia did the same, but on the right side.

Hunter knocked three times.

No answer.

Another three knocks.

Still no answer.

'See? I told you, *ese*.'

'OK.' Hunter nodded. 'You can use your key now.'

As Moreno unlocked the door and pushed it open, it creaked just as loudly as the one down at the entrance lobby.

From the outside, they could only see as far as the light that seeped in from the hallway allowed them to, which wasn't far. Most of the room lay in shadow as all the curtains were drawn shut.

'Lights?' Hunter asked, once again pulling Moreno back a few steps.

'On the wall.' Moreno indicated from outside. 'To the right of the door.'

Garcia reached in and flipped the switch.

At the center of the ceiling, a bulb flickered twice before coming on, bathing the small room in crisp, bright light.

'Mathew Hade?' Hunter called from the door.

No reply.

'Mathew Hade?' Hunter called again. 'This is the LAPD. We would like to ask you a few questions.'

There was no one there.

As both detectives finally stepped inside, they paused, their eyes searching the room. It smelled slightly of bleach and disinfectant, with a hint of orange, as if somebody had spring-cleaned it not that long ago.

Intrigued, Garcia turned and checked the number on the door again – 211. They were indeed in the right apartment.

The room was completely bare, save for a simple wooden desk by the window on the north wall, a single chair and a two-drawer cabinet to the left of it. There was no sofa, no rug, no table and chairs, no TV, nothing hanging from the walls, none of the items one would expect to see in a living room.

'Like I said, *ese*,' Moreno said again. 'He's not here. I haven't seen him for several days.'

'It looks like he's *never* been here,' Garcia said, still looking around.

The living room offered two other doors, one that led to a small kitchen and the other to the bedroom and the bathroom.

While Garcia walked over to the window to pull open the curtains, Hunter moved into the bedroom. It was just as bare as the living room, with a single bed pushed up against the east wall, a bedside table with no drawers and a two-door wooden wardrobe.

There was no bedding on the bed, as if no one had ever slept there. Resting against the wardrobe were an empty plastic bucket and a string mop.

Hunter grabbed a pair of latex gloves from his pocket before pulling open the wardrobe doors.

Empty.

One drawer at the bottom of it.

Also empty.

Hunter got down on his knees and took a look under the bed and the wardrobe.

There was nothing there. There was nothing anywhere.

He lifted the mattress and checked under it.

Clear.

He ran his hand across the top of the wardrobe.

Nothing but what was expected – dust.

He pulled the wardrobe away from the wall and checked behind it.

Nothing on the wall.

Nothing on the back of the wardrobe.

Hunter reached for the plastic bucket and checked inside it. Completely dry. Not even a drop of water. He brought the bucket to his nose. It carried the same faint smell of bleach and disinfectant with a hint of orange as the living room.

Hunter put the bucket down and checked the string mop. There was still a little bit of moisture on its strings. It smelled identical to the bucket, only not as faint. Hunter guessed that it had been used no more than four, maybe five days ago.

He returned the mop to its place, turned and stepped into the small, white-tiled bathroom. There was a washing basin on the left with a fixed mirror on the wall above it. The toilet was against the wall opposite the basin, with the shower enclosure to its right. On the basin, Hunter found a shaving razor and a half-used tube of toothpaste – no toothbrush. The piece of soap inside the shower enclosure looked like it had only been used a couple of times. There were no towels of any sort inside the bathroom, paper or otherwise. No toilet paper either.

Hunter paused in front of the mirror and stared at his tired reflection for a moment, as though if he stared at it long and hard enough, the mirror would either tell him a story or reveal the reflection of who had last been standing before it.

Neither happened.

Hunter returned to the bedroom.

There was no doubt that apartment two-eleven was nothing more than a crash pad, a place Mathew Hade used from time to time and for only a day or so at a time. This was not where he lived – and if he really was who they were looking for, it certainly wasn't the place where he kept his victims.

Sixty-Five

While Hunter searched the bedroom and the bathroom inside Mathew Hade's apartment, Garcia checked the rest of the flat.

At least, this won't take long, he thought, approaching the only three furniture items in the barren living room.

The desk and chair seemed relatively new, but the old-looking two-drawer cabinet looked as though it had been salvaged from the city dump. It was covered in nicks and scratch marks. The good news was that the drawers had no locking mechanism, which made things a lot easier.

From his pocket, Garcia retrieved a pair of latex gloves and slipped them on before pulling open the cabinet's top drawer. Inside it, he found several sheets of regular, white printer paper, nothing else. He removed the sheets from the drawer and quickly fanned through them.

They were all blank.

Just to be sure, he swapped hands and fanned through them again from the other side.

Yes, all blank.

He returned them to the drawer before closing it and moving on to the bottom one. It slid open a lot less smoothly than the first drawer, as if one of its runners had been severely damaged.

From the look of the cabinet, Garcia didn't find that at all surprising.

The drawer came open only about halfway before jamming. Garcia tried again.

Same result. It was certainly jammed.

He tried once more, giving it a firm pull this time, but it made no difference, the drawer got stuck at the exact same point. But the firm pull made something that was lying at the back of the drawer roll forward – a red, BIC Cristal, ballpoint pen.

A millisecond later, Garcia's memory spat out images of the note the killer had sent Mayor Bailey, and the one that had been slid under Hunter's door. Both had been written on crisp white sheets of printer paper, and forensics had identified the pen used as a red, BIC Cristal, large ball-point pen.

Garcia reached for the pen inside the drawer and for a quick instant he felt the hairs on the back of his neck stand on end. On the body of the pen, in tiny white letters, he saw the BIC logo, followed by the words 'Cristal 1.6 mm'.

In his hand, he was holding a red, BIC Cristal, *large* ball-point pen.

Garcia curbed his excitement and retrieved a plastic evidence bag from his pocket. He dropped the pen inside it, sealing the bag.

Squatting down, Garcia looked inside the jammed drawer. It seemed empty. He stuck his hand inside it and felt around. Nothing. He closed the drawer and reopened the top one. From the paper pile inside it he retrieved the topmost sheet, before lifting it up to the window to study it against the light.

He was looking for impressions that could've been left behind. Depending on the pressure a person applies to a pen when writing, if a second sheet of paper is used as a base for the one that is being written on, partial and sometimes even full indentations might be left behind.

The sheet of paper was completely clear. No impressions of any kind.

Garcia reached for the sheet at the bottom of the pile and repeated the process, just in case he had returned the pile to the drawer the wrong way around after fanning through them.

Nothing.

Still, together with the red BIC Cristal, they would all be taken back to the forensics lab for further analysis.

Garcia left the living room and entered the kitchen. It was even more barren than the living room. There was a fridge-freezer at one end of the short kitchen worktop, a sink at the center of it and a small stove at the other end. Just under the worktop, Garcia saw two drawers together with three cupboards. Three other cupboards were mounted on to the wall above the sink. The only item on the chrome-plated dish rack to the left of the sink was a sponge. An electric kettle was to the left of the stove. There was no dishwasher, no washing machine and no microwave oven. Just like the rest of the apartment, a faint smell of bleach and disinfectant with a hint of orange lingered in the kitchen.

Garcia started by checking the fridge. There was nothing inside it except two small and unopened bottles of water. The inside of the fridge was sparkling clean. The freezer was completely empty.

Next he checked the three cupboards on the wall.

First one on the left.

Empty.

Middle one.

Empty.

Last cupboard.

Garcia found a can of tomato soup, a jar of coffee and a small pack of sugar, nothing else.

He moved on to the cupboards under the sink.

First one on the left.

He found a bottle of bleach, one of washing-up liquid, one trigger spray bottle of Orange Plus, two large sponges and a pack of cleaning cloths.

Middle one.

There were two plates, two tumblers and one coffee mug, all of them plastic.

Last cupboard.

Empty.

Garcia closed them all and reached for the sponge and the dish rack. Both were completely dry. No one had used either in a while.

He placed the sponge back on the rack and opened the drawer by the fridge.

Empty.

He walked to the other end of the kitchen worktop and opened the final drawer. All he found was one fork, one knife and a teaspoon – again, all of them plastic – together with a plain black book of matches with no logo on the front or back cover. He picked it up and flipped it open. The matches were also black with a bright red head. Five of them were missing. The inside of the book of matches differed from the outside because it was white instead of black.

Garcia stared at it for a couple of seconds before he finally realized what he was looking at.

Goosebumps rose on the back of his neck again.

'Fuck!'

Sixty-Six

With his back flat against the wall, Squirm sat alone in the darkness of his cell. His knees were pulled up against his chest and his arms hugged his legs so tightly they were starting to go pale. The tips of his toes were moving up and down robotically, as if tapping to the beat of a slow song only he could hear. Despite the darkness, the boy kept his one good eye open, staring at nothing at all. The pain in his left eye was still there but Squirm simply didn't care anymore.

'The Monster' had left soon after he had told Squirm how much money he'd been paid by the boy's father to take him away.

'Do you know what your father said to me?' the man had asked Squirm back in the kitchen. 'He told me that once I had taken "that plague" away from his life, I could do with you whatever I wished – kill you in whichever manner pleasured me most – as long as your body was never found. Now, what sort of father says something like that about his own child?'

Squirm had trembled at those words. Not because of the threat of death – in his own way he had already accepted that that was what was going to happen to him – but because he then knew that the story 'The Monster' had told him was true. That was exactly what his father used to call him – 'plague'.

Immediately, an avalanche of memories came crashing down inside the boy's mind.

All of them bad.

You're like a fucking disease, you hear? A goddamn plague that torments my life.

You are the reason your mother left, did you know that? You are a plague. No wonder you have no friends. Nobody likes you. Nobody wants you.

Get the hell out of my face, you fucking plague, or I will tear you a new asshole.

'I would've done it for nothing, you know?' 'The Monster' had said, bringing the boy back to reality. His next words, though delivered in a chillingly cold voice, were overflowing with what could only be described as a morbid passion.

'What can I say? I like killing people. I like looking into their eyes as life leaves them. I like to savor every drop of their fear. I like how they beg *me* for mercy . . . not God . . . *me*. I like how they cry. How they promise to do whatever I want. Yes, I like it all, Squirm, but most of all I like the way it makes me feel.'

The man had paused for a moment. Just talking about it had filled him with such exhilaration he was practically shaking.

'Do you know how killing someone makes you feel, Squirm? Powerful . . . strong . . . special. No one can ever again tell you that you don't matter because right at that moment you know that you matter more than God.' 'The Monster' moved his head from left to right and as he did so he shivered in a creepy sort of way. 'You are their God.'

'The Monster' had laughed at how spooked Squirm looked.

After that, 'The Monster' had locked Squirm back in his cell, telling him that he would see him later that night. That had been hours ago. Squirm had then sat down on his dirty mattress, hugged his legs and not moved from that position since.

The boy's rational mind didn't want to believe it but the more he thought about it, the more it all made sense.

Due to his father's inability to hold down a job, brought on by his struggle with alcohol, they had moved five times in the past three years. Eight times in the past five years, which made making friends a very difficult task and keeping them damn right impossible. That fact alone placed Squirm in a not very desirable category – the category of 'loner'. He had no friends and, since his mother left them, no family either, with the exception of his father. No one really knew who he was because he'd learned to play the 'loner' part terribly well. He kept himself to himself as much as he could, especially in school. He was, in everyone's eyes, the proverbial 'invisible boy' and that fitted his father's plan like a glove. All he had to do was drop by Squirm's school to let them know that they had to move again. That was it. Problem solved.

No one would find that odd due to the family history.

No one would ask any questions.

And no one would miss him.

His father could then move to a different city and start a new life as a single, childless man, because 'the plague' had finally been removed from his life.

The emptiness Squirm felt inside was so devastating it

made him break his promise to himself. Tears came to the boy's eyes and, alone in his cell, he cried.

Now he knew that no one was coming to save him, because no one was looking for him.

No one had ever been.

Sixty-Seven

Garcia was still in the kitchen when Hunter exited the bedroom and walked back into the living room of apartment two-eleven. He immediately spotted the two evidence bags that Garcia had left on top of the small desk by the window – one holding the red BIC Cristal pen and the other the sheets of white printer paper. As he checked them, the same splinter of excitement that had made the hairs on the back of Garcia's neck stand on end grabbed hold of Hunter for just a millisecond, but he knew better than to let excitement cloud his objectivity. They needed to get those evidence bags to the forensics lab ASAP.

'Robert!' Hunter heard his partner call. 'Come check this out.'

Hunter placed the evidence bags back on the desk and made his way into the kitchen.

Garcia was standing by the stove, with an urgent look on his face.

'What have you got?' Hunter asked.

Garcia flicked the book of matches Hunter's way and he caught it midair.

'Have a look inside,' Garcia urged him.

Hunter thumbed it open and paused. An annotation had been made on the cover's flipside. Hunter stared at it as if hypnotized, his heart beating just a little bit faster than a moment ago.

The annotation read – *Midazolam, 2.5 mg.*

'Do you know what that is?' Garcia asked.

'I think it's an anesthetic,' Hunter replied, his eyes never leaving the text.

Though Garcia didn't know the drug, he had guessed it to be some sort of sedative, but that wasn't what had excited him, or kept Hunter so transfixed.

The handwriting was.

The handwriting that they both had stared at for hours on end over the past few days.

The killer's.

Sixty-Eight

Hunter and Garcia's first stop after leaving Mathew Hade's apartment was the LAPD Scientific Investigation Division's Criminalistics Lab in El Sereno, East Los Angeles. On their way there, Hunter called Doctor Brian Snyder, the lead forensics agent who had attended Sharon Barnard's crime scene in Venice. He had just come back from a double homicide scene in Westlake.

Doctor Snyder came out to meet the detectives at the lab's reception lobby.

'Detectives,' he said, shaking their hands. 'Nice seeing you again. How can I help?'

Hunter gave him a quick summary of everything that had happened in the past twenty-four hours, before handing him the evidence bags he had with him.

Doctor Snyder studied them for a short moment, his eyes lingering over the book of matches for a little longer than they did the other items.

'Midazolam,' he read out loud, his voice full of concern.

'Do you know what that is?' Garcia asked.

Doctor Snyder nodded. 'Yes. Midazolam is a Benzodiazepine-based anesthetic with hypnotic properties.'

Garcia blinked twice.

'There are three Benzodiazepines in common anesthetic

use today,' he explained. 'Diazepam, Lorazepam and, especially, Midazolam. It is the most lipid-soluble of the three, which means that it's the fastest to be absorbed by the body and, therefore, also the quickest acting. Its main properties are sedation, relatively little respiratory and cardiac depression, anti-panic, anti-anxiety, anti-convulsant, and it's also a very strong, centrally acting muscle relaxant. It will induce unconsciousness, or a hypnotic state, in under thirty seconds, producing a very reliable level of amnesia very similar to the "black hole amnesia" caused by Rohypnol, the rape drug. The patient, or victim, will remember nothing.'

'So, in short,' Garcia commented, 'it's the perfect drug to quickly immobilize a victim.'

Doctor Snyder agreed with a nod. 'Or, depending on the dosage, to pacify them enough so they would offer no resistance. A person under a mild dosage of Midazolam would act as if he or she were drunk – very drunk, actually. To a passer-by, a perpetrator dragging a victim in that state would just look like somebody helping a drunken friend. That's all.' His gaze returned to the book of matches for an instant. 'But the dosage described here – two point five milligrams – is more than enough to completely subdue a subject as tall and as heavy as any of us.'

'How difficult is it to obtain?' Hunter asked.

'Not very. Especially with the clandestine sites you find on the net today. If you know where to search, it won't take long.'

'Perfect,' Garcia said.

'How long do you think it will take to process those, Doc?' Hunter asked.

The face Doctor Snyder made didn't fill them with confidence.

'I can put them through right now with an "urgent" request,' he told them. 'And I promise that I'll do all I can to move them as close to the top of the pile as possible. If I get lucky, I can probably have the result of the handwriting analysis back to you by tomorrow, or the day after.' He reflexively checked his watch as he mentioned the time frame. 'As for the rest, I'm really not sure. Maybe two days . . . maybe more.'

Hunter and Garcia knew that there was nothing more they, or Doctor Snyder, could do. The Criminalistics Laboratory was part of the Hertzberg-Davis Forensic Science Center at the LA Regional Crime Lab and the whole facility was shared jointly by five different organizations, all of them wanting results back by yesterday. Their technicians had more work than they could possibly handle. An urgent request by one of their own sure was an advantage, but not a guarantee. For now, all they could do was wait.

Sixty-Nine

Hunter managed only three and a half hours of sleep before his brain was fully awake again. He kept his eyes shut for another minute or two, hoping, willing, but deep inside he knew that it was a futile exercise. No matter how hard he wished, no matter how tightly he squeezed his eyes, sleep would not come back.

Finally giving up, he rolled over in bed and opened his eyes. Unorganized thoughts collided against each other inside his head, creating an undecipherable mess that only served to confuse him more. He breathed out a leaden breath, swung his feet off the bed and sat at its edge, giving his eyes a chance to get rid of the stupor of sleep. He checked the digital clock by his bed – 4:55 a.m.

In the bathroom, Hunter washed his face and brushed his teeth before regarding himself in the mirror just above the washbasin for an instant. He looked exhausted. His eyes were half bloodshot and the circles under them were starting to look like badly applied makeup.

Entering his living room, and without even thinking about it, he checked the floor by the front door.

Nothing.

No envelopes.

He shook his head as he considered the silliness of what he'd just done.

But was it really? he heard the little voice at the back of his mind ask. The killer had done it once, and there was nothing to keep him from doing it again. In his entire career as an RHD detective, Hunter had never dealt with a more unpredictable predator.

He crossed the living room and entered the kitchen. After pouring himself a glass of water from the tap, he pulled open the fridge door and looked inside. Its emptiness made him chuckle. All he had was the still-untouched energy drink, a couple of apples and three dried-up slices of pizza – hot pepperoni. The beef jerk pieces were all gone, but cold pizza was probably Hunter's favorite breakfast. He had practically lived on it throughout his college years.

He grabbed a pizza slice and walked back into his living room. Once again, he checked the floor by his front door.

Nothing.

'OK, Robert, you're going to have to stop doing this,' he said to himself as he took a bite of his pizza. To him, it actually tasted better than when it was piping hot.

He walked up to the window and peeked outside, searching for nothing at all. He lived in a quiet corner of Huntingdon Park and, as far as he could see, the streets still looked dead.

He had another bite of his pizza and turned away from the window. On the table by his small bar was a photocopy of the killer's third note. He'd read it so many times that he could probably recite it backwards, word for word.

He checked the clock on the wall – 5:11 a.m.

Hunter finished eating his pizza slice, went back into the kitchen and grabbed a second one. On his way back, he checked the floor again.

Nothing.

He cursed himself for his paranoia and paused by the note. He decided not to sit down. From his standing position, he read it again a couple of times. Just like before, nothing stood out.

He concentrated on the last part of the note.

Do you want to know who I am, Detective Hunter?
Do you really want to know?

He paused.

Well, the clues are in the name.
FOR I AM DEATH.

Hunter was sure that it wasn't an attempt at being funny or sarcastic.

He read the whole thing one more time.

Zilch. He could think of nothing.

Hunter gave up.

As he looked away from the note and in the direction of his bar, his gaze grazed the last few lines. It was as if, for some reason, his brain decided to mix up the words and the letters in a peculiar way. For a split second he saw something that made him freeze in place.

'What the hell?'

Hunter stared at it again, his breathing calm, his eyes searching for what he had just seen.

Nothing.

'Where is it?' he breathed out, trying again, willing his eyes to find it.

He couldn't see it.

Had he imagined it?

Hunter looked away, blinked a couple of times and then looked back at the note.

Not there.

Maybe he had imagined it.

He did it again, but this time he only allowed his gaze to just scrape over the letters.

His breathing caught in his throat.

There it was.

Seventy

Garcia pulled into an empty space in the Police Administration Building parking lot, shut off the car's engine and checked the screen display on his cellphone for the tenth time since he'd gotten out of bed that morning. It showed nothing. No missed calls. No text messages.

Even without confirmation from the forensics lab, what they'd found yesterday in Mathew Hade's apartment was enough to send alarm bells ringing everywhere. An APB had been sent out to every police station and sheriff's department in the Los Angeles area. A design expert from the LAPD IT Division had used the mugshot they had of Mathew Hade and created a series of variations to the way he might now look, adding different hairstyles, hair colors and facial hair. A note was added to the APB alerting everyone to keep in mind that the subject had, very possibly, become quite skillful with makeup and disguise and that the images were to be used mainly as guidelines.

After a lengthy meeting with Hunter and Garcia, Captain Blake authorized an around-the-clock surveillance operation on Mathew Hade's apartment. The first LAPD Special Investigation Section team had been dispatched to the address last night.

The LAPD SIS was an Elite Tactical Surveillance squad

that had existed for more than forty years, despite efforts from various human rights and political groups to shut it down. The reason for such efforts was that their kill rate was higher than that of any other unit in the department, including SWAT. SIS teams were mainly used to stealthily watch apex predators – individuals suspected of violent crimes who would not cease until caught in the act. Masters of disguise and surveillance, every SIS officer was an expert in close-quarters combat as well as a distinguished marksman. Their main tactic was to wait to observe a suspect committing new crimes before moving in to make arrests. Due to the fact that most suspects would not surrender without a fight, lethal force was often used. With that in mind, all SIS teams for this operation were under specific orders that if Mathew Hade was sighted, he was not to be approached. Their job was to keep him under surveillance and not lose him until the detectives in charge of the investigation got there.

As Garcia took the elevator up to the fifth floor, he checked his phone one more time.

Still nothing.

He'd been at his desk for less than a minute when Hunter pushed open the door and stepped inside. Despite how exhausted Hunter looked, Garcia picked up something else in his expression – a mixture of doubt and excitement.

'Have you heard anything?' Garcia asked, instinctively peeking at his cellphone yet again. He had nothing.

'Not yet, have you?'

Garcia shook his head. 'Nothing from the SIS team, the sheriff's department or any other LAPD station. I'm just about to check emails, but if we had anything from forensics I'm sure Doctor Snyder would've already called one of us.'

'I've received nothing either,' Hunter confirmed, also checking his cellphone. His 'silent' switch was off and his ringer volume was cranked up to the maximum. 'But I'd like you to have a look at something and tell me if I'm losing my mind or not,' he added, returning his phone to his pocket and approaching the picture board.

'OK.' Garcia swiveled his chair around, intrigued.

'This morning,' Hunter began. 'I thought I saw something on the note that I hadn't picked up before.'

The intensity with which Hunter delivered his statement made Garcia get to his feet.

'And what was that?' He joined Hunter by the board.

'What does the killer call himself?' Hunter asked.

Garcia frowned. 'What?'

'On the notes, what does the killer call himself?'

Garcia looked at all three notes on the board before his gaze moved back to Hunter.

'Death,' he replied, flipping his palms up, as people do when giving an obvious answer.

'So why doesn't he sign them as "Death"?'

Garcia's expression was one of total confusion.

'OK, maybe you have lost it, Robert. That's exactly how he signs his notes.'

'No, it isn't,' Hunter came back. 'He signs them "I am death", not just "Death". Why?'

Garcia regarded the notes again. 'What? I'm not sure I'm following you?'

'Just look at them, Carlos.' Hunter tapped the board. 'They all end with the phrase "I am death", not just the word "death". No other killer who has ever taunted the police with notes or messages has done that – Jack the Ripper, the BTK Killer, the Zodiac Killer, Son of Sam, whoever, it doesn't matter: they all signed their notes with just a name, not a sentence.'

Garcia pondered this for a moment before accepting it. 'OK, fine, but what difference does it make?'

'Probably none, if not for what he wrote in his last message.' Hunter indicated the note.

Well, the clues are in the name.
FOR I AM DEATH.

'I see that,' Garcia said, lifting his hands again in a surrendering gesture. 'But I'm still not sure where you're going with this, Robert.'

'This guy likes to play,' Hunter said. 'We all know that by now. The notes are part of his game and, if we are correct in our assumption, he considers himself too smart for us. Actually, too smart for anyone. Playing a game against someone who is so much inferior to him is no fun. And he wants to make this fun.'

'OK,' Garcia agreed.

'At first, you believed this could be his way of being funny or sarcastic, remember? But what if he isn't being funny? What if he really is giving us a clue?'

The blank stare on Garcia's face remained.

'Look at this,' Hunter said. 'He wrote: "the clues are *in* the name".' He emphasized the word 'in' and at the same time tapped it on the board with his index finger. 'Not the name. He also uses the word "clues", not clue, indicating that there's more than one.'

Garcia looked at the note again. This time, his expression showed concentration.

'*In* it,' Hunter said again and paused.

Garcia kept his attention on the board, a few dots just starting to connect in his mind. '*In* it . . . You mean, like an anagram?'

'Precisely,' Hunter said, his voice just a little more excited than a moment ago. 'But don't look only at the word "Death". Look at the whole sentence. "I am Death" – that's how he signs every note. That's what he placed inside Nicole Wilson's throat. That's what he left us at Sharon Barnard's crime scene.'

Without waiting for Garcia to start trying combinations, Hunter picked up a marker, wrote the sentence 'I am death' on an empty space on the board and, as he used a letter from that phrase, he crossed it off the original sentence. When he was done, he put the marker down.

Garcia had been following everything with the utmost attention. When Hunter stopped, Garcia looked at what he had written, then back at the original sentence, then back to the board.

Without noticing, his jaw had dropped open.

'No fucking way.'

Seventy-One

Alison coughed and spluttered awake with a jolt as freezing water was splashed on to her face. Her natural reaction was to shake her head, but she immediately regretted it. The pain that the movement awakened inside her skull was so acute she believed her brain was being squeezed by a giant pair of pincers. But the pain she felt inside her head was nothing compared to how her body agonized as the water dripped down from her face and made contact with the tens of open wounds on her torso, arms and legs. One would be forgiven for believing that the animalistic scream she let out belonged to some dying beast.

She coughed again, this time trying to open her eyes, but her eyelids felt heavy and sticky and it required an effort of will to force them open. Water trickled into her gasping mouth and she finally understood why it made everything hurt so much. The water was heavy with a salty, vinegary taste.

A single drop made it past her right eyelid and as it coated her cornea it stung at her eyeball. Immediately, her eyes shot closed once again before she started blinking ferociously, which she did for almost a full minute.

Pain now came at her from all angles and she grunted as her body began shaking, unable to handle the brutality of it all. She braced herself for another bucket full of vinegary water over her head but it never came.

Alison finally blinked her eyes open again. The sting was still there but not as incapacitating as before. The blurriness was now very subtle.

The man was standing directly in front of her. Immobile. Staring.

They finally locked eyes. The feeling of familiarity was still there, but no matter how hard she tried, her brain just couldn't place him.

The man had lowered the chain that held her arms by a few inches. Alison's feet could now properly touch the ground, but her legs carried no strength. The bulk of her weight was still being held by her arms and the chain shackled to her wrists – which had now lost their skin. Metal was resting against unprotected raw flesh. Her hands felt like blood-filled balloons and a tiny prick was all that was needed for them to burst spectacularly.

Because Alison kept slipping in and out of consciousness, she had no way of telling the time. No way of knowing how long she had been held captive.

In silence, the man continued to study Alison. Her naked body had been made even more beautiful by all the small cuts and lacerations he had made. At least that was how he saw it. The blood that had flowed from them had recolored her skin in beautiful crimson and that vision filled him with an almost uncontrollable excitement, and his body responded accordingly.

They stared at each other for a long while until, surprisingly, the man was the first to break eye contact. He turned and walked over to the workshop table in the corner.

The action caused panic to erupt inside Alison. She had

already been whipped and flogged like an eighteenth-century slave, until she had passed out. She had never experienced pain that deep, that debilitating.

'Oh, please, no.' The words stumbled out of her cracked lips, as her eyes were once again filled with tears. 'No . . . not again.'

Alison had no idea why she was there, why the man had taken her or why he was punishing her in the way he was. Was he connected to her father? He had barely said a word to her. All he did was either watch her or beat her up.

'Please, talk to me . . .' she pleaded. 'Why are you doing this to me?'

Ignoring her, the man picked up something from the workshop table.

Every muscle in Alison's body tensed up. She wanted to plead again but she couldn't speak anymore. Her sobs were too intense for that.

The man turned to face her again.

Alison squinted, trying to focus on what he held in his hand, but whatever it was it was too small for her to see.

The man got closer.

Three steps.

Two.

One.

Alison caught a glimpse of something metallic between his fingers.

A knife?

A scalpel?

What?

There was nothing she could do but cry uncontrollably. She closed her eyes and held her breath, bracing herself.

A moment later, she heard the sound of metal scraping against the concrete floor.

Her eyes squeezed tighter.

A few seconds after that, she felt her body swing forward just a little but, surprisingly, it was accompanied by no further pain.

Her first thought was that maybe her body was already so battered that it just hadn't registered the pain yet.

She waited.

The pain finally came.

And from where else but her arms? So powerful, she felt consciousness slipping away from her again. Her eyes fluttered as she exhaled and, in her mind, her body began a slow descent into a dark and cold abyss.

But before she hit its bottom, something, or someone, caught her. Right at that moment, her legs turned to jelly and she slumped down on to something hard and uncomfortable. She breathed in a full mouth of hot, humid air, and that was when she realized that she wasn't imagining it. She wasn't falling down into an abyss, she was simply falling down.

The man had grabbed a set of padlock keys and freed her from her shackles. The metal scraping sound she'd heard earlier was a fold-up chair he had dragged and placed under her legs.

As she collapsed into the chair, her arms dropped down to her sides and the sensation that followed was a mixture of total relief together with immeasurable pain. Blood began to freely flow through them for the first time in who knew how long. The feeling was so intense that her body couldn't take it. She curved forward and vomited on to the floor.

Surprisingly, that did not upset her captor. When she was

done, he grabbed her by her hair and pulled her back up into a sitting position.

Slobs of vomit dripped down from her lips on to her naked torso and legs. She started breathing deeply, her chest rising and falling in a broken rhythm. Her arms now began to feel like they were on fire. One million pins and needles found their way into her hands and fingers.

Alison's head slumped forward again, her chin coming into contact with her chest. The man, realizing that she was about to pass out, grabbed her by the hair and pulled her head back.

'No, no, no. Stay with me, Alison. I need you awake. I need you to feel *everything*.'

Her jaw fell open and he spat inside her mouth.

'Are you listening to me?'

She half coughed, half gagged on his spit. It tasted like sour milk and rotten eggs, but it had the desired effect. It brought Alison back to consciousness.

'That's my girl,' the man said, letting go of her hair and taking a step back.

This time Alison was able to hold her head in place by herself, but something made her doubt that she was one hundred percent conscious. As the man moved toward the workshop table once again, she caught a glimpse of something that froze her soul. In one of the corners of the basement, hidden in the shadows, she could swear that she saw a little boy. He was staring straight at her. The terror in his eyes easily matched the fear in hers.

Seventy-Two

'I'm not sure why,' Hunter said. 'Maybe it was because I was so tired when I reread the note again in the early hours of this morning, but for some reason my brain mixed up the letters in a strange way and for a split second, I saw it . . . Then it was gone.'

Garcia was still staring at the board.

'I thought I was imagining things, but I kept on blinking, looking away, then looking back at it again.' Hunter paused, following his partner's gaze. 'And then, as if it were a dream, the letters just moved around right in front of my eyes.' He tapped the board one more time. 'And I saw this.'

From the letters in 'I Am Death' Hunter had created three new words: 'I Mat Hade'.

'No fucking way,' Garcia said again, his eyes finally leaving the board. He faced Hunter.

'I also found it hard to believe, but it's there.'

'I know this killer is fucking bold,' Garcia said. 'He's daring and all, but this is ridiculous, Robert.' He pointed at the board. 'It's unprecedented. He's not giving us a clue. He's giving us his name. Why would he do that?'

'Because he doesn't know we know,' Hunter said. 'He doesn't know we know about Fresno, about Sacramento, or about his place in East LA. He has no idea that we have a suspect on the books and that suspect is Mathew Hade – Mat Hade. In fact, when he delivered the note to my door we didn't have a suspect. We didn't know who Mat Hade was, remember? That came later.'

Garcia began making all the connections.

'So,' he said. 'Even if we had figured out then that the clues he was referring to in his note were in the form of an anagram, we didn't know what to look for – a word, a couple of words, a phrase, a name, what? We had no way of knowing that what he was giving us was his actual name. With that in mind, how many possible words or combinations of words could we make from those letters?'

'Exactly.'

Garcia looked back at the sentence: 'I Am Death'.

'And of those,' Hunter added, 'how many do you think could form some sort of a name, or a contraction of a name, like "Mat", or "Ted", or whatever? And remember, this is Los Angeles. This place is an international hub. This name we're talking about doesn't necessarily need to be an American name.'

'And even if we did come up with the phrase "I Mat Hade",' Garcia said, 'we would've probably discarded it because, in all truth, we would've had no idea that it was an actual name. Family names can come in all shapes and forms . . . and spellings.'

'Precisely. It would've been unrealistic for us to verify every possible anagram. What would we have done, run background checks on every combination that spelled out a name or part of one? Not likely.'

Garcia chuckled at the cleverness of it all.

'So he created the anagram because he was never expecting us to find out about him, about Mathew Hade,' Garcia theorized. 'Why would we? The odds of us finding out about him were bordering on zero. He was never arrested. Never charged with anything. He was just a person of interest in three different abduction investigations, two in Fresno and one in Sacramento, but never here in LA. And all that happened years ago. Not in a million years was he expecting us to find out about any of that.'

'Probably not,' Hunter accepted it. 'All we need is for that phone to ring now.'

As if on cue, Hunter's cellphone rang loudly, rattling against his desktop.

Garcia's eyes widened.

'You've got to be kidding.'

Seventy-Three

Hunter couldn't remember ever taking a call so quickly. He dashed toward his desk, his feet almost scuffing against the floor, his hand shooting out in the direction of his cellphone.

'Detective Hunter, Robbery Homicide Division.'

'Detective,' the male voice at the other end of the line said. 'It's Brian.'

In his excitement, it took Hunter a second to match the name to the voice, and then both of them to a face.

'Doctor Brian Snyder, with SID,' the doctor clarified, picking up on Hunter's hesitation.

Maybe it had taken Hunter more than just a second.

Garcia looked at Hunter, the question practically written in his eyes.

'Doctor,' Hunter said, shaking his head at Garcia. 'Of course. I'm sorry.' He paddled back fast. 'It's been an eventful morning so far.'

'Have you found your suspect?' he asked, his voice shifting from calm to half-excited.

'No, not yet, but we're hopeful. Have you got something for us?'

'I do,' he confirmed. 'The results of the handwriting analysis.'

'OK. Just a sec, Doc. Let me put you on speakerphone.' Hunter keyed in the necessary command and placed the phone back on his desk.

Garcia stepped closer.

'All right,' Doctor Snyder began. 'Graphologists will need on average thirteen to fifteen different letters out of the twenty-six we have in the English alphabet to achieve a "one hundred percent" positive match. As I'm sure you're aware, the annotation inside the book of matches you gave me – Midazolam, 2.5 mg – contains only eight different letters, and two numbers.'

Garcia glanced at Hunter.

'So for us to achieve that indisputable positive match, you'd need to find something else with his handwriting on it.'

'Well,' Garcia said, before Doctor Snyder was able to continue. 'For now, that's pretty much out of the question, Doc. Any sort of partial confirmation?'

'I was just about to get to that.'

'Oh sorry,' Garcia said, lifting his hands and quickly using Hunter's 'paddle back' excuse. 'Eventful morning.'

'Our graphologist said that though legally he cannot one hundred percent confirm it as a match, by analyzing the curvature of some of the letters, together with the way in which the person who wrote them connects them to one another, he would stake his professional reputation on the assumption that whoever jotted down that annotation is the same person who wrote both of the notes. In short, he's your killer.'

Seventy-Four

Los Angeles 9-1-1 Emergency Response System operator Talicia Leon removed her curved-frame glasses, placed them on her desk just next to her empty coffee mug and rubbed her tired eyes with her thumb and forefinger. She was about to tell Justin, the operator sitting in the booth to her right, that she was taking a five-minute coffee break when a brand new call came onto her monitor.

Talicia quickly reached for her glasses again.

Coffee would have to wait.

'Nine-one-one, what's your emergency?' she said as she took the call, adjusting her headset.

'Yes, I have a problem.' The voice at the end of the line was female. Though she sounded a little distressed, Talicia got the feeling that the woman was trying hard to keep it all together. 'For some reason, my savings accounts seems to have been blocked. I can't get to my money and I need to transfer funds from one account to the other ASAP.'

Oh great, Talicia thought. *Another dumbass call.*

On average, Talicia answered around ten completely non-related emergency calls a week. Some of them were damn right stupid.

'Ma'am, you've reached nine-one-one emergency,' she replied calmly. 'Not your bank.'

'Yes, that's right,' the woman replied. 'It's not allowing me to do it over the Internet, that's why I'm calling. I need this problem fixed ASAP, please.' This time, the woman emphasized the letters 'A-S-A-P' and the word 'please' came out a little shaky. 'Do you think you can help me?'

'I don't think so, ma'am. This is nine-one-one emergency, not Bank of America. Do you have an emergency or not?'

'Of course. I wouldn't be calling otherwise. My name is Vivian Curtis.'

All of a sudden it dawned on Talicia that this might not be a crank call at all. Her voice became a lot more serious.

'So, Vivian, you do have an emergency.' She didn't phrase it as a question.

'Yes.'

'And at the moment you're unable to talk because there's someone there with you?'

'That's correct, I've already keyed in my account number and passcode. The address registered to the account is 13605 South Vermont Avenue, Gardena, 90247.'

'Got that, Vivian.' Talicia was already typing as fast as she could, and she was fast. 'Are you under any physical threat?'

'Yes.'

'Are you hurt?'

'Yes. Will this take long? I need to attend to my daughter.'

'Your daughter is also hurt and under physical threat?' Talicia pressed 'enter' on her keyboard, dispatching the primary emergency message.

'Yes, that's right. Of course I authorize it. It's my money. I would like to transfer the whole amount. How soon will it be before either myself or my partner can withdraw the money from an ATM?'

'The threat is your partner?'

'Um-hum.'

'OK, Vivian, help is on its way. Just hold tight. They'll be with you in less than four minutes. Can you stay on the line with me? Calls to banks tend to be lengthy and we can pretend there's some sort of minor complication before the funds are able to be released.'

'OK, I'll wait.'

'How old is your daughter, Vivian?'

'I think that was on the twelfth of this month.'

'Do you or your daughter have any life-threatening injuries?'

'No. I haven't received anything yet.'

The word 'yet' worried Talicia.

'Are there any firearms in the house?'

'Yes, I have entered it *twice* already.'

Two weapons. 'Is your partner in possession of any of them?'

'No, not at the moment. Thank you.'

Talicia quickly typed in some new instructions.

'Is the front or back door, if you have one, unlocked, Vivian? Help is almost there.'

'Yes. As I've said, transfer *everything*.'

Both doors unlocked.

'So, is it OK to just drop by an ATM and withdraw the funds now?' Vivian's voice was getting more and more distressed.

'They're seconds away, Vivian. Just turning into your street now. Even if you tell him right now that he can go and get the money out, he won't make it past your front porch.'

'OK. Thank you very much for your help.'

The call disconnected.

Talicia immediately checked the history for calls related to Vivian's address. There had been six in the past eight months. All of them for domestic violence.

Before Talicia could even breathe out, a new call lit up her screen.

'Nine-one-one, what's your emergency?' She pushed her glasses up on to the bridge of her nose.

'She's dead.' This time, the voice at the other end of the line was male. The serenity with which he delivered those words made Talicia feel a little uncomfortable.

'Are you reporting a murder, sir?' Talicia's fingers were already cruising over her keyboard once again.

'There's so much blood. Her screams were so full of pain and fear. It was beautiful.'

Every inch of skin on Talicia's body turned cold. She coughed to clear her throat.

'I'm sorry, sir. Who did you say is dead?'

'Number three.'

Talicia halted her typing for just a moment.

'Are you saying that there are three people who are dead?'

'You are not listening to me, are you?' the man said calmly, but didn't give Talicia a chance to reply. 'Number three is dead. Her name is Alison. Number four will soon follow. A lot sooner than you think . . . for I am death.'

This time, the thought that came to Talicia's mind was the opposite of what she had thought about the previous call. What had started seriously was now beginning to sound bogus.

'Did you get that? Alison. Her name is Alison. Make sure you have it. Make sure they know it.'

Talicia couldn't risk it.

'Alison. Yes, I got it, sir. Do you have a last name for her?'

'Good. Now write this down. Are you ready?'

'Yes, sir, I'm ready.'

'I. Am. Death. Tell that to the cops when you dispatch them.'

'I got it,' Talicia said. 'What address shall I dispatch them to?'

'Run your trace. Find this phone and you'll find her.'

'Sir? Hello? Sir?

The line didn't disconnect but the caller was gone.

Seventy-Five

Lopez Canyon Road, in Lake View Terrace, stretches out from Foothill Freeway all the way into the small western tip of the Angeles National Forest, before sharply bending right and reaching Kagel Canyon Road, where it finally ends. Less than a mile after the sharp right bend, a disused and uneven road forks out and to the right of it, going up a small hill. The call that Talicia had taken had come from there; more specifically, from inside an abandoned wooden building right at the top of that road.

It was past two in the afternoon when Hunter and Garcia received a second call from Doctor Snyder. He had just arrived at the crime scene and, as he entered the building, the first thing he did was reach for his phone and call the UV detectives.

Even with the sirens on, the twenty-five-mile drive that saw Hunter and Garcia cutting through South Central before hooking on to Glendale Boulevard, and finally to the western tip of the Angeles National Forest, took them an hour.

Thanks to the isolated location, and the fact that the whole of the disused road was flanked by nothing more than rough terrain and dense, impassable shrubs, the LAPD could set a perimeter right at the road's entrance. No reporter or press van was able to get within a mile of the building.

Garcia flashed his credentials at the officers by the outer crime-scene tape, took a right and drove up the bouncy road.

'Is this place secluded and out of the way enough for you, or what?' Garcia asked as he parked by a forensic-van at the top of the road.

Hunter had just checked his cellphone – still no news about Mathew Hade.

As they exited Garcia's car, Hunter took a moment to study the building.

It was a relatively small, rectangular, wooden structure, with an old-style gable roof. Entrance was through large double doors at the eastern end of it. Both Hunter and Garcia's first impression was that the building very closely resembled a barn, with the exception that its roof wasn't as high as one would expect it to be. The outside had once been painted white but, after years of being battered by sun and rain, only small patches of color remained. Also, as a result of their harsh contact with the elements, a few planks of wood from the south wall, the one that they were facing, were either partially missing or broken.

Three police officers stood to the right of the double doors. All three of them looked like they'd just been sick.

As Hunter and Garcia approached the yellow crime-scene tape that further restricted the entrance to the building, they were greeted by a peculiar smell that came from inside – a mixture of rotten food and a sweet, metallic odor. Both detectives recognized the smell immediately because they'd been around it too many times.

Blood.

And lots of it.

They flashed their credentials at the lone officer with the crime-scene log book, who handed them a Tyvek coverall and a pair of latex gloves each.

Hunter and Garcia suited up, stooped under the yellow tape and pushed open the doors. They'd taken only two steps inside before the force of the image that met their eyes sucked all the air from their lungs, and held them fast.

They now understood why the officers outside looked like they'd been sick.

But the savagery of what stood before them wasn't what had driven Hunter and Garcia to a stunned silence, or made their hearts skip a beat.

It was the fact that they both knew who the victim was.

Seventy-Six

Hunter and Garcia stood at the entrance to a large open area. Just like the impression they'd got from the outside, the inside also reminded them of a ranch barn, only to a smaller scale. The harsh sun in the sky outside, beating down on the building's old wood walls and black gable roof, made its interior feel like an oven. They had been inside for less than ten seconds and beads of sweat were already starting to form on their foreheads and on the back of their necks.

Doctor Snyder was standing toward the back of the room, talking something over with one of his forensics agents. As he saw the detectives come through the doors, he made his way over to greet them. He had to travel around the edge of the room to avoid all the blood.

'Robert. Carlos,' he said with a small nod. His coverall was zipped up to the base of his neck but the hood was down, resting against the back of his shoulders. Once again, he had no nose mask.

Both detectives returned the gesture but kept their attention focused solely on the female victim before them. Her head was slumped forward, with her chin touching her chest, but her face was still visible. And that was what Hunter and Garcia seemed so transfixed by.

Doctor Snyder narrowed his eyes at them. Something wasn't adding up. Despite the brutality of the entire scene and the amount of blood splashed around the place, their gaze was cemented firmly on the victim's face. Why? The doctor spoke again.

'Her name is—'

'Alison,' Hunter said almost robotically. 'I don't know her last name.'

Intrigue turned to surprise in Doctor Snyder's eyes. 'You know her?'

'We both do,' Garcia said. 'She's a waitress at Donny's.' He paused, closed his eyes, subtly shook his head and corrected himself. '*Was* a waitress at Donny's, a diner two blocks away from the PAB. We sometimes eat there.'

Doctor Snyder processed that information in silence before adding, 'Atkins. Her name was Alison Atkins. She was twenty-eight years old.' He read the way Garcia looked at him and added, before he could ask the question, 'The killer used her cellphone to make the nine-one-one call. Once he was done, he put the phone down by the door but never disconnected. He wanted it traced so we could find her.'

Hunter immediately made a mental note to get a copy of the 911 call as soon as they got back to the Police Administration Building.

'She was a very sweet woman,' Hunter said. 'Always smiling. Always very polite. The type who loved life.'

There was a new emotion in Hunter's voice that Doctor Snyder failed to properly identify. Sadness? Anger? He couldn't tell.

'Do you think that she became a victim because you knew her?' he asked.

Hunter's focus hadn't yet diverted from Alison's face. He gave Doctor Snyder the slightest of shrugs. Right at that moment, he really didn't know the answer to that question.

The doctor looked again at the victim.

Alison had been stripped naked. Her arms had been shackled together at the wrists by a long metal chain, which in turn had been looped around the thickest of the three wood beams that ran across the ceiling. The loop was kept in place by a small padlock. Alison's arms were fully extended above her head. Her feet grazed the floor beneath them just enough to stop her body from moving around.

There was so much blood on the floor directly under her body that, at first guess, Hunter would have said that she had bled to death. But what Hunter and Garcia knew had made the police officers outside lose their lunch by the side of the building was the way in which she had bled out.

A horizontal incision, which crossed her body from side to side, had been made across her lower abdominal area. Once the incision had been made, her lower gastrointestinal tract, or small and large intestines, had been removed from her abdominal cavity and left on the floor in front of her. But neither her small nor her large intestine had been completely severed from her body. They were still attached at the highest point – the stomach.

'The killer disemboweled her?' Garcia asked disbelievingly, his eyes now moving to the large pool of blood on the floor.

'That's exactly what he did,' Doctor Snyder confirmed.

The killer had cut open the victim's abdomen, reached inside and gutted her while she was still alive.

As Garcia breathed in, he felt his body shiver.

'I've seen disemboweled bodies before,' he said, his

voice restrained, 'but I've never seen one where the intestines have been completely stretched out this way. How long can it get to?'

Doctor Snyder kept his eyes on Alison Atkins' eviscerated body for a moment longer before following Garcia's.

'Both intestines together will measure about twenty-five feet in length,' he said, the tone of his voice matching the detective's.

The killer hadn't only dragged her small and large intestines out of her abdominal cavity. He had also stretched them to their full extent, twisting and looping them around at points. The visual result was as unbelievable as it was grotesque. As the victim hung in the air with her arms stretched out above her head, the entirety of her lower gastrointestinal tract could be seen exiting her body as if it were an oversized, alien, umbilical cord. It then lay extended, twisted and looped outside her body, splashed on to the floor, lying in an enormous pool of blood.

But what boggled the mind was that all this had been done while she was still alive and, most probably, conscious. Death would've come very slowly and in agonizing pain. Neither Hunter nor Garcia needed to ask. They both knew those facts very well.

'I wanted both of you to see her *in situ* before we cut her down,' Doctor Snyder said. 'As you can tell, this place feels a like a sauna, which will speed up the decomposition process. Rigor mortis had just started to set in when we got here, which means that the killer waited for her to die before making the call. She died no more than three to five hours ago.'

Hunter finally allowed his attention to deviate from Alison. Garcia did the same. As they turned around and faced the large doors behind them, they paused.

There it was.

Written in blood across the inside of both doors was the killer's signature – I AM DEATH.

'Do you think he filmed it again?' Doctor Snyder asked, also facing the morbid script.

'Probably,' Garcia replied. 'Filming it, or taking pictures, or whatever, is his token. His trophy. His sick way of keeping them alive for ever. To him, the recording itself would be just as important as the attack, or the victim, or the violence.'

In silence, all three of them looked around for another full minute before the doctor spoke again.

'The place is an absolute mess. It's been abandoned for years. There's debris here dating back to who knows when. If we decide to look at everything, we might be here for days.' He paused and made a face.

Hunter had no idea if they'd find anything in there. If they did, it was because the killer wanted them to, but it now made no difference. What the killer didn't know was that they already knew who he was. They just needed to find him.

Seventy-Seven

Hunter and Garcia spent the rest of the afternoon at the crime scene in the Angeles National Forest. They watched as Alison Atkins was freed from her shackles, placed inside a body bag and loaded into a coroner's van. Her intestines were carefully collected by one of Doctor Snyder's forensic agents. Despite all his years of experience, at times he looked like he was about to be sick.

Both detectives were still checking their phones every five minutes or so. Still no sign of Mat Hade. Hunter had also checked with the State of California Department of Motor Vehicles – Mathew Hade had no vehicles registered under his name at present. His last one had been a used 2003 black Ford Escape, which he'd acquired in February 2007 and kept until October 2014. After that, nothing. He also had no outstanding fines.

At 8:30 p.m. Hunter and Garcia received another call from Doctor Snyder. He had the first of the two test results they'd been waiting for – the pen ink analyses. Forensics had first collected a small ink sample from the note the killer had sent Mayor Bailey and chemically compared it to the ink in the BIC Cristal Garcia had found inside Mat Hade's apartment. The result had been inconclusive. But forensics hadn't given up. They'd placed the ballpoint pen under a Leica digital microscope and found out that the roller ball at its tip had a couple of faults – scratches. Those scratches, though invisible to the naked eye, would certainly show on any sort of stroke made by the pen. When they'd placed the note under the same microscope, they'd got a perfect match. The killer's note had been written with that exact same pen.

They had their guy.

They just didn't have their guy *yet*.

With this new discovery, a new APB had also been sent out. Orders had been updated from 'observe and inform the case detectives' to 'carefully approach and apprehend'. All they had to do now was sit and wait until Mat Hade was arrested. They just had to hope that this would happen before he claimed another victim.

Garcia went home at around 9:00 p.m., but only after Hunter practically ordered him to.

'Get the hell out of here, Carlos,' he said, pointing at the door. 'Because if you don't, Anna won't be angry with you, she'll be angry with me. And I'd rather face the wrath of a serial killer any day than that of a pissed-off woman, especially Anna.'

'That is a very wise decision, my friend,' Garcia said as he powered down his computer. 'Because when she gets angry, she could make the devil look like Casper the friendly ghost.' He paused as he reached the office door. 'How about you, Robert? You're not going to spend the night in here again, are you? There's nothing else we can do but wait. He'll get picked up soon enough. We have the whole of the LAPD and the Sheriff's Department looking for him. He can't hide for ever.'

'Yeah, I know. I'll be leaving soon. I just need to check on a few more things first and I'll be right behind you. Ten, fifteen minutes max.'

'Do you need any help?'

'No, man, I'll be fine. Send Anna my love, will you?'

Over an hour later and Hunter was still at his desk.

He swiveled his chair around to look at the picture board again. They had already added several new items to it – the two photographs they had of Mathew Hade and a number of new crime-scene shots from that afternoon. Operations was still gathering a full dossier on Alison Atkins.

Hunter breathed out as he stared at the crime-scene shots. He hadn't exactly known Alison, but he had seen her go about her job, full of life, smiling at every customer, and that had inevitably altered the way in which seeing her hanging from that wood beam had affected him – first total sadness, then absolute rage.

'Where the fuck are you, you piece of shit?' Hunter said between clenched teeth, moving his attention to Mat Hade's photographs.

He checked his cellphone again. Still nothing.

He pushed his chair away from his desk, leaned back and rubbed his face with both hands. He felt tired, hungry and drained. Garcia was right. There was nothing else they could do. Maybe it was time to go home, but as that thought entered his mind he remembered something he'd forgotten about – the 911 call. The killer had been the one who had called it in, using Alison Atkins' phone.

Hunter needed to listen to that recording.

He quickly pulled his chair back to his desk and began typing commands and navigating through folders and locations. It took him just over a minute to find it. He cranked up the volume on his computer speakers and double-clicked on the sound file.

As he listened to the recording and to how calm and collected the killer sounded, Hunter could feel his heartrate doubling because he knew that Mat Hade had just eviscerated Alison Atkins prior to making that call. As he'd spoken to the 911 operator he had probably been standing in a pool of her blood, treading over her gutted intestines and staring at her lifeless face.

How could anyone be that cold, that senseless?

Once the recording had played, Hunter rewound it and played it again. Then again. Then again. That was when something struck him as odd.

'Wait a second,' Hunter whispered to himself as he played the call one more time.

'Why?' he said out loud, mulling over something specific the killer had said to the operator. 'Why would he do this? It makes no sense.'

Hunter got up, approached the picture board and reread the note the killer had pushed under his door.

Something began moving the gears inside his head.

He stepped back and stared at the whole board for a minute. Then his eyes began moving from victim to victim to victim. Back and forth, back and forth, back and forth.

He read the note one more time. The gears in his head were now moving at full speed.

'That is one dumb idea, Robert,' he said, shaking his head to try to ban a new thought.

It didn't work.

He looked at the wall clock – 10:48 p.m. 'Fuck!' he said as he sat back at his computer. 'Here goes nothing.' He began searching.

Seventy-Eight

Whatever result it was that Hunter had first imagined he'd get from his search, it sure as hell wasn't what appeared on his screen. As pages and pages of material began loading, he leaned forward, placed both elbows on his desk and rested his chin on his knuckles.

Hunter was a fast reader. Actually, he was a very fast reader and as soon as he began devouring the chunks and chunks of information he knew he had stumbled upon a complete minefield.

And then the first bomb went off.

He reread the paragraph twice over before he was certain he had it right. And it staggered him.

The second bomb followed almost immediately.

Hunter had to pause and take a deep breath. He could practically hear adrenalin dripping into his veins – and then he found the images. They came at him like an angry heavyweight champion and hidden among them was the knockout punch.

As the final image loaded on to his screen, he felt a sickening shiver kiss the nape of his neck.

'This can't be.'

And then that was it.

No more information.

With the same speed with which it had all appeared, it all stopped.

Hunter tried something else. Being a Special LAPD Detective had its perks but the words that came up on his screen made him jerk back.

RESTRICTED ACCESS.

'What the fuck?'

He tried again.

RESTRICTED ACCESS.

One more time.

RESTRICTED ACCESS.

'You've got to be kidding me.'

He backtracked and reread some of the information he'd gotten from his initial search.

And then it dawned on him.

Just like the killer's note to Mayor Bailey, the information had mentioned the FBI.

Hunter checked his watch – 11:58 p.m. In Virginia it would be 02:58 a.m. It didn't matter.

Hunter reached for his phone.

Seventy-Nine

Adrian Kennedy was the head of the FBI's National Center for the Analysis of Violent Crime and its Behavioral Analysis Unit. He was also a good friend of Hunter's.

Despite the late hour, Kennedy didn't even blink when his cellphone rang inside his jacket pocket. As the head of the NCAVC he was used to getting calls at godforsaken hours. Sleep was a luxury that didn't come as part of his job description.

He reached for the phone and was very surprised to see Hunter's name on the display screen.

'Robert?' he answered it, still sounding a little unsure.

'Hello, Adrian.'

'Well, this is a surprise.' His naturally hoarse voice, made worse by over thirty years of smoking, sounded tired but relaxed. 'Are you back in LA?'

'I am.'

Kennedy checked his watch. 'What time is it there? About midnight?'

'That's about right, yes.'

'So I guess you're not calling for a chitchat.' Adrian coughed a laugh. 'What can I do for you, old friend?'

'Are you in your office?'

'Well, I'm sure as hell not home in bed where I should be.'

'I need to ask you for a favor,' Hunter said.

Kennedy's interest grew. If there was one thing he knew about Robert Hunter, it was that he wasn't a man who asked many people for favors.

'What do you need?' Kennedy leaned back in his leather chair.

Without going into too much detail, Hunter told him.

Kennedy sat forward. 'Are you kidding?'

'Not even a little bit.'

'There's no way, Robert.' Kennedy's voice turned morbidly serious. 'That kind of information is as restricted as it gets. It's under the same sort of lock and key as our witness protection program.'

'To someone like me, yes,' Hunter replied. 'But not to the head of the NCAVC.'

'Still, Robert. We have protocols and rules here.'

'Yeah, I have an egg.'

Kennedy frowned. 'Excuse me?'

'I thought that we were just mentioning things that we can easily break.'

'Oh, that's cute.'

Hunter said nothing.

'Listen, Robert, I can't just go accessing that sort of information without leaving a log trail as long as Route Sixty-Six.'

'So? Leave a trail.'

'Easy for you to say.'

'What difference would that make to you, Adrian? All you'll be accessing is information and that's what your job demands, isn't it? Acquiring it, processing it and understanding it. No one will care.'

'I will. I'll still be breaking protocol to access extremely restricted information to then pass it on.'

'To a fellow law enforcement officer, Adrian. What do you think I'm going to do with it, sell it to the press? And, after all, you owe me.'

Kennedy did owe Hunter. He also knew the LAPD detective well enough to know that he wouldn't ask for anything unless it was absolutely imperative. He breathed out.

'This is more than I owe you, old friend.'

Hunter remained quiet.

'OK. Fuck it,' Kennedy finally said. 'Give me about half an hour.'

Eighty

Hunter spent the next twenty-two minutes rereading everything he had found, and for him it only served to underline something he already knew – that reality was much, much more perverted than fiction. The problem was, if he were right in his hunch, reality was just about to get a lot more twisted.

He recalled all the photographs he had found with his initial search less than an hour ago and studied them again, this time a lot more carefully. The last photograph was the one that had triggered an avalanche of thoughts inside Hunter's head. The one that had made him call Adrian Kennedy.

Despite his best efforts, that was the only photograph of that subject he could find. It had been taken years ago and from a considerable distance. The angle also didn't help, making the subject blurry and unclear.

Hunter tried using a photo-enhancing application to enlarge it on his screen, but the bigger he made it, the more pixelated it got and the blurrier it became. Still, something about its subject made him very uneasy.

Hunter had become so absorbed by the image that he almost didn't notice his cellphone rattling against his desktop.

The screen display told him that the caller was unknown.

Had Mat Hade been arrested?

'Detective Robert Hunter, Robbery Homicide Division,' he said as he brought the phone to his ear.

'Robert, it's Adrian.'

Hunter breathed out. 'Did you have any luck?'

There was a heavy pause.

'Adrian?'

'Yes. I got the files you're after. I'm emailing them to you right now.'

'Thanks, Adrian. I'll owe you for this.'

'Yes, you will. Robert?' Adrian called before Hunter could put the phone down.

'Yes.'

'Be careful, old friend.'

Hunter disconnected and opened his email application. Seconds later, Kennedy's email arrived. The subject field was left blank. The body of the email showed only two words – *Good luck* – but the message came with three separate attachments. Hunter opened the first one and began reading through it. The information it contained was very similar to what he had already found out, only much more detailed.

The second attachment consisted of a single black and white photograph. A photograph of the same subject Hunter had been studying before he'd received Kennedy's telephone call. As the picture filled Hunter's screen, he stopped breathing for a moment. It was an old photograph, but not as old as the one Hunter had found. It had been taken inside a controlled environment, not from a considerable distance, and the subject was staring straight at the camera.

Hunter could barely believe his own eyes.

It took him more than a minute to get over the shock of what he was looking at. Once he had, he finally opened the last attachment. The most secretive of all the documents Adrian Kennedy had sent him.

And the most devastating.

As Hunter read through it, he felt as if life had lost its logic.

He got up and began pacing the room, trying to put his thoughts in order. What to do next?

The clock on the wall showed 12:59 a.m.

There was no way he could wait until the morning.

Reaching for his cellphone, Hunter placed two calls. The second one was to his partner.

Eighty-One

Garcia had gotten home at around a quarter past nine in the evening. He had called Anna from the office to let her know that, once again, he wouldn't be home in time for dinner. Like always, Anna had told him that it was OK. She said that she wasn't planning on going to bed early anyway, so she would keep their dinner in the oven and they could heat it up when he got home, and still dine together.

Garcia and Anna had been together since their senior year in high school, and Garcia couldn't have asked for a more supportive wife. Anna knew how much he loved his job. She'd seen how hard he'd worked for it and how dedicated he was. She understood the commitment and the sacrifices that came with being a detective in a city like Los Angeles, and she fully accepted them. But despite her incredible psychological strength, it was only natural that Anna felt scared sometimes. Scared that one day she'd get that phone call, or that knock on the door in the middle of the night, telling her that her husband wouldn't be coming home again.

The truth was, after Hunter and Garcia's last case, the one that had prompted Captain Blake to demand that they both take a two-week break, Garcia had been ready to quit the RHD Special Section.

Garcia was as fearless as fearless got, but his last

investigation had brought Anna to within a whisker of death and that had scared him senseless. She meant everything to him, and if he lost her he would lose himself. He'd told his wife about his decision and Anna had been the one who had made him go back.

Tonight, after dining with his wife, Garcia dragged Anna into the shower with him. It reminded him of how they'd made love for the first time. After that, they both collapsed in bed, feeling completely exhausted.

Garcia thought he was dreaming when he heard a clattering sound coming from his right. He turned his face in that direction but kept his eyes closed.

Brrrrrrrrrrr.

There it was again.

He let out a confused sigh, opening his eyes just enough to see his cellphone vibrating against the surface of his bedside table. It took another two seconds for his tired and sleepy brain to understand what was happening before he finally reached for it.

'Hello?' he answered in a drowsy voice, quickly getting to his feet and making his way out of the bedroom so as not to wake Anna.

Too late, she was already turning in bed.

'Carlos, it's Robert.'

'Umm, Robert?' Garcia asked, sounding a little unsure as to who Robert was. Suddenly, his brain engaged. 'Robert.' His voice urgent. 'What's going on? Have we got him? Have we got Mat Hade?'

'No. Forget about that, Carlos. Nothing is what we thought it was. We were wrong.'

'Wrong? Wrong about what, Robert?'

'Everything.'

Eighty-Two

Hunter had been driving for almost an hour when he finally spotted the tiny dirt path hidden between bushes to the left of the road he was on. With no signs, no indications of any sort and no illumination whatsoever, even someone who'd been looking for it, like Hunter had, could've easily missed it. Like Hunter had. He had driven back and forth along that same stretch of road twice before he at last saw the gap between the bushes.

He stopped and directed his headlights toward it.

'Is that it?' he asked himself, leaning forward against the steering wheel. 'It must be. There's nothing else out here.'

He left the road and his car disappeared between the bushes as if it'd been swallowed by the night.

The uneven path was full of bumps and holes and that, together with pitch-black darkness, forced Hunter to slow down to a tense crawl. After about three quarters of a mile and two bends, one left, one right, the shrubs and bushes that lined the sides of the dirt road became less dense, giving way to endless fields of nothing at all except dirt, foxtail cactuses and desert marigolds.

Hunter drove on, being as careful as he could to avoid the larger potholes. The smaller ones were inevitable. They practically were the road.

After another half a mile, the road bent left again before going up a small hill. As Hunter drove down the other side, the vegetation changed again. The marigolds were swapped for Joshua trees and desert willows. Dirt and foxtail cactuses were still everywhere. As Hunter drove around a denser concentration of cactuses, he thought he spotted something in the distance. Some sort of massive shadow. He immediately brought his car to a full stop and switched off the headlights. Reaching for the pair of binoculars he always kept inside his glove compartment, he stepped out of the car.

As luck would have it, it was a cloudy, moonless night. No stars were visible either, which made it all way too dark for him to be able to see anything from where he stood. Looking for higher ground, Hunter climbed up on to the hood of his car, then on to its roof.

Still he saw nothing.

He needed to get closer.

Hunter got back into his Buick and, keeping the headlights turned off, began moving again, this time even slower than before. He drove for another quarter of a mile before stopping, climbing on to his car and scanning the terrain before him as carefully as he could.

Nothing to his right.

Nothing directly in front of him.

Nothing to his...wait. He paused, leaned forward. There it was. Way up ahead and slightly to his left.

Eighty-Three

From that distance, and in almost total darkness, Hunter struggled to understand what he was really looking at. It was some sort of construction. From the size of its shadow, it could be a medium-sized, two-storey house – the only issue was, it didn't look like a house. The building was square in shape, like a big box, and dusky in color, which on such a dark night, out there in a desert, made it practically invisible. Hunter was surprised that he had managed to spot it, even with a pair of binoculars.

He calculated the distance between the building and where he was standing to be about a quarter of a mile. He got back into his car and reached for his cellphone.

Nothing. Not even half a bar of signal. Moving it about also made no difference. He was slap-bang in the middle of nowhere.

'Great!'

Hunter decided to leave his car by the side of the dirt road and continue the rest of the way on foot. He'd be a lot quieter, and a lot less visible, that way.

He checked his HK Mark 23 pistol. It had a full clip loaded on to the weapon but Hunter was taking no chances. From the glove compartment, he picked up a flashlight and a second, fully loaded clip.

Despite still being another quarter of a mile away, Hunter moved stealthily, hiding himself as best as he could behind cactuses, trees and willows. He moved about fifteen to twenty yards at a time in a half-crouched position, stopped, got as close to the ground as possible and used his binoculars to check ahead. Everything looked as still as death.

He'd repeated the process five more times before he was able to spot something he hadn't seen before – a black GMC Yukon parked to the right of the construction.

From his window, Marlon had seen the fake telephone engineer climb into a black GMC Yukon after he'd collected the Wi-Fi camera he had placed high up on the telephone pole.

Hunter breathed in, wiped the sweat from his forehead, and carried on moving forward, getting closer and closer until he was no more than forty yards away from the building. He positioned himself behind a cluster of willows and used his binoculars again. He'd been right. The building looked nothing like a house.

Hunter figured that he'd been approaching it from its side instead of its front. He'd come to that conclusion because he could see no doors on that end of the building. With the Yukon parked around to the right, it seemed only logical that whoever had been driving it had parked by the front door.

Hunter was about to move closer when he noticed something else. On that whole side of the building there was only one window. It was way up high and a little to the left, but what made Hunter pause suddenly was the fact that, despite how far from the ground it was, thick, metal bars had been fitted to the outside of that lone window.

That building wasn't a house.

It was a prison.

Eighty-Four

Still hiding behind the cluster of willows, Hunter used his binoculars to check the property's grounds, its roof and all the corners he could see from his shielded location. He found no surveillance of any kind, at least not around that side. Satisfied, he moved closer, reaching the building in front of him in less than twenty seconds. As he did so, he placed his back flat against its west wall before checking left.

Nothing.

Right.

Nothing.

So far, so good.

He then began scooting south, toward where the Yukon was parked. Once he got to the edge of the wall, he crouched down, unholstered his weapon and flash-peeked around the corner.

He saw nothing.

He waited a few more seconds, then peered around again. This time, not so fast.

The Yukon was parked about eleven yards from the building's entrance – a heavy-looking wooden door. That was it. There was nothing else there.

Great, Hunter thought. *Now what, Robert? No way that that door will be unlocked. This is a prison, not a house.*

Whatever security has been put in place here, it hasn't been used to keep anyone from getting in. It's to stop people from getting out.

There was nothing else Hunter could do but get closer and have a better look. And that was exactly what he did. Still with his gun in hand and his back flat against the wall, he rounded the corner and slowly slid his way toward the heavy door. As he got to it, he felt his guts beginning to churn inside him.

There was something definitely evil about this place. Even the air immediately around it felt denser, harder to breathe.

Hunter studied the lock on the door. It looked old, but solid. He took another deep breath and looked around him again.

Nothing but darkness and silence.

He stretched out his left arm, placed his fingers on the door handle, twisted it downwards and gave the door a slow but firm push.

He was wrong.

To his bewildered surprise, the door moved inwards. It was unlocked.

'What the hell?' he whispered under his breath.

Hunter held the door in that position for a long moment, his brain quickly trying to figure out what to do next.

He'd come too far to turn back now.

As cautiously as he could, he pushed the door just another inch. Then another. Then another. Then another. Until the gap was wide enough for him to peek inside.

He saw nothing. Whatever this first room was, it seemed to be completely empty.

Hunter held his breath, pushed the door just a couple

more inches and furtively slid into the building, slowly closing the door behind him.

The air inside was warm and dusty, heavy with the smell of bleach and disinfectant, very similar to the odor that he and Garcia had picked up inside Mat Hade's apartment in East Los Angeles.

Hunter stood still for a moment, his back now flat against the inside of the door. His eyes were already used to the moonless night outside so it took them no time at all to acclimatize to the darkness inside, which suited him perfectly. He wanted to avoid using his flashlight as much as possible.

Hunter found himself standing at the entrance to a wide corridor, which had been stripped of all furniture and decorations. The walls were gray and made of cinder blocks, the floor and the ceiling of solid concrete. The entire hallway looked like a square, concrete tunnel – claustrophobic and airless.

It extended about seven yards in front of Hunter, leading to a second door, which lay ajar. A faint light came from somewhere behind it.

With watchful, soundless steps, Hunter quickly moved to it, pausing by the wall to the right of the door. He stood there motionless, waiting, listening.

One minute.

Two minutes.

The silence was deafening.

He finally twisted his body, craned his neck and very carefully peeked through the gap. The light source, which Hunter was unable to identify, was extremely weak, keeping most of the room in shadow. From where he stood, he could only partially see one half of the room without exposing himself, and it looked almost as sterile as the corridor he was in. Toward the back of it, a dark fabric armchair faced a blank wall. To its left, Hunter saw a small, wooden coffee table. On the floor, just in front of the armchair, a rectangular, black and white rug bridged the gap between the armchair and the wall. That was it. Hunter could see nothing else other than dark corners.

With his back still against the wall to the right of the door, he waited another two full minutes.

No sound or movement from inside.

Time to move on.

Hunter took a deep breath and, in a noiseless and well-rehearsed movement, rotated his body into the room, his arms extended in front of him, his gun searching for a target everywhere . . . anywhere.

He found none.

The second half of the room was even emptier than the first.

Hunter's eyes were still frantically searching the barren space for some sort of target, but he was looking the wrong way. The movement came from the shadow directly behind him.

Fast.

Precise.

Unstoppable.

As Hunter began turning back toward the door he had come in by, he received a blow to the back of the head that was so powerful it propelled him forward and against the wall.

A millisecond later, all thought was swallowed by total darkness.

Eighty-Five

Hunter's consciousness returned to him slowly and painfully. With every heartbeat, his head throbbed with an intense pain, like a spiked ball was pulsating at the center of his brain. He blinked a couple of times, but his eyelids felt too heavy for him to be able to fully open them, so for now he kept his eyes closed. He took a deep breath and as the warm air inflated his lungs, it seemed to also inflate that damn spike ball in his brain. Agonizing pain exploded inside his head like a furious thunderstorm and brought with it a second, searing and debilitating pain. This one ran the length of his arms, stretching and pulling at both ends as if his arms were about to be violently ripped from their sockets.

Hunter blinked again, but this time he finally found the strength to force open his eyes. Through the pain and the confusion, it took him a moment to understand what he was looking at – his bare feet resting on the floor, limp as if they belonged to a dead man. That was when he realized that he had been tied up in the exact same position they had found Alison Atkins inside that barn-like building. His arms were stretched high above his head. His wrists had been shackled together by a shiny steel chain and then looped around a metal pipe that ran across the ceiling. Two different padlocks kept it all in place. The chain was supporting the whole of his weight and it was biting deeply into his wrists. Thin lines of blood had run down his bare arms and over his shoulders.

Fighting the sickening pain in his head and arms, Hunter lifted his head and looked up. There was no way he was getting out of those shackles by himself.

'I must admit that you've surprised me, Robert.'

The voice came from somewhere in the shadows in front of him. Hunter looked in that direction but saw no one.

'I never thought you'd get here. I never thought you'd figure it out.'

Despite the voice sounding somewhat different from the one in the two 911 recordings he'd heard, Hunter was still able to recognize it. He'd heard it enough times.

That was why he showed no surprise when the man walked out of the darkness and stopped directly in front of him.

'Hello, Robert.'

Eighty-Six

Squirm hadn't slept at all. How could he? Every time he closed his eyes he saw her. Naked. Arms stretched out above her head. Her body dangling from that wooden beam while suspended by the chain shackled to her wrists. He would never forget the way in which she had looked at him.

The terror in her eyes.

The despair in her expression.

The fear that oozed from every pore in her body.

Alison. That was her name. Just like with the previous two women, 'The Monster' had made him repeat it until it was engraved on his brain.

'The Monster' had dragged Squirm out of his cell, tied him to a chair and made him watch as he slit that poor woman's abdomen open. A cut so wide Squirm thought the man was about to sever her in half.

Blood cascaded through the cut in large crimson sheets, recoloring her legs before dripping down on to the floor, creating the biggest pool of blood Squirm had ever seen. And the smell that came with it was like nothing he had ever experienced before – sweet and metallic, as if the blood were made out of copper.

But all that blood was nothing compared to what had come next. With a bright smile on his lips, 'The Monster' had approached the woman, looked straight into her eyes and slowly shoved his hands deep inside the opening he had made. Seconds later, they came out holding on to her insides.

Squirm had felt bitter bile shoot up from his stomach and travel up his throat, but by now he knew better than to puke in front of 'The Monster'. Clenching his teeth and squeezing his eyes tight, Squirm managed to swallow it all back down.

But 'The Monster' wasn't done yet. He carefully began pulling and twisting whatever it was that he had ripped from inside her, creating some sort of visceral string and allowing it to drop down into the ever-growing pool of blood on the floor.

It became so long, Squirm could hardly believe it had all come from inside her.

But what had terrified Squirm to the point that he had wet himself was the fact that, through all of that, the woman was still alive. She was still conscious. Despite the devastating pain that she was going through, she also had to watch as 'The Monster' exenterated her like an animal, and spread her guts all over the floor like play dough.

'This, Squirm, takes skill,' the man had said to him as he plopped another piece of her insides on to the floor. Every time she looked like she was about to pass out, 'The Monster' would either slap her face or bring a small flask to her nose so she stayed awake.

Squirm wanted to look away but he'd found it impossible to. It was like he had been hypnotized by the savagery of it all.

Now, back in his cell, Squirm had a new thought and that thought carried with it a sliver of hope. The police might not have been looking for him but they sure as hell would be looking for those women. Unlike his own, their fathers hadn't paid 'The Monster' to get rid of them. Squirm was certain of that. So, if the police were searching for the man who was abducting and killing those women, the police were searching for 'The Monster'. And if they found him, they would find Squirm.

That thought planted a new seed of hope inside the boy's heart.

Eighty-Seven

Hunter's shirt was soaked through with perspiration and he felt beads of sweat dribble down the back of his legs. He looked around the space, trying to understand the room he was in.

Despite the faint light that came from somewhere above his head, the space was dark and shrouded in shadow, just like the room Hunter had found himself in before the killer had gotten the best of him. But this certainly wasn't the same room. The walls were made out of cinder blocks, the floor of solid concrete. Several metal pipes crisscrossed the ceiling in different directions. Over to Hunter's left he saw a short flight of stairs leading up to a closed door. Hunter had no doubt now that he was down in the basement of this godforsaken house. If the place could even be called a house.

The man who had stepped from the shadows paused directly in front of Hunter and waited.

Hunter didn't even look at him. His hands felt stiff and swollen. The chain around his wrists was constricting the blood flow. He tried moving his fingers. He could flex them, but the movement brought with it excruciating pain.

Hunter groaned.

The man smiled.

'Please tell me, Robert,' Detective Troy Sanders, the head

of the LAPD Missing Persons Unit's Special Division, said, 'How did you figure it out?' His posture was relaxed, his voice calm.

Hunter's eyes moved to look at him.

Sanders waited.

'You told us,' Hunter said. His voice, on the other hand, sounded hoarse and fatigued.

'Did I?'

'The notes you sent us. First to Mayor Bailey, then to me. They were full of clues.'

Sanders smiled. 'They certainly were.'

'We just didn't know what any of them meant ... Until tonight.'

'So what gave it away, Robert? What made you understand what the clues meant?'

Hunter coughed and it made the spike ball inside his head stab at his brain again.

'Your last nine-one-one call,' he finally replied.

That answer seemed to surprise Sanders. 'Really? How so?'

Hunter licked his cracked lips, trying to get some moisture from his face. 'Cut me down and I'll tell you.'

Sanders laughed as he walked around Hunter, disappearing behind him.

'Well, I can't do that, Robert. But let me see what I can do.'

All of a sudden, Hunter heard the sound of metal on metal. The chain shackling his wrists lost some of its tautness and his feet were finally able to touch the ground. Just. That allowed him to teeter on his toes and use his legs to support a small percentage of his weight, relieving some of the tension from his arms. It felt like heaven.

'Better?' Sanders asked.

Hunter said nothing.

'So tell me, Robert, how did my last nine-one-one call help you figure it all out?'

Hunter breathed in slowly. 'The victim's name,' he replied. 'Alison.'

Sanders walked back around to face Hunter.

'You mentioned it three times,' Hunter said. 'You made sure that the operator had that down. Why would you do that? It made no sense, because that would've been one of the first things we would've found out anyway, especially since you used her cellphone to make the call.'

Sanders remained silent, but the ghost of a smile began to play on his lips.

Hunter tiptoed a little to his left to better support his weight. 'The fact that you were so insistent that the operator write her name down – something didn't sound right about that. So I went back to the note you sent me and studied it again.'

Sanders waited.

'"The clues are in the name,"' Hunter said. 'You wrote that.'

Sanders nodded. The ghost of a smile grew.

'The clues *were* the names,' Hunter said. 'The victim's names.'

Clap, clap, clap.

Sanders applauded Hunter. 'Very good, Robert. I'm impressed.'

Hunter licked his lips again. 'You also wrote that you were –' he coughed one more time and had to endure the spike ball for several seconds – 'rewriting history.'

The smile finally appeared.

'So you searched through history, using the victims' names as your guideline. All of them.'

Hunter's silence was a resounding 'yes'.

'Let me guess,' Sanders said. 'What you found out made your head spin.'

Hunter swallowed and the saliva fought to get through his swollen throat. 'What I found out made almost every clue in both notes come alive. Suddenly, everything began making sense. The puzzle began to sort itself out.'

'I'm glad,' Sanders said. 'But no matter what you searched for, Robert, I *know* that whatever result you got wouldn't have answered every question. A very important piece of that puzzle is still missing.'

'Yes,' Hunter admitted.

'So the picture is still incomplete, Robert. You still have no idea who I really am, do you?'

Hunter and Sanders locked eyes as if in a battle. Hunter blinked first.

'Your real name is Richard,' he said. 'Richard Temple.'

Sanders looked back at Hunter in bewildered surprise. It took him several seconds to overcome the shock of what he'd heard. As he did so, he laughed again, but this time it was a strange laugh that disturbed Hunter. It gurgled up from the depths of his body as if he had chewed it for a long time in his lungs before spitting it out. It was raucous with pain. Emotional pain. When he spoke again, his voice was coated with a macabre tone.

'You're wrong, Robert. My name isn't Richard. My name is . . .'

Sanders paused and moved his neck first left then right in an anxious manner.

'Squirm.'

Eighty-Eight

Six years had passed.

Squirm's hope that the police would one day capture 'The Monster' for any of the heinous crimes he had committed over the years had died a long time ago. He would never be saved. 'The Monster' would never let him go.

Squirm was eighteen years old now. He was still scrawny, but almost as tall as 'The Monster'. He'd expected to be dead by now, but it seemed that 'The Monster' enjoyed having him around.

Every year, on Squirm's birthday, 'The Monster' sat with him in the kitchen and talked to him as if they were old friends. Squirm listened more than talked, but still, that was the only time 'The Monster' treated him like a human being.

Today was Squirm's eighteenth birthday.

'The Monster' had woken him up early – 5:45 a.m. – like he had done every single day in the past six years, shackled him (by a single wrist only) to one of the metal rings in the kitchen and allowed Squirm to eat breakfast. Not from the floor. Not with his hands. But like a civilized person.

'I have a question for you, Squirm,' 'The Monster' had said as Squirm finished his piece of chocolate cake.

For the past five years, as a present to Squirm on his

birthday 'The Monster' had brought him a single slice of chocolate cake. It had become a sort of ritual.

Without making eye contact, Squirm nodded shyly.

Squirm had grown up shrouded by interminable fear and completely stripped of all self-confidence. A comparison to a scared puppy wouldn't have been far from the truth.

'How would you like to possess a woman?'

Squirm paused and this time looked back at his long-term captor.

'You are officially a man now. So I think it's time you learn what it is to be a real man.' 'The Monster' slapped his own chest twice. 'How about I give you some time with the next piece of trash I bring in here, huh? You would like that, wouldn't you?'

Squirm froze.

'Actually,' 'The Monster' continued carelessly, 'thinking about it, we can do better than that. We can do much better than that. How about, after you're done with the piece of trash, you get rid of her? And you know just what I mean when I say get rid of her, don't you?'

The pause that followed was so heavy that Squirm thought it would put a hole through the earth.

'I know you know what to do, Squirm. You've had plenty of classes over the years, haven't you?'

For six years, 'The Monster' had made Squirm watch every single one of his murders. Thirty-three in total. And he had made Squirm memorize the name of every victim. Squirm would never forget their names. He would never forget their faces. He would never forget how they died.

'You can hurt her as much as you like, Squirm. How does that sound, huh?'

Squirm broke eye contact again. He could feel his throat constricting.

'I know you have a lot of anger inside you.' 'The Monster' scratched his crotch. 'Well, maybe it's time you set that anger free, Squirm, and I say punish her with everything you have. Make her scream with fear, with pain, with suffering and I guarantee you'll feel liberated . . . vindicated . . . cleansed . . . powerful. You will feel like God.'

Squirm's heartbeat picked up speed.

'And that is my present to you, Squirm. Tonight you'll not only become a real man but you'll become God.' 'The Monster' let out a throaty laugh. 'On this earth, there's no feeling more powerful.'

Tonight?

His heart began thundering against his chest.

Tonight?

Faster still. Squirm felt like his heart might explode out of his body.

Tonight.

That one word terrified him.

He began feeling dizzy.

Tonight you'll not only become a real man, but you'll become God.

He couldn't breathe.

Fear flooded every atom in his body.

Ironically, that fear, that immeasurable fear, was what finally gave him the courage he'd been lacking for six years. Courage that every night had boiled inside his brain but every morning had failed to materialize in his veins.

Today was Squirm's birthday. It was the only day throughout the entire year when, for a very brief period of time, 'The Monster' shackled him to the wall by a single wrist.

For the past three birthdays, Squirm had thought about lashing out against 'The Monster' when he wasn't looking, but right at that last second his courage had always failed him. And if courage had been what Squirm was depending on that day, it would've failed him again, but sometimes the only thing that can overcome fear is fear itself.

Squirm looked at 'The Monster' who was sitting to his left. This time, what collided inside of him wasn't fear against courage but fear against fear.

As 'The Monster' turned to look at the clock on the wall, Squirm tensed, closed his eyes and allowed fear to guide him.

Squirm had never heard of an 'out of body' experience. But there was no other way he could describe how he saw the scene play out before his eyes.

As if he were watching a movie on a big screen, Squirm saw himself sitting in that kitchen, just to the right of 'The Monster'. Suddenly, and as if the movie had been slowed down to a fraction of its original speed, he saw his right arm swing out. Not the arm that had been freed from its restraints but the one with the thick metal cuff around its wrist, from which a long chain crossed the room and connected to a metal ring on the east wall.

The shackled arm slowly gained ground, agonizingly inching closer and closer towards his captor's face.

The spectator Squirm could barely watch. *What are you doing? Have you lost your mind? Stop it. Stop it.*

But the Squirm in the movie couldn't hear him. He was aiming to hit 'The Monster' square across the jaw, but 'The Monster' turned to look at the clock just in time. Luck seemed to be on Squirm's side that day. The metal cuff around his wrist struck 'The Monster' at the center of his right temple.

The spectator Squirm saw the man's eyes flicker, then roll back into his head. The scene shocked and excited him in equal measures.

Was this really happening?

Time trickled away.

Time that he didn't have.

He screamed at the screen.

Hit him again. Hit him again.

This time, it seemed like the Squirm in the movie heard the loud shouts because he brought his right hand back and swung it against 'The Monster' once again. Harder this time. It hit him almost exactly in the same spot as before.

His head and arms shook as if he was having an epileptic attack.

The spectator Squirm could barely believe his eyes.

One last time. Do it. Do it now.

Squirm swung a third and final blow.

Lights out.

'The Monster' collapsed to the ground completely unconscious, blood dripping from the gash on his head.

The spectator Squirm flew through the air, back into the movie Squirm.

The eighteen-year-old boy didn't care if 'The Monster' was dead or not. He didn't check. All he did was grab the keys from 'The Monster's' trouser pocket and transfer the bloody cuff from his wrist to that of 'The Monster's'.

Seconds later, he unlocked the front door and stepped out into a world he never thought he would see again.

Eighty-Nine

The FBI file that Adrian Kennedy had sent Hunter contained Squirm's complete deposition, together with a single photograph of the then eighteen-year-old boy. He looked a lot thinner, and his head wasn't completely shaved like Detective Sanders' was, but the facial features were still the same, especially those piercing pale-blue eyes. Hunter had recognized him as soon as he had seen the picture.

Hunter coughed again, sending another ripple of searing pain through his brain.

'Squirm.' He repeated what Sanders had told him. 'That's the name your captor used to call you, right? I read that on your file. You used to call him "The Monster".'

Upon hearing those words again, Sanders took a step back.

Hunter noticed it.

'You read the FBI file?' Sanders asked, surprised. 'How? I was part of the FBI Victim Relocation Program. That program is as secretive as the Witness Protection Program. Not even FBI agents have access to it, with the exception of a few top guns. That's how I was able to join the LAPD.' He lifted both palms up. 'The program assigned me a completely new identity, with a full, totally legit background history that would stand scrutiny from anybody, anywhere. Banks, insurance companies, private investigators, government agencies, you name it – and that includes the LAPD.'

'Being a cop was the perfect cover,' Hunter said.

Sanders glared at him, half amused.

'Oh, no, no, no, no. Don't disappoint me, Robert. You were doing great with the figuring-out thing. You think I joined the LAPD so I could start killing people?'

Hunter tiptoed again. This time a little to the right.

'I joined the LAPD because I genuinely wanted to help people.' Sanders' voice became a little harsher. 'I *wanted* to become a Missing Persons investigator so I could try to help people like me. So I could arrest people like 'The Monster'. You, more than anyone, know that he wasn't unique. The world is full of monsters like him.' He paused and locked eyes with Hunter again. 'Monsters like me.'

Hunter drew a deep breath and the air hurt his lungs.

'Do you want to know what changed me?'

Hunter already knew.

'Your file,' he said.

Sanders snapped his thumb and forefinger together, then pointed at Hunter with a *Eureka* gesture. 'Exactly, Robert. My file. Being a cop, especially being the head of an LAPD department, gives you access to certain restricted files. Files that, as a civilian, I would never normally have seen. Files on the investigation of certain murders, certain disappearances. They didn't know it then but they all had one common denominator. Would you like to guess what that common denominator was, Robert?'

'"The Monster".'

'"The Monster",' Sanders agreed. 'And what I found out from those files changed me for ever. Do you know what that was?'

Hunter's eyes blinked a silent 'no'.

'Seven times, Robert.' His eyes narrowed. 'In the six years I was kept locked in that disgusting cell, between the LAPD and the FBI "The Monster" was questioned by the authorities seven times. SEVEN TIMES.' Sanders yelled those two last words at Hunter's face, spit flying from his mouth.

Hunter flinched but it was too late. Some of the spit got into his mouth.

Sanders was breathing heavily now. Words were coming from between clenched teeth. 'I was just a boy when I was taken, Robert. I was eleven years old. I was intelligent. I had a future. And for six years, that boy was sodomized and beaten up *every day*, as if I were nothing more than just a piece of rotten meat.'

Sanders took a step back, grabbed hold of his shirt with both hands and ripped it off his body. Buttons were propelled high up in the air before bouncing down against the concrete floor.

Despite the pain and how fatigued he was, Hunter's eyes widened. Sanders' torso was completely covered in scars – some small, some big, some enormous. Many of them hadn't healed well and the scars looked leathery and lumpy. Some looked like huge welts.

Sanders turned around. His back looked even worse.

Hunter remained silent.

'During those six years, they had seven chances to end it all. SEVEN.' Sanders began pacing the room in front of Hunter. Tears looked like they were about to well up in his eyes but they never materialized. Squirm was still keeping true to his promise. His voice became deep, full of gravel. 'Seven times, Robert. The LAPD and the FBI looked straight into the eyes of pure evil seven *different* times. The eyes of a complete maniac, and yet they didn't see the monster inside him.' He stopped pacing. 'They were supposed to be the best at what they did. The experts.'

A paragraph of Sanders' first note to Mayor Bailey popped into Hunter's head.

Those agencies are supposed to be the best of the best. The experts when it comes to reading people and discerning good from evil. But the truth is that they only see what they want to see. And the problem with that is that when they play at being blind men, people suffer . . . people get tortured . . . and people die.

Sanders began pacing again.

'They could've saved me from my nightmare, Robert. They could've saved me from becoming what I have become. They could've saved all those women. They could've saved all of these women.'

Hunter knew he was referring to his own victims.

'In those six years, he killed thirty-three women. And he made me watch them all die. He made me memorize all of their names.'

Hunter remembered the file he had read just hours earlier. Once 'The Monster' had been arrested, after Squirm finally directed the police to his hiding place, he had confessed to over sixty murders. He'd been killing women for more than ten years.

'So finding out that you could've been saved changed you,' Hunter said.

'Wouldn't it have changed you?' Sanders shot back. 'How could the best of the best make so many mistakes that cost so many so much?'

Hunter didn't reply.

'Those women are dead, Robert. They're not coming back. My life was *ripped* from me.' Sanders smiled a humorless smile. 'Mistakes have a flip side to them, Robert – repercussions. You know that. The bigger the mistake, the more devastating the repercussions. *I* am the repercussion of the mistakes that were made twenty-five years ago.' Sanders opened his arms as if he were welcoming a gift from the skies. 'And here I am. I knew that if a similar case happened today, those same mistakes would repeat themselves because people only see what they want to see. *You* only see what you want to see.'

Hunter's toes were becoming exhausted and the chain around his wrists was starting to dig deep into his flesh again, shutting down the blood flow to his hands.

'So, to prove a point, you became "The Monster" yourself,' Hunter said. 'You retraced his steps and you began killing women. Women with the exact same name as the ones he killed. In the exact same order. Using the exact same methods. Even the filming.'

Sanders' intrigued stare returned. He had no idea Hunter knew about the filming.

'You're not a trophy collector. The films mean nothing to you. You did it because "The Monster" did it. You even found a place hidden away and transformed it to look similar to the place in which he kept you.'

'With a few modern modifications, of course,' Sanders admitted. 'How do you think I knew that you were approaching the house at this time in the morning?' His eyebrows arched. 'There are hidden sensors all around this place.'

Those words filled Hunter with dread.

'Why do you think that the front door was unlocked, Robert? I was waiting for you. I wanted you to get inside.'

Hunter's arms were starting to feel like meat lumps.

'But I'm impressed, Robert,' Sanders continued. 'You are right. I became "The Monster" to prove a point. *My point*. But I didn't just take to the streets and start killing people. I began devising my plan years ago. I didn't want to rush it. And I planned everything to the very last detail. The first victim had to be the result of an over-the-top, daring abduction. That way, I could guarantee that the Missing Persons Unit's Special Division would get the call. *I* would get the call.' He chuckled at his own cleverness. 'I even managed to find the person who, if the detective assigned to the murders investigation didn't make a complete fuck-up of everything, would become the perfect scapegoat. The perfect prime suspect.'

'Mat Hade,' Hunter said. 'I Am Death.'

The surprise in Sanders' eyes was sincere.

'Wow! You figured that one out too?' He nodded approvingly. 'OK, now I'm really impressed. I knew you were good from the first time we met in my office to discuss Nicole's case. You were asking all the right questions, but I must admit that I wasn't expecting you to ask for a history search on similar abductions. I thought that you would just grab the files and leave. But your request gave me the perfect opportunity to bring Mat into the equation and to run my first quick test on how good you really were.'

'You called me and told me you hadn't found anything,' Hunter said.

'Exactly. And that was when you figured out what we were doing wrong. We were searching only for concluded cases. That really impressed me, Robert. Obviously, I already had it all covered from the beginning. The idea was to suggest that search to the detective in charge of Nicole's murder investigation myself, but you saved me the trouble. And if you hadn't brought the "concluded case" mistake to my attention, I would've just said that I thought better of the search you had asked me for and had come up with that idea myself.'

Hunter's mouth was starting to feel bone dry.

'I knew I needed a scapegoat and it took me years to find him, but Mathew Hade fitted my plans like a glove,' Sanders said. 'But not even the best-laid plans could've delivered his name. That was pure luck. How perfect was it? Can you imagine how surprised I was when I figured out that I could make the perfect anagram out of it?'

Sanders laughed another throaty, macabre laugh before continuing. 'That also gave me the perfect opportunity to drop the best hint into my note.'

'"The clues are in the name",' Hunter said.

'Wasn't it perfect?' Sanders boasted. 'A clue with a double meaning: I MAT HADE or I AM DEATH. But in the end, that wasn't the *name*, or *names*, the clue was referring to. That was genius, if I might say so myself.'

'So once you knew you would hand us Mat Hade's file,' Hunter said. 'You took care of him.'

Sanders applauded Hunter again. 'Of course I did. I didn't want you finding him. That would've spoiled all my plans.'

'And you planted those items in his apartment – the red pen, the sheets of paper, the book of matches.'

'Another genius move, don't you think?' Sanders replied. 'This whole case was supposed to have stretched for a very long time, Robert, and with every new victim I gave you, a new cryptic clue would've once again pointed to one person, and one person only – Mat Hade. How frustrating do you think it would be for you to chase a ghost, Robert?'

Silence reigned for several seconds before Sanders spoke again.

'But though you were good, Robert, very good indeed, you weren't good enough. Because you made the same deadly mistake that was made twenty-five years ago. You know what that mistake was, don't you?'

'I looked into your eyes and I didn't see it.'

'Correct again. You and your partner looked straight into my eyes. I sat in your office. You sat in mine. We conversed and you still didn't know. Admit it.'

Before Hunter could say anything, an electronic beeping sounded in the room.

Hunter's eyes scanned the place.

'They're here,' Sanders said, grabbing the double-barreled shotgun he had left on the workshop table that was half hidden in the shadows.

Hunter looked at him with deep concern.

'I knew that you wouldn't turn up here by yourself, Robert. You're not that dumb. Sure, you might turn up here first to check things out, but the cavalry would be right behind you, correct?'

Hunter breathed out.

Sanders smiled. 'I know I've got no way out of here. But I don't need a way out. I don't want a way out. My life ended when I was eleven, and whatever hell I go to from here, it will feel like paradise compared to the last twenty-five years of my life.'

He cocked the hammer on both barrels.

'One for you, one for me. Congratulations, Robert. You managed to stop the murders. And, believe me, I would've carried on until someone corrected the mistakes that were made twenty-five years ago. But you still failed me. You failed to identify the monster in me when you looked into my eyes.'

The beeping got louder and more frantic.

'They are inside,' Sanders announced with a smile, pointing the shotgun at Hunter.

Hunter looked straight into Sanders' eyes. He would not give him the satisfaction of closing his eyes or looking away.

The door at the top of the staircase creaked.

Sanders squeezed the trigger.

Ninety

As Garcia pushed open the basement door, he heard the second shotgun blast. Both had happened in very quick succession. The confined space made them sound louder than normal, almost like a double bomb going off.

Garcia dropped to his knees, his weapon in a firm double-hand grip. Instead of returning fire, as he had no fixed target he used the door as cover and waited.

Two seconds.

Five.

Ten.

Nothing. No other shots.

Garcia pushed the door open further and glanced inside. His weapon was still searching for a target, searching for Troy Sanders. All he saw was a staircase going down into a basement and some gun smoke floating around at the bottom.

'Robert?' he called.

No reply.

'Robert? Are you down there?'

Not a sound.

'Fuck!' Garcia drew in a deep breath and slowly started down the stairs.

'Robert?' he called again after three steps.

Still nothing.

Garcia moved down another five steps. He now had a better look at the basement but gun smoke and the dark shadows still made everything unclear.

'Robert? Are you down here?'

The place was still.

'ROBERT?'

'I'm here. I'm here.' Garcia heard Hunter's voice. 'Everything is OK, it's all clear.'

Garcia didn't fight the smile that stretched his lips. He didn't want to fight it.

He went down the last few steps in a hurry and paused at the bottom, his eyes widening in shock.

On the basement floor, just a few feet in front of a workshop table, lay an almost headless body. Fresh, steaming blood was still pouring out of the recent wound.

Hunter was also on the floor, his hands shackled by a metal chain speckled with blood, but there was no blood on the floor around him.

'Are you OK?' Garcia asked, quickly moving to him. 'Are you shot?'

'No, I'm OK,' Hunter replied, pushing himself up into a sitting position.

Garcia helped him.

'I heard two shots,' he said.

'He aimed the first one at the chain,' Hunter explained, looking up at the metal pipes. A piece of chain still hung from one of them.

'If you were alive, why the fuck didn't you answer when I called your name?' Garcia asked. 'I thought you were dead.'

'My ears were still ringing from the shots. They sounded loud as fuck down here.'

Garcia laughed for almost a full minute.

'I think we better call this thing in. This is going to be one long report.'

Hunter nodded. What he never told Garcia was that, just before pulling the trigger, Squirm had looked deep into his eyes and mouthed the words 'thank you'.

Ninety-One

'So he was copying everything, to be just like his captor all those years ago?' Captain Blake asked. She was still completely stunned by Hunter's report.

'Pretty much,' Hunter replied. His wrists were still bandaged. 'Everything except taking a boy captive.'

'And if nobody had stopped him, you think that he would've claimed thirty-three victims?' Chief Bracco asked. He had been the one who had called for this particular meeting inside Captain Blake's office.

'Maybe more,' Garcia replied. 'What he wanted was for someone to stop him. To end his nightmare.'

Chief Bracco frowned at Garcia.

'It never ended for him when he escaped all those years ago,' Garcia explained. 'All that happened was the second part of his nightmare began.' He looked at Hunter, who agreed with a subtle nod. 'If no one had stopped him, he would've just carried on going. Reaching thirty-three victims wouldn't have brought it to an end.'

'Forensics is still running tests inside that house of horrors,' Captain Blake said. 'They found all the video footage, together with a list of victims' names. There were exactly thirty-three names on it but I think Carlos is right. If no one had stopped him, he would've carried on way past thirty-three.'

'Nobody,' Hunter added, 'no matter how mentally stable they think they are, could go through six years of such torment and come out the other side unscathed, never mind a boy who was eleven at the beginning of it all. So the trauma was always there. Troy Sanders did manage to keep it under control for a hell of a long time. But finding out that the reason why he'd had to suffer so much for so long had been negligence, a series of mistakes made by the police and the FBI, tipped him over the edge. In a way, he had put his trust in those law enforcement agencies to keep him safe and to right him when he'd been wronged. Everybody does. And they –' Hunter paused and corrected himself – '*we* failed him.'

No one said anything for a long while.

'How did you find that godforsaken place?' Captain Blake asked Hunter. 'It's not registered to anyone. It practically doesn't exist.'

'Sanders' car,' Hunter replied. 'All LAPD vehicles are equipped with trackers. Once I found out that he was Squirm, I placed a call to Operations before calling Carlos and asked them to give me Sanders' car location. I had to manually enter the coordinates into the navigation system.'

'Well.' Chief Bracco got to his feet. 'All I can say is congratulations on a fantastic job.' He shook Garcia's hand, but Hunter just lifted both of his, showing the bandages.

'Sorry, sir.'

'No need,' he said, approaching the door. 'Now, back to work, or do you think Troy Sanders was the only psychopath in this town?'

Ninety-Two

Marlon Sloan was shaking a little as he began walking.

The detective that had come to his house that day had intrigued him. He had told him to disregard the advice of his therapist. He had told him that he could do this himself, all he needed to do was to walk about a block outside his comfort zone and take it from there. Marlon had decided to try it.

He carried on walking past the end of his road, his comfort zone. About a block and a half later, he reached a small park at the top of a hill. His breathing was labored, but not because he was tired.

The detective had told him that that would happen.

Marlon found a bench, which faced a small green area, and had a seat. He concentrated on his breathing and on how much he was shaking. He was scared, no doubt about that. He wanted to run back but he forced himself not to.

'You can do this,' he told himself, focusing his attention on a cluster of trees. 'You can do this.'

A few minutes later, the shaking had subsided and he was breathing just as if he were sitting inside his own bedroom.

Marlon could barely believe it.

He sat on that bench for about half an hour until he had mustered enough courage for the second part of his task.

As an elderly gentleman walked past the bench Marlon was sitting on, the boy turned and faced him.

'Excuse me, sir.' His voice was a little unsteady.

The older man stopped and looked at the boy.

'Do you have the time, pl . . . please?'

'Certainly.' The man consulted his timepiece. 'It's ten past two.'

'Thank you.' Marlon breathed out, relieved, his hands still shaking.

The man went on his way.

As Marlon got to his feet and began walking back home, an enormous smile filled his face. He couldn't remember the last time he had smiled like that.

Acknowledgements

I am tremendously grateful to a number of people without whom this novel would've never been possible.

My agent, Darley Anderson, who's not only the best agent an author could ever hope for, but also a true friend. Everyone at the Darley Anderson Literary Agency for their never-ending strive to promote my work anywhere and everywhere possible.

Jo Dickinson, my fantastic editor at Simon & Schuster, for being so amazing at what she does, and for all her guidance and support. Jamie Groves for his incredible promotional ideas, and for creating the most 'glute-kicking' task force there is. Everyone at Simon & Schuster for always working their socks off on every aspect of the publishing process.

My unconditional love goes to Kara Irvine, for all her patience and understanding, but most of all for her companionship, for keeping me sane, and for making me smile again – I love you.

I would also like to say a massive thank you to Sharon Barnard from Tuffley, in Gloucester, who has very kindly taken part at the auction created by CLIC Sargent, a Children with Cancer charity, to become a character in this novel. Thank you so much for your generosity, Sharon.

Chris Carter
An Evil Mind

A freak accident in rural Wyoming leads the Sheriff's Department to arrest a man for a possible double homicide, but further investigations suggest a much more horrifying discovery – a serial killer who has been kidnapping, torturing and mutilating victims all over the United States for at least twenty-five years. The suspect claims he is a pawn in a huge labyrinth of lies and deception – can he be believed?

The case is immediately handed over to the FBI, but this time they're forced to ask for outside help. Ex-criminal behaviour psychologist and lead Detective with the Ultra Violent Crime Unit of the LAPD, Robert Hunter, is asked to run a series of interviews with the apprehended man.

These interviews begin to reveal terrifying secrets that no one could've foreseen, including the real identity of a killer so elusive that no one, not even the FBI, had any idea he existed . . . until now.

Chris Carter
One by One

'I need your help, Detective. Fire or water?'

Detective Robert Hunter of the LAPD's Homicide Special Section receives an anonymous call asking him to go to a specific web address – a private broadcast. Hunter logs on and a show devised for his eyes only immediately begins.

But the caller doesn't want Detective Hunter to just watch, he wants him to participate, and refusal is simply not an option. Forced to make a sickening choice, Hunter must sit and watch as an unidentified victim is tortured and murdered live over the Internet.

The LAPD, together with the FBI, use everything at their disposal to electronically trace the transmission down, but this killer is no amateur, and he has covered his tracks from start to finish. And before Hunter and his partner Garcia are even able to get their investigation going, Hunter receives a new phone call.

A new website address. A new victim. But this time the killer has upgraded his game into a live murder reality show, where *anyone* can cast the deciding vote.

Chris Carter
The Death Sculptor

'Good job you didn't turn on the lights...'

A student nurse has the shock of her life when she discovers her patient, prosecutor Derek Nicholson, brutally murdered in his bed. The act seems senseless – Nicholson was terminally ill with only weeks to live. But what most shocks Detective Robert Hunter of the Los Angeles Robbery Homicide Division is the calling card the killer left behind.

For Hunter, there is no doubt that the killer is trying to communicate with the police, but the method is unlike anything he's ever seen before. And what could the hidden message be?

Just as Hunter and his partner Garcia reckon they've found a lead, a new body is found – and a new calling card. But with no apparent link between the first and second victims, all the progress they've made so far goes out of the window.

Pushed into an uncomfortable alliance with confident investigator Alice Beaumont, Hunter must race to put together the pieces of the puzzle . . . before the Death Sculptor puts the final touches to his masterpiece.

Chris Carter
The Night Stalker

When an unidentified female body is discovered laid out on a slab in an abandoned butcher's shop, the cause of death is unclear. Her body bares no marks; except for the fact that her lips have been carefully stitched shut.

It is only when the full autopsy gets underway at the Los Angeles County morgue that the pathologist will reveal the true horror of the situation – a discovery so devastating that Detective Robert Hunter of the Los Angeles Homicide Special Section has to be pulled off a different case to take over the investigation.

But when his inquiry collides with a missing persons' case being investigated by the razor-sharp Whitney Meyers, Hunter suspects the killer might be keeping several women hostage. Soon Robert finds himself on the hunt for a murderer with a warped obsession, a stalker for whom love has become hate.